CW00867938

I Keep Myself Safe

Safety Actions for Young Children

Rebecca A. Timmins

Archway Publishing books may be ordered through booksellers or by contacting:

Archway Publishing
1663 Liberty Drive
Bloomington, IN 47403
www.archwaypublishing.com
844-669-3957

ISBN: 978-1-6657-0844-9 (sc)
ISBN: 978-1-6657-0845-6 (hc)
ISBN: 978-1-6657-0846-3 (e)

Print information available on the last page.

Archway Publishing rev. date: 08/09/2021

To my parents, for lovingkindness and a passion for learning every day.
To the dogs, for giving us unconditional love and making us smile.
To my colleagues around the world, who are passionate about helping
others practice protective behaviors and prevent injury.

Dear Grown-Ups:

This book seeks to help children develop protective behaviors from a young age. Childhood injuries are many, ranging from minor to catastrophic. It's notable that the protective behaviors that reduce childhood injuries are the same protective behaviors needed through our lives to prevent injuries as adults, including in the workplace.

Here are common protective behaviors:

- Keeping your hands so you can always see them
- Learning to sense heat and stay away
- Keeping your hands at your sides and out of pinch points
- Going up and down stairs while keeping three points of contact, such as holding handrails or holding a grown-up's hand
- Using all the steps or stairs at a deliberate pace
- Looking where you are going
- Looking where you put your feet
- Washing your hands
- Keeping your hands away from your face
- Using a seat restraint such as a seat belt or car seat

This guide should help children build self-confidence and learn protective behaviors to help keep themselves safe.

The story is about three dogs—Bella, Finn, and Daisy—and what they are learning to keep themselves safe.

Something powerful happens when we combine physical movement and saying things aloud. Many grown-ups do this. Before leaving home, we run through what we need for the day: "Got my keys? Got my water? Got my phone?" We point to the item and say, "Check." This is a common example. We do this because it increases our chance of getting it right—and reduces the chance we end up without what we need for the day.

This technique is particularly fun for children because they love to move and use their voices; it's like a game, but it's a powerful way to engage children and build important behaviors.

Throughout the book, Bella, Finn, and Daisy illustrate how to do this, and the children can practice with them. Grown-ups can encourage and reinforce the ideas presented here; positive feedback is a great way to build desired behaviors.

Meet Bella, Finn, and Daisy. Bella is seven, Finn is five, and Daisy is four. They have their very own grown-ups. Today they each learn how to keep themselves safe.

How do I keep myself safe?

"I keep my paws where I can see them! When getting in and out of the car, I keep my paws at my sides." Bella points to the car door and then looks at her paws and says, "My paws are at my sides and safe from getting trapped!"

Bella's grown-up says, "Great job, Bella! Paws are very important. I am so happy you keep your paws safe."

What are some fun things you do with your hands? Hold cookies? Pick flowers? Pet baby animals? Hands are very handy!

How do I keep myself safe?

"In the car I stay in my car seat. Where am I safest in the car? In my car seat!" Daisy points to her car seat and says, "I am in my seat and safe in the car!"

Daisy's grown-up says, "Daisy, I am so proud of you! You are smart to sit in your seat and stay safe."

What is fun about sitting in your car seat? Can you see out the window better? Does it make you taller? Is it your very own seat? What else do you like about your car seat?

How do I keep myself safe?

"I look where I am going and watch where I put my paws. Where do I look?" Finn points to the sidewalk and says, "I look where I am going!"

Finn's grown-up says, "Finn, you are getting to be such a big boy! I love that you look where you are going.

Do you look where you are going on the playground? What about in the grocery store?

How do I keep myself safe?

"I wash my paws. I wash them before I eat, when I come inside, and when they are sticky. I keep my paws clean, clean, clean!" Bella points at her paws and says, "My paws are clean!"

Bella's grown-up says, "Bella, great job washing your paws! This will keep germs from going from your paws into your food."

Do you wash your hands after using the bathroom? What about after playing with animals?

How do I keep myself safe?

Bella and Daisy love, love, love the pool!

"We never, never, never go near water without a grown-up. At the lake, at the pool, at the river—what do we do? We never, never, never go near water without a grown-up." They point to the water and say, "We never, never, never go near water without a grown-up!"

Bella and Daisy's grown-up says, "Bella and Daisy, it makes me happy to hear that you always have a grown-up with you near water."

Do you have a grown-up with you when you are in the bathtub? What about other places with water?

How do I keep myself safe?

"When I go up or down the stairs, I always hold the handrail. What do I do? I look where I put my paws, and I hold on." Daisy points to the stairs and says, "I look where I put my paws, and I hold on to the handrail!"

Daisy's grown-up says, "Daisy, you are very smart to hold the handrail. I like how you look where you put your paws on every step—good job!"

Where else do you go up and down stairs?

How do I keep myself safe?

"I love to make cookies! Cooking in the kitchen is fun, fun, fun, but beware—things can get hot." Finn points to the oven and says, "I can sense when the oven is hot before I touch it. The oven can be hot, hot, hot!"

What does Finn do when the oven is hot? He points to the stove and says, "Stand back, stand back. The oven is sizzling."

Finn's grown-up says, "Finn, you are a great cookie maker, and you know how to protect yourself. You stand back and say, 'Stand back, stand back. The oven is sizzling.' Excellent job! May I have a cookie?"

What else can get hot and sizzle? The stove? The fireplace? The barbecue? Candles? Matches? Firepits?

How do I keep myself safe?

"We always hold a grown-up's hand when we are near the road or alley. What do we never do? We never run into the street, no matter what—not for baby animals, not for balls, and not to see our friends!" Bella, Finn, and Daisy point to the road, and Bella says, "We never run into the road, no matter what—not for baby animals, not for balls, and not to see our friends. We always hold a grown-up's hand when we are near the road."

Their grown-up says, "Great job, Bella, Finn, and Daisy! Thank you for never running into the road, no matter what. Can you run in parking lots?"

"No!" they answer.

"Can you run near the school bus stop?" their grown-up asks.

"No! We never run near the road!" they answer.

Learning to keep yourself safe takes thinking.
Let's take a break. It's time for a snack!

Bella, Finn, and Daisy dream of all the fun things they will do tomorrow. And they know how to keep themselves safe!

The Pride of Pirton

The Men of Pirton, Hertfordshire
Who Served in The Great War
by Tony French, Chris Ryan and Jonty Wild

This book is dedicated to:

The memory of the men from Pirton who served in the Great War.

Lynda Smith, who was closely involved with the website www.roll-of-honour.com,
sadly died in 2007. She generously gave the information she had gathered to the Pirton website
and that was the original inspiration for this book.

The research for this book was undertaken by Tony French(Centre), Chris Ryan(Left) and Jonty Wild(Right)
and documents the Pirton men who served in the Great War, their lives and their experiences
of the war. We hope that in some small measure we have done them justice.

Published 2010 version 1.00
ISBN No. 978-0-9566816-0-7

Published by the Pirton Heritage Support Group *1

Copies can be obtained via www.pirton.org.uk/books or by contacting
Cats' Whiskers, 14a High Street, Pirton, Herts, SG5 3PS or history@pirton.org.uk

*1 The aim of the Pirton Heritage Support Group is to conserve, preserve, record and where possible, to make the
history of Pirton accessible to Pirton residents and other interested parties. Further details can be found at
www.pirton.org.uk/phsg.

CONTENTS:

Foreword

The Pirton World War 1 Project - How did it start?

The names of the war dead from the village memorial were printed in the 2002 Pirton Magazine just before Remembrance Sunday. I saw the names and noticed the difference in numbers between the two wars, 30 and 6 respectively, and thought about some of the quotes I had heard about World War One – 'the Great War', 'a lost generation', 'the carnage of the trenches', 'lions led by donkeys', but in truth I knew nothing about it.

As the editor of the village website, I decided to include the names, but felt that they deserved a little more information. A search of the internet found an excellent website www.roll-of-honour.com and an email to one of the people responsible, the late Lynda Smith, received a generous response giving permission to use their information. It occurred to me that it might make an interesting series of articles for the Pirton Magazine and I suggested that to the editor.

Talking about the subject to Chris Ryan in our local pub 'The Fox' led to an introduction to Tony French. He was then new to the village, but soon became a well established member of the Pirton community. Tony has a long standing interest in the First World War and is passionate about the need to remember the men whose names appear on the memorials. These talks turned to actually planning a trip to visit and photograph the men's graves and memorials. The idea for a Pirton book was discussed by Tony and me on that first trip in 2004.

Chris, Tony and I have since made the pilgrimage to Belgium and France on many occasions. These visits have made us all realise how important they are to understanding the men and the horrors that they experienced. They are the reason why we formed the book team, undertook the work involved and remained with the project.

Between us the book team has visited all the cemeteries and memorials for the men on our Village War Memorial - they lie in Pirton, Belgium, France, the Netherlands and Egypt.

On the first visit I told Tony that I would not let myself get too involved, but the visits, reading many books and time spent time with the men in the cemeteries and at the memorials that bear their names, but perhaps most of all, attending the Menin Gate ceremony in Ypres, made me change my mind. I now feel connected to those Pirton men and have a continuing urge to return to where they lie. To coin another phrase, one that meant so little before, but that now means so much:

"Lest We Forget"

We agreed the mission statement early in the project: *"We are seeking to publish a book documenting the men from Pirton who served in the Great War, their lives and their experience of the war."* The book team felt very strongly that, as far as possible, all men with a Pirton connection should be included and we have stuck to that principle.

We are very grateful for the help and support of members of the Pirton Heritage Support Group, which has raised money and facilitated this book.

I am also personally grateful to the other members of the book team and the Pirton Heritage Support Group for their support through some difficult times with the book and I am especially grateful to Irene, my life partner, who has put up with the many, many hours that I have spent in front of the computer and abroad at the expense of DIY and decorating the house.

One lasting affect of researching and producing this book is that all the book team now feel a responsibility to these men and their memory. We hope that, in some small measure, this book does the men's service and sacrifice justice.

Jonty Wild

If you have any additional information, which might add to the information in this book, no matter how seemingly insignificant, e.g. documents, photographs or artefacts, please contact any member of the book team or Jonty Wild via jontywild@pirton.org.uk, so that we can discuss capturing this for the future. We do not ask for the original item, just to capture it by scanning, copying or by photography.

If any relative would like a copy of a photograph of any Pirton World War One war grave or memorial, please contact us. Where possible we will supply digital copies free of charge for personal use by relatives; hard copies can be provided for a nominal charge.

The First World War
'THE GREAT WAR?'

There was no single act that caused the First World War and speculation over the relative importance of the many and complex combining factors, still to this day, generates great debate amongst historians. However, all would probably agree that they sprang from the key countries' mistrust and jealousies of each other and a variety of patriotic desires. These included underlying resentment over gains from previous wars - Germany held the Alsace region, taken from France in a war some forty years earlier; concern over strategic alliances between Great Britain, France and Russia; and those between Germany, Austria and Italy. These were further complicated by the seemingly less important alliances of Austria and the Balkans, and Great Britain and Belgium.

Germany also had a great desire to be seen as a world power, which for them meant surpassing the strength of Great Britain's navy – the most powerful in the world - and winning and controlling a large empire. From Great Britain's point of view this was a worrying challenge to her supremacy. The result was that for years Europe's politics simmered away dangerously, with the heat slowly rising and, in 1914, the single act of the assassination of Austria's Archduke Franz Ferdinand in Sarajevo caused it to boil over.

The connection was convoluted, but resulted in Germany declaring war on France and the German invasion of neutral Belgium to outflank the French. Britain had promised to protect Belgium and, as a result, our direct involvement in the conflict began on August 4th 1914, when we declared war on Germany.

Field Marshal Earl Kitchener was appointed Secretary of State for War on August 5th and, despite the popular belief of the country, he did not expect that the war would be 'over by Christmas'. He began recruiting for a 'New Army' and by the 25th he had raised the first 100,000 men. On August 28th he began raising the next 100,000 and so it continued.

In 1914, the population of Pirton was around 810 with 411 being male and about 146 of those of an age to serve; 91 more became so during the next four years of war. The men from Pirton would have read the news and seen Kitchener's plea - "*Your Country Needs YOU*" in the local newspapers. It would have been discussed around the village and in the pubs and ale houses. Many enlisted, and they did so out of duty to King and Country and for adventure. Those who knew them must have been so proud; their sons, brothers, friends would be serving their country in its hour of need.

At the time, travel was still not commonplace, and the young lads from Pirton were probably too poor or too busy earning a living to have travelled far. For most, the extent of their travel would have been a trip to the nearest town, or occasional visits to relatives further afield, perhaps further still if they had a job on the railways or were specialist workers. The prospect of going to a foreign country, France or Belgium, and teaching the Germans a lesson, must have seemed like the adventure of a lifetime. So belief in duty, the cause and the expectation of adventure drove them, but how horrific the realities must have been. The immense bombardments, the sounds of battle, the unimaginable carnage and horror. Seeing your friends and comrades fall, and then, for it to go on and on, week after week, month after month. And how sad to think that, set against their initial high ideals and the spirit of adventure, so many would never return.

There are 30 names on the War Memorial from the First World War, '*the Great War*' and the research for this project identified another 8 men who died and 190*1 men who survived, all with a connection of some kind to Pirton – *there are probably more, yet to be discovered, in records that were not available to the book team at the time of researching and writing.* Clearly, the war had a huge impact on this small Hertfordshire village.

A Modern War: No one really knew what to expect from this war; nothing like it had been fought before, not on such a scale, not with such modern weapons, and not with such equally matched forces. Some of the first battles began with old-style engagements and even cavalry charges, but that quickly changed.

The Belgians and French fought fiercely and bravely and were joined by a small British Expeditionary Force (the BEF), only 120,000 strong but highly trained. The BEF faced overwhelming numbers, but fought beyond what could have been reasonably expected of such a small force. Initially, the Germans were hugely successful and forced the French and the British back at the Battle of Mons, which could only be described as a major defeat. However, the BEF withdrew fighting, rather than in full scale retreat. Miraculously, the French and British were given time to reorganise and for a short while the success of the Germans was partially reversed and they were forced back, but then, when no great gains were made, lines were drawn and, within a matter of a few weeks, troops had 'dug in' and formed the 'Western Front' and as the armies tried to outflank each other the front line extended, eventually reaching from the Belgian coast to the Swiss border, around 400 miles.

The trenches were sometimes a few hundred yards apart, sometimes just tens of yards apart and, in many locations, only small changes would occur for much of the rest of the war. By the end of October 1914 the BEF had lost 90,000 men.

Battles and the conditions in which they were fought: Men fought over a few hundred yards of land, perhaps trying to gain control of a slight rise in the ground, a hill or a small wooded area. Today, it is hard for us to understand the battles and tactics, and why some land was seen as strategically important, let alone vital, but it was. Indeed, it is difficult to understand why some battles were fought at all and, perhaps even more difficult for us to comprehend the conditions in which they were fought.

There were three major battles around Ypres, also know as Ieper and pronounced '*Eepra*', but '*Wipers*' to the British soldier; the first began in October 1914 and, by November, the troops of both sides had had their first experience of fighting in mud. It was here that a German corporal named Adolf Hitler won the Iron Cross.

In the following year the second battle of Ypres began. The Allied soldier miners had spent weeks digging tunnels underneath the German lines and had packed them with explosives. In all, nineteen mines were detonated, and it is said that the explosions were heard in London.

The third battle, more commonly known as the Battle of Passchendaele, was fought in 1917. Despite all that had been experienced before, this was the true '*battle of the mud*'. Roads became impassable and trenches waterlogged. Wooden walkways to the trenches were constructed, but it was not unknown for soldiers to miss their footing, fall into the mud and drown.

Conditions in the trenches were often awful; with no drainage possible they filled with water. An order was reportedly issued that '*soldiers should not stand waist deep in mud for more than four hours*'.

'*The water in the trenches through which we waded was alive with a multitude of swimming frogs. Red slugs crawled up the side of the trenches and strange beetles with dangerous looking horns wriggled along dry ledges and invaded the dugouts, in search of the lice that infested them.*' - An unknown journalist

Exploding shells formed craters in no-mans land and they also filled with water. Men running forward to attack often fell into them or tried to use them for cover and death by drowning was not uncommon.

Over 20,000 men in the British Army suffered from Trench Foot, which is an infection brought on by feet being constantly wet, cold and in generally unhygienic conditions. Infections could become gangrenous and this resulted in many amputations.

> 'If you have never had trench foot described to you, I will explain. Your feet swell to two to three times their normal size and go completely dead. You can stick a bayonet into them and not feel a thing. If you are lucky enough not to lose your feet and the swelling starts to go down, it is then that the most indescribable agony begins. I have heard men cry and scream with pain and many have had to have their feet and legs amputated. I was one of the lucky ones, but one more day in that trench and it may have been too late.'
> - Harry Roberts

There was little more comfort in drier conditions, when the men in the trenches suffered from lice and rats.

Men became infected with lice and acted as their unwilling larder - imagine hundreds of lice living with you, on you, in your clothes and bedding, biting you at every opportunity. The irritation must have been terrible. The lice were known as chats and when the men were standing down they would sit 'chatting' - trying in vain to beat the lice by killing them off one by one.

Rats infested the trenches, feeding on the bodies of men that lay on or just beneath the ground. Their food was plentiful, so the rats grew to unprecedented proportions and were often quoted to be 'as big as cats!'

> 'We must look out for our bread. The rats have become much more numerous lately because the trenches are no longer in good condition. The rats here are particularly repulsive, they are so fat - the kind we call corpse-rats. They have shocking, evil, naked faces, and it is nauseating to see their long, nude tails.'-
> - Erich Maria Remarque

Most major attacks were preceded by massive artillery bombardments - incredibly frightening and destructive and yet, when their purpose was to destroy the enemy's barbed-wired fortifications so that troops could attack, often useless.

In the seven days before the Battle of the Somme, the British artillery fired 1,750,000 shells non-stop at the enemy lines. That is an average of 250,000 a day or nearly 10,500 an hour. The noise was horrific and could be heard clearly for many miles behind the lines by those living there or waiting to move to the trenches.

The shelling at the Somme was supposed to give the British Army a walkover, but the enemy's wire was undamaged. The Germans were better prepared and held better ground. They had deeper trenches and bunkers and during the bombardment retired to them for better protection. They emerged when the bombardment stopped, knowing it to be the signal for the attack and were ready with their machine guns.

In the early days, few realised the impact that the mechanised guns would have. Each could fire hundreds of rounds a minute and the Germans had far more than the allied forces. Many men emerging from the British trenches to attack the enemy were cut down within a few yards. At the Battle of the Somme, on the first day, 120,000 men of the British Army advanced at walking pace; thousands were cut down by machine guns in the first few minutes – by the end of the day there were 57,470 casualties, including 19,240 dead *2.

> 'The next morning we gunners surveyed the dreadful scene in front of us......it became clear that the Germans always had a commanding view of No Man's land. The attack had been brutally repulsed. Hundreds of dead were strung out like wreckage washed up to a high water-mark. Quite as many died on the enemy wire as on the ground, like fish caught in the net. They hung there in grotesque postures. Some looked as if they were praying; they had died on their knees and the wire had prevented their fall. Machine gun fire had done its terrible work.'
> - George Coppard, German machine gunner at the Battle of the Somme.

Artillery also fired shrapnel shells, which could cause the horrific destruction; in the open, men were killed or injured over a wide area and, if in a trench, for a significant distance along its line. Terrifyingly a shell blast could completely destroy men's bodies and, even if not destroyed, continuous shelling buried men's bodies deep under ground. 527,183*3 men from the British Army are commemorated on memorials because they have no known grave.

'To die from a bullet seems to be nothing; parts of our being remain intact; but to be dismembered, torn to pieces, reduced to pulp, this is the fear that flesh cannot support and which is fundamentally the great suffering of the bombardment.'
Written by a French soldier at Verdun.

Gas was used for the first time in warfare at Ypres; no-one had believed it would ever be used, it had been thought too terrible. However, its first use was not, as commonly believed, by the Germans, but actually by the French, although this was just in the form of an irritant intended to disable the enemy. Perhaps the Germans interpreted this as a signal that the gloves were off and later were the first to use poison gas. Their gases were much more potent and destructive. Chlorine was the first of this type to be used, then phosgene and finally mustard gas. Externally, mustard gas caused blisters and blindness and, internally, caused blisters on the lungs and other internal organs, which were excruciatingly painful. Phosgene was also particularly nasty; it had little immediate effect, but once inhaled, it was usually too late, and its affects would only become apparent after about four hours.

Gas! GAS! Quick, boys! - An ecstasy of fumbling,
Fitting the clumsy helmets just in time,
But someone still was yelling out and stumbling
And flound'ring like a man in fire or lime -
Dim, through the misty panes and thick green light,
As under a green sea, I saw him drowning.
From the poem 'Dulce et Decorum est'
by Wilfred Owen

Gas was launched by several methods, but one of the most common was simply to wait until the wind was blowing in the right direction and open the containers. Of course, if the wind changed . . . . ? The British Army suffered some 188,000 casualties and

a further 8,100 deaths from the use of gas by both sides. How many died after the war as a result of the effects, or suffered ill health or disability problems for the rest of their lives, was never recorded.

The Generals are frequently criticised and it is true that some were slow to learn or worse, completely ignored the facts; for instance, later in the war when tanks were considered to be the *'new great weapon'*, reconnaissance surveyed a proposed battlefield, and mapped the areas considered to be too waterlogged for tanks in blue. Staggered by the huge areas marked, and realising the implications, the maps were urgently forwarded to those in command. They were returned with a simple note *'stop sending any more ridiculous maps'*. The tanks were sent in and many simply stuck in the mud.

Much of the criticism however, uses hindsight and ignores significant facts; for instance, communication from the Front, on which orders and tactics were based, was always slow and often poor. There was, of course, no front line radio or satellite communication, so information was incomplete and often hours out of date. Even more importantly, although hard to accept, some battles were fought simply because they had to be. It can be argued that the Battle of the Somme, one of the most heavily criticised episodes of the war, was fought because there was a very real danger that the French would be defeated at Verdun and, if so, would have been forced out of the War. At that time, Britain with the other Allied forces, but without the French, could not have held the Germans, let alone defeat them. It is equally true though that some of those in command chose not to learn from the terrible results of their tactics, and went on to repeat them time after time.

The Great War is one of staggering statistics. Consider the numbers of men; for example, the British Army*4 mobilised 8,904,467 men, of which 908,371 were killed and 2,090,212 wounded. Of our allies France had 1,357,800 soldiers killed and 4,266,000 wounded, Russia 1,700,000/4,950,000, Italy 650,000/947,000, the USA 126,000/234,300 and Belgium 13,716/44,686. Germany lost 1,773,700 men and had 4,216,058 wounded, Austria-Hungary 1,200,000/3,620,000.*5

As with so much of the Great War, little is as simple as it might first appear. It should be remembered that winning the war saved the French and Belgium nations and much more, but the fact remains that for many, the criminal aspect of this war was that, even when the nature and scale of losses was beginning to be understood, those in authority, from the safety of a desk well behind the lines or in a cabinet office in London, made a simple calculation; *Great Britain and France with their great empires could simply 'afford' to lose more men than the Germans and their allies.* The war of attrition was accepted; no need for new tactics, and the high hopes and ideals of Britain's and Pirton's youth counted for little as individuals.

The soldiers brave, idealistic and therefore glorious, the generals and politicians . . . . ?

*1 194 names appear in this book but 4 appear to be duplications.
*2 British Army numbers usually include all Commonwealth soldiers.
*3 Figures from the Commonwealth War Grave Commission – numbers change if men's bodies are found and identified.
*4 Soldiers of the British Empire.
*5 Source - Microsoft Encarta 2002 and other websites.

Were they lions led by donkeys?

Top - the Bedfords are on the march. Bottom 'Herts Are Trumps' taken on January 24th 1916. Both taken during training. One wonders whether any Pirton men are amongst them?

THE LOCAL SITUATION

WAR INCIDENTS IN TOWN AND DISTRICT.

All calamities come as with a swift blow, and the news of the declaration of war between Britain and Germany was received in Hitchin

THE TERRITORIALS.

CALLED ON FOR HOME DEFENCE.

STIRRING SCENE AT HITCHIN STATION

The Hertfordshire Territorials were called from their summer encampment amid the beautiful surroundings of Ashridge Park for

1914 - The Rush to War

The causes of the war were many and complicated to the point of being intellectually challenging. However, very simplistically, and from the British perspective, Germany invaded 'neutral' Belgium as part of their great plan to outflank the French. Consequently Britain, who had promised to protect Belgium, declared war against Germany on August 4th 1914.

There were two immediate impacts; first there was an immediate tidal wave of public indignation and patriotic fervour, and secondly, in the way of the world, there was a '*shopping*' panic.

The Hertfordshire Express of August 8th, referring to Hitchin, reported a '*stupid rush for provisions*'. Whether price increases caused this, or the panic buying resulted in the price increases is perhaps debatable, but the affect was the same; high prices, rationing of goods, the sudden depletion of stocks and early closing of shops. '*Self preservation in this case became selfish greed*'.

The same paper, referring to an incident in Letchworth, reported a meeting held '*to protest against England being dragged into a European War*'. This was a controversial move with speakers being shouted down or drowned out by the singing of '*Rule Britannia*' and '*God Save the King*'.

By the 15th the paper was presenting a more reasoned, but perhaps also a more politically acceptable line. Lord Robert Cecil wrote that '*Though we have wished and worked for peace we have been forced to go to war. Germany has attacked France and invaded Belgium*'. The latter '*has appealed to us for help and reminded us that over and over again we have promised to defend her*'. . '*Those*

of us who can fight should volunteer for the war, and those who remain at home must help relieve the suffering and distress which war must always bring.'

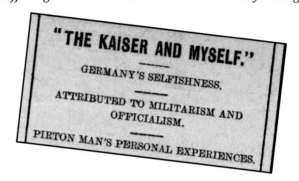

In September, a lecture was given by Mr W A Newbery to a large gathering in the Pirton National School; he was described as an '*old Pirtonian*', who had been living in Germany. The event was chaired by the vicar, Rev. E W Langmore. Mr Newbury warned that "*people failed to understand how stupendous was the war*'". He then, perhaps bravely, admitted to having been "*received with hospitality*" (in Germany) and that he had "*left many friends there*". However, this was balanced with comments on the Germans' extreme selfishness and their underestimation of the British Army. The talk ended with the Vicar uttering a protest against the brutality of the Germans and with Mr Grotian's summing up, to the appreciation of the audience. He added that "*An outstanding statement of his* (Mr Newbury) *in reference to Germany was that of autocracy and despotism of the mailed fist in Germany was unbearable.*"

The Hertfordshire Express of September 19th reported that in Hertford alone between August 14th and September 4th 2,000 men had enlisted.

Our Pirton men would have been aware of all this and much more. Talk would have been of little else. To our young men, it would have seemed the adventure of a lifetime; defend your King and Country, be the pride of the Pirton and a previously unimaginable opportunity to visit another country and 'be home by Christmas'. By the end of the year, at least thirty-six Pirton men had joined up.

Those who delved deeply into the smaller reports of the Hertfordshire Express towards the end of the year might have read a report on a local man, which gave a salutary warning of the affects of war and how desperate the experience for the men fighting it.

'A verdict of "Suicide during temporary insanity" was returned on Wednesday at an inquest on the body of Joseph Edward Line, aged twenty-six, a private in the 2nd Battalion Bedfordshire Regiment, who died in a London hospital from the effects of a razor wound in the throat. The evidence was that Line had returned home from the Front wounded in the shoulder. On Thursday he was very strange in his manner. During the night he cut his throat with a razor, jumped out of a window, ran along the Hendon-broadway, where he placed himself on the tramway metals in front of a car, but the cow-catcher caught him and he was not injured. He then tried to place himself in front of two passing motor-cars, the drivers of which avoided him, and finally jumped in front of a motorcycle with side-car, which knocked him down and ran over him.'

After the first few months of the war, it was clear that this would be a war like no other, there were no 'quick wins', in many areas even small gains had been impossible. The troops dug in and the armies, men and generals began to learn the lessons of trench warfare and machine guns. Perhaps the generals learned more slowly than others?

RECRUITING AT HITCHIN.

MEN URGENTLY NEEDED.

Recruits are still being enlisted at the Drill Hall, Hitchin, 60 men having joined the force since August 13. Most of them have gone the new Army for the duration of the war.

In the last few days of the year there were still signs of good wishes between men on both sides in the spontaneous and now infamous *'1914 Christmas Truce'*. Many readers will have some knowledge of this event and, as some of the Bedfordshire Regiments in which many of the Pirton men served were involved, it is possible that at least some Pirton men experienced at least an element of the *'Truce'*.

The event was unplanned and the extent of the truce varied from a simple cease-fire to fraternising with the enemy in no-man's land. Because of the nature of the event, details are vague. In some locations there was no sign of a truce, but there are numerous reports of soldiers from opposing sides (British and German) meeting in the middle, sometimes exchanging gifts and, in at least one location, playing a football match. In some areas the truce lasted a few hours and, in others, a few days, with the occasional volley of shots to satisfy senior officers, often with advance warning and aimed over the heads of the enemy. To varying degrees it involved hundreds if not thousands of troops. Senior British officers were livid; some more junior ranks who had turned a *'blind eye'* were disciplined. Battalion war diaries often did not fully report events. The Bedfordshire Regiment, 2nd Battalion records the following entry for Christmas Eve/Day:

'On evening of 24th December 1914 at about 8pm the Germans were singing in their trenches. There were numerous lights on their parapets apparently on Christmas trees. A voice shouted from their trenches & could be distinctly heard "I want to arrange to bury the dead. Will someone come out & meet me". 2/Lt. de Buriatte went out with 3 men & met 5 Germans the leader of whom spoke excellent English but was not an officer. He said he had lived in Brighton & Canada. This German said they wished to bury about twenty-four of their dead but would not do so at night as they were afraid their artillery might open fire and they could not stop them and this would not be fair to us. No arrangement was made at the time' .... 'This morning 25th inst. at 10am a German officer and two men unarmed came out of their trenches with a white flag and were met by Captain H. C. Jackson and asked to be permitted to bury their dead so we said we would not fire till 11.30am to give them time and this was done.'

The *'Christmas Truce'* probably occurred because for many soldiers there was not yet any great 'personal' animosity between them. Losses had not yet been so terrible as to cause deep seated resentment and the widespread urge for revenge. Also shelling had not yet been underway for long enough to have caused total devastation of trenches, towns and villages. At any rate it never happened again.

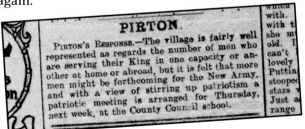

PIRTON.

PIRTON'S RESPONSE.—The village is fairly well represented as regards the number of men who are serving their King in one capacity or another at home or abroad, but it is felt that more men might be forthcoming for the New Army, and with a view of stirring up patriotism a patriotic meeting is arranged for Thursday, next week, at the County Council school.

The Men on the Village War Memorial

It is important that all of the men documented in this book should be remembered for their service to our country. Duty and patriotism may not always be fashionable and may not always be good, but these men, many of whom volunteered, served out of duty for their King and their country and for the freedom of Belgium, France and, perhaps ultimately, us.

Not all the reasons for the war were sensible and not all were honourable, but if these men had not fought, the world would be a very different place today.

The 30 men appearing in this chapter are special because they gave the ultimate sacrifice, their lives. There could easily have been many, many more. The chapter on those who survived lists 192 men, at least 41 of whom were wounded, some seriously, some more than once and they too could so easily have died.

The men who died are specially remembered and their names are read out at each annual Remembrance Service. Think about them then, next year and every year.

LEST WE FORGET
REST IN PEACE

Research Notes:

More complete details of the research for this book are given in the reference section of this book and at www.pirton.org.uk. For a more comprehensive understanding of the following pages and of potential errors, it would be wise to read those notes before continuing.

Additional Notes:

Serjeant, rather than sergeant, is the spelling used because it reflects the use by the Commonwealth War Graves Commission on the headstones and memorials.

Abbreviations commonly used in the following text include: b = born, bapt = baptised, c = circa, d = died, DCM = Distinguished Conduct Medal, MM = Military Medal, *OR = Other Ranks (i.e. not commissioned officers)*.

As with a number of the men on the Pirton War Memorial, Frank's connection to Pirton is not immediately obvious. In fact, it was not until his connection to West Mill was discovered that Frank's listing on the Village War Memorial was explained - West Mill lies near Ickleford and adjacent to Oughtonhead Common and the River Oughton and lay within the Pirton parish boundary.

Frank was born on November 8th 1885 in Hitchin and it is the Hitchin records that provide most of the following information.

His parents were John and Martha Cannon, who were born in Hitchin and Therfield respectively. The 1891 and 1901 censuses identify nine children; three girls and six boys, all born in Hitchin. They are named below*1. The 1911 census does not add any more names, but gives the total number of children as thirteen and sadly records that five had died.

In 1891 and 1901 the family was living at 14 Church Yard, Hitchin. John (senior) was listed as a grocer in 1891 and then later as gardener and fruiterer. By 1911 most of the family, including Frank, had grown up and left home. The remaining family had moved to 16 High Street, Hitchin; John (senior) now recorded as a fruiterer and nurseryman, with his wife, John (junior), Annie and Ralph all listed as assisting in the business.

It is not clear when Frank left home, but after leaving school he worked in one of Hitchin's firms of solicitors as a clerk, in fact for Mr Francis Shillitoe the coroner. He was a keen swimmer and diver and also played football for Hitchin Town. He was described as a *"dashing player and good dribbler with a fine shot"* and he had a County Cap – meaning he was selected to play at least five times. Queens Park Rangers spotted him and he signed for them in April 1907, although he continued his *'day job'*. He played for them against Manchester United in the 1907/08 Charity Shield. The match was played between the Football League champions (Manchester United) and

Company Serjeant Major Frank Cannon

the Southern League champions (QPR), the score was one all, so it was replayed and Frank also played in that game which Manchester United won four nil.

In April 1908, playing centre forward, he scored three goals against West Ham; that must have impressed them because by 1909 he had been persuaded to transfer to them, where oddly he was known as *'Fred'*. It was about this time that he married a young woman called Violet Maud, who was born in Potters Bar, and they moved into 87 Walsworth Road. He debuted for West Ham against New Brompton on January 1st 1910 and in his next game, against Norwich, he scored. That was to be his only goal and after only four appearances, all in January, he left the club. Their daughter Margaret Grace was born later in 1910 and he must have continued playing, because in the 1911 census, when he was boarding with his wife and daughter in the home of George and Annie Eve, 107 Gillingham Road, Gillingham, Kent, his occupation was given as *'Nurseryman's son working on nursery and professional footballer'*. In fact he went on to play for Gillingham, then Colebridge - located in the Potteries - and for finally for Halifax in Yorkshire.

After his return to Hertfordshire, his name appears

in connection with the war, in the Parish Magazines of September and October 1914 and by then he and Violet had three children. So it was some time after 1911 that he returned to Hertfordshire, moving to West Mill and taking on a smallholding. Both magazines record him as serving in the Bedfordshire Regiment and the Hertfordshire Express of November 14th 1914 lists him as one of the men of a local rifle club who had enlisted. All the men from the rifle club seem to be from Pirton and by that time Frank had been transferred to the 11th Service Battalion, Essex Regiment and held the rank of serjeant. We know from his Commonwealth War Graves Commission records that he later became Company Serjeant Major.

The 11th Essex was a service battalion – a battalion created specifically for the duration of the war. It was formed at Warley in September 1914 as part of K3 – Kitchener's third army, and was attached to 71st Brigade in the 24th Division. The following January (1915) they were moved to Shoreham and then to billets in Brighton. In March they returned to Shoreham and then in June moved again, this time to Blackdown Barracks, Deepcut, Camberley, Surrey. They were ordered to the Front in August and landed in Boulogne on August 30th 1915. Unfortunately the Battalion's war diary, obtained from the National Archives, starts on January 1st 1916 so Frank's experience before that date is uncertain. However, in January the 11th Essex were in the Line at Potijze in Belgium, so it is likely that they went straight there and fought in the defence of Ypres (Ieper). Ypres is pronounced 'Eepra', but was known as 'wipers' to the British Soldier.

Frank was killed in action on Tuesday February 15th 1916 and the war diary records the preceding days. The 11th Essex had been in the trenches around Potijze, with rest periods away from the trenches spent in Ypres. Whether this could be described as rest is arguable as although they were behind the front line the town was constantly shelled and while 'resting' they still had to form working and carrying parties.

Frank returned to the trenches for the last time on the 11th. The bombardment was heavy and there were seven casualties that day. The shelling continued on the 12th and they observed an aircraft flying low over the enemy trenches before a gas alarm was called and a heavy cloud drifted towards them. It seems that it was smoke and not gas, but not knowing that and fearing that it was hiding an enemy attack they had no choice but to bravely stand their ground and pour rapid fire into the smoke. There were six casualties that day, but the next day was quieter with only three. The 14th was more eventful, more shelling, two mines*2 were blown somewhere to their right and the trenches were subject to enfilading – fire from the flank, along the line of the trench - very dangerous. Casualties included three officers and eight other ranks. On the 15th the enfilading continued, their front line was hit by shrapnel shells and they suffered thirteen casualties. It was the shrapnel that wounded Frank. The diary makes a simple statement '*D Company had Serjeant Major Cannon wounded*' - it was fatal.

He did not die in one of the recognised Battles of Ypres, of which there were three, but rather in the general and bloody defence of the salient*3 to the east of Ypres. This prevented the Germans from taking Ypres and moving west to capture the British supply ports. By the end of the war 1,700,000 men from both sides had been wounded or killed in this area of Belgium.

Various local newspaper reports record his death and confirm his connection to Pirton. One records two families in bereavement, and notes that one was from the war '*the sudden death at the Front of Sergt* (actually Company Serjeant Major) *Frank Cannon whose family had been residing in West Mill for some time.*'

The reports that appeared in the North Herts Mail add detail from a letter written by Quarter Master Serjeant, L P Martin. The 13th Essex had been in the trenches for sixteen days and were just about to be relieved, '*He was just ready to leave the trench when several shrapnel shells burst over him, wounding him and several others. Although his wound was rather serious – he was wounded in the back – it was quite thought he would get to England and recover, but I am sorry to say he died on his way to the dressing station about an hour after he was hit.*' It also confirms that Frank's brothers, Harry (actually Charles Harry), Robert and Ralph were all serving, and that Ralph was serving in the same Battalion as Frank. His brothers do not have a known connection to Pirton, at least not before the war, although after the war Robert moved to West Mill and worked as a dairyman.

The 13th Platoon Commander, H Aylmer Burdett

also wrote to Frank's wife expressing how sorry he was for her loss.

The Parish Magazine of May 1918 lists some of the subscribers for the War Memorial Shrine and it includes a donation of ten shillings, a substantial sum, from Mrs Cannon of the High Street, presumably his widow.

Frank Cannon is buried in Potijze Burial Ground Cemetery, Ypres, West-Vlaanderen, Belgium. The cemetery lies to the north-east of the town and holds 584 Commonwealth burials from the First World War, of which 565 are named graves. It is a large space considering the number of burials and with low walls has an unusually open and exposed feel. Now it is surrounded by private housing, but at the time was an area which suffered constant shell fire.

It was close to Potijze Chateau, which contained an advanced dressing station and this may be where Frank spent his last hours. His family chose an inscription for his headstone *'Always Remembered by Those at Home'*.

Frank is also remembered on the Hitchin Town War Memorial.

[1] John Herbert (b c1883), Charles H (probably Harry, b c1884), Frank (b 1885), Alice (b c1887), Robert (b c1888), Annie (b c1882), Ralph (b c1884), Ida (b c1889) and Cecil V (b 1890).
[2] Armies mined under their enemy's lines, packed them with explosives and blew them up to dramatic affect causing a massive death toll.
[3] A salient is an area protruding forward from the rest of the line and therefore liable to attack on three sides.

Company Serjeant Major 14982, Frank Cannon, Potijze Burial Ground Cemetery, Ypres (Ieper), West-Vlaanderen, Belgium. Ref. H. 10.
'Always Remembered by Those at Home'

ALBERT ABBISS
PRIVATE 429011, 7TH BATTALION, CANADIAN INFANTRY
(BRITISH COLUMBIA REGIMENT).
DIED: WEDNESDAY, MARCH 29TH 1916, AGED 28.
BURIED: BERKS CEMETERY EXTENSION, COMINES-WARNETON, HAINAUT,
BELGIUM. REF. III. B. 20.
BORN IN PIRTON, LIVED AND ENLISTED IN NEW WESTMINSTER
BRITISH COLUMBIA, CANADA.

Albert Abbiss was born in Pirton on November 16th 1887*1 and was the son of Frank and Elizabeth Abbiss who lived around Great Green. Although the family were in Pirton in 1887 they are absent from the 1891 census, but present again in 1901 and 1911. Frank was a farm labourer and probably followed the seasonal work on local farms which may explain the family's absence.

Their children were Annie, Albert, Rose, Thomas William and Alice*2. The 1911 census confirms five children, but also records that one had died. It must have been Annie who died as she is absent from the later census records.

Albert is recorded on the Pirton School Memorial to the Great War, so we know that he attended the school. By 1901, and still just thirteen, he had left the classroom and was working as a ploughboy on one of the local farms. A few years later, probably in 1906 or 1907, he emigrated to Canada, but he seems to have returned for a period in 1910. Perhaps his visit also persuaded his brother Tom to emigrate as Edna Lake, from Victoria British Columbia, informs us that in 1912 five Pirton men, including Tom, emigrated to Canada together. The others were Albert William (Toby) Buckett, Edward Lake, Charlie Stapleton and one of the Walkers, possibly Arthur Robert Walker. Most settled in New Westminster, British Columbia and, perhaps surprisingly, during the time that Albert was there, he managed to return to visit Pirton three times. Once war had started, most of the Pirton men, who had emigrated to Canada, felt duty bound to return and defend their homeland and in all nine men returned, including Albert, Toby and Edward.

The Parish Magazine of September 1915 notes Albert as enlisting during 1915 before August. In fact it was on March 13th 1915 that he swore the oath; 'I *hereby engage and agree to serve in the Canadian Over-Seas Expeditionary Force, and be attached to any arm of the service therein, for the term of one year, or during the war now existing between*

Private Albert Abbiss

Great Britain and Germany should last longer than one year, and for six months after the termination of that war provided His Majesty should so long require my services, or until legally discharged.'

Albert Abbiss was now in the Canadian Army as Private 429011, 7th Battalion, Canadian Infantry (British Columbia Regiment). His attestation papers help complete the picture of Albert. He was twenty-seven, 5' 8" tall, had grey eyes and brown hair. He had been working as a labourer and was unmarried. His distinguishing marks were three vaccination scars on his left arm and a tattoo on his right, '*THC*' over a heart, cross and anchor. His religion was given as Church of England.

By the time Albert enlisted, his Battalion had already been to Belgium and had moved to France and was serving with distinction. Albert would have gone for training and during that time the Battalion continued fighting in both Belgium and France. The date that he joined them, and the fight, is uncertain. The war diary only records two drafts of men being received; a draft of 5 officers and 262 men on May 6th 1915, but that would have been too soon for Albert who must have still been in training; the second entry records a draft arriving on August 28th. It is by no means conclusive, but the latter date certainly seems more likely.

A couple of days before August 28th the Canadians had received the new helmets, which were now being issued – a bit better for protection than the caps worn previously. They had returned to the trenches around the Grande Mungue Ferme in Belgium wearing them and probably feeling a little safer. That feeling might not have lasted too long as the enemy artillery was recorded as 'very active' and the diary notes that there were many casualties and German snipers were active all day. They were relieved and within a few days were repositioned on Hill 63. This was a very important part of the British line; Ypres could be seen in the distance, but the military significance was that it protected the railhead at Steenwerck and the main road running between Bailleul and Armentières. They spent September there, moving between the reserve and support lines and the front line trenches.

In October they entered the Le Rossignol trenches, which was not a surprise to the Germans as they welcomed them with shouts of "Hello Canadians" and, strangely "Wait till October 13th and you can have the damned war". The Canadians spent the month there, recording significant enemy rifle and trench mortar activity in the periods when they were manning the trenches. Casualties at the end of the month were, one officer suffering from shock, 5 other ranks killed and 25 wounded. In November the trenches that they had moved to were in the area of the Douvre River, which was in flood and the trenches were badly affected. Both sides suffered and consequently the Germans were unusually quiet. To obtain information about the enemy's defences, the battalion was ordered to supply an attack party as part of a two point attack, planned for the night of the 16th/17th. They succeeded in entering the German trenches, killing about 30 men and bringing back 12 prisoners. It would have been a total success had it not been for a man killed when a rifle was fired accidentally as a soldier tripped on the wire and another who was slightly wounded. The total casualties for November were light; 3 men killed, 4 later died of wounds and another 26 were wounded. From the next day to December 9th they were given time away from the front line.

When they returned to the fighting they were at Neuve Eglise briefly and then went back to Hill 63. The condition of the trenches had not improved, the river was still in flood, parapets were in poor condition and only isolated parts of the lines behind the front line were considered defendable. Every effort was made to drain the trenches, but with only limited success. The artillery

*2 The newspaper article refers to Alfred not Albert; however this is a misprint.

16

bombarded the enemy lines, but that just drew retaliation and made matters worse. They were withdrawn for five days, returning on December 22nd to spend Christmas in the trenches, but at least Christmas Day and Boxing Day were quiet.

Between January and the beginning of March Albert and his Battalion improved the conditions by hard work. They also continued to hold the familiar trenches at Hill 63 and spent time resting, training or working in the Divisional Reserve at Grande Munque Farm and Bulford Camp. Late February was particularly cold with snow followed more by rain. During this time the German activity seems to have been restricted to artillery shelling and rifle fire and casualties were very light.

The diary records little in the way of activities before Albert's death on March 29th 1916. There were only general movements between camp and trenches. In fact there is no entry for the 29th, but on the 28th they had moved out of the front line to Bois de Boulogne. The only details of his death come from a newspaper report, which confirms that he was not in the front line, but billeted and being held in reserve when a shell landed on a road quite close by and killed him.

On April 2nd just four days after his death, the Rev. Louis W Moffit, one of the chaplains, wrote to Albert's mother. Some of the text of that letter was reported in the local paper*3 and that report appears here. He wrote that "*It will be a little comfort to you to know that he was instantly killed and did not suffer*". Sadly, while it may be true in this case, the expression is one that seems to appear in almost every such letter sent from the Front and was often just a kindness to the ones left behind.

The report records that he was buried in the Battalion cemetery on the slope of Hill 63 near Plug-street Wood - actually Ploegsteert which was another British colloquialism replacing the difficult local pronunciation. It seems likely that Albert's body was moved from the original location to the Berks Cemetery Extension where he now lies.

This cemetery is about eight miles south of Ypres and was not the location of any major battles, but rather the 'normal' trench warfare – shelling, sniping, small scale skirmishes. In spite of this, the cemetery and its extension, where he lies, holds 876 graves and the impressive open roofed memorial remembers 11,000 Commonwealth servicemen who died in the surrounding area and who have no known grave.

*1 *16th on his Attestation papers, 9th in other sources.*
*2 *Annie (bapt 1884), Albert (b 1887), Rose (b 1891), Thomas William (b 1893) and Alice (b 1896).*
*3 *The newspaper article refers to Alfred not Albert, but this is a misprint.*

Private Albert Abbiss,
Berks Cemetery Extension.

Private 429011, Albert Abbiss,
Berks Cemetery Extension, Comines-Warneton,
Hainaut, Belgium. Ref. III. B. 20.

FRANK HANDSCOMBE
PRIVATE 22173, 6TH BATTALION, BEDFORDSHIRE REGIMENT.
KILLED IN ACTION: TUESDAY, JULY 11TH 1916, AGED 22.
BURIED: GORDON DUMP CEMETERY, OVILLERS-LA BOISSELLE,
SOMME, FRANCE. REF. 5. J. 5.
BORN AND LIVED IN PIRTON, ENLISTED IN MILL HILL, MIDDLESEX.

Frank was the son of George and Martha Handscombe (née Dawson) and born in 1893. He seems to have had fifteen siblings or half-siblings. His father was married twice, the first time to Eliza Pearce. They were married in 1866 and had seven children*1. These would all be half brothers and sisters to Frank. Eliza died in 1882 and George remarried a year later. His new wife was Martha Dawson and she had one son already, Harry Dawson.

Together George and Martha had nine children*2 including seven boys and of those four served. Two, Charles and Hedley, both survived the war and two died; Frank who is the subject of this chapter and Joseph who is documented in a later chapter. All the family members listed were born in Pirton.

Frank and his parents lived in a thatched cottage set back from Shillington Road and which was near to the present number fifteen. We know from newspaper cuttings that Frank was secretary for the Wesleyan Chapel Sunday School and also taught the children there. The Chapel stood towards the bottom of the High Street in an area known as Burge End and next to where the Hammond's Almshouses stand today.

Private Frank Handscombe

The Wesleyan Chapel.

The Parish Magazine of September 1915 confirms that he enlisted in 1915 before July 31st and was serving in the 2nd Battalion, Bedfordshire Regiment. However, when Frank was killed in action on July 11th 1916 he had moved to the 6th Battalion of the

Bedfords and was just twenty-two years old.

The 6th Battalion was another service battalion formed for the duration of the war. After training they left for the Front, boarding trains at Ludgershall Station, which lies to the west of Andover and travelled to Southampton. Then they boarded the Empress Queen at 6:30pm and by 7:00am on July 31st 1915 they had landed at Le Havre, France. They marched to No. 5 Camp on the outskirts of Le Havre and later they gathered at St. Omer before moving to the Front. It is not certain if Frank was with them at that time, as that would depend on how early in 1915 he actually enlisted.

19

Frank's Battalion served entirely on the Western Front. In the first twelve months, the period up to Frank's death, they saw a significant amount of action. In 1915 they manned the trenches around Hannescamps and Bienvilliers. They had a mini heat wave in September followed by rain and then hard frosts. In late November when the thaw came they were knee-deep in water and mud. The cold and the rain continued into December. During this time artillery and snipers were active on both sides and, in the 6th, casualty numbers slowly mounted. They saw in the New Year while in the trenches before being relieved on New Year's Day 1916.

The action of 1916 continued on the level that they had become used to, as did the conditions in which they fought, but the war diary seems to indicate that the rate of casualties was increasing. In February they saw Zeppelins and increased aircraft activity and the month ended with snow, a thaw and a lot of hard work to keep the trenches in reasonable condition. On March 20th they were given three days of complete rest as a reward for seven months in and around the trenches. This was followed by training and the formation of working parties of up to 500 men and, apart from a short time in the trenches, April was mostly work and training.

In May they moved to new trenches at Monchy-au-Bois where they were welcomed with a hostile bombardment, followed by an enemy raid at 3:00am. When things calmed down they counted 66 casualties and 8 men were missing, presumably taken as prisoners. After relief they formed working parties and then moved to Bailleumont for more work and a period of training. For most of June they moved between Bailleumont and the trenches at Bienvillers. On the 25th they had 5 men killed and 16 wounded.

The Battalion's war diary helps establish the detail of Frank's last days. Although they served in the Battle of the Somme, which has an infamous place in our history, they were not part of that horrendous first day, July 1st 1916, when there were 57,470 casualties including 19,240 men killed. They were in reserve, moving into the line east of Albert on the 8th. That day 4 men were killed and 14 wounded. The fighting quickly escalated and on the following day when 14 men were killed and 75 wounded with 1 missing. The 10th saw 6 more killed, 40 wounded and 4 men listed as missing. Then on the 11th, the date of Frank's death, they moved to the support

PRIVATE. FRANK HANDSCOMBE KILLED IN ACTION.—The following letter from Sergt. W. H. Austin, received by Mr. Geo. Handscombe, on Tuesday, conveyed the sad news that his son, Pte. Frank Handscombe, Beds. Regiment, had been killed on July 11th:—"I very deeply regret to have to inform you of the sad death of your son Frank, who was killed on the morning of July 11th. He did not suffer any pain, as death was instantaneous. I was his platoon sergeant, and thought it my duty to write to you. He was a good soldier and always did his duty, and I was sorry to lose him, 'as he was liked by all. I might mention that myself and two of my men buried him, and we put a cross over his grave with his name upon it. Must now close, offering you my very deepest sympathy. I beg to remain, yours sincerely, W. H. Austin, Sergt." Private Frank Handscombe, who was 22 years of age and a promising young man, went over to France about two months ago. His was a fine, sensitive nature, and his influence with the children in the Wesleyan Sunday School, where he was teacher and secretary, was great. He frequently mentioned the Sunday school and the work in his letters from the Front. Much sympathy is expressed in the village for the parents; who have two other sons in khaki—one, Pte. Joseph Handscombe, arriving in France on July 11th.

trenches and a working party was formed. It is not clear if Frank was in the working party or even if they are the ones that suffered the day's casualties, but there were 9 confirmed casualties of whom 2 died; sadly Frank was one of them.

He is buried in Gordon Dump Cemetery. It lies about 1 ½ miles north-east of Albert in France. It is an exceptionally peaceful place, accessed by a long rough grass path and completely surrounded by farmer's fields. Originally it was a small cemetery, but after the war, as was common practice, it was expanded as the men from scattered burial sites were brought together. It now holds the graves of 1,676 First World War servicemen, 623 are identified and 1,053 remain unidentified, although 34 of the named men are commemorated as buried in the cemetery amongst the unidentified graves.

The special inscription for Frank's headstone, chosen by his family reads *Blessed Are The Dead That Die In The Lord*.

A memorial for Frank was held at the Wesleyan Chapel and conducted by the Rev. R E Parker. It was well attended and a solo, 'Oh rest in the Lord' was sung by Miss Bunyan. The collection was used for the Y.M.C.A. Huts' Fund.

*1 *Miriam (b c1866), Caleb (bapt 1867), Emma (bapt 1868), Elijah (bapt 1869), Elizabeth (bapt 1871), Arthur G (b c1876) and Bertie (b c1879).*

*2 *Frisby (b c1881), Charles (bapt 1884), Jane (b 1885), Fred (b 1888), Emma (b 1890), Sidney (b 1891), Frank (b 1893), Joseph (b 1896), and Hedley (b 1900).*

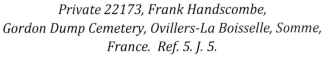

Private 22173, Frank Handscombe,
Gordon Dump Cemetery, Ovillers-La Boisselle, Somme,
France. Ref. 5. J. 5.
'Blessed Are The Dead That Die In The Lord'

JOSEPH FRENCH
PRIVATE 14223, 1ST BATTALION, BEDFORDSHIRE REGIMENT.
KILLED IN ACTION: MONDAY, SEPTEMBER 4TH 1916, AGED 27.
COMMEMORATED: THIEPVAL MEMORIAL, SOMME, FRANCE.
PIER AND FACE 2.
BORN AND LIVED IN PIRTON, ENLISTED IN HITCHIN.

Joseph French, the son of William Henry French and Mary Ann Maria (née Reynolds) was baptised in Pirton on August 4th 1889. When his parents married in 1879 both were recorded as *'from Pirton'* and they are present in all the censuses between 1881 and 1911 and most list William as born in Kings Walden and Mary as a Pirton girl. The 1911 census confirms that they had nine children*1, but that six had died.

Joseph began his schooling in Pirton in 1891 at just two, and was still at school in 1901, but by 1911 he was twenty-one, living with his parents around Little Green and working as a farm labourer for Thomas Franklin on Walnut Tree Farm. From his military records we know that their home was one of Holly Tree Cottages, which sit in Hambridge Way.

In response to one of Jonty Wild's pleas for information, Brenda Dawson (of Pirton) wrote confirming that Joseph was her mother's only brother and that he and her father, Arthur Castle, had enlisted at the same time. They must have been one of the first to do so, probably answering Lord Kitchener's call to arms, *'Your Country Needs You'*.

Joseph, like many other Pirton lads, had been in the Hertfordshire Territorials. Their motivation to join was probably the mix of soldiering, socialising and a summer break away in a training camp. When war was declared, as a Territorial he would have been mobilised, but they were only required to defend home soil and could not be ordered to undertake overseas duty. As with many, if not all of the other Pirton 'Terriers', Joseph must have felt that it was his duty to volunteer.

He was first reported by the Parish Magazine, as being in the 3rd Battalion of the Bedfordshire Regiment and if that was the case then he was presumably transferred to the 1st. The fact that he joined the Bedfordshires was a little unusual as most of the Hertfordshire Territorials went straight into the 1st Battalion of the Hertfordshire Regiment.

Private Joseph French

The 1st Bedfords were a part of the regular army with a proud history and not a battalion created to service the war. They were in Ireland when war was declared, but were called to action very quickly. They landed in France on August 16th and fought in two of the very early engagements, Mons and Le Cateau. That includes them as part of the *'Old Contemptibles'* - so called because the British Expeditionary Force (BEF) was so small that Kaiser Wilhelm II called it *'General French's contemptible little army'*. In August 1914 the BEF was tiny in comparison to the German Army, just 110,000*2 men facing vastly superior numbers, but they fought incredibly bravely and with immense discipline. They were continually forced back by what should have been overwhelming numbers, but fought so well that the Germans believed they were a much larger force with substantial reserves. It is probable that Joseph joined the Battalion some time later in order to replace losses. The Division of which they were part had suffered 5,000 casualties by the end of November and took up a purely defensive role before moving first to Ypres in Belgium early in 1915, to Loos later in 1915 and then to the Somme in 1916. Whenever it was that Joseph joined them, he would have quickly been in the thick of the action.

He was killed in action on September 4th 1916 and the Battalion's war diary provides the details of their movements up to that date. After some heavy fighting in July they were bivouacked on August 2nd. They had a good rest with some training, a church parade, boxing and football tournaments and a Regimental sports day. Officers were even granted 48 hours' leave. As they were preparing to move back into the trenches the weather deteriorated with heavy rain and storms between August 28th and the 30th. On the 31st they moved to the reserve section of the Silesia trenches and then at 8:00pm, when they relieved the 12th Gloucesters, were welcomed with '*gas and tear shells*' – presumable gas and tear gas shells.

The recent weather had been very wet and the trenches required improvement, so on September 1st 276 men formed working parties working day and night. After more gas shelling, the British Artillery retaliated on the 2nd with bursts of rapid fire from the 18-pounder guns. That evening, nine men were wounded from a single shell, recorded as '*a peculiar type, it burst on the parapet and burst in reddish light and formed no crater.*'

Strangely, given Joseph's death on the 4th, the war diary records nothing of interest between the 3rd and the 6th, but that was because they were too busy fighting. An investigation of the Battalion's war orders reveals that they were part of the 13th Infantry Brigade Operation attack on Falfemont Farm due to start on the 3rd, the day before Joseph died. Without any other information it seems most likely that he was killed in that attack.

This attack formed part of the Battle of Guillemont and Falfemont Farm was a key German stronghold to the south-east of Guillemont. The bombardment, as preparation for the attack, began on the Saturday, September 2nd. Early on the 3rd, before zero hour, two battalions from the 20th (Light) Division crept forward and took the Germans by surprise. The main attack was launched at noon and they succeeded in advancing, but only after very hard fighting. They took Guillemont, but not Falfemont Farm. On the 4th, the day Joseph died, another attempt was made and the farm finally fell early on the next day.

His comrade and chum in the Bedfordshires, Private Kilby from Stevenage, wrote to his sister asking her to let Mrs French of Pirton know that her boy had been killed. Whether as fact or kindness is uncertain, but he said that he was killed instantly: '*Pte French was going over the parapet of the trench in the attack when a bullet entered the centre of his forehead*'. Private Kilby said that he visited his grave. If true then his grave must have been lost or destroyed in later action, because Joseph is commemorated on Thiepval Memorial meaning that he has no known grave. This often means that the body was buried, destroyed by shelling or lost in no-man's land when recovery was too dangerous to

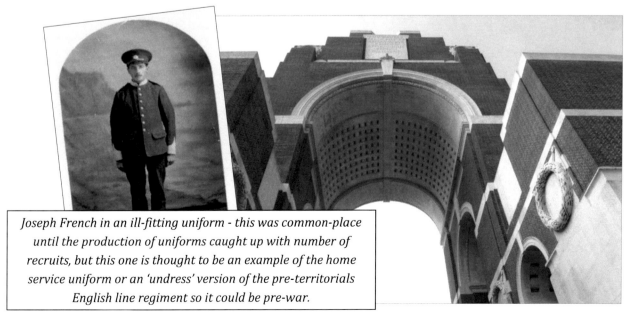

Joseph French in an ill-fitting uniform - this was common-place until the production of uniforms caught up with number of recruits, but this one is thought to be an example of the home service uniform or an 'undress' version of the pre-territorials English line regiment so it could be pre-war.

be attempted, but it can also apply to men who were buried, but their graves or markers were subsequently destroyed in later actions.

Thiepval is an awe-inspiring memorial near the village of the same name in France. A huge brick-faced structure, which dominates the surrounding countryside, but it is difficult to understand its visual impact if you have not been there. It is 'the' memorial to the missing of the Somme and names 72,092 men, of which ninety percent died between July and November 1916. Even with this great number they are only the men with no known grave from the United Kingdom and South Africa. The remaining men from other Commonwealth countries who shared a similar fate are commemorated elsewhere.

In the first Battle of the Somme, which lasted from July 1st to November 1916, the total British Army casualties were 654,751, including 127,419 dead*3. French casualties were 204,253 and German casualties estimated as 465,000 to 680,000. In some

places the allies had gained as much as 7 miles, in others nothing at all.

*1 *Only seven can be named at this time and they are Emma (b 1879, d 1880 age 16 months), John (b 1881, d 1882 aged twenty-one months), Kate (b 1883), Annie (bapt 1885), Joseph (bapt 1889), Henry (b 1891, d 1901 aged nine) and George (b c1895, d 1901 aged six). The two who are unnamed probably died at a much younger age.*
*2 *Of those 110,000 men over 86,000 were wounded or killed.*
*3 *British Army numbers usually include all Commonwealth soldiers.*

Private 14223, Joseph French. Commemorated on Thiepval Memorial, Somme, France. Pier and Face 2.

ALFRED RAYMOND JENKINS [1]

PRIVATE 24100, 1ST BATTALION, GRENADIER GUARDS.
KILLED IN ACTION: SUNDAY, SEPTEMBER 10TH 1916, AGED 21.
COMMEMORATED: THIEPVAL MEMORIAL, SOMME, FRANCE. PIER
AND FACE 8 D.
BORN IN PIRTON, ENLISTED IN HITCHIN.

[1] *He was baptised Alfred Raymond, but appears as A. Raymond on the Village Memorial. As that is how they wished him to be remembered, that is how he appears here..*

Although born Alfred Raymond Jenkins on April 4th 1895, it seems that the village knew him as Raymond or perhaps Ray.

His parents were Alfred Jenkins and Elivina Elizabeth (née Carter), although in the 1911 census she appears as Elizabeth. According to the census from 1891 and 1901 they were born in Stondon and Pirton respectively. They met and were married in June 1887 when both were listed as from Pirton, so presumably Alfred had moved to Pirton some time before. He was a bricklayer and she a strawplaiter – a common occupation within the village. Children quickly followed and according to the 1911 census they had a large family[2], eleven in all, but two died. At least seven were sons and, in all, four sons served and all survived except Raymond. They lived in the Little Green area of the village.

The Pirton School's Roll of Honour confirms that he attended, which would have been in the late 1890s. After leaving school he became an engine cleaner on the railway, probably working in Hitchin. When war was declared he was still working on the railway. As a railway employee he would not have had to join up, but apparently was anxious to do so. Twenty-one and single he gave a week's notice and enlisted. He was 6' 1¾", but he must also have had other qualities because he was accepted by the proud and prestigious Grenadier Guards. The October 1915 issue of the Parish Magazine acknowledged this in a list including fifteen others - *'May God bless, defend and preserve them and bring them safe home!'*

He went to France in June 1916 and sent cheerful letters home. One asked relatives to send a Christmas pudding *'there was nothing like asking in time'*. His last letter was sent on September 6th, just four days before the date recorded for his death. He

said that he had been in the trenches and that he and about twenty others were resting in a barn before returning to them again.

There was a quiet start to June, training in the area behind Poperinge, Belgium before moving to the Yser Canal not far from Ypres. They watched heavy bombardments, had warnings of gas attacks and took part in raids on the enemy trenches. Even though it was June, it was noted as wet and cold. July was similar, starting with training and then back into the trenches before moving some twenty miles from Poperinge to Bollezelle. Then on the 29th they moved again, by train to Halloy, France, via Cassel and Frevent. At the beginning of August they moved to a camp in a wood near Bus-les-Artois. There they had daily training in bayonet fighting, bombing and wiring, but in a complete change from routine they were honoured with a visit from the King on the 9th. The next day, probably still talking about the visit, they moved into the notorious trenches at Beaumont-Hamel on the Somme.

They recorded the trenches as being very quiet, despite the 'hostile trench mortars'. They were only there for three days before returning to billets and more training. Between the 19th and the 25th they moved on, marching first to the original camp in France, then to Sarton, Longuevillette and Vignacourt, where they caught a train to Mericourt, and then marched to their new billets at Ville sous Corbie. They undertook more training until the end of August, including two days of open warfare training, presumably in preparation for an attack.

The Battalion's war diary records them as billeted at Ville sous Corbie between the September 1st and 9th. The 10th saw them move back to the Front, part of the Battalion going to the front line East of Ginchy, and part to Guillimont. On the 11th they were ordered to attack an enemy strong point and occupy a line of trenches known as Ginchy Telegraph. The writing is not clear, but it looks like the attack commenced at midnight and some time shortly after 10:00am they had managed to fight their way to within 100 yards of the strong point. Here they were then held up by the enemy's wire. They regrouped and attacked again just after 6:00pm. The casualties are not recorded in detail, but they certainly lost seven officers and presumably many more other ranks. They were withdrawn on the 13th and then, the next day, marched to the trenches at Trones Wood. On the 15th a new zero hour of 6:20am was ordered and the Guards Division went into the attack. The 1st Battalion were used as carrying parties for the rest of the day supplying the leading Brigades. On the 16th, at 9:00am, the 1st Battalion advanced to the trenches and at 1:30pm went into the attack with the Welsh Guards to their left. They advanced to attack the trenches called Les Boeufs, but without artillery or other support. The losses during this period and for the rest of the month were awful. For the period from the 15th to the 26th for the 1,000 men that formed a Battalion, the war diary records the following casualties; 84 officers and men killed, 445 wounded and 86 were missing - a total of 611 men.

His exact date of death may be in doubt as the 'Soldiers Died in the Great War' database records

that it was between the 10th and 12th and another man, Private F Adams, wrote to his wife in Hitchin that he had heard that he died on the 16th. The exact date is perhaps of little consequence and officially remains the 10th.

We know that Raymond was killed in action, his body never found or at least never identified. Probably left behind in the attack and then not recovered, another casualty of the Somme, another name on the massive, imposing and memorable memorial at Thiepval.

As A R Jenkins he is also commemorated on the Hitchin War Memorial.

*2 *From the records available only ten can be named, they are Annie (b c1886), Alice Alma (b 27/10/1887, d 1890 aged two years and three months), Montague Harold (b 1889), Arthur Alfred (b 1893, d 1894 aged ten months), Raymond (Alfred Raymond, b 1895), Edward Victor (b 1897), Leonard Cyril (b 1899), John (b c1902), Norman (b c1905) and Emma (b c1909). Montague, Edward and Leonard all served and survived.*

PTE. A. R. JENKINS KILLED.—The sorrow of many has been evoked at the death in action of a fine soldier Private Alfred Raymond Jenkins, Grenadier Guards, son of Mrs. Jenkins, Brampton Cottage, Brampton Park-rd., Hitchin. Pte. Jenkins was 21 years of age and single. He was employed on the railway, and left there in June, 1915, in order to join the Guards. As a railway employee he would not necessarily have had to join up, but he was anxious to do so, and he gave a week's notice and joined. He stood 6ft. 1¾in. high. He went out to France last June, and always wrote home cheerfully. Recently he asked his relatives to send him some Christmas pudding this year, saying there was nothing like asking in time. His last letter home, dated September 6, stated that he was resting in a barn with about twenty others for a few days after being in the trenches, and expected to go back to the trenches shortly. Pte. F. Adams, Grenadier Guards, writing to his wife, Mrs. Adams, of West-alley, High-street, Hitchin, states he had heard "that poor old Ray Jenkins was killed on the night of Saturday, Sept. 16," and had seen a postcard that came from up the line, sent by one of his old chums, who was close to him when it happened. Another of Mrs. Jenkins' sons is in the Royal Engineers at Chatham, and there are younger sons.

Private 24100, Alfred Raymond Jenkins.
Commemorated on Thiepval Memorial,
Somme, France. Pier and Face 8 D.

JOHN FREDERICK PARSELL
PRIVATE 2366, 1ST BATTALION, HERTFORDSHIRE REGIMENT.
KILLED IN ACTION: SUNDAY, SEPTEMBER 10TH 1916, AGED 18.
BURIED: KNIGHTSBRIDGE CEMETERY, MESNIL-MARTINSART, SOMME, FRANCE. REF. F. 28.
BORN IN STOTFOLD, BEDFORDSHIRE, LIVED AND ENLISTED IN PIRTON.

John was the son of John and Sarah Parsell. The first Pirton record for John (junior) was the 1901 census. That gives the birth places for John (senior) and Sarah as Wormley, Essex and Guilden Morden, Cambridgeshire respectively and Stotfold, Bedfordshire, for young John. He was just thirteen and so was born around 1898. It also lists Katherine Maude and his elder sister and she had been born in Stapleford, Herts. John (senior) was working as a shepherd. The same census confirms that they had three children, but that one had died. From this information it is possible to find the family in 1901, when they were living in Aston, Hertfordshire. John (senior) was now a cattle stockman on a local farm. This census reveals the third child, and their eldest son, William G. He was then eight and born in Bennington, Hertfordshire.

They had clearly moved around the area and as John (senior) worked on farms he moved to where the work was. They moved to Pirton some time after the 1901 census and certainly in time for John to attend the school as he is listed on the their memorial.

Newspaper articles reveal that before the war John (junior) had begun working at Timothy White's chemist shop in Hitchin, where his services were *'highly appreciated'*. In February 1914 he was one of the Pirton contingent who joined the Hertfordshire Territorials. In fact he was at camp with them when war was declared. At sixteen he was too young to serve and had to wait until July 1915 to go to France and even then would have been too young officially. The Parish Magazine records that he was one of the men who *'had come forward to uphold the honour of our King and Country'* and was with the 1st Battalion of the Hertfordshire Regiment.

John wrote home from Hertford, presumably in late 1914. He was pleased that the Pirton soldiers were not forgotten: *'I am very happy and comfortable and getting on well'* and he wished all a *'Happy Christmas'*.

Private John Frederick Parsell

If he joined up with the Battalion in July 1915 and was probably in the draft of seventy men plus one officer who arrived from England on the 14th. Two other Pirton men*1, Arthur Walker and Harry Smith, were already serving with the 1st Hertfordshires, and had been since the November 1914; John would have known both.

At that time two of the Hertfordshire companies were in the front lines at Cuinchy and two held in reserve. The men were alternated every 48 hours, so John would have been in the frontline very soon after arriving. They were relieved on the 21st and marched to Montmorency barracks, near Bethune. The period to the end of August was spent in and out of the trenches, turn and turnabout with the Coldstream Guards.

John fought for a year with this pattern - in and out of the trenches, trench warfare and shelling. He would have been part of, or seen and heard much of, the following action, which is extracted from the Battalion's War Diary.

On September 25th 1915 they were standing ready to supporting the 1st Kings who attacked the German trenches, but they were cut to pieces by machine gun fire and the Hertfords were ordered not to advance. On the 27th they launched a gas attack on the Germans, but it had little effect so they did not follow it up. In fact the diary suggests that it was a failure, with two officers and a number of other ranks wounded or gassed – presumably the wind changed. In December they suffered unusually heavy shelling, but were lucky enough to be in Bethune away from the Front for Christmas Day.

January 1916 saw 126 replacement drafts arrive, and for the period between January and September they spent most of their time in and out of the trenches around the Bethune area of France. Many of the names of where they were located are an important part of the World War One's history and include Givenchy, Festubert, and Ancre. John did have some respite, however, because the North Hertfordshire Mail of February 17th 1916 reported that he had been home on leave and had 'returned to the front last Saturday after several days' leave'. He had brought with him some souvenirs of war; a German cap, a spent Allies hand grenade and a Jack Johnson - a 'Jack Johnson' was the British nickname used to describe the black German 15 cm artillery shell. It was named after the popular black American world heavyweight boxing champion. He returned fit and in good spirits.

In July, on the 12th Germans attacked with Minenwerfen fire*2 during the day and then at night followed up with a raid. They were driven off with Lewis gun fire. A few days later the Hertfords returned the compliment and raided the German lines. They found the section they attacked to be empty, but were then bombed from the German support line. Three officers were wounded, along with 12 other ranks, 3 other men were killed and 1 listed as missing.

On September 3rd there was an attack on the German trenches north of Ancre, but it failed. The Hertfordshire trenches suffered badly from shelling and that night, despite the Germans using gas shells from 11:30pm to dawn, they worked to consolidate the line and improve its condition. For the 10th, when John was killed, the only entry records a draft of seventeen other ranks joining the Battalion.

In fact we know that John was not present during some of this because the newspaper reporting his death noted that he had only been back with the Battalion a few hours, having been in hospital ill. The report quotes from the letter from Ted Goldsmith to John's mother that brought the sad news of his death. He had written at the request of Corporal Harry Smith, both Pirton men. Harry was too affected by the death to write himself. Ted wrote that just before his death, John had been 'very cheerful having seen Fred Baines and Arthur Odell of the Royal Sussex and George Thompson of the ASC' (Army Service Corps) another two Pirton men. It goes on to confirm that John was killed by a shell and that literally at the time of his death he had been with yet another two Pirton men, George Roberts and Arthur Walker. Both were wounded by the same shell. In fact Arthur's wounds were so serious that he died later.

In Memoriam.

The following lines appeared in the local Press in memory of John Parsell, who was killed on September 10th, 1916. They were written by a comrade who had been at school with him and who had enlisted at the same time. They are a tribute from his sorrowing father, mother and sister, and his comrade :—

"Sleep on in peace in that unknown grave,
For you fought and died, when your years were best :
You left all you loved to sail o'er the wave,
You fought the good fight, then were called to rest.

"Sweet memory now lives in the heart,
Of your mother, who mourns for her boy ;
With the hope to meet and never to part
In the peace of eternal joy."

Ted wrote that he had been close by and 'It may be small consolation to you to know that his death was practically instantaneous.' Similar words were used often to save the relatives' distress, but perhaps in this case, with an exploding shell being the cause of death, they may well have been true. Of the other Pirton men mentioned, Ted Goldsmith and George Roberts survived the war. Arthur Walker died of the wounds he received. Arthur Odell, Harry Smith and Fred Baines*3 were killed later.

John's was another death in the Battle of the Somme. He was buried in Knightsbridge Cemetery, named after one of the communication trenches. The cemetery is more remote than most; it stands quietly in the middle of fields 1 ½ miles north-east of Mesnil and is accessed by a 1 ½ mile farm track, the second half of which is a dirt track, unsuitable for cars and then 200 yards of a mud and grass path. Here there are 548 First World War burials, 141 of them unidentified men '*Known Unto God*'. John's grave is marked with his name, rank and Regiment and a simple message from his family '*Rest In Peace*'.

He is also commemorated on the Hitchin Town War Memorial and the Hitchin Hertfordshire Territorials' Memorial.

*1 *Both died and more complete details for the earlier period are provided under Arthur Walker.*
*2 *Minenwerfen were trench mortars.*
*3 *There were three Pirton men called Fred Baines who served, two of whom survived, another died and*

because of the Regiment mentioned it would be the man whom John had met earlier.

Private 2366, John Frederick Parsell,
Knightsbridge Cemetery, Mesnil-Martinsart,
Somme, France. Ref. F. 28.

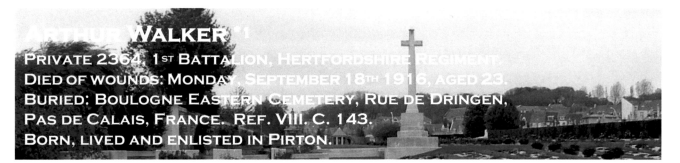

ARTHUR WALKER *1
PRIVATE 2364, 1ST BATTALION, HERTFORDSHIRE REGIMENT.
DIED OF WOUNDS: MONDAY, SEPTEMBER 18TH 1916, AGED 23.
BURIED: BOULOGNE EASTERN CEMETERY, RUE DE DRINGEN,
PAS DE CALAIS, FRANCE. REF. VIII. C. 143.
BORN, LIVED AND ENLISTED IN PIRTON.

*1 *Arthur Walker is the man mentioned in the previous
chapter on John Parsell, who died from the wounds
received in the same shell explosion.*

Arthur was born on November 13th 1892. The
Commonwealth War Graves Commission records
confirm him to be the son of George and Sarah
Walker of Pirton and husband of Mrs A. Walker of
Pirton. George and Sarah Walker (née Odell) had
seven children*2; three girls and four boys, all served
and all survived but Arthur. J

The family lived in Bury End, near Great Green, and
like his elder brothers, Sidney and Herbert, Arthur
attended the Pirton School and appears on its war
memorial. George worked as a farm labourer and
Sarah a strawplaiter, but they knew nothing of the
war or the service of their sons because they died
before the war; Sarah at fifty-nine in March 1907 and
George at sixty-four in 1911.

Sidney married a girl called Susan some time
around 1908, and moved out of the family home.
Herbert remained and in the 1911 census is listed
as the head of the household with Gertrude and
Arthur still living there. Arthur was working as a
labourer on one of the local farms.

He was another Pirton born man and another in
the Hertfordshire Territorials and signed his
attestation papers for them in February 1914, six
months before the war. He was twenty-one at that
time and an agricultural worker, working for Mr
Knowles at Oughton Head, near Hitchin.

When war came the Territorials were only obliged
to undertake home defence duties, but Arthur, like
a number of other '*Pirton Terriers*' volunteered, and
he signed the papers agreeing to overseas service
with 1st Battalion of the Hertfordshire Regiment, on
August 31st 1914. Before leaving for France he
became very friendly with a Pirton girl called Rose
Males. Perhaps the fact that Arthur was going to war
was involved, but they became close and Rose
became pregnant. Whether he managed to see her

*Arthur Walker's next of kin memorial plaque,
more commonly known as the 'death penny'.*

before his embarkation to France on the November
5th is not known, but it is likely, and perhaps that is
when he learnt of her pregnancy and a future
marriage was discussed.

The Battalion war diary records that just before
embarkation they were issued with the new, short
magazine Lee Enfield rifles. They arrived at Le Havre
and marched to rest camp before moving to St. Omer
by train and then motor bus to Vlamentinghe in
Belgium, arriving on the 11th. They came under
shrapnel fire as they marched through Ypres and two
men were slightly wounded. The next day, while
bivouacked, another shell landed, but fortunately it
failed to explode. On the 14th they moved into the
trenches for the first time and their first death in
action occurred on the 18th - it rapidly got worse as
the next day eight men were killed and more
wounded.

They were only in Ypres briefly and quickly moved
to France where the Hertfordshires saw a great deal
of their war action. They fought in the trenches
around Bethune - Givenchy, Cuinchy, Vermelles,
names that mean much to students of the war. This
whole area, along with great swathes of France, was

a fierce battlefield and by the end of the war, towns and the surrounding villages were destroyed and the land laid bare. The war diaries, which provide much of the following information, rarely dwell on the terrible conditions in which the men fought or the fierceness of the fighting.

In the North Herts Mail of February 4th 1915, he is recorded as in "G" Company and in a letter he wrote on January 4th, he confirmed that they were all alive and kicking and in the best of health. They quote from his letter, *'We can all think ourselves lucky,'* explaining *'to be in good health after being in so much mud and water for eight days.'* and of Christmas *'We were happy all the time, and had a good sing-song to keep the Germans in good spirits, for they could easily hear us, as their trenches were only twenty yards away in one place. But the Germans were careful not to show their heads for us to get a shot at them.'*

They went turn and turnabout in the trenches with Guards' battalions (Grenadier, Coldstream and Irish), but they were not 'Regulars'. It would have been understandable if the regular troops, particularly the Guards, with their proud reputation, had thought themselves a cut above the 'Territorials', but the Hertfords dug in (literally) and earned their respect. In February 1915 The G.O.C. (General Officer Commanding) sent the following message to the Hertfordshires: *'The GOC received with unqualified satisfaction your report of the steady soldier-like bearing under heavy fire of the 1st Bn Herts. Regt. (TF) both in support of the attack on the 6th February and again during the bombardment in the afternoon on the following day. He will be glad if you would convey to Major CROFT and the Officers, NCOs and men his appreciation of their action.'*

In April 1915 Arthur would have received news of his son, Stanley Arthur, born to Rose on March 31st. The Hertfords continued with their dangerous existence, in and out the trenches around Bethune, Givenchy, Sailly le Bourse and Vermelles. The North Herts Mail of May 27th 1915 reported that Arthur was with Privates Smith and Roberts, also from Pirton, when they had been hit by shrapnel. Arthur had escaped injury, but had been covered by debris.

They continually supported the Guards, relieved them and held the trenches. The Guards had a proud reputation; they were a cut above everyone, smarter, more disciplined and feared by the enemy. By the end of June, Brigadier General the Earl of Cavan, C.B., M.V.O. who was relinquishing command of the 4th (Guards) Brigade wrote: *'On leaving the Brigade to take command of a Division it would not be seemly to recall the various actions since 18th September in which it has been my privilege and delight to command you but I may say – whether in action, in the trenches or in billets, no unit of the 4th (Guards) Brigade has ever disappointed me, nor has any battalion ever fallen short of that great standard set by our predecessors. We welcomed the 1st Herts. Territorials at YPRES and most worthily have they borne their part with the rest of us. To you all I convey the gratitude of a very full heart and I wish you Goodbye and Godspeed.'*

In August, when the Guards Battalions left the area, their route was lined with other regiments. Colonel Page-Croft of the Hertfordshires Regiment noted that *'the Herts. were given pride of place'*. The Hertfordshire men cheered louder than anyone else as the Guards marched past. The Colonel of the Grenadiers gave the order *'Eyes right'* to his Battalion and saluted them as they went. In military terms high praise indeed.

The Hertfords continued fighting in the trenches of Northern France and in late September they were ordered to provide close support to an attack by the 1st Kings, but they never made it to the enemy

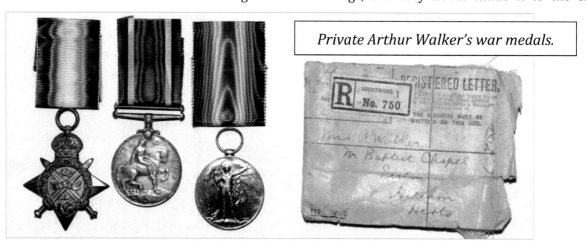

Private Arthur Walker's war medals.

trenches – the Kings were cut down by machine gun fire and the Hertfordshires were ordered not to advance. Two days later the Hertfordshires launched a gas attack, but that had little effect on the Germans, so they did not advance. In fact it seems that the wind may have changed as they had a number of their own men recorded as casualties to the gas.

Later, another letter written by Arthur was reported in which he mentioned that a friend from Lilley had died. This could be Herbert Clarke, who is included in the chapter *Should these names be on our War Memorial?* If that is the case then his letter would have been written in late September or October 1915. Arthur says that '*they had been in the firing-line for thirty-six days, with one day out.*'

He was given some respite in November when he was given nine days leave to return to Pirton to meet his son and marry Rose. A number of Arthur's comrades from the 1st Herts were at the wedding and after their experience they were probably determined to enjoy the event. Perhaps their over exuberance could have been forgiven in the circumstances, but, as can be seen in the Parish Magazine article reproduced here, the vicar was not very understanding and was disappointed that they treated the event with merriment and not the solemnity it deserved.

A Disgrace to Pirton.

We are sorry to say that the conduct of some of those attending the wedding on Nov. 22nd was disgraceful. They showed respect neither for God's Acre nor God's House, and seemed to come for "merriment," instead of attendance at a solemn Service. All such need to be reminded of our Lord's action in driving the irreverent out of His Father's House. "The Lord is in His Holy Temple, let all the earth keep silence before Him."

Value of a Clear Head.

Mr. H. J. Andrews, who lives at Hertford, in his C.E.T.S. address to us said that in the recent Zeppelin raid he observed that Temperance people were the calmest people in the district. Others who were inclined to drink seemed to lose their heads; they crowded into each others' houses and did'nt know what to do. With regard to the Temperance movement he stated that never had there been so much encouragement before: it was advancing with rapid strides.

Holy Matrimony.

" *Let marriage be held in honour.*"—
1915.   Heb. xiii., 4. (r.v.)
Nov. 22.—Arthur Walker to Rose Males.

Note the pointed positioning of the article on temperance between '*A Disgrace to Pirton*' and the announcement of their marriage '*Holy Matrimony*'. Whatever the vicar thought, '*Private Walker and his bride received the hearty congratulations of many khaki-clad and civilian friends.*'

Arthur returned to the war and his Battalion and they fought on, but they were lucky enough to spend a good period out of the trenches at Christmas including Christmas Day.

January 1916 began with training and the arrival of new drafts of men and then returned to the normality of their war, regular turns in and out of the trenches, holding the front line and casualty numbers continually rising. In February they added Festubert to their collection of infamous French areas of trench warfare.

On April 4th the Hertfordshire snipers claimed ten Germans killed. In May Serjeant G. Gregory was awarded the Military Medal for gallantry at Givenchy, '*carrying two wounded men to a place of safety during a hostile artillery barrage of fire following the explosion of a mine.*'

In July, the Germans attacked with trench mortars during the day and then at night attempted a raid on the British lines, but were driven off with Lewis gun fire. A few days later the Hertfords raided the German lines.

On September 3rd the Hertfordshire trenches suffered badly from shelling, the Germans using gas shells from 11:30pm to dawn and on the 10th yet another shell exploded which wounded Arthur. It was reminiscent of his near miss from a similar explosion in May the previous year, but this time it was much more serious. One wonders how many other unreported near misses they had each experienced. The event is described in detail in the chapter on John Parsell, who was killed, but it also wounded George Roberts, and, more seriously, Arthur - both had also been present at the previous incident in 1915.

Arthur's wounds were to his left shoulder, wrist and right hand and the first indications for Arthur were not too bad. The Rev. E J Welsher, Chaplain of the hospital where he was taken, wrote to reassure his wife. '*Your husband was brought in wounded yesterday, and he thinks you might worry until you hear, so he has asked me to write and so relieve your mind. He asks me to say there is no need to worry, that he is doing quite well, and hopes soon to be on the way to the base of England.'* It was meant in kindness, but the result was cruel. His wife was led to believe that he would recover, but he died from his wounds on September 18th 1916.

He died in one of the hospitals local to Boulogne or on his way back to England. Arthur was buried in Boulogne Eastern Cemetery, Pas de Calais. It is a large cemetery in a built-up area of the town and it contains 5,577 Commonwealth burials of the First World War, almost all of whom are identified. Its entrance is a very unusual design, with predominantly low stone walls and railings together with a gatehouse.

Over the years the nature of the ground caused the headstones to move and resulted in an untidy line, unacceptable to the normal formality of the Commonwealth War Graves and disrespectful to the men. So the very unusual solution of laying headstones flat was adopted. When compared to what is almost universally applied elsewhere, this gives the cemetery an odd feel, still very respectful, but slightly disconcerting when recalling the usual style.

After the war all the next of kin were sent the fallen man's medals and a memorial plaque, often called a death or dead man's penny. The one pictured here was provided by Andy Males who is Arthur's grandson. It was originally sent to Rose, Mrs A Walker, nr Baptist Chapel, Pirton, Hitchin, Herts.

Arthur is also commemorated on the Hertfordshire Territorial Army Memorial in Hitchin.

[2] John (bapt 1868), Alice (bapt 1871), Frederick (bapt 1882), Gertrude (bapt 1885), Sidney (b 1888), Herbert (b 1890) and Arthur (b 1892).

Private 2364, Arthur Walker, Boulogne Eastern Cemetery, Rue de Dringen, Pas de Calais, France. Ref. VIII. C. 143.

SIDNEY BAINES
PRIVATE 26026, 4TH BATTALION, BEDFORDSHIRE REGIMENT.
KILLED IN ACTION: MONDAY, NOVEMBER 13TH 1916, AGED 23.
BURIED: ANCRE BRITISH CEMETERY, BEAUMONT-HAMEL,
SOMME, FRANCE. REF. I. C. 26.
BORN AND LIVED IN PIRTON, ENLISTED IN BEDFORD.

Sidney was the son of Albert and Emma Elizabeth Baines (née Weeden), their fifth child and born on March 27th 1891. The 1911 census confirms ten children*1, but by then one had died. Five were sons, but only Sidney and Fred, who survived, appear to have served. Both attended the Pirton School and are remembered on its memorial.

Their father worked on the local farms until some time after 1901 when he became a roadman for Hertfordshire County Council. They lived in one of the cottages known as 'Ten Steps', which were a row of four small cottages in Shillington Road. They were built in the mid 18th century and demolished in 1980 to make way for new houses near where number 13 is today. After leaving school Sidney also became a farm worker.

David Baines, who has a particular interest in the local soldiers appearing on the Hitchin War Memorials, was able to add that 'As an adult Sidney moved to Hitchin and married Ethel Lily Elms'. Ethel formerly lived at the Grange, Shillington, Hitchin, Herts. A local paper recorded that he had been working at Letchworth Woodworkers and then at Phoenix – probably Phoenix Motors Ltd, who made the Phoenix motor car in Letchworth, before enlisting on February 9th 1916. According to the Parish Magazine he enlisted in Bedford and served in the 4th Bedfordshires. He survived approximately eight months, but that of course included some months of training.

The terrible losses in the early days of the Battle of the Somme*2 (July 1916) meant that large numbers of troops were desperately needed to return to strength. The 4th Battalion of the Bedfordshire Regiment was a special reserve battalion providing home defence around Harwich, but men were needed so they were called to France and landed there on July 25th 1916. Sidney was probably with them.

The Battalion's war diary held by the National

Private Sidney Baines

Archives does not start until September 1916 and so they seem to have entered the firing line for the first time on the 11th as relief for the Royal Fusiliers at Calonne. They came out of the line on the 15th, moving to reserve trenches at Bully Grenay, then moved to Coupigny, Dieval and then Orlencourt. The month of October is not available, but they would have seen action. November 2nd saw them in the front line at Knightsbridge – a trench system named after Knightsbridge Barracks and near where John Parsell had been buried two months earlier. On the 3rd they were relieved at 11:00am and moved to Englebelmer, resting until the 7th, when they marched to Hedeauville and then Puchvillers where they stayed until the afternoon of the 11th when they once again moved on, this time to Varennes. Here they waited in the assembly trenches near Bedford Street and Victoria Street (trenches), for the forthcoming major attack being launched between Beaumont Hamel and the River Ancre on the 13th – this was in the Somme and this battle became known as the Battle of the Ancre.

After a nerve-racking night the heavy barrage commenced on the enemy lines at 5:45am. The enemy responded, killing men in the support line. After an hour the men were ordered to attack. *'The Battalion advanced with the remainder of the Brigade at 6.45am and sustained heavy casualties among Officers and NCOs in and near the enemy front line from a strongpoint established between enemy front line and second line which had been passed over by the leading Brigades. Battalion advanced to enemy second line and from there parties pushed forward to Station Road and beyond.'*

Fourteen officers were killed and in the other ranks 108 men were wounded, 16 were missing and 48 killed, including Sidney. He may have died in the attack or from the earlier shelling of the support line.

Officially his wife was told that he was missing, but Private Stapleton from Holwell wrote to her telling her he had been killed. She must have desperately hoped that he was mistaken. She had just received a letter from him written on the 10th, only three days before his death.

His body lies in Ancre British Cemetery, which is about 1 ½ miles south of the village of Beaumont-Hamel. It lies to the side of a quiet country road between Albert and Achiet-le-Grand. The graves are unsighted from the road, but it has an impressive, formal, brick and stone entrance with double rising steps leading to the elevated cemetery. Its proportions are long and thin and set at right angles to the road. As you mount the steps long lines of headstones, edge on, lead the eyes away into the distance.

It is another cemetery to which men from other burial sites were brought after the war. It originally held 517 graves, but now contains the graves or memorials to 2,540 Commonwealth casualties of the First World War. 1,206 men's graves are named, memorials commemorate 43 casualties known or believed to be buried among them and there are special memorials to 16 casualties who were known to have been buried in other cemeteries, but whose graves were destroyed by shell fire. The rest are *'Known Unto God'*.

1 Charlie (bapt 1885), Mary (b-1886), Ida (b 1888 and who died in infancy), Fred (b 1890), Sidney (b 1891), Rose (b 1895), Edward (b 1897), Lily (b 1900), Harry (b 1902) and Hilda (b 1906).
2 By the end of the first day of the Battle of the Somme (July 1st) there had been 57,470 casualties, including 19,240 men killed. It had been, and still is, the blackest day in the British Army's history.

Private 26026, Sidney Baines,
Ancre British Cemetery, Beaumont-Hamel,
Somme, France.

EDWARD CHARLES BURTON [1]
PRIVATE 28050, 2ND BATTALION, BEDFORDSHIRE REGIMENT.
KILLED IN ACTION: THURSDAY, DECEMBER 21ST 1916, AGED 19.
BURIED: BERLES POSITION MILITARY CEMETERY,
PAS DE CALAIS, FRANCE. REF. B. 1.
BORN AND LIVED PIRTON, ENLISTED IN BEDFORD.

[1] *He was baptised Edward Charles, but appears as E Charles on the Village Memorial and as that is how they wished him to be remembered, that is how he appears here.*

Goliath and Mary Ann Burton had nine children, the fifth being Ellen. Edward Charles Burton was her son, born on Christmas Day 1896, when she was about twenty-one and unmarried. She later married George Pearce, some time around 1898 or 1899. While it is possible that Edward was also George's son the gap of two or three years between his birth and their marriage suggests that this is unlikely.

In most records Charles retained the surname of Burton, while children born after the marriage had the surname of Pearce. Establishing his siblings or half-sibling[2] is important because one of them also served, but it is not straight-forward. The 1911 census records that they had five children and all were living, but confusingly the investigation of parish, baptism and census records seem to suggest seven. The 1901 census reveals Edward ('Charles' Burton), John and George. Then in the 1911 census, John ('Francis John'), Frederick, Lilian, Stanley and Laurence. Their son George is not listed in the latter. Only John, who is given as Francis John, is confirmed by the available baptism records. This number was added to when Phyllis was born in 1913 – Phyllis still lives not far from Pirton. Francis John was the brother or half-brother of Charles and also served and died.

Private Edward Charles Burton

Charles went to the Pirton School from the early 1900s and then seemed to disappear from the records until it became apparent that his grandfather, Goliath, married more than once, the last time to Charlotte Weeden in 1905. He died in 1909 leaving her recorded as a widow in the 1911 census. This reveals that Edward Charles Burton was then known as '*Charles*' and was living with Charlotte. He was only fourteen and has no employment given, but as Charlotte was a widow and listed as a cow-keeper it seems likely that he was helping her, but when war came he was working for his uncle Mr H Burton who was another local farmer.

He enlisted on April 1st 1916 and according to the Hertfordshire Express went to France some time around June, but that is unlikely as fresh recruits were supposed to receive six months' training, according to the infantry training manual and reservists four, which presumably would also apply to Territorials.

The 2nd Battalion were regulars and were already in France, having gone there in September 1914 as soon as they could be recalled from South Africa where they had been stationed. It is likely that Charles joined them some time around September 1916. In fact, a draft of 160 other ranks joined the Battalion on September 21st so it seems likely that is when Charles arrived. At that time they were billeted on the Somme in France until October 10th, either in Vignacourt or Dernancourt, and so it would have been a gentle start for Charles.

He probably watched the football matches in late September when the 2nd Bedfords beat the 20th King's Own Liverpool Regiment four goals to one, and the 19th King's Own Liverpool Regiment one - nil, but all that would have been a distant memory by October 11th when they went into the front line completing the relief of the 20th Cheshires at 2:30am. The war diary records that they were heavily shelled twice on the way. At 4:00am they were ordered to take over the adjacent trenches between 6:30am and 3:30pm. On the 11th their casualties were 5 men killed and 7 wounded. They were also told that they would be attacking the enemy's trenches the next day.

That day before they were due to attack, the diary records a strange incident when some fifty Germans seemed to want to surrender and appeared without arms. Bravely one of the British officers, 2nd Lieut. H.G. Fyson, went out to speak to one of the German officers among them. After the discussion the German officer returned to his trench, but a shot was fired from the British lines and so nothing came of this episode.

The attack went ahead in the early afternoon. The German trenches were about two hundred and fifty yards away and the Bedfords, with others, went over in four waves. There were mixed results; the first wave came under terrible machine gun and rifle fire. Despite this they got within about fifty yards, but the casualties were so great that they had to lie out until nightfall before they could make their way back. In another section about two hundred yards of trench were captured and held. The war diary notes '*The Battalion did magnificently and were the only Battalion to gain any ground on the whole of the Corps Front, all the others having to withdraw to their front trenches.*' They were relieved on the 14th and went to the reserve trenches. The casualties for the period were recorded later; 5 officers were killed, 1 died of wounds and 4 others were wounded. In the other ranks the casualty total was 242, 49 men killed, 49

wounded, 2 listed as wounded and missing, another 137 wounded and 5 were recorded as shell shocked.

In the following period they occasionally occupied the trenches, but more frequently worked improving the reserve trenches and moved to the area around Mametz Wood before continuing to move, by train, to Doullens via Mericourt and then back into the front line trenches at Berles-au-Bois at the end of October. November was spent in and out of the trenches in that area of France.

Charles died on December 21st 1916, just a few days before the birthday that would have been his 20th, so the month of December is an important part of his story and the Battalion's war diary provides relevant information. On December 1st the 2nd Battalion was billeted in Humbercamps where they had been since November 28th. The weather was freezing cold. They stayed there until the 4th when they moved to relieve the Kings Liverpool Regiment in the first line trenches at Berles-au-Bois Billets, near Humbercamps. This was complete by 3:30pm and it was followed by a quiet night with no casualties.

On the 5th snow turned to rain, probably making the conditions even more uncomfortable. The Battalion HQ was shelled receiving seven casualties and eight other ranks were wounded in the trenches. From the 6th to the 9th they were in the front line, but with little happening. The 10th saw them relieved by the Kings and billeted; there were further falls of snow. The normal turn and turnabout with Kings continued and Charles was back in the trenches on the 17th. Again it was quiet by the standards of the war, but presumably the 'normal' shelling claimed six casualties in the other ranks on the 21st and two were killed. Charles Burton was one of them.

The Hertfordshire Express reported that the news was conveyed by another Pirton man, Charles Furr who was in the same Battalion. He wrote that Charles Burton and another soldier were *'killed instantly by an exploding shell while at tea.'*

The trench in which Charles died was close to Berles-au-Bois, about nine miles south-west of Arras. It remained in allied hands throughout the war, but suffered severe shelling at times.

Berles Position Military Cemetery, where his body lies, is tiny holding under sixty graves. Enclosed by a low stone wall, it nestles in the middle of fields, in the middle of nowhere and is only accessed by a sombre walk along a grass path that is almost bowling green standard, and which leads you through the ploughed fields – it is one of the most poignant cemeteries to visit anywhere.

Berles Position Military Cemetery is between Berles-au-Bois and Monchy-au-Bois, two miles south of the main road from Arras to Doullens and 100 yards south-west of the road between the two villages.

² *Harry (b 1881 or 1882), Annie Jane (bapt 1885), Albert*

Vincent (b 1886), Florence Rose (b 1888), Alice (b 1891), Helen (b 1891), Millie Ellen or Eleanor? (b 1893), Katie or Kate (b 1895), Frank (b 1896) and Phillip (b 1902).

³ *Edward ('Charles' Burton, b 1896), Francis John (b 1898), Frederick (b c1900), George (b 1901), Lilian (b c1904), Stanley (b c1907) and Laurence (b c1911).*

*Private 28050, Edward Charles Burton,
Berles Position Military Cemetery,
Pas de Calais, France. Ref. B. 1.*

HARRY CRAWLEY
PRIVATE 33153, 6TH BATTALION, LEICESTERSHIRE REGIMENT
(FORMERLY 6539 5TH BATTALION, BEDFORDSHIRE REGIMENT).
DIED OF WOUNDS: MONDAY, FEBRUARY 26TH 1917, AGED 35.
BURIED: BETHUNE TOWN CEMETERY, PAS DE CALAIS,
FRANCE. REF. VI. B. 75.
BORN AND LIVED IN PIRTON. ENLISTED IN HITCHIN.

Harry was the son of an Offley man*1, Henry Charles Crawley, and a Pirton woman, Minnie Cherry. They married some time around 1882. Henry worked as a farm labourer and then a horse keeper and by 1911 they had ten children*2, although one had died. They lived at Middle Farm on Crabtree Lane roughly where 16 Crabtree Lane is today.

After leaving Pirton School, Harry followed in his father's footsteps to become a horse-keeper. Probably, as the Parish Magazine report appearing here suggests, for Mr Thomas Franklin of Walnut Tree Farm.

Harvest Home Supper.
MASTER AND MEN SPEND A HAPPY EVENING.

On Friday, Sept. 8th, Mr. T. Franklin generously entertained his employees to a supper in the Church School. The repast was admirably served by Mr. Cooper, of the Angel Vaults, Hitchin, and amply done justice to by the Company. The tables having been cleared, Mr. Franklin took the chair. The usual loyal toasts were heartily responded to, some old-fashioned English songs followed, in which Messrs. H. Crawley, D. Titmuss, E. Males, Geo. Males, F. Anderson and others, distinguished themselves. The health of the Chairman and his family was proposed by an old servant on the farm and most heartily drunk by all.

The Chairman thanked them for their good wishes, and hoped the cordial relations at present existing between himself and the men would always continue. "God save the King" finished a most enjoyable evening.

When war came, Harry was still living with his mother in Middle Farm, his father had died some time between 1911 and 1915, and on December 9th 1915 he enlisted. His brother Frank also heard the *call to arms* and followed him, some time between March 2nd and July 1916. Frank survived the war.

Although he joined the 5th Battalion of the Bedfordshire Regiment, he was transferred to the 6th Battalion of the Leicestershire Regiment at some point. They were another service battalion formed for the duration of the war and to train Lord Kitchener's first wave of men raised for the war. They were ordered to France and landed on July 29th 1915, but Harry did not go to France until December 10th 1916 and it was on December 21st that he joined his new Battalion in the field.

Private Harry Crawley

They were at Auchel in northern France and out of the line, so Harry had a quiet start. The Battalion had Christmas dinner together, in the local theatre, and on New Year's Eve the Battalion band played the old year out. On January 27th they were due to go back into the trenches, but that order was cancelled and instead they were ordered to move to the area round Hazebrouck. They marched to Lillers, caught a train to Proven in Belgium, about thirty miles to the north, and then marched the three miles to Houtkerque. This is about fifteen miles from Ypres and quite probably they were being held in reserve and despite their Commanding Officer reconnoitring the defences, they did not go into action. Instead, on February 14th they went back to France, first to Chocques and then to Bethune and by the 18th they were in the Lancashire trench at Noyelles. The war diary for the 22nd to the 25th describes their activity as '*Normal trench warfare. One wounded on 23rd and died of wounds.*'

That man was Private Harry Crawley and that is confirmed by his service record. As he was initially only wounded he was probably taken to a hospital near or in Bethune. The Commonwealth War Graves Commission notes that: '*Bethune was comparatively free from bombardment and remained an important railway and hospital centre, as well as a corps and divisional headquarters. The 33rd Casualty Clearing Station was in the town until December 1917*'. It is probably this clearing station where Harry was taken and just three days later on the 26th, only a little over two months after he first joined the Battalion, he died.

The Hertfordshire Express newspaper of March 10th 1917, under the heading '*3rd Year of War, 32nd Week*' and, referring to local men, lists 4 men killed, 2 men died of wounds, 1 man missing and 8 wounded. Under '*Killed*' is '*Private Harry Crawley, Pirton*'.

As the name suggests, Bethune Town Cemetery serves the town. The war graves lie in a large separate area holding 3,004 Commonwealth burials from the Great War, including Indian soldiers. It also contains some French burials and, interestingly, some German graves – probably all these men died in the hospital.

It is formally laid out, as one might expect, with large areas of grass and the soldiers are carefully grouped in their various nationalities. The Great Cross sits behind the large War Shrine, rising above and encouraging eyes upwards, but the War Shrine carries the important message and reminds visitors that '*THEIR NAME LIVETH FOR EVERMORE*'.

His few remaining effects were returned to his mother, who recorded their receipt on May 4th 1917 and three years later on October 9th 1920 she received his Memorial Scroll, bearing the signature of the King.

*1 *Although confusingly his birth place is given as Offley (1911 census), Ickleford (1901) and Kings Walden (1891).*
*2 *Harry (b 1881 or 1882), Annie Jane (bapt 1885), Albert Vincent (b 1886), Florence Rose (b 1888), Alice (b 1891), Helen (b 1891), Millie Ellen or Eleanor? (b 1893), Katie or Kate (b 1895), Frank (b 1896) and Phillip (b 1902).*

Private Harry Crawley's War Medals and Memorial Plaque.

Private 33153, Harry Crawley,
Bethune Town Cemetery,
Pas de Calais, France. Ref. VI. B. 75.

GEORGE THOMAS TRUSSELL
PRIVATE G/22199, 6TH BATTALION, THE QUEEN'S
(ROYAL WEST SURREY) REGIMENT.
KILLED IN ACTION: TUESDAY, APRIL 10TH 1917, AGED 28.
COMMEMORATED: ARRAS MEMORIAL, PAS DE CALAIS,
FRANCE. BAY 2.
BORN AND LIVED PIRTON, ENLISTED IN HITCHIN.

The Commonwealth War Graves Commission records give Mrs. Elizabeth Trussell, of Burge End, Pirton, Hertfordshire, as George Trussell's mother. She was formerly Elizabeth Pitts and recorded in the 1881 census as the daughter of James and probably Ellen Pitts. At that time she was unmarried, a spinster of the parish with two children: James (b c1875) and Alice (b 1880). On April 6th 1885 she married George Trussell and home was recorded as 'near Burge End' - a name given to a much larger area than the current road of that name. They had three children*1 together, Ellen, Emily and George Thomas Trussell who was born in October 1888. By then Elizabeth was a widow, as George (senior) died on April 19th 1888 and so George Trussell (junior) never knew his father.

The School Memorial confirms that he attended the school and by 1911 George he had left and was earning a living as a stable groom. A very brief Parish Magazine article, dated August 1916, confirms that he had joined up in 1916 and therefore he probably did not go to France until early 1917.

The Battalion's war diary records the period leading up to George's death on April 10th 1917. March started off with the Battalion in the area around Lignereuil. On the 1st and 2nd they were in practice trenches near Givenchy-les-Noble where they rehearsed for an attack. They would not have known, but they were preparing for the Battle of Arras. On the 3rd and 4th they marched to Arras, billeting over night at Lattre St. Quentin. Between the 5th and the 15th they were in constant demand for working parties preparing the way for the launch of the major offensive. They were fortunate to only have three men were wounded during this period. On the 14th they did not finish their work until midnight and then marched for over six hours to reach billets in Montenescourt. One of the entries records the strength of the Battalion in France as 45 officers and 1,129 other ranks. After their efforts they remained in billets until the 19th.

On the 20th they marched for 3 ¼ hours to Lignereuill and they must have known that something big was in the air because the next four days were again spent practicing for a major attack. Heavy traffic on the roads meant a difficult march to Arras where they relieved the 9th Battalion, Essex Regiment who were in billets. Between the 26th and 29th they formed working parties and only suffered light losses and on the 30th moved into the front line, relieving the 6th Royal West Kent Regiment at 7:30am. They recorded a quiet night.

During the night of April 1st, the German artillery became more active and four other ranks were wounded. The next night they sent patrols to reconnoitre the German barbed wire and found that previous gaps they had made had not been repaired. It is possible that this was a deliberate strategy by the Germans as it would allow them to concentrate their machine gun fire on exactly the positions where the British would concentrate their troops. They were relieved on the 3rd and went to billets in the museum in Arras.

The British plan for the Battle of Arras moved into a new phase on April 4th and 2,800 British guns began a bombardment of the enemy lines on a fourteen mile front. The war diary notes the commencement of the bombardment and it seems that there was retaliation and there was a direct hit on the museum where the Battalion were billeted. That single shell buried some men, killed 6 and wounded 26. A further 4 were killed and 3 wounded while fetching rations.

On the 5th half the Battalion went into the front line. The next day they stood to, concerned about a possible German attack, but it came to nothing. Acting on orders they sent two parties to the German trenches to try and capture prisoners - presumably to gain intelligence before the attack, but they were seen and were lucky to get back with no casualties. On the 7th they were ordered to send out two strong patrols because they had received information that the enemy were withdrawing. Each patrol consisted of one officer and thirty men. One party reached the first line and indeed found it lightly defended and they captured two Germans. The other party continued to the second line, but were not so successful with one man wounded and five men, including the officer, captured. On the 8th, perhaps because the Germans were now anticipating the forthcoming attack, the diary recorded that the enemy was nervous all day.

On the April 9th at 5:30am, after five days of bombarding the enemy lines, the Battle of Arras started with a creeping barrage. This was a standard tactic, the artillery aimed to land their shells just in front of the advancing men, moving the barrage forward in front of them. In theory the enemy would then be forced to keep their heads down and so the advancing men were protected. In practice the men were often advancing over difficult ground and the speed at which they could move was not always predictable. When they got it wrong the men were either shelled by their own guns or, often more likely, the curtain of shells left them behind and the Germans simply stood up at the posts and fired into the advancing troops.

On this day, at least for George's Battalion, it seemed to work; they were in the front line of the advance and their final objective, the Glasgow Trench, was reached. Amazingly, during their action, they only had 2 officers and 4 other ranks killed, although 7 officers and 88 other ranks were wounded and 19 more listed as missing, but they now held the Glasgow Trench.

Although George Trussell is officially recorded as 'killed in action' on the 10th, the Battalion's war diary clearly states 'Casualties NIL'. We know that his body was never found so it seems almost certain that he was one of the missing nineteen men of the day before, and so that was probably the real date of his death, April 9th – the first day of the Battle of Arras.

Officially the battle lasted from April 9th to May 16th. The Commonwealth War Graves Commission estimates the number of British troops dead, missing or wounded as nearly 170,000, but that figure does include the losses from the reduced level of fighting, which continued to the end of May.

The men whose bodies were never found or never identified are recorded on individually unique memorials. George Thomas Trussell's name appears with four other Pirton men on the impressive Arras Memorial, which stands on the western edge of Arras. The names on this memorial and the associated cemetery lie behind huge brick and stone walls, and they are protected from the bustle of the modern world by this impressive fortress-like structure. The cemetery holds 2,651 Commonwealth burials from the First World War, but George is amongst the 34,717 names of the men from the United Kingdom, South Africa and New Zealand who died in the Arras sector between the spring of 1916 and August 7th 1918. None of these men have any known grave.

*1 *Ellen (bapt 1885), Emily (b 1886) and George Thomas Trussell (b 1888).*

JOSEPH HANDSCOMBE

PRIVATE 23086, 4TH BATTALION, BEDFORDSHIRE REGIMENT.
KILLED IN ACTION: MONDAY, APRIL 23RD APRIL 1917, AGED 20.
COMMEMORATED: ARRAS MEMORIAL, PAS DE CALAIS, FRANCE.
REF. BAY 5.
BORN AND LIVED IN PIRTON, ENLISTED IN AMPTHILL.

Joseph Handscombe was the younger brother of Frank who was killed in action on July 11th 1916. They shared Regiments, but were not in the same Battalion; Frank was in the 6th and Joseph in the 4th. They were the sons of George and Martha Handscombe (née Dawson). George was married twice and the offspring from his first marriage and his marriage to Martha are detailed in the chapter on Frank. All, parents and children, were born in Pirton.

Like a number of Pirton families the George and Martha saw a large number of their children go to war. In their case it was four. Frank and Joseph both died and their brothers Charles and Hedley survived. Joseph was born on June 16th 1896. He, like all their children, went to Pirton School and again, like most of the children or at least the boys, went to work on the local farms when he left school. In Joseph's case he was just fourteen; this is confirmed in the 1911 census.

After his brother went to war, Joseph took on his brother's position as secretary of the Wesleyan Sunday School until he too joined up to serve his

TWO SONS KILLED.

PIRTON BROTHERS' SUNDAY SCHOOL WORK.

Great sympathy is felt for Mr. and Mrs. George Handscombe, of Pirton, in the loss of their sixth son, Private Joseph Handscombe (20), recently killed in action. He had been in France ten months, arriving on the day his other brother Frank was killed. Both were in the Beds. Frank was formerly secretary of the Wesleyan Sunday-school, and when he joined up he was succeeded in this position by Joseph, till the latter enlisted in November, 1915. Joseph formerly worked for Mr. E. R. Davis, Rectory farm. Another son, Charles, has been discharged from training through illness. A fourth is in the Army. The family live at Burge-end, Pirton.

MR. AND MRS. G. HANDSCOMBE return thanks for the many expressions of kind sympathy.—[Advt.]

'King and Country'. The Parish Magazine records that as being some time between October 21st 1915 and March 2nd 1916. The Hertfordshire Express published in May, after his death, confirms that he had been in France for ten months. So, after a period of training, he would have arrived there some time around July 1916. In fact the 4th Battalion landed in France on July 25th and he probably travelled there then with Sidney Baines, also from Pirton and in the same battalion. Their experience, up to the date that Sidney died, would have been much the same*1. Luckily they missed the first days of the Somme and the tragic and massive losses. In fact they were brought to the Front to help replace them. They suffered the same shelling, fought in the trenches and nervously waited to go 'over the top' in the major attack on November 13th. Sidney died on that day, but Joseph survived and carried on.

The survivors of the 4th Battalion withdrew to Hamel to be resupplied and then moved back to the reserve trenches in the Beaucourt Sector. On the 14th they formed carrying parties and supplied bombs and sandbags etc. up to the front line and were still in great danger. They moved to bivouacs and huts on the 16th before carrying out the sad, painful and very dangerous task of clearing the dead from the battlefield. At least in this case the bodies had only lain there for a few days; in other locations they lay for months before they could be collected, identified if possible and then buried.

On the 18th they moved to Longuevillette and were driven there by motor omnibuses. Although the roads were probably in poor condition, they may have managed to get some rest on the journey. At least they were not on foot and that was fortunate because the next day they started on a 55 mile route march over four days moving from Longuevillette to Nouvion-en-Ponthieu.

Unfortunately the December 1916 and January 1917 months are missing from the diary, but February 1917 saw more marching. This time to

Forceville and then Englebelmer, where they were billeted before moving into the reserves trenches at Beaumont-Hamel on the 6th. These were the old 1st and 2nd German lines. They moved forward and held the front line in support of the 189th Infantry Brigade who were in action. On the 11th they were ordered to 'push forward their line of posts', which they did, although they were held up by barbed wire and heavy machine gun fire. Between the 6th and 16th they had 68 men killed, 90 wounded, 3 were missing and 45 missing believed killed. They were in and out of the front line until the 24th when they were ordered to advance the line of posts from the Sunken Trench. This they did with 1 man killed and 10 wounded.

March was quieter with lots of marching, training and a little well earned rest. In April they moved to Arras and on the 14th took over part of the front line. The next day 2 officers were killed and 58 officers and other ranks were wounded. On the 23rd at 4:45am they attacked and captured the village of Gavrelle, but were heavily shelled during the day and then the Germans counter attacked. Afterwards 2 more officers were dead and 13 wounded. The war diary records 260 casualties amongst the other ranks, it does not say how many died, but Joseph Handscombe was one of them. He was the second Pirton man to die in the area. George Trussell of the 6th Royal West Surrey Regiment had been killed thirteen days earlier.

Like George and three other Pirton men in this area, Joseph's body was never found and his name appears as one of 34,717 names of the missing on the Arras Memorial which stands with imposing and quiet dignity alongside one of the main routes into Arras.

*1 *More details appear in the previous chapter on Sidney Baines.*

Private 23086, Joseph Handscombe. Commemorated on Arras Memorial, Pas de Calais, France. Ref. Bay 5.

HARRY SMITH

CORPORAL 265408, 1ST BATTALION, HERTFORDSHIRE REGIMENT.
KILLED IN ACTION: TUESDAY, JULY 31ST JULY 1917, AGED 27.
BURIED: TYNE COT CEMETERY, ZONNEBEKE, WEST-VLAANDEREN,
BELGIUM. REF. 10. D. 5.
BORN, LIVED AND ENLISTED IN PIRTON.

On September 5th 1869 James Smith married Lydia Pearce and by 1911 they had eight children. Research of the records available has only succeeded in naming seven so far and their details are provided*1. This was another family in which all members were Pirton born and bred. Harry was the youngest and was born on August 15th 1889.

Harry went to the Pirton School and followed his father to work on the local farms when he left, but by 1914, before the war, he was working for Spencers' Engineering Works in Hitchin. Also around that time he joined the Hertfordshire Territorials.

The Territorials could not be ordered to serve abroad - their duty lay in home defence, but when war came Harry, like most if not all the other 'Pirton Terriers', volunteered to do so and on August 31st 1914 he signed his papers accepting overseas service. The Hertfordshire Regiment was purely a Territorial Army unit, but was preparing for war service and was the obvious home for the local men. The men from the Territorials were partly trained and could be sent to fight sooner than most recruits, but they still required a period of training before facing the enemy. The 1st Battalion were stationed at Bury St. Edmunds and received orders on November 1st 1914 to be ready to go to France on the 5th. They left camp in the morning and by the evening were on the City of Chester sailing for Le Havre. Harry shared the journey with at least one other Pirton man, Arthur Walker. They entered the war almost immediately and Harry would have shared much of the action with Arthur and later another Pirton man, John Parsell, who joined them in the middle of 1915.

The Battalion's war diary is comprehensive and provides a lot of detail, although typically, rarely mentions the true horrors and conditions of the war. For the period from November 1914 to September 1916 more detail is provided in the chapter on Arthur Walker. However, during that period Harry

Corporal Harry Smith

must have been recognised as a capable man for, on November 9th 1915, he was promoted to the rank of acting Lance Corporal. He was given nine days' leave, which coincided with Arthur Walker's, so they travelled back together and presumably Harry attended Arthur's wedding to Rose Males. In February 1916 his rank was confirmed and then in July he was promoted again, this time to acting Corporal.

In September the Pirton men, John Parsell and Arthur Walker, who were serving with Harry, were hit by the shell explosion, which is described in detail in the chapters on those men. John died almost instantly and Arthur was wounded. Understandably Harry seems to have been deeply affected and he had to ask another Pirton man, Edward Goldsmith, to write to John's mother on his behalf. Soon afterwards Arthur Walker also died.

Loss, of course, of friends and comrades, did not

prevent the war from continuing. In October the Battalion took over the trenches at Hamel and were then very close to the Schwaben Redoubt - one of the German heavily fortified strongholds on the Somme. However, apart from one platoon, they were not involved in attacking it, but they did suffer some of the shelling by the Germans in its defence.

They played their part in the Battle of the Ancre between November 13th and 18th. The British attack was launched in the darkness of early morning and in fog. The men had to move through deep mud in poor visibility, although the scene would have been lit to a certain extent by the tremendous bombardment which accompanied the attack. The war diary says '*At 5.45am on the 13th just before dawn and in a thick mist the guns opened fire, the Bn went forward, the Cambridgeshires on the left and the East Lancs (19th Division) on the right.*' Sidney Baines of the 4th Bedfords (and Pirton) died on this day in the same battle.

The battle itself was not a huge success and, although gains were made, there were significant losses. The Hertfordshires did better than most, they advanced 1,600 yards, took 250 prisoners and killed many Germans, but between the 13th and 15th the Hertfordshires had 7 officers wounded, 20 other ranks killed, 5 other ranks missing and 115 other ranks wounded. On the 14th, probably as a result of losses, Harry was appointed to acting Lance Serjeant in the field. On December 4th, upon completion of his duties he reverted to Corporal, but was appointed to Lance Serjeant again on the 15th.

In the latter half on November they were on the move, marching to Worloy, Orville and then Candas. There they boarded a train to Esquelbecq and billeted nearby. After a draft of over 150 men had arrived, they moved again by road and rail to Esquelbecq. By the 28th they were in Belgium at Poperinghe and then the next day they were in the dugouts in the Canal Bank, north of Ypres. It was in this area that Harry was to spend the rest of his war.

1917 opened with them back at trenches around Ypres and under an intense barrage as cover for a German raid. The Germans were successful; they took 3 men prisoner, killed 5 more and wounded 14. In February the Hertfords returned the favour, entered the German trenches, capturing 2 Germans, at the cost of 5 men wounded. Harry missed the latter event as at the end of January he caught

influenza and was hospitalised in Boulogne. It turned into bronchitis and he was moved to Calais, arriving on February 22nd. His war service record is unclear at this point. He was appointed to the rank of acting Serjeant, probably in early March, and then between March 17th and 31st he appears to have been away from his Battalion, but the explanation is not clear. He rejoined his Battalion on April 1st, the day that they relieved the 1/1st Cambs at Hooge.

They stayed around Ypres and were in and out of the dugouts on the Canal Bank in the Hill Top sector of Ypres for most of May, June and July. He reverted to Corporal '*at own request*'; Harry would have had his reasons but we could find no record of them.

The British were planning a major attack on July 31st. This would later become known as the 'Third Battle of Ypres' and the Hertfordshires were to play a major part. On the 30th they were assembled east of the river Steenbeek and ready to advance towards the Battalion objective of Langemarck.

They moved off at 3:50am in four lines and moved forward behind the 116th and 117th Infantry Brigades. The war diary records that to that point '*casualties had been very slight indeed*', but as they continued, casualties became heavier from sniper and machine gun fire. They continued and at the halfway point they came to a German stronghold, which they charged, capturing it and killing or capturing all the defenders. They continued forward reaching the enemy wire, but the diary records a simply statement '*On reaching the enemy wire this was found to be practically undamaged (except in one place) and very thick.*' Usually the military tactic was to shell the wire in advance of an attack, using ammunition designed to cut the wire, but so often this simply failed. Using simple language, the war diary describes the horrific results, '*a handful of men of No. 3 Coy got through the only gap and got into the enemy trench & killed a lot of Germans. The remainder of the Bn, being unable to get through the wire and suffering severe casualties from enfilade MG (machine gun) fire & the Germans making a strong counter attack from our left flank about this time, had*

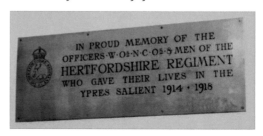

to fall back having suffered exceptionally heavy casualties.'

Harry had survived over 2 ½ years of fighting, but fell, becoming one of the many who died that day; *'He was seen to fall just before reaching our final objective.'* The Battalion casualties were 12 officers killed, 2 men missing and 7 wounded. In the other ranks numbers were estimated at 29 killed, 5 missing believed killed, 132 missing, 68 wounded missing, 223 wounded and 2 died of wounds. This made an incredible total of 478 casualties – nearly half the Battalion strength - a terrible, terrible day.

Harry's body was found and is buried in the largest of all Commonwealth War Cemeteries, Tyne Cot - huge, sadly impressive, yet beautiful and peaceful.

Tyne Cot lies about five miles north-east of Ypres. It holds the bodies of 11,954 Commonwealth servicemen of the Great War, of which 3,588 lie in named graves. Its rear walls form the memorial for the names of nearly 35,000 men whose bodies were never found.

In recent years a new car park and entrance have been built to the rear and as you walk along the rear wall to the entrance, sombre voices slowly and respectfully read the names of the men within. This, together with the realisation that this is the single largest concentration of graves for the British Army, brings incredible poignancy and emotion to a visit. Even if you never visit another cemetery you must visit this one.

[1] Mary Pearce (born before the marriage, bapt 1869), Emma (bapt 1871), James (bapt 1874), Ruth (bapt 1879), John (b 1882, d 1911), Frank (bapt 1885) and Harry (b 1889).

Corporal 265408, Harry Smith, Tyne Cot Cemetery, Zonnebeke, West-Vlaanderen, Belgium. Ref. 10. D. 5.

WILLIAM BAINES

PRIVATE 204361, 12TH BATTALION, EAST SURREY REGIMENT
(FORMERLY 20341, 5TH BATTALION, BEDFORDSHIRE REGIMENT).
KILLED IN ACTION: WEDNESDAY, AUGUST 1ST 1917, AGED ABOUT 40.
COMMEMORATED: YPRES (MENIN GATE) MEMORIAL, YPRES (IEPER),
WEST-VLAANDEREN, BELGIUM. REF: PANEL 34.
BORN IN PIRTON, LIVED IN LETCHWORTH AND ENLISTED IN HITCHIN.

William was the fourth child of Edwin and Annis Baines (sometimes listed as Baynes) who married on October 26th 1872. The 1911 census records that they had thirteen children, but one had died and that number seems to miss Herbert Charles Goldsmith, born to Annis before her marriage. The full list of children is given below*1 and all were born in Pirton.

William attended the Pirton School and at fourteen was working on a local farm. By 1901 he had left the village, but by using the census, can be found lodging with Emma Smith and her two daughters Mary Rebecca and Jane, in Norton Street, Baldock. William was working as a domestic groom. The 1911 census identifies two William Baines of a similar age, one living in Pirton and the other in Union Road, Hitchin. From marriage records, which list the father, the latter is proved to be our man. William was working as a hotel cab driver and had been married to Mary for nine years. Mary was born in Baldock, so it seems likely that he married the daughter of Emma Smith with whom he had previously lodged. Her ages in the various censuses also fit.

By 1915 he was still working as a groom and living with his wife in 56 Shott Lane, Letchworth, Herts. The Parish Magazine of October 1915 records that William had enlisted, which is odd because his Attestation papers give the date he took the oath as December 12th 1915. He was thirty-nine and actually a shade over the upper age limit at the time.

He enlisted in the 5th Reserve Battalion of the Bedfordshire Regiment and went to France on June 21st 1917. He was posted to the 7th Battalion and then transferred to the 12th Battalion of the East Surrey Regiment on July 13th. This may have been to bring the East Surrey Regiment up to strength, but both battalions saw considerable action while he was with them.

The 12th Battalion (Bermondsey) was a service battalion formed for the duration of the war and, as the title suggests, was formed at Bermondsey, East London, on May 14th 1915 by the Mayor and Borough. They landed at Le Havre on May 2nd 1916, but as explained William did not go to France until June 1917. The Battalion's war diary provides information on the period up to William's death.

July started with the Battalion on working parties. They moved to a location near Vierstraat, which lies about 4 ½ miles from Ypres. It may not have been on the front line, but they would have clearly heard the shelling and would have seen it at night. They continued on working party duty, before marching for 5 hours to La Roukloshille for training on the 6th. That night they witnessed an air raid on Bailleul. They rested until the 9th then training began and a few days later William joined them. Training continued on and off until the 23rd when they moved to a military location called Wood Camp and prepared to occupy the front line. The Battalion was now recorded as 'at battle strength'. With 500 men they moved to the Ecluse Trench at 9:15am on the 24th, leaving the other men in camp. By then the bombardment of the enemy lines was well under way. Of course the German guns were retaliating, but only one other rank was wounded. This artillery duel continued and the Battalion received orders on the 29th that they would be moving to their advance position the next day in preparation for an attack. They managed to do this with the loss of only one man.

The initial target of their attack on July 31st was a stronghold at Hollebeke and this was taken along with sixty-four prisoners and only seven casualties were reported. Conditions were bad in this area, with a lot of heavy rain falling in the previous days, making all movement difficult. On August 1st the East Surreys moved to forward positions in front of Hollebeke. The war diary plays down the difficulty of these operations and does not record the casualties on the 1st, but it does record that their forward and back areas were continually and indiscriminately shelled. Their attack was part of the Third Battle of Ypres or the Battle of Passchendaele and was notorious for the mud and the terrible conditions in which it was fought. The soldiers called it the '*Battle of Mud*' and, such were the conditions that some men died, drowning in the mud.

William's death was recorded as August 1st and his body was never recovered. He, like 54,321 other men with no known grave, is remembered on the beautiful memorial at Menin Gate in Ypres, but to this number can be added another 35,000 names of men who shared a similar fate and who are remembered on the Tyne Cot memorial, just a few miles away.

The Menin Gate is special, not only because of its impressive and beautiful design, but because it is in Ypres, and spans the road leaving the town over which so many men marched to their deaths. It is very special because at 8:00pm on every single day of the year, a moving ceremony of remembrance takes place for the fallen; such is the gratitude of the Belgian people for what our soldiers did for them. This has happened almost every night since November 11th 1929; only the German occupation between May 1940 and September 1944 prevented it.

Such is the significance of events in this area of Belgium to British history that anyone with a serious interest in our history, and especially the history of the Great War, must visit at least once. The British Army defended Ypres, and the path to the coast, and was prepared to pay almost any price. In the immediate area surrounding the town over 1,700,000 soldiers on both sides were killed or wounded. Ypres was all but destroyed, and in 1919 Winston Churchill said "*I should like to acquire the whole of the ruin of Ypres . . . a more sacred place for the British race does not exist in the world.*" That was not to be; instead it was rebuilt as it was, maintaining its original character and heritage.

William is remembered on this fine memorial. His wife's legacy was a few possessions, a pension of 13 shillings and 9 pence a week, his war and victory medals, a memorial scroll and a brass plaque, commonly known as a Death Penny.

*1 *Herbert Charles (Goldsmith, bapt 1871), Clara Baynes (bapt 1873), Ruth (bapt 1874), Martha (bapt 1876), William (bapt 1877), George (bapt 1879), Ellen (bapt 1879), Elizabeth (b 1880), Kate (b 1882), Alice (bapt 1884), Emily (b 1887), Anne (b 1889), Ida (bapt 1891) and Violet Anne (b 1898).*

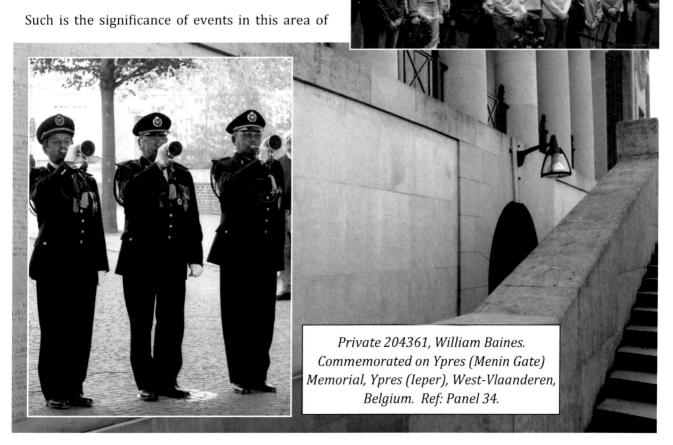

Private 204361, William Baines. Commemorated on Ypres (Menin Gate) Memorial, Ypres (Ieper), West-Vlaanderen, Belgium. Ref: Panel 34.

The Menin Gate Memorial.
'Impressive and beautiful'

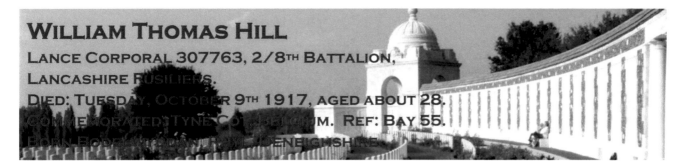

WILLIAM THOMAS HILL

LANCE CORPORAL 307763, 2/8TH BATTALION,
LANCASHIRE FUSILIERS.
DIED: TUESDAY, OCTOBER 9TH 1917, AGED ABOUT 28.
COMMEMORATED: TYNE COT, BELGIUM. REF: BAY 55.
BORN BODELWYDDAN, RHYL, DENBIGHSHIRE.

William's connection to Pirton might have remained a complete mystery, but for one small notice found in the Parish Magazine; in October 1914 a wedding was reported between a Pirton born girl, Florence Rachel Carter, and William Thomas Hill.

This simple clue, together with a report in the August 1918 Parish Magazine listing him with Charles Wilsher as missing, and which gave his Regiment as the Lancashire Fusiliers, enabled the rest of the information appearing here to be found.

William was born in Bodelwyddan, Rhyl, Denbighshire, some time around 1888, and he was very probably christened in the famous marble church of that village, which was erected at a cost of sixty thousand pounds by Lady Willoughby de Broke in memory of her husband. His information was found in the 1891 census and in that census his age is given as three. By then, William's parents, who were James Arthur and Eliza Hill, and William's two younger brothers James (b c1889) and Clement (b 1891) had moved to Shirehampton in Gloucestershire. James was working as a watchman on the railway. The family remained living in Shirehampton, in 1901 in 1 Ivy Cottage and then later in 2 Avon View Cottage, Pembroke Road. James continued to work on the railway, but now as a platelayer. The family had expanded with a daughter, Nancy (b c1893).

It is not entirely clear, but it seems possible that William's mother, Eliza, died some time before 1900

and that James subsequently remarried. This suggestion comes from the various censuses; in 1891 James was married to Eliza, in 1901 to Annie E and in 1911 to Annie Elizabeth – the former born in Bridgnorth and the latter two from Weston under Lizard. As there is a similarity in names and the two locations are only a few miles apart, it is possible that Eliza and Annie Elizabeth are the same person. However, the 1911 census records the marriage as only eleven years old and, despite four children being listed it records only one child from the marriage. Based on this information it seems likely that James had remarried and that the youngest daughter, Elesia (b c1900) was a half-sister to William.

At fifteen, William left school and was learning to be a domestic gardener. He must have worked hard and gained a good reputation as he moved on to become one of the gardening staff at Highclere Castle in Newbury, Berkshire - an important and historic property. The 1911 census confirms this and also lists a Florence Rachel Carter aged twenty-four, as a housemaid and from Pirton. So it seems that they met there and that their marriage is William's connection to Pirton.

The owner of Highclere was the 5th Earl of Carnarvon who became famous for participating in and funding excavations in Egypt. This he did from 1907, so William and Florence were probably there during his less successful ventures, but not for his most famous – his meeting and funding of Howard Carter and the subsequent discovery of the Tomb of Tutankhamun.

The Fusiliers' Museum was very helpful in providing information on William's war service. He was conscripted in late 1916 and sent to the 4th Training and Draft Finding Battalion at Barry Docks in South Wales. After a few months, with training completed, he had joined the 2nd Company, 8th Battalion and was preparing for embarkation to France.

On February 28th 1917 they arrived at Le Havre and then travelled to Thiennes, Paradis, Lestrum and then Béthune. By March 19th they were in the trenches on the front line at Givenchy. In April, May and up to mid-June they continued with the 'normal' and dangerous cycle of front line trenches, support and reserve, much of the time in the thick of the fighting around Givenchy. For the latter half of June and the first half of July they were stationed around Dunkerque, either on coastal defence duties or in camp, but by the 24th were back in the trenches, this time at Nieuport. This pattern continued, in and out of the fighting or at the coast, with the only change being the country, as at the end of July they moved to Belgium.

From the beginning of October, William's last days were spent moving forward and positioning for an attack on Passchendaele – on one of our visits the locals told us to pronounce it 'passion-da-la'. This was to be part of the Third Battle of Ypres, also known as the Battle of Passchendaele and to the soldiers, from the conditions in which they suffered and fought, the *'Battle of Mud'*.

For the Lancashire Fusiliers, October 9th was the first time in their history that two Regular Battalions had fought, shoulder to shoulder, and in all six were fighting that day. Their objective was to take Poelcapelle (now Poelkapelle). Poelcapelle is located about five miles north-east of Ypres and was a strongly fortified German position. This operation was to have its own name, the Battle of Poelcapelle.

Conditions were appalling. It had rained for weeks, the ground was waterlogged and trenches flooded, as were the many shell holes. Men fought and some drowned, especially if they fell, seriously wounded, in no-man's land. The Commonwealth War Graves Commission's website explains the conditions succinctly: '*Aspects of the ensuing fighting conformed to the classic imagery of Western Front trench warfare in which the dominant elements of mud and rain generated a degree of misery for participants which is almost impossible to describe.*'

William's Battalion were due to be in position to attack at 3:20am on the 9th, 'zero' hour being 5:20am, and to avoid daylight they moved forward in order to get to position by 6:30pm on the previous evening. Despite allowing nearly nine hours to cover just two and a half miles, the conditions were so bad – men were often up to their waists in water or up to their knees in mud - they failed to meet their deadline. However, by 5:50am it was 'optimistically' decided that enough men had arrived to attack. They moved forward and amazingly by 7:20am their first objective had been taken. Casualties were bad, the men kept trying, but by the middle of the day the German defensive fire forced the British withdrawal and, by afternoon, exhausted survivors were back on their start lines and hardly any of the objectives had been won and many men had been lost.

The action was heroic, many medals were won and some of the 2/8th managed to reach the outskirts of Passchendaele – this was proved because their bodies were found when the village was finally captured on November 6th, nearly a full month later - perhaps William got that far. The 2/8th had 35 men killed, 213 wounded and 139 missing (probably killed). William was one of those killed. The sad news was conveyed to his wife who was living at 156 Cronin Road, Commercial Road, Peckham, London.

Tyne Cot is the largest of all Commonwealth War Cemeteries and contains 11,954 graves of the British Army of the Great War. The sheer size of the cemetery brings deep emotion, but in William's case, as his body was never found, it is not the cemetery that is of primary interest but the memorial wall - the 'Memorial to the Missing'. This wall is at the back of the cemetery and it is now the rear of this wall that you pass from the

Lance Corporal 307763, William Thomas Hill. Commemorated on the Tyne Cot Memorial Wall, Bay 55.

car park to gain entry. So many names are listed that, in order to include them all, a number of bays were created. William is commemorated in Bay 55 on the north-eastern boundary, one of 34,885 names. The bays offer a sanctuary for peaceful and secluded contemplation and a chance to come to terms with what you have seen in the cemetery.

ALBERT JOHN TITMUSS

CORPORAL L/37084, "B" BATTERY, 189TH BRIGADE*1, DIVISIONAL AMMUNITION
COLUMN, ROYAL FIELD ARTILLERY.
KILLED IN ACTION: TUESDAY, OCTOBER 23RD 1917, AGED 32.
BURIED: PERTH CEMETERY (CHINA WALL), YPRES (IEPER), WEST-VLAANDEREN,
BELGIUM. REF. 6. J. 7.
BORN IN PIRTON, LIVED IN FINSBURY PARK, LONDON AND ENLISTED IN LONDON.

*1 T*he Commonwealth War Graves Commission lists Albert as
serving in "B" Battery, 169th Brigade, Royal Field Artillery;
however his service record is quite clear and his final listing,
at his death, records the 189th Brigade Ammunition Column.*

Albert was the fifth child and first son of George
and Emma Juliana Titmuss (née Cherry). Both
parents and all their eight children*2 were Pirton
born and bred. Between 1891 and 1911 the family
lived in Burge End, Bury End and then Church Baulk.

After attending Pirton School, Albert followed his
father to work on the farms around Pirton, while his
mother earned extra money as a strawplaiter. Sadly
she died in 1909 aged fifty-three.

By 1911, Albert was recorded as working as a
general labourer, but by 1915 we know from his war
service records that he was 30, living at 39 Charteris
Road, Finsbury Park, London and working as a
railway carman – a driver of a horse-drawn vehicle,
usually making local deliveries and collections.

He heeded the call to arms and enlisted, signing his
attestation papers in Hampstead on August 16th
1915, becoming Driver 37084, 183rd Howitzer
Brigade, Royal Field Artillery (RFA). He went for his
training and it was during this period that he
returned to Pirton for his wedding to Elsie Goldsmith
on March 20th 1916. He was probably aware that he
would soon be posted to the war, and when he was
his new wife remained in Pirton living around Little
Green.

By May he was fully trained and on the 2nd he
embarked from Southampton arriving in Le Havre
the next day. He was posted to the 41st Divisional
Ammunition Column (DAC) on the 23rd and
appointed as acting Bombardier on June 9th.

The ammunition columns were manned by the
members of the Royal Field Artillery (RFA) and could
be called upon to supply any unit requiring
ammunition. In addition the men employed in the
Ammunition Column could be required to replace
casualties in the artillery batteries. The work

Corporal Albert John Titmuss

supplying the guns would have meant travelling
supply routes which, if identified, would then have
been targeted by the enemy's guns. Delivering the
ammunition to the guns meant going to locations
also targeted and potentially close to the front line
– all dangerous situations.

We do not know how close to danger Albert came
during the next few months, but it was probably very
close and it would have been with great relief that
he received news of his allocation of leave to England
and he set off for two weeks' leave, starting on
November 27th. Shortly after his return, his section
of the ammunition column became the 189th Brigade
Ammunition Column and at the end of January,
confusingly, he seems to have been appointed acting
Bombardier for the second time. A Bombardier was
qualified to lay a gun for use or perhaps even a whole
Battery, which might number three or four guns.
However, while working in the ammunition column
he may not have used that skill, at least not regularly.

Albert continued doing his duty, probably experiencing much more of the same hard work and danger. His appointment to Bombardier was confirmed on March 31st. After another six months, he got the news of more leave to the UK, relatively short though, September 27th to October 7th 1917, but a newspaper report confirms that he managed to get back to Pirton. Upon his return he received the good news that he had been promoted to acting Corporal.

The events leading up to Albert's death are not clearly documented. There are no entries in his service records to suggest that he was permanently posted away from the 189th Brigade Ammunition Column to a 'firing' battery of the RFA. However, the local newspaper reporting his death referenced a letter written by Serjeant Gay and it seems conclusive and that he was serving with the guns when he died. Perhaps this explains the fact that the Commonwealth War Graves Commission and the Soldiers Died in The Great War database record Albert as in "B" Battery, 169th Brigade, Royal Field Artillery, which conflicts directly with his service records. They have 189th Brigade written clearly against 'Killed in Action' and also in their letter, dated March 19th 1918, requesting that his personal possessions be dispatched to his wife.

The clue that explains this confusion may be his recent leave. When he returned from leave in October, a short time before his death, he may not have been able to return to his normal duties, his situation may have been confused and transportation may have been scarce so he may have temporarily been assigned to the guns. It is also possible that after supplying the guns he was ordered to assist them. As mentioned above, soldiers serving in ammunition columns were required to assist the guns when necessary due to casualties etc. So it can be surmised that he was 'helping out' at the guns and that they were the 169th. We shall probably never be certain, but we do know that Serjeant Gay wrote that 'he had not been long with us in the battery' and that the 'posting' was not properly recorded and therefore may not have been official, but it is certain that he was with them for only a brief period before his death.

Working on the assumption that one of the situation described above is correct, then it is appropriate to give a little information on the 169th and their whereabouts in October 1917.

In 1916 the 169th Brigade consisted of four batteries, "A" to "D" and twelve 18 pounder guns and eight 4.5 inch howitzers and in 1917 that was probably still the case. Although they had been in France, by October 1917 they were in Belgium, and were involved as artillery support in the Battle of Passchendaele, or Third Battle of Ypres. Artillery support typically included shelling the enemy lines and key targets, support for the infantry when enemy movements were spotted and increasing in intensity during the preparation for attacks. The RFA Batteries were often at risk of retaliation from their enemy counterparts.

Albert's death was first reported in the Hertfordshire Express dated November 11th under the headline 'True and Honest Comrade – Pirton Man Who Fell by His Guns' and then again on December 1st 1917. Both reports had the date as 'on or about October 31'. Although the date may have been wrong they were quoting from the letter written by Serjeant Gay, who was in the same Battery, to Albert's wife, 'They were getting the guns in action when a shell exploded near the battery.' Albert was hit and badly injured. They took him to a place of safety, but 'he expired before he reached the dressing station.' It seems likely that he was killed in one of the commonplace artillery 'duels' of the war.

His date of death is officially recorded as October 23rd 1917. At that time the Third Battle of Ypres was nearing its end, but still being fought in appalling

TRUE AND HONEST COMRADE

PIRTON MAN WHO FELL BY HIS GUNS.

We regret to include another gallant Pirtonian in the roll of honour—Corporal Albert Titmuss (32), R.F.A., whose death in action took place on or about October 31. Writing under that date Sergeant Gay, in whose battery he was, informs deceased's wife that they were getting the guns in action when a shell exploded near the battery. They got her husband to a place of safety and a doctor dressed his wounds, but he expired before they got him to the dressing station. He adds, "His last thoughts were of you. He gave me your address and I promised him I would write. Please accept deepest sympathy from myself and comrades who respected him as a brave and fearless man. He had not been long with us in the battery, but we found him a true and honest comrade, respected by all the N.C.O's, and men in the battery." Corporal Titmuss enlisted on August 16, 1915, and went to France the following May. He only left England on his last home leave on October 7. He worked at the G.N. station at Finsbury Park. He was a son of the late Mr. and Mrs. George Titmuss, Church-walk, Pirton, and his wife, with whom much sympathy is felt, lives with her mother at Little Green, Pirton. Photograph next week.

conditions – the soldiers called it the Battle of Mud. The losses on both sides were huge, the British had lost 310,000 men and the Germans 260,000. The vast majority would have been from the front lines, but as Albert's story proves, the artillery also suffered. The shock for his wife must have been compounded by the fact that his death was so soon after he had been home to Pirton on leave.

His body was buried in the Perth Cemetery (China Wall), located two miles east of Ypres' town centre. The cemetery is another one holding men brought together from a surprising large number of smaller cemeteries, but was used in its own right for front line burials until October 1917. It now contains 2,791 burials or commemorations to Commonwealth servicemen, 1,422 are identified.

Visitors are met by the Cross of Sacrifice which immediately demands one's attention. Then the avenue of trees drags one's eyes to the distance, but as they descend the realism of the headstones, heading towards the horizon, begins to focus your thoughts on what they represent. Albert's headstone bears the inscription chosen by his family which reads 'Death Divides Sweet Memories Cling'.

*2 Mary (bapt 1876), Elizabeth (bapt 1878), Peggy (b 1879), Ellen Rose (b 1882), Albert John (bapt 1884), Sidney (b 1888), Lilian (b c1891) and Frederick (b 1895).

Corporal L/37084, Albert John Titmuss, Perth Cemetery (China Wall), Ypres, West-Vlaanderen, Belgium. Ref. 6. J. 7.

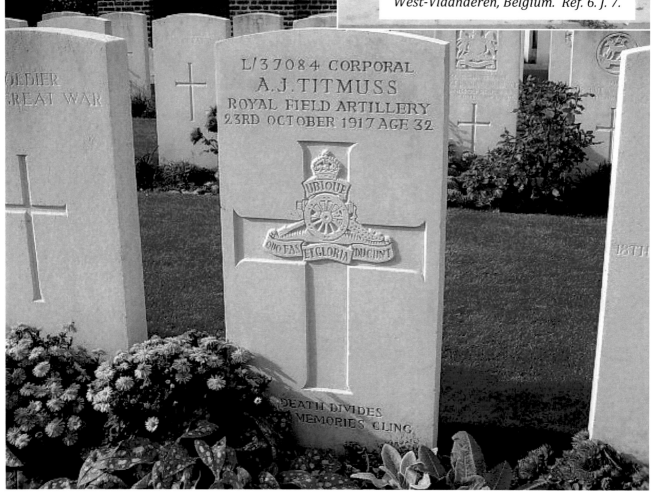

FRED BURTON

SERJEANT 200950, 2/4TH BATTALION, PRINCESS CHARLOTTE OF WALES'S
ROYAL BERKSHIRE REGIMENT.
KILLED IN ACTION: ON SUNDAY, DECEMBER 2ND 1917, AGED 29.
BURIED: FIFTEEN RAVINE BRITISH CEMETERY, VILLERS-PLOUICH, NORD,
FRANCE. REF. VIII. D. 17.
BORN AND LIVED IN PIRTON, ENLISTED IN READING, BERKS.

The records of the Commonwealth War Graves Commission confirm Fred's parents as David and Rose (Fanny*1) Burton (née Walker). They married some time around 1880 when he was an agricultural worker and publican, running The Red Lion in Crabtree Lane. This property is still there, near the entrance to the church and is now called Red Lion Cottage. They had four children*2; Beatrice Ruth, Sydney Charles, Fred, born on January 29th 1888, and Thomas.

Pirton School records show that he was admitted in 1890 as Freddie Burton. By the 1901 census the family had moved to Great Green and David was working as a farmer and cowkeeper. Curiously Fred is absent and even with the power of the internet he was difficult to locate, as his birth place of Pirton was recorded as Parton. Eventually he was located in Trumpington Street, Cambridge where, at just thirteen, he was a domestic page to a Cambridge University professor of Sanskrit.

His family remained in Pirton. By 1911 Fred had moved on and was now a footman at Binfield Manor in Berkshire. He first worked for Mr Erskine and then later for his daughter upon her marriage to Mr Luard. The house was a large thirty-seven roomed property, originally built for William Pitt the Elder, so it is safe to assume that his employers were wealthy. The household consisted of 21, nine family members and 12 servants. A later newspaper reported that by the time Fred enlisted he had risen to the position of the family butler.

Both Fred and his brother, Sidney, enlisted – Sidney is detailed in the chapter on the survivors of the war. Fred enlisted some time around November 1914, joining the 2/4th Battalion of the local Regiment, the Princess Charlotte of Wales's Royal Berkshire Regiment. This Regiment had only been formed in September and was established to accommodate the Territorials who had not signed up for overseas service and the many new recruits. They initially undertook UK service and were

Serjeant Fred Burton

stationed at Gateshead from mid-January to late March 1916 and it was during this period that Fred's father died.

In May, the Territorials who accepted overseas service and the other recruits moved to Luggershall on Salisbury Plain to wait for embarkation to France, where they arrived on May 27th 1916.

Their first action was in June, close to the Belgium border, and then they moved to the Somme in November, but were not involved to any great extent in that battle. During the early part of 1917 they were training in France. Fred was lucky to be given leave during February and was able to return to Pirton for a brief visit.

They remained in France and their next action was in April 1917. On the 1st, while they were in defending Vermand, 5 other ranks were killed, 15 wounded and 1 suffered shell shock. The next day they joined in the attack and the capture of the enemy line at Bihecourt-Ponne Copse, but 11 more men were wounded, 2 of whom later died.

In August they returned to Belgium and on the 23rd Fred and the Berkshires were in fighting in the mud at Passchendaele. Thirteen platoons of the 2/4th Royal Berks attacked a number of known strong points including Pond Farm, Hindu, Schuler, Somme, Hill 35 and Gallipoli (all trench names). After consolidating their position they fought off three counter attacks. During these two days, 7 officers were wounded and 2 killed or missing. In the other ranks 32 were killed, 111 wounded, 25 wounded or missing and 54 missing. On the 24th they rested.

The following three months were relatively quiet and spent first in Belgium, and then, from September 19th, in France. In October the Berkshires were in and out of the trenches, but it was still relatively quiet. On the 28th they marched to Arras for a period of training, returning to the line between November 11th and 30th, in the Chemical Works Sector, Arras. During this period 7 more men were killed and 14 wounded. Fred would have experienced most if not all of the action and by now he was probably battle-experienced and battle-hardened.

At 3:45am on December 1st 1917 the Battalion marched in the bitter cold, through mud and water, to Fins where they prepared for the next battle. On the 2nd, they were told that the Guards had retaken Gouzeaucourt and they were to join them to resist any counter attacks. They were in position by 5:30am and operational orders were given. About lunchtime Fred went to Battalion HQ with food for the officers and was killed on his way back to the mess cart. This was during the Battle of Cambrai; the Battalion's participation was described as '*marginal*', but that was not so for Serjeant Fred Burton.

Fred Burton was first recorded officially as missing and the North Hertfordshire Mail of December 20th reported the anxiety of his family at Great Green Farm and particularly that of his mother, who was a widow and had been ill for some time. They obviously hoped for the best, but received the unofficial news of his death on Wednesday December 19th. It came from his former employers, who had been notified by another soldier. Just three days later his mother died without receiving the official notification. She was only fifty-six and perhaps she was another, indirect victim of the war.

The remaining family produced this memorial card with its touching poem that appears here. They also

PIRTON.

OBITUARY.—We regret to report that Mrs. Burton, Great Green farm, passed away on Saturday, after a long illness, patiently borne. The event cast a gloom over the district, especially as tidings of her youngest son, who has been unofficially reported killed in action, is anxiously awaited.

In Loving Memory of our dear Brother,

SERGT. FRED BURTON,

2nd/4th Royal Berks Regt.

THE YOUNGEST SON OF THE LATE Mr. & Mrs. DAVID BURTON,

Who was killed in Action near Marcoing,
in the great Cambrai Battle on December 2nd, 1917,
after nobly serving his country for 3 years and 1 month,

AGED 29 YEARS.

There on the field of battle,
He nobly took his place ;
And fought and died for Britain,
And the honour of his race.
He sleeps besides his comrades,
In a hallowed grave unknown ;
But his name is written in letters of love
In the hearts that he's left at home.
A dreadful shock, a painful blow,
As only those who loved him know.
There is a link death cannot sever,
Sweet remembrance lasts for ever.
We cannot take your hand, Fred,
Your dear face we cannot see ;
But let these few lines tell, dear,
How we remembered thee.
But the hardest part is yet to come,
When the warriors they return,
And there among that smiling throng
Our dear one we ne'er shall see.

ensured that his name was added to their parents' headstone in St. Mary's churchyard.

Fred's body was recovered and lies in the Fifteen Ravine British Cemetery to the east of Villers-Plouich - a village about eight miles south-west of Cambrai. It lies in beautiful rolling French countryside within sight of the village church. Originally it began as a very small cemetery, but was enlarged after the war to bring together scattered graves. It now contains 1,264 Commonwealth burials and commemorations of the Great War of which only 525 are identified, but there are special memorials to 44 casualties known or believed to be buried among them.

*1 Recorded as Rose Mary at Sidney's baptism, but Rose Fanny in the 1901 census and on the family headstone in St. Mary's churchyard.
*2 Beatrice Ruth (b 1881), Sydney Charles (b 1883), Fred (b 1888, January 29th) and Thomas (b 1886).

Serjeant 200950, Fred Burton, buried in Fifteen Ravine British Cemetery, Villers-Plouich, Nord, France. Ref. VIII. D. 17. and remembered in St. Mary's churchyard, Pirton.

WALTER REYNOLDS
PRIVATE 242137, 2/5TH BATTALION, GLOUCESTERSHIRE REGIMENT
(FORMERLY 002361, 1ST BATTALION, HERTFORDSHIRE REGIMENT).
KILLED IN ACTION: SUNDAY, DECEMBER 2ND 1917, AGED 23.
COMMEMORATED: CAMBRAI MEMORIAL, LOUVERVAL, (DOIGNES),
NORD, FRANCE. REF. PANEL 6.
BORN, LIVED AND ENLISTED IN PIRTON.

The family of Lewis and Mary Ann Reynolds (née Catterell) was a large one. Baptism and census records list fifteen children*1, born in the space of fifteen years, but by 1911 five had died. Walter, born on September 20th 1894, was their youngest, one of six to serve, and the first of two to die. A newspaper commented, '*Few families can show a better record of war service*'.

The family lived in 3 Wesley Cottages - the group of cottages behind the terrace which now contains the village shop and Walter grew up following the common Pirton pattern; Pirton School then labouring locally. By the time war came his mother had been an invalid for several years and he was working for his father on the family's smallholding. He joined the Hitchin Territorials with other friends from Pirton, and was one of the first to volunteer to serve overseas and so joined the 1st Hertfordshire Regiment.

Although he joined the 1st Battalion, Hertfordshire Regiment as Private 002361, he was attached to the Gloucestershire Regiment and was eventually amalgamated into it as Private 242137. A newspaper article reports that he '*went to France May 24th 1916*' and elsewhere it is recorded that the 2/5th Battalion of the Gloucestershire Regiment landed in France on May 23rd 1916. With two such similar dates it seems likely that he was already in the Gloucestershire Regiment by that date or was transferred on arrival.

The Gloucesters had battalions in France from the very beginning of the war and in 1915 had battalions at the Second Battle of Ypres, Loos and Gallipoli, but they were all before Walter's service. By the summer of 1916 they were at the Somme. However they were lucky and were not in action on the first day, when in the confused carnage there were nearly 60,000 casualties in the British Army.

By March 1917 they must have felt that they were winning as they pursued the German Army from

Private Walter Reynolds

Caulaincourt to Vermand, but this was a planned withdrawal to the heavily fortified Hindenburg Line. This advance was described by Captain R.S.B. Sinclair of 2/5th Battalion:

'*. . . patrols were sent forward to ascertain if the village of Vermand had been evacuated. This was found to be the case and "A" Company was sent up to consolidate east of the village. Whilst digging we saw Uhlans*2 skirmishing in Holnon Wood . . . they made off towards Bihecourt, about a mile east of Vermand and our rifle fire had no effect on them. This was the first and only time that I saw German Cavalry in the War.*'

Interestingly, three celebrated war poets came from Walters's Regiment; Captain Cyril Winterbotham, Lieutenant Will Harvey and Private Ivor Gurney. Will Harvey (DCM) was captured in August 1916 and completed a slim book of his poetry called 'Gloucestershire Friends: Poems from a German Prison Camp', which surprisingly his

German captors forwarded, untouched, for publication in England in 1917.

In the summer of 1917 they were involved in their next big battle, the three-month long Third Battle of Ypres. The appalling conditions in which the battle was fought have been described earlier, for the other Pirton men who died in it. Here it is enough to say that it was fought in a quagmire of mud.

In between, major attacks, raids and counter-raids were launched. One of the captains of Walter's Battalion, Captain M.F. Badcock, wrote to his wife describing a typical example; perhaps Walter was part of it:

'I have done a raid show. It did not go badly: we collared some prisoners, one machine gun, and did in about twenty. . . . . . . The wretched Germans were simply mad with fright and it seemed sheer butchery, all poor youths of eighteen and nineteen. We got ten prisoners, but six were killed going across No Man's Land by their own shells; one fool surrendered to me and thrust at me with his bayonet; it went through my trousers, tore my pants, and never touched me. There was nothing to do but to shoot him. It's the first life I have ever taken in this war to my certain knowledge and it was beastly. We did not have a single fellow killed, only four slightly wounded and all got in safe, so it was a success. Our fellows absolutely saw red and we had a job to stop the killing. We blew up three of their dugouts, which they would not come out of, so I suppose they were buried and suffocated.'

By the end of this battle, which was November 10th 1917, the British and their Allies had advanced about 4 ½ miles. The British had lost about 310,000 men and the Germans 260,000.

Perhaps surprisingly, Walter did get some respite from this battle. He was home on leave in late October, but upon his return he was heading towards another – The Battle of Cambrai.

This battle commenced in the 'usual' manner. At 6:20am key German targets were hit with heavy artillery fire. This was followed by smoke to confuse and blind the enemy and then a creeping barrage – intended to stay just ahead of the attacking force and act as a protective curtain by forcing the enemy to take cover. The difference in this battle, compared with others, was the significant use of tanks. Some 350 attacked supported by the infantry. The attack was initially very successful and some five miles of ground was won and, most importantly, the Hindenburg Line, which the Germans had believed to be impregnable, was breeched. The Germans reorganised, reinforced and then counter attacked on November 30th and, as had happened so many times before, the gains were lost. By December 3rd, General Douglas Haig ordered the troops, who were still near Cambrai, to withdraw to shorten the ragged front line into a more defensible position. By then 179 tanks were out of action and there had been 44,200 casualties on the British side and a similar number for the Germans.

Walter died on the 2nd while on his way to the front line, the day before Haig ordered the withdrawal. He and others were resting near an ammunition dump, which was not a good position to choose, because it exploded, presumably due to a shell hit. The Rev. J Panton, a Wesleyan chaplain wrote to his parents with this information. He added that *'Death was instantaneous'* – it is hoped that this was true, but this phrase was all too often used so that relatives did not think their boy had suffered.

His Commanding Officer, CF Hamilton also wrote, *'These men are all so splendid out here and you have every reason to be proud of them, but it is hardest of all for you at home, as the men themselves say. You must try and keep a brave heart as he would wish and a bright hope for the future. God bless and comfort you.'*

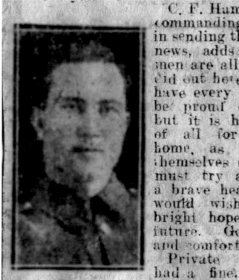

C. F. Hamilton, his commanding officer, in sending the painful news, adds: " These men are all so splendid out here and you have every reason to be proud of them, but it is hardest of all for you at home, as the men themselves say. You must try and keep a brave heart as he would wish and a bright hope for the future. God bless and comfort you."
Private Reynolds had a fine, upright character, his considerateness and kindliness being a comfort to those dear to him. He helped his father in the small-holding work. He joined the Hitchin Territorials before the war, and went to France May 24, 1916.

Although the Rev. J Panton confirmed that Walter's remains were interred, this may also have been a 'kindness'. In any case, either his body was not found or the burial site was lost or destroyed after their withdrawal, because after the war Walter's grave was not recorded and so he is remembered on the Cambrai Memorial. It is smaller than some, but this memorial's entrance is still imposing and it stands on the side of a country road between Bapaume and Cambrai, near the small village of Louverval. His name appears on Panel 6, situated on the rear boundary, beyond a small number of burials - one of 7,043 names of men with no known grave.

Officially he died on December 2nd, but the family believed that it was the 3rd, and that there was a grave that they could visit.

Apart from Walter five other brothers were also serving; William, Albert, George, Harry and Jacob. All survived except Albert who features later in this book.

Walter and Albert are also remembered on their parents' grave in St. Mary's churchyard.

*1 *James (bapt 1870, d 1871 aged seven months), Clara (bapt 1872, d 1874 aged two years), Maria (bapt 1874), Jacob (bapt 1876), Peggy (bapt 1877), Daisy Emma (b 1879, possibly d 1900 aged twenty), Mary (b 1881), William (b 1883), Albert (bapt 1884), Abigail (b 1886), Sarah (b 1888), George Thomas (b 1890), Harry (b 1890 and George's twin), Emily Agnes (b 1893) and Walter (b 1894).*
*2 *The Uhlans were the German light cavalry.*

He wept not himself
That his warfare was done,
The battle was fought,
And the victory won;
But he whispered of those
Whom his heart loved the most;
"Tell my brethren from me,
That I died at my post."

Victorious his fall,
For he rose as he fell,
With Jesus his Master
In glory to dwell;
He has passed o'er the sea,
He has reached the bright coast,
For he fell like a warrior—
He died at his post.

IN LOVING MEMORY OF

Our dear Son,

WALTER,

Youngest Son of Lewis and Mary Ann Reynolds,

Who was Killed in Action on December 3rd, 1917,

And is buried in a British Cemetery in France.

Aged 23 Years.

My Great Uncle

Private 242137, Walter Reynolds.
Commemorated on Cambrai Memorial, Louverval,
(Doignes), Nord, France. Ref. Panel 6.

ARTHUR ODELL
LANCE CORPORAL G/15640, 13TH BATTALION, ROYAL SUSSEX REGIMENT.
KILLED IN ACTION: TUESDAY, FEBRUARY 26TH 1918, AGED 21.
BURIED: FINS NEW BRITISH CEMETERY, SOREL-LE-GRAND, SOMME, FRANCE. REF. IV. C. 10.
BORN, LIVED AND ENLISTED IN PIRTON.

The official records held by the Commonwealth War Graves Commission record Arthur as the son of Mrs. M. (Mary) Odell, of 2 Royal Oak Lane, Pirton, Hitchin, Herts., but fails to mention her husband, and Arthur's father, John Odell, although he was certainly living at the time.

Mary's maiden name was Dawson and she married John Odell on November 27th 1880. The family, including eleven children*1, is identified from the various censuses of 1891, 1901 and 1911. They were recorded as living near Little Lane and in Dead Horse Lane, later renamed as Royal Oak Lane - in fact these could all have been the same house.

Three of their children served in the Great War; James, the eldest son, served in the navy and survived, Arthur, the subject of this chapter, and his younger brother Fred, both served in the army and both died.

Arthur was working as a farm labourer in 1911, but before the war he began working for a company that produced yeast in Bucklesbury, Hitchin. He joined the Hitchin Territorials six months before the war and then, when war came, quickly volunteered for overseas service and joined the 1st Hertfordshire Regiment. The September Parish Magazine records that he did this before the end of 1914 and later the Hertfordshire Express reported that he had gone to France with the Herts. Regiment in August 1914. The latter was incorrect as the Hertfordshires did not embark for France until November 5th. At that date Arthur was only eighteen and officially should not have gone abroad to fight until the age of nineteen.

The Hertfordshire Express reported that Arthur had been wounded, shot in the arm before his 19th birthday. That would have been before May 4th 1915. The Parish Magazine of September 1915 records him as still with the 1st Hertfordshires, so presumably, it was some time after that date that he was transferred to the Transport Section of the 13th

Lance Corporal Arthur Odell

Battalion, Royal Sussex Regiment. The exact date of that transfer is not known, but it must have been before September 10th 1916, because a newspaper cutting about the death of John Parsell on that date mentions that they, and another Pirton man George Thompson, had all met earlier that day and notes Arthur's Regiment was the Royal Sussex. He was not with John at the time of his death, but other Pirton men were, George Roberts who was injured and Arthur Walker who was wounded so seriously that he died later.

Arthur must have seen action with the Hertfordshires, probably in Belgium and France, and he would have shared the experiences described in other chapters with the Pirton men of that Regiment. Here, as we know that he was with the Royal Sussex from September 1916, seems an appropriate date to record his experience with them. On the 10th when he had met John Parsell, the war diary records that the Battalion was in the Beaumont Hamel sector of Bertrancourt. They relieved the 1/5th Gloucesters in the trenches, leaving "C" Company in support and "D" Company in reserve. Arthur may have met John on the way to the trenches or while waiting in support or reserve.

During September they moved locally in the area of the Somme between the Beaumont Hamel sector, Mailly-Maillet and Redan Ridge, sometimes in the trenches, but often providing working parties to improve drainage or lay duck boarding, with the obvious inference that it was very wet and muddy. They experienced danger from artillery shelling and trench mortars and sometimes continuous bombardments. An interesting entry on the 30th reflects other, more widespread concerns elsewhere, over the quality of the shells being supplied to the British artillery - '*22 shells were fired, 15 of which failed to explode*'; examples of the latter are still being found in French and Belgian fields today.

The first part of October was much the same as September, until the middle of the month when they relieved the trenches and other battalions involved in the capture of the German stronghold, the Schwaben Redoubt. On the 17th they began preparations for an attack of their own on Stuff Trench. On the 21st, along with the 11th Royal Sussex, they attacked in three waves along a 250 yard front. For the most part the resistance was light - '*In the main not much opposition*' - nevertheless the 11th Battalion suffered considerably but took the trench and held it. The next day the 13th Battalion recorded their losses and although recording '*not much opposition*', they had 3 officers wounded and in the other ranks 25 men killed, 71 wounded and 30 men were missing. The diary comments, '*Our losses were not unduly heavy*'.

At the end of the month the entire Battalion was withdrawn to dig new reserve trenches, and for the early part of November, with the weather deteriorating with heavy rain. Most of their time was spent in working parties, sometimes of up to 250 men. The work included the salvage of any useful material from the old battlefields and burying the dead from earlier battles. The weather began to improve, new drafts arrived replacing the Battalion's losses, and preparations began for a new attack. This would later become known as the Battle of the Ancre.

On the evening of November 12th they assembled and everything was in place by 3:00am for the attack. At zero hour, plus four minutes (5:49am), in thick mist and deep mud, they captured their first objective, with little opposition, apart from a small party of German machine gunners and snipers in No Man's Land. Again casualties were considered '*slight*', although a volunteer party from "A" Company were recorded as doing excellent work recovering twenty-seven men. The Royal Sussex considered that the battle was a great success '*one of the most successful attacks of the "Great Push" and was a fitting conclusion to the operations of the 39th Division on the Somme*' and the Battalion was withdrawn to billets in Warloy.

In fact, while the 13th Royal Sussex may have been successful, the final objectives of the overall battle were not achieved. The conditions had been appalling, the battleground was very wet with deep mud and, with more winter rains arriving, further offensive action was called off. This was the last major battle of the Somme during 1916. They had started with the terrible losses on July 1st (60,000 British Casualties) and the total British and Commonwealth casualties for this period were calculated as 419,654 (dead, wounded and missing); French losses as 204,253 and German casualties at between 437,000 to 680,000 – in total somewhere between 1 million and 1.3 million men.

Between November 15th and the 18th they moved from France to Poperinge in Belgium and entered an extended period of rest and training, only returning to the forward area on December 11th. They went first to the dug-outs in the Canal Bank, north of Ypres and then in the Turco Farm sector, also north of Ypres. They noted the front line '*being to all intents and purposes non-existent and badly waterlogged.*' They spent the period up to Christmas in the front line, but were lucky to have Christmas Day away from the Front and then several days of training.

For the first four months of 1917 they remained in Belgium playing their part in the defence of Ypres and preventing the Germans breaking through to the coast and the allied supply ports. They rotated in, out and around the trenches of Ypres, Poperinge, Zillebeke and Hooge. They experienced periods of constant shelling by the enemy, gas attacks, terrible conditions in the trenches, watched aircraft fight in the skies above and, although not detailed in the war diary, they must have received very significant numbers of casualties. It must have been to the Battalion's great relief that they were withdrawn to northern France and away from the front line for almost all of May.

They returned to Belgium in June, to much improved weather and, although still out of the trenches, were welcomed with a gas attack at 11:00pm, which forced them to wear gas helmets until 3:00am the following morning. They were back in the trenches, and on the 10th the war diary records that since they had returned to the front line, 2 men had been killed, 2 died of wounds and 27 were wounded.

War diaries rarely go into detail of how men became casualties, particularly in the case of other ranks, but unusually the entry for June 13th gives a description which would have been fairly typical and Arthur is likely to have experienced similar events, even if not this particular one. Captain A C Taylor was leading his working party back after a night's work, a shell burst in front of him, he lost the lower half of his right leg and doctors confirmed that had they been slower in getting him in, he would have died from loss of blood. The total losses between June 2nd and the 24th were given as 1 officer died of wounds, 1 officer wounded, 11 other ranks killed, 6 died of wounds and 85 more were wounded – about eight or nine a day and probably not considered to be too bad. They were again withdrawn to France for another extended period away from the Front.

On July 22nd they returned and were back in the dugouts at Canal Bank for the British attack launched on the 31st, which became known as the Third Battle of Ypres, and which lasted until November 6th, 1917. Arthur and the 13th Royal Sussex fought in this and one of its first major battles - the Battle of the Pilckem Ridge, which was fought between July 31st to August 2nd. Their casualties for those three days were 14 officers and 250 other ranks. It is likely that it was during this battle that Arthur was wounded for the second time. This time in the leg and in November he was home on leave, probably as part of his recovery. He rejoined his Battalion some time in December, but would have had to catch up with them as they had moved from Belgium to France and were at Coulomby, away from the fighting between the 11th to the 29th before returning yet again to Belgium.

Following training at the beginning of January

1918, the Battalion moved to Hilltop Farm, taking over the camp from the 1st Hertfordshire Regiment. They formed working parties and undertook carrying duties between the 7th and 14th. On the 15th the Battalion moved to relieve the Cheshires. The weather was atrocious with gales and rain storms. The war diary records that they had *'Great difficulty in reaching front line posts, owing to the PADDEBEEK* (a stream in Belgium near Passchendaele) *being flooded. Men swept off feet. Arrived drenched through. Posts over knee-deep in mud and water.'* They completed the relief at 4:00am on the 16th and stayed in the line in those awful conditions until relieved on the 18th. The following day was spent cleaning up and foot rubbing in an effort to avoid trench foot. They were back in the line on the 20th, but moved to their camp the following day for a period of baths, rest and training.

Between January 21st and February 1st the Battalion moved by route march and rail from Belgium to France and back to the Somme. The route was, Wieltje, Railhoek, Proven Héricourt, Sailly Laurette, Peronne, Haut Allaines and then to Church Camp, Heudicourt, where they took up position as reserve to the front line. It seems that the weather remained extremely wet as there are frequent entries in the Battalion diary of foot rubbing parades. From this position they provided working parties and improved trenches before moving into the front line on the 4th. Patrols were sent out and working parties continued to repair the damage to trenches that the recent awful weather and enemy action had caused.

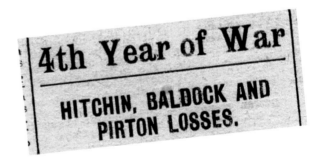

Arthur died on February 26th, but the exact circumstances are not clear. For most of the month the Battalion continued with the established norm, taking turns in the front line trenches with the 1st Hertfordshire Regiment, working on the trenches, salvaging, sending out patrols, burying cables and foot rubbing parades. There is nothing in the diary to suggest any special event on the 26th, but that was the date Arthur died.

He was in the Transport Section so he may well have been away from the front line or was perhaps supplying it. In either case, he would still have been subject to the danger of enemy shelling or sniping. The newspaper reports his death with little detail. Having died on the 26th, a funeral was held two days later. It must have been a quiet period, and he must have been popular, because it was attended by his two serjeants, NCOs and twenty-one of his comrades. Serjeant J Watt sent the news to his parents. *'A cross marks the spot.'* and he added *'Everything that we could do was done for him; he was esteemed by us all.'* His Chaplain, Captain H Collinson sent his condolences and added that he *'was killed bravely doing his duty.'* – which was probably of little comfort to his parents, brothers and sisters.

His body lies in the Fins New British Cemetery, situated in the Somme area of France and on the outskirts of the village of Sorel-le-Grand. The village can be seen to its right hand side, with other views over open beautiful rolling countryside.

It holds 1,289, First World War casualties - 208 remain unidentified and a further 276 foreign national casualties are also commemorated.

Arthur is also remembered on his brother Fred's headstone in St. Mary's churchyard. Fred was the last Pirton man to die.

[1] Jane (bapt 1881), James (b 1883), Martha (bapt 1885), Robert (b 1886), Nellie (b 1888), Frank (b 1890), William (b c1894), Arthur (b 1896, May 4th), John (b 1898, died at seventeen days), Frederick (b 1899) and Marjorie (b 1902).

Lance Corporal G/15640, Arthur Odell, buried in Fins New British Cemetery, Sorel-le-Grand, Somme, France. Ref. IV. C. 10. and remembered in St. Mary's churchyard.

CHARLES WILSHER [1]

LANCE SERJEANT G/15042, 21ST BATTALION, MIDDLESEX REGIMENT.
KILLED IN ACTION: SUNDAY, MARCH 24TH 1918, AGED ABOUT 40.
COMMEMORATED: ARRAS MEMORIAL, PAS DE CALAIS, FRANCE. BAY 7.
BORN IN PIRTON, LIVED IN FINSBURY PARK, MIDDLESEX AND ENLISTED
IN HOLLOWAY, MIDDLESEX.

[1] *Recorded as Wilsher by the Commonwealth War Graves Commission, on the Soldiers Died in the Great War database and on his memorial in Arras, but as Wilshere on the Village Memorial. His great niece confirms that Wilsher is the correct spelling for this man.*

Parish and census records confirm seven children for James Wilsher and Sarah (née Larman), but by 1911 one had died. At this time we can only name the six detailed below[2]. Charles was baptised in 1878 and, presumably, born the same year.

It was not without good reason that the local papers used the headlines *'Pirton's Patriotism'* and *'Pirton's Sacrifice'*, as many Pirton families had more that one son serving his country. The Wilsher's were another such family and Charles, Frederick, Arthur and Bertram, all served. Apart from Charles, all survived, but Frederick was badly wounded and sadly lost a leg.

In 1891 Charles was working as a farm labourer. He is absent from the next Pirton census, but he can be found at 169 Cornelia Street, in the London census of Islington for 1901. He was boarding with the Walker family, also from Pirton, and was working as a general labourer. Confusingly, he seems to be absent from the 1911 census. There is a Charles Wilsher living in Islington of the right age, but he is recorded as being born in Islington. No corresponding record for this man, born in Islington, was found in the 1901 census and no record for the man, born in Pirton, was found in the 1911 census, so it could be an error and he could be our man. However, this information should be treated with caution because the later census records Charles as having been married for eleven, or possibly twelve years – the census entry has been amended, and consequently that fact should have appeared in 1901, but did not. If this is our man, then he was living at 32 Canonbury Avenue, Islington, his wife's name was Evelyn and they had six children, Irene, William, Albert, Basil, George and Elesie(sic) all aged between eight and one. This man was working as a milk carrier at a nearby dairy hall.

Charles was not one of the first to enlist, but was not far behind. The Parish Magazine recorded his enlistment in the 21st Battalion, Middlesex Regiment in 1915 and before August. This would have been his local Regiment and a service battalion formed for the duration of the war. It was actually formed on May 18th 1915 at the request of the Mayor and his Borough. They were stationed in Aldershot and Witley for training and went to France in June 1916.

At this time his parents were living in Andrew's Cottages - the three cottages at the bottom of the High Street. By April 1917 they heard that another son, Frederick had lost a leg. Then came more worrying news; Charles wrote from the First Australian General Hospital in France, to let them know he had been wounded (on Easter Monday) *'We were advancing, when the Germans let the machine guns go, and I got a bullet. It went in at the top of the buttock and stopped just above the back of the knee.'* They took the bullet out on the 14th he added bravely and reassuringly *'I feel much better now. Nothing to worry about.'*

He returned to Pirton for recuperation and, although it should have been a happy prospect, he must have had mixed feelings when he found that his visit coincided with two of his brothers also being in Pirton – Frederick, waiting for his formal discharge following the loss of his leg, and Arthur, who had also been wounded.

Charles recovered and returned to service and we have no more news of him until a newspaper report of May 2nd 1918, under the heading *'Three Men Missing'* Charles Wilsher's name is one of them. This information was repeated two days later, on June 6th and then again in the August Parish Magazine. Without any firm news the family must have hoped for the best and feared the worst.

We know that Charles died on March 24th 1918 and that date was during the period of the German Spring Offensive, which may explain some of the delay in getting news back to Pirton, but why the family could not be informed sooner is not known. Sometimes news of the deaths of non-commissioned officers and the lower ranks, given its importance to their families, travelled at an uncomfortably slow pace, especially when compared to the telegram which normally informed of an officer's death. The Battalion's war diary helps piece together the last three or four days of his life.

On March 21st the Germans launched a huge offensive, with sixty-five Divisions attacking along a 60 mile front. They knew that massive numbers of American troops would be entering the war and they needed to strike a decisive blow before they could change the outcome. General Erich Luderndorff masterminded and ordered the offensive. '*We must strike at the earliest moment before the Americans can throw strong forces into the scale. We must beat the British.*' He had reinforced his army with 500,000 battle-hardened troops from the Russian front. The British were targeted with the aim of splitting the French and British troops. They concentrated crack troops on the weaker sections of the lines and almost ignored the stronger sections, effectively leaving them isolated to be strangled at will when the line along the Western Front had been broken.

Initially they were hugely successful, the British were forced further and further back to shorten the defensive line and to avoid being outflanked. The retreat varied from a structured withdrawal to near rout, but they fought all the way. By the end of the first day the British had nearly 20,000 dead and 35,000 wounded.

By the 24th, the date given as Charles Wilsher's death, the Germans were jubilant and claiming almost complete success, but they had moved forward at such speed and with such success that their troops were exhausted, they were running out of supplies of all kinds and the attack began to peter out between the end of March and early April.

In those few days the Allies lost 255,000 men and the Germans 239,000. It was near chaos and so it is not surprising that facts surrounding Charles Wilsher's death are confused.

The war diary of his Battalion provides more specific information on what Charles experienced, although still describing a very confused situation. At the start of the offensive (March 21st) they were at Boisleux-au-Mont South of Arras. Charles and his Battalion were ordered to move to Henin Hill before the Germans could occupy it. They moved in the early evening, taking up position by 3:00am, but later that day they were ordered to Sensée Valley, north-east of Ervillers, where they were to be the reserve for the 121st Brigade, who were holding a position near St. Leger. At 2:00pm they were ordered to reinforce the Welsh Regiment at Croisilles Switch and by 6:00pm they recorded that the troops in front of them were being driven back and, very soon afterwards, the Middlesex were fighting the German advance troops. It seems that they held position or at least were not forced back too far because on the 23rd the war diary records that they counterattacked.

The situation was chaotic and the fighting and shelling was fierce; between the 21st and then 25th the Middlesex diary records their losses as 2 officers and 21 other ranks killed, 6 officers and 189 other ranks wounded, 6 other ranks wounded and missing, and 2 officers and 80 other ranks missing. As Charles Wilsher's body was never found he was amongst the missing.

He, like 34,749 other men with no known grave, and who died in the Arras sector between the spring of 1916 and August 7th 1918, is commemorated on the Arras Memorial. This memorial is hugely impressive and stands fortress-like on the western outskirts of the town. Its high walls protect the honoured names, the 2,651 Commonwealth burials and the peace within. It has ten bays to record the names. Charles Wilsher's name is in Bay 7, not that far from five other men listed who appear on Pirton's memorials or who at least have some Pirton connection.

*2 *Martha (b c1876), Charles (bapt 1878), Frederick (b 1882), Robert (bapt 1885), Arthur (b 1887) and Bertram (b 1890).*

Lance Serjeant G/15042, Charles Wilsher. Commemorated on Arras Memorial, Pas de Calais, France. Bay 7.

BERTRAM WILLIAM NEWBURY WILSON *1
PRIVATE 23187, 4TH BATTALION, BEDFORDSHIRE REGIMENT.*2
KILLED IN ACTION: WEDNESDAY, MARCH 27TH 1918,
AGED ABOUT 24.
COMMEMORATED: ARRAS MEMORIAL, PAS DE CALAIS,
FRANCE. BAY 5.
BORN AND LIVED PIRTON, ENLISTED IN HITCHIN.

*1 *Bertram appears as Bert on the Village memorial and, as this is how they wished him to be remembered, that is how he appears here.*

*2 *4th Battalion in official records, 8th Battalion on Pirton memorial.*

Bert was the only recorded son of Martha Matilda Wilson. He was baptised on May 13th 1894 and it is reasonable to assume that he was born earlier that year. Wilson was the surname of Martha's parents, James and Hannah, so she was unmarried. Newbury is an unusual middle name and as there were a number of families with the surname of Newbury living in Pirton, it could be a clue to the father. James and Hannah died in 1900 and 1899 respectively leaving Martha, their eldest child, the head of the family.

In 1911 the family consisted of Martha, Bert and Martha's siblings Ellen, Emma and Charles. Martha's work is not recorded, but Charles and Bert were earning money as farm labourers. Bert enlisted some time between October 21st 1915 and March 1st 1916, joining the Bedfordshire Regiment. Official records give his Battalion as the 4th when he died, although the 8th is given on the Pirton War Memorial. This cannot be correct because the 8th were disbanded in France on February 16th 1918, which was about six weeks before his death. It is possible that he was in the 8th and was one of the 299 other ranks who moved from the 8th to the 4th Battalion on February 7th 1918, but it is also possible that this detail is an error and that he was never in the 8th. For this reason a very brief history for both Battalions is given below and then more detail from February 7th 1918 when he must have been in the 4th Battalion. Hopefully in the future we can be more certain of Bert's exact experience.

8th Battalion

The 8th was formed in October 1914 as part of Kitchener's 3rd Army. It was a service battalion formed for the duration of the war and after training was ordered to mobilise in August 1915 and then left for France on the 28th and arrived in Boulogne on the 30th.

During their service in the Great War, the Battalion saw action in the following major battles:

The Battle of Loos - September 1915, the defence of Ypres - 1916, the Battle of the Somme - July to November 1916, the Battle of Arras - April and May 1917 and the Battle of Cambrai - November and December 1917

Given that Bert enlisted between October 21st 1915 and March 1st 1916, he could not have been involved in the Battle of Loos, but could have seen service in the others.

Ypres was a bloody area, with the British holding on to a small salient*3, preventing the capture of the Belgian town of Ypres and the Germans from reaching the coast and the British Army's supply ports. The Battalion's war diary gives the losses between January and July, as 94 killed, 205 wounded, 91 missing believed killed and 550 sick in hospital or evacuated to base.

In August 1916 they moved to the Somme where casualties from the Battle of the Somme had been horrendous, but at least they had missed the first few bloody days. Here they saw action in the trenches in the infamous areas of Auchonvillers, Beaumont Hamel, Thiepval, Guillemont, Ginchy and others, and between August 1916 and March 1917 casualties were 149 killed, 367 wounded, 103 missing believed killed and 1,209 sick in hospital or evacuated to base.

They moved to Arras and in the next 2 months another 59 men were killed, 263 wounded, 8 missing and 206 sick. The final actions of this Battalion were around Cambrai in December 1917 with another 57 men killed, 246 wounded 16 missing in action and 246 sick in hospital.

The remaining time, until the Battalion was disbanded in February 1918, was thankfully quieter, but during their service in the First World War some 700 men were killed and 5,000 became casualties*4.

4th Battalion
Their service in the Great War included the following battles:

The Battle of the Somme - 1916, the Battle of the Ancre - 1916, the Battle of Arras 1917, the Third Battle of Ypres (Passchendaele) - 1917, the German Spring Offensives - 1918 and the final "Hundred Day" offensive – 1918.

The 4th (Extra Reserve) Battalion, in existence long before the war, was effectively a training unit. Within a few days of the beginning of the war they were moved to Felixstowe for home duty with the Harwich Garrison and to stand ready to supply replacements for the front line troops.

The disaster of the losses in the first day of the Battle of the Somme has been mentioned before, but obviously the numbers of casualties continued to rise over the next days and weeks so the 4th were called to service and landed at Le Havre in France on July 25th 1916.

Their first experience in the front line came on September 11th 1916. The casualty figures for the 4th were not recorded as comprehensively as those of the 8th Battalion above, but the following perhaps gives a sense of their part in the war.

In November 1916 they were at the Somme, in the tail end of the action known as the Battle of the Somme. The war diary records that on the 13th they attacked the Germans between Beaumont Hamel and the River Ancre.

'Bn attacked at 6.45 am Operations on the North Bank of the ANCRE - Nov 13th 1916 The Battalion advanced with the remainder of the Brigade at 6.45 am and sustained heavy casualties among Officers and NCOs in and near the enemy front line from a strongpoint established between enemy front line and second line which had been passed over by the leading Brigades. Battalion advanced to enemy second line and from there parties pushed forward to Station Road and beyond.' In this action 14 officers and 48 other ranks were killed, 9 more died of wounds, 108 were wounded and 16 men were missing.

In the same area, between February 11th and 16th 1917, they were ordered to 'push forward their line of posts'. An artillery barrage started at 9:00pm; it was to be a creeping barrage, with shells moving forward in front of the men. They were held up by uncut barbed wire and heavy machine gun fire - presumably the creeping barrage had continued forward, passing over the enemy, and allowing them to return to their machine guns. They achieved their target, but many died. Between the 6th and 16th, 68 men were dead, 90 wounded, 3 missing and 45 missing believed killed. Most of these were in the above action.

On April 14th 1917 they moved to Arras by motor bus. They took over the front line and were immediately in the thick of it, 2 with 2 men killed and 58 wounded. On the 22nd they assembled to attack and capture the main road through a village called Gavrelle. The attack was launched the following day at 4:45am. They were successful, but were shelled heavily during the day, and were counter-attacked in the afternoon. They held on, at the cost of 2 officers killed, 7 more wounded and 260 other ranks wounded or killed. Despite the losses it was not all fighting - in June the men had long rest periods, periods of training and even attended the Brigade's horse show, taking five first and two second places in seven events!

In October they were involved in the Third Battle of Ypres (specifically in the Second Battle of Passchendaele) and on the 30th they were in position by 3:30am for an attack at 5:50am. The British barrage commenced, but the Germans replied with their own barrage aimed 100 yards to the rear of the British lines, where the support lines were positioned. This did enormous damage, almost completely wiping out the support line consisting of the Artists Rifles within five minutes. The Bedfordshire and Royal Fusiliers pressed on, but, as detailed elsewhere, the conditions were atrocious and their progress was held up by the mud. This allowed the creeping British barrage to get too far in front and when it had passed over the enemy's machine gun posts the Germans had time to raise their heads and return fire. The Battalion came under fire from their front and their exposed flanks - 100 men and officers were killed and 400 more wounded, 11 of whom later died.

By January 1918 they were back in France fighting around Villers-Plouich and by the end of the month another 18 men had died, 39 were wounded and 28 had been gassed, but they did receive a draft of 111 men to help bring the Battalion back to some sort of fighting strength.

At this point, we do not know which of the above was Bert's service experience; however from February 7th he was certainly in the 4th Battalion. He would have known fellow Pirton men Sidney Baines and Joseph Handscombe who had all been in the 4th, but they had died long before February 1918. If Bert had been in the 8th he would probably have received news of their deaths, but if he too had been in the 4th Battalion, he may even have seen them.

In February the men drafted from the 8th Bedfordshire Battalion arrived and they all had a relatively easy time, even reaching the final of the Division's football cup, but losing out to the Hawke Battalion.

March saw them back at the Front and the worst experience of the month was on the 13th when they were shelled with mustard gas. Five officers and 264 other ranks had to be evacuated, but that was not Bert's fate. On the 21st the German's launched their Spring Offensive (more details can be found in earlier chapters). When the front line was attacked the 4th were in reserve and not immediately involved. Even so they were soon forced back, first to the second line, then, between the 21st and 23rd, to Havrincourt Wood, Neuville and to Ytres, but they fought all the way. The withdrawal continued under heavy machine gun fire, until the 25th, when they paused, regrouped and counter attacked. They

forced the Germans back from Thiepval to High Wood, but when all their ammunition had been fired, they were again forced to retire and returned to Thiepval to defend the ridge. On the 26th they marched to Aveluy Wood where they were relieved, but were then ordered to Bouzincourt. So on the 27th they were west of Albert, where they attacked the railway at 7:30am. If the official date of Bert's death is right then this is the action in which he died, but obviously records around this time were very confused. Between the 20th and 28th they had 21 men killed, 88 wounded and 124 missing. Bert was one of the missing.

Although Bert was recorded as killed in action on March 27th 1918, there was a long period of uncertainty for family and friends. Newspapers dated May 2nd and 4th and July 6th all recorded that he was only missing and cruelly the Parish Magazine suggested that he was a prisoner of war – if fact he had been dead for over three months. His body was not found and his name is recorded on the Arras Memorial along with five other men with a Pirton connection. He is the last Pirton man to be recorded there and consequently this memorial is described many times elsewhere in this book. Perhaps in Bert's case it can just be said that although it is terribly sad that his body was lost, there is no finer memorial for a man's name to be recorded than Arras. He shares that honour with 34,749 other men.

*3 an area protruding forward from the rest of the line and
therefore liable to attack on three sides.

*4 To put the casualties into perspective they need to be set
against the strength of a battalion, which in ideal
circumstances would be about 1,000 men. Numbers obviously
include new drafts and men who returned to service following
recovery from wounds or illness.

> **". . . there is no finer memorial for a man's
> name to be recorded than Arras."**

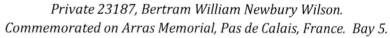

*Private 23187, Bertram William Newbury Wilson.
Commemorated on Arras Memorial, Pas de Calais, France. Bay 5.*

HENRY GEORGE CHAMBERLAIN D.C.M.
PRIVATE 20655, 2ND BATTALION, SUFFOLK REGIMENT.
DIED OF WOUNDS: SATURDAY, APRIL 20TH 1918, AGED 39.
BURIED: PERNES BRITISH CEMETERY, PERNES EN ARTOIS,
PAS DE CALAIS, FRANCE. REF. 1. C. 2.
BORN IN PIRTON AND ENLISTED IN HITCHIN.

The Commonwealth War Graves Commission lists Henry's next of kin at the time of his death as Elizabeth Gazeley. She was his aunt and the sister of his mother Rose who had died in 1895.

Rose was the daughter of Thomas and Dinah Chamberlain, one of their eight children*1 and did not marry. Henry was baptised in 1878 and so presumably he was born earlier that year. Records seem to show that he had two siblings, Albert Thomas (b 1879) and Ellen (b 1888). Ellen died aged twenty-one months in 1890 and as Albert does not appear in any later census perhaps he too died young.

Rose and Henry lived with his grandparents somewhere around Burge End and he attended the Pirton School. Like most other young men he went on to labour for the local farmers when he left school. His grandfather died in 1894 and then his mother, Rose, just a year later, when Henry would have been seventeen. Rose's sister, Elizabeth, married Frederick Gazeley in 1896 when she would have been about thirty and then four years later, Henry's grandmother and Elizabeth's mother, died. The 1901 census records Elizabeth, her two children, her nephew Henry and boarder, all living around Burge End – her husband Frederick is absent from the records. Just three years later he also died leaving Elizabeth, just twelve years Henry's senior, as head of the household.

Henry remained living with his aunt and working as a farm or agricultural labourer and living in one of Andrew's Cottages - the three cottages at the bottom of the High Street. This does not necessarily indicate that they had moved as this area was then known as Burge End.

War was declared in August 1914, but Henry did not join up straightaway. In fact two months later he was in trouble with the law. The Hitchin Express of October produced a dramatic report headed '*WAR AGAINST SPECIAL CONSTABLES*' and then to add to the impact, sub-headed it '*Exciting Night Scenes at*

Private Henry George Chamberlain D.C.M.

Pirton' .... '*Batch of Defendants at Hitchin Sessions*' . . . . '*Strong Measures by the Bench.*'

The report is an interesting read and several other men featured in this book are named: Frederick Buckett, Reginald Lake and Bertram Walker all fought and survived the war. Henry was a key figure in the story so his part in it is highlighted here, but because of the interest and relevance the full report is included in the reference section of this book.

Frederick Buckett was summoned for assaulting Bertram Walker, who was a special constable. At 9:45pm on October 3rd Bertram and another special constable, George Charlick*2 entered The White Horse*3. Whether drink was responsible is not clear, but Frederick struck Bertram and warned both

constables not to go near his property threatening to 'blow your brains out'. The constables withdrew, but were followed by Frederick and some of his mates; Henry was one of them. They continued to swear and make threats and the confrontation continued with Henry hitting both of them. This was all brought out in court and the matter was considered all the more serious because of the war and the fact that the special constables were considered to be serving their Country during the emergency. Frederick was ordered to pay £2 or go to jail for a month. Henry was summoned for the assault and pleaded guilty, he was fined £2 7s 6d or go to jail for a month. In another related incident, later the same night, Henry had also assaulted Alfred Hubbard, who was protecting his wife, so he was fined another £1, with another fourteen days being added to the jail term, if he did not pay. This fine would have been a large sum for a farm labourer to find and one wonders if this was connected in some way to Henry's decision to join up, which he did in June 1915. At this time he was working for James Walker at Little Green Farm.

The North Herts Mail dated July 1st 1916 and the Parish Magazine of September 1915 both record that he joined one of the Suffolk Bantam Brigades. This would indicate that he was a small man, less that 5' 3" and such small men were not accepted for service in the early stages of the war. However, he was Private 20655, in the 2nd Battalion, Suffolk Regiment and the Suffolk Regiment's Museum confirms that this was not a bantam battalion. The 12th Battalion was and it is possible that he transferred from them; if this was not the case then the reports would seem to be misleading.

When Henry enlisted, the 2nd Suffolks had already been in France for many months, having been mobilised on the declaration of war. They had seen action in the early major battles at Mons and Le Cateau, where they formed part of the rear guard to the 5th Division, fought overwhelming numbers of Germans and lost more than 700 men. Subsequently they spent most of their service in France and took part in all the major battles.

Henry went to France in May 1916 and would have been one of the 144 reinforcements that arrived at various times during the month. He would probably have gone into the trenches within a few days of his arrival and although the war diary recorded 'in trenches, quiet time' 15 men were wounded and 3 killed.

June was quiet, mostly training. They moved to St. Omer area and then in July moved on again, by train to Doullens, then between the 3rd and the 6th they marched to Longuevillette, Naours, Coisy, Francvillers and Bois Celestine on the Somme. Some men went into the front line and between the 6th and the 19th 12 more men were killed and 65 wounded.

On August 14th, the war diary notes that of 17 officers and 700 other ranks, only 4 officers and 350 other ranks had been in action before. They were near Bois de Talus and suffered another fifteen casualties. By midnight they had moved to their trenches. The next day was spent improving the trenches, which was difficult because of congestion caused by too many men. It was also noted that 'the carrying of water and rations and removing the dead was no easy matter'.

On the 16th they were preparing for an attack; bombers were to rush the German Block (a concrete bunker) while snipers were detailed to keep the German machine gunners occupied. The artillery commenced a creeping barrage and the Company on the left closely followed its advance. They got within about 120 yards before all their officers were killed by machine gun fire – they had to fall back having lost three officers and 90 other ranks. The Company on the right also met machine gun fire and lost 1 officer and 85 other ranks - they had gained 250 yards in one location and captured seven Germans. The following day at 4:00am, one company was in support of another attack, this time by the 10th Royal Welch Fusiliers; the report notes *'It is uncertain how far they got. Their casualties were 2 officers 60 Other Ranks.'* - companies were normally made up of about 220 men.

Between August 21st and the 31st they marched from Morlancourt to Mericourt L'Abbe, took a train to Candas, were transported by road to Le Meillard and then marched to Houchin; about 65 miles and they marched the last fourteen in heavy thunder showers. The following day they continued on to Mazingarbe. During September and October they were frequently in the trenches, but it was quieter, only averaging one or two men killed or wounded per day while they were in the line.

In November, they were ordered to capture the German Trench called Serre. When read the order must have sounded straight-forward, but the attack failed, 17 men were killed, 94 wounded and 161 were missing. It seems likely that Henry was hurt in this action because by January 1917 he was back in England having been injured and rendered unconscious.

He did not recover sufficiently to return until July 1917 and that was lucky, because it meant that he missed the Battalion's involvement in the Battle of Arras, where between the April 9th and 11th their losses were 32 men killed, 163 wounded and 31 missing. Although Henry missed this battle, they later moved in 1917 to Belgium to take part in the Third Battle of Ypres.

Having seen so much action, death and injury and having already received a bad injury Henry could have been forgiven for trying to avoid danger where possible, but that does not seem to have been the case. The local papers reported that, on his own initiative, he went into No Man's Land to search for a German sniper who had been harassing his battalion - he found three and killed them all. They also reported that he *'was further instrumental in the capture of a "pill-box" containing twelve Huns'* and that *'he also bayoneted several Germans who feigned death.'* It is not clear if all this happened on the same day. Whether he acted out of duty, anger, revenge or the wish for glory, who knows, but he must have been incredibly brave and in November 1917 it was announced in the London Gazette that he had been awarded the Distinguished Conduct Medal (D.C.M.) - the next highest award to the Victoria Cross.

PIRTON MAN'S EXPLOIT.

STIRRING RECORD OF VALOUR.

The London Press has recounted the stirring story of valour performed by Private H. G. Chamberlain, D.C.M., Suffolk Regiment, of Pirton. Entirely on his own initiative he went in search of a German sniper, and found three in a shell hole. He killed them and returned with the viery lights and a trench lamp. He afterwards accounted for three more snipers. He was further instrumental in the capture of a "pill-box" containing twelve Huns, who had been overlooked by the front line troops. He also bayonetted several Germans who feigned death.

His D.C.M. citation read, *'For conspicuous gallantry and devotion to duty. During operations an enemy aeroplane flew low over our lines and fired a white light, which was answered by a hostile sniper nearby. Entirely on his own initiative he went in search of the sniper, found three in a shell-hole, killed them all, and returned with Verey lights (flares) and a trench lamp. He afterwards accounted for three more snipers [by] lying out for hours in No Man's Land, and stalking them when they declared themselves.'*

The Distinguished Conduct Medal (D.C.M.).

The Suffolk Regiment Museum used an account written by Colonel C C R Murphy to identify the likely date for his action '*The 27th (*September 1917*), except for sniping activity, was a day of comparative quiet until the evening, when the enemy launched another counter-attack. The 28th passed in a like manner, except that our troops were further harassed by hostile aircraft flying very low.*' They add that '*As the fighting was in full swing on 26th September, and there was a counter-attack on the 27th, it seems likely that the action he was commended for was on the 28th.*' The 2nd Suffolks had captured Zonnebeke on the 26th. Losses between the 25th and the 30th were 41 men killed, 192 wounded and 25 missing.

In October they moved back into France where they remained for the rest of Henry's service. From March 21st 1918, the start of the German's major Spring Offensive, there were more terrible losses. They were holding the line along the Arras to Cambrai road when, at 5:00am, the German attack started. For the Suffolks it began with a large explosion, initially thought to be a mine, but subsequently it was judged to be a projector discharge (gas). Shelling, gas and infantry attacks continued throughout the following day and night. At 1:30am they were ordered to withdraw - probably to prevent them being outflanked and cut off. This pattern continued for the next few days; as the Germans made advances they continued to outflank the sections of British troops who were able to defend successfully, forcing them to also withdraw in order to shorten and straighten the line for a better defensive position. Between the 21st and the 29th the 2nd Suffolks suffered 428 casualties.

During the early part of April they were able to withdraw from the fighting to rest and regroup, before once again returning to the fighting line. On the 11th they were busy preparing new defensive positions around Hinges and although this would have been behind the main fighting it was still dangerous, with heavy shelling and barrages being laid down by both sides. On the 20th, although recorded as a quiet day, there would have been more shelling and 2 other ranks were killed and 6 wounded. Henry was one of those wounded. He was evacuated to either the 6th or 22nd Canadian Clearing Station, where, although partially conscious he had a severe head wound and a fractured skull. The Chaplain of the Clearing Station wrote on the 23rd, confirming that he had died soon after being brought in and that he had been buried in the local cemetery

with his comrades. He concluded the letter '*We have been having a dreadful time.*' Henry was thirty-nine.

He was buried in Pernes British Cemetery, which served the clearing stations. It is near to the small town of Pernes-en-Artois alongside a country road at the foot of a gentle slope which gives a backdrop of grass and trees. The views are much like those around Pirton. There are 1,078 burials from the First World War and as the men mostly came from the clearing station almost all are identified. Intriguingly, because he died in the hospital or, perhaps because of this, he lies in a single 'trench' grave containing several men, denoted by the close grouping of headstones. His headstone reads '*Henry George Chamberlain D.C.M. God is Love, In Paradise*'.

Additional notes: *The 1918 newspaper reports seem to contain errors; firstly they suggest that he won the D.C.M. in February of that year, but that was when the citation was printed, he was actually awarded it in November of 1917. They also suggest that he was brought up from a baby by his Aunt Elizabeth. While as a family member she undoubtedly helped, his mother did not die until he was about seventeen and the 1881 and 1891 censuses record him as living in the same household as her and, as a strawplaiter she would have been working from her home, so it is more likely that he was brought up by his mother with help from her family.*

*1 Confirmed by the Chamberlain family tree provided by Alan Males.
*2 Probably the father of the man of the same name that served and died.
*3 The White Horse PH was where The Motte and Bailey PH now stands.

Private 20655, Henry George Chamberlain D.C.M.,
Pernes British Cemetery, Pernes en Artois,
Pas de Calais, France. Ref. 1. C. 2.

GEORGE THOMAS CHARLICK

PRIVATE 698133, 1/22ND BATTALION, LONDON REGIMENT 'THE QUEEN'S'.
(FORMERLY 452330, 2/11TH BATTALION, LONDON REGIMENT).
KILLED IN ACTION: MONDAY, JUNE 17TH 1918, AGED 30.
COMMEMORATED: POZIERES MEMORIAL, SOMME, FRANCE. PANEL 89.
BORN AND LIVED IN ENFIELD, ENLISTED IN HOLBORN.

George shared his name with his father, who was also George Thomas Charlick and his mother's name was Elizabeth. He was their eldest son, born around 1888, and had two siblings; Ernest Nugent (b 1889) and Louisa M (b c1892) - Ernest was recorded as Edward in the 1901 census.

In order to establish George's connection to Pirton it was necessary to analyse information for the rest of the family. His parents were from Enfield, Middlesex and Eaton, Bedfordshire respectively. They married in 1887 and the 1891 census shows them to be living with their young boys in 4 Cleveland Terrace, Totteridge Rd, Enfield. George (junior) was born in Ponders End, Middlesex and the other children in Enfield. George (senior) worked as a gunsmith and his younger brother Alfred J shared their house and also worked as a gunsmith. Quite probably both men worked at the Royal Small Arms Factory at Enfield Lock. By 1901 the family had moved to Warley Road, South Weald where George (senior) had become a publican in an ale house, possibly called The Brass Hare, but the census writing is hard to decipher.

It was hoped that the early release of the 1911 census data would help with George's details, but there are no George Charlicks (or similar names) with sufficient corresponding information to attribute their details to George (junior) with any confidence. His sister is missing, but she had probably married and changed her surname. Ernest had become a policeman and was boarding with the Cartwright family at 265 Monega Road, Forest Gate and their parents had moved to Eynesbury, St. Neots, Huntingdonshire (now Cambridgeshire). George (senior) was 'working on own account' as a beer retailer in The Hare and Hounds – presumably the same pub that still exists today in Berkley Street. It is possible that they had first moved to The Jolly Plough Boys beer house in Chawston, Bedfordshire, in 1904, as the landlord is recorded as George Charlich – a possible transcription error. There are no Charlicks listed in Pirton in 1911 so it seems that

the family connection with Pirton began some time between 1911 and October 1914, when George seniors name appears in the Hertfordshire Express newspaper report featured in the previous chapter on Henry Chamberlain 'WAR AGAINST SPECIAL CONSTABLES' - the full report is included in the reference section of this book. Although George (senior) was fifty-one and could not have been in Pirton for very long, he had become a special constable and would therefore have been a well known and respected member of the community. His part in the 'Exciting Night Scenes at Pirton' is mentioned elsewhere. In later years, long after the war, George's brother Ernest came to Pirton to live and George and Ernest's parents, as well as Ernest and his wife, Minnie Flora Agnes, are buried in St. Mary's churchyard.

This, of course, only offers information about George's family, not him. His name does not appear in the lists of local men joining up, which suggests that he never lived in Pirton, at least not for any length of time. His parents did however, and in 1918, just one or two months before his son's death, Mr G Charlick donated two shillings to the carved oak War Memorial Shrine being constructed and which still sits inside Pirton Church.

When George enlisted he was living in Rosebery Avenue, Holborn, and this is where he joined up. He was initially Private 452330, 2/11th Battalion, County of London Regiment (Finsbury Rifles). He was later transferred to the 1/22nd Battalion, County of London Regiment (The Queen's), becoming Private 698133. We know little of George Thomas Charlick's personal life, so perhaps it is fitting that his service experience is given more prominence as so much of what he experienced would have been similar for many of the Pirton men who served.

Although it is not certain when he enlisted, in 1915 George would have been about twenty-seven, so it is reasonable to assume that he enlisted early in the war. With this assumption, and the details provided by the war diaries of the two battalions, it seems almost certain that George transferred to the 1/22nd on January 30th 1918 and that what follows was his experience of the war.

The war diary of the 2/11th Battalion confirms that they were part of the 58th Division, 175th Infantry Brigade. In September 1915 they were in training at Woodbridge and Melton and their experience of war was limited to watching Zeppelins flying over Woodbridge and home defence work. The war diary has a gap from February 1916 to January 1917, but other sources indicate that in May 1916 they moved to Bromeswell Heath and then to Longbridge Deverell.

On January 19th 1917 the Battalion finally received its long-awaited entraining orders and a railway timetable. They were ordered to Warminster, Southampton and to Le Havre, France. They arrived in two parties on February 5th and 6th. Within a week they had entered the trenches, where they immediately experienced 'moderate enemy activity', watched aerial warfare and saw the British bombardment of the enemy trenches. But on the 16th it was their turn; they had their first experience of an enemy bombardment and they were shelled with heavy, medium and light artillery. Some of the shells contained gas. This was repeated the next day and '3 men were badly gassed before their respirators could be adjusted. These 3 died later and another 8 other ranks from the same party were admitted to hospital.' - their first casualties. They were relieved on the 17th.

Having moved to Halloy, on February 25th and been billeted, they were told that the enemy had retired along the whole front and orders were given: 'All troops to be ready to move at short notice after 5:00am tomorrow.' The Germans had begun a planned withdrawal of 25 miles to their prepared 'impregnable' defensive positions along the Hindenburg Line. They burnt or destroyed everything as they retreated, leaving a waste land, where, if items of interest or battleground souvenirs were found, they were often booby trapped.

George's Battalion did not move until the 27th, when over two days they marched to Gaudiempre and then to Riviere, some 16 miles and presumably the location of the new front line. They were back in the lines on March 1st and the diary for the first half of March records a lot of artillery action by the Germans, a good proportion of which included gas shells. The weather cannot have been good as the rain seriously damaged the trenches and some were becoming impassable. In fact they became so bad that they had to withdraw to the support line, but at least the enemy's activity eased off for a few days in the middle of the month. The relief was temporary as their activity returned with increased ferocity and included machine gun sniping and trench mortars. Explosions were also heard in the German trenches and it was suspected that they were about to withdraw further. They were right and it turned out to be another phase of their planned withdrawal.

From March 18th to May 3rd the 2/11th Battalion were out of the line, and frequently assigned to working parties of up to 300 men. Often the work related to the repair and maintenance of roads and railways. This was vital because of the pressing need to extend the British supply lines to the new front line. Also during this period they had moved from Buire au Bois to Miraumont and then to Achiet le Petit.

On May 4th they moved another eleven miles forward and returned to the trenches. The normal terrors of war were restored over the next two days and the diary records 'a great artillery activity by both sides . . . . . . trench mortars . . . . . .' but 'comparatively quite little shrapnel.' After eight days, with only 7 men wounded and 1 killed, they marched out of the trenches for six days' training and rest. By the 20th they were in the right sector of Bullecourt. Having just arrived, their war diary, with unusual frankness, gives an insight into the conditions 'Trenches were in a very bad state many decomposed bodies lying about and trenches were practically shell *holes joined together. Enemy artillery shelled our front support lines intensively from 3:45 – 4:30am with shrapnel and gas causing several casualties. Total for 24 hours 3 killed and 19 wounded other ranks.'*

When trench warfare falls into a pattern of apparent monotony, it is difficult to do justice to the men's experience. From May to July 1917 they were in the trenches for a few days, then rested, formed working parties, carried supplies to the Front or trained and then returned to the fighting. When in the trenches they were in constant danger; just about every day the diary records artillery activity, sometimes light, sometimes heavy, sometimes during the day, sometimes at night, sometimes both. The truth of their experience is indicated by the almost daily punctuation of entries, with casualty figures; *'several casualties . . . . . 6 other ranks killed, 9 other ranks wounded . . . . . . 3 other ranks killed 4 wounded . . . . . . 2 killed 3 wounded'. 'Keep your head down'* would have been the sound advice given by the old hands, but you might well be selected for a trench raid such as the one on June 13th: *'Raiding party consisted of 3 offs (officers) 60 other ranks & was successful killing 20 Germans & capturing 1 off & 2 other ranks'* – usually dangerous, but on that occasion *'Our casualties 1 other rank wounded.'* After their efforts they were given much of August to train and to recover, and the danger of this area of France disappeared as they marched to Arras station, to board a train to Belgium and the Third Battle of Ypres.

By August 28th 1917 they were in the dug outs at the Yser Canal, near Ypres. The country was different, but the conditions probably worse and the warfare familiar: *'6 killed & 10 wounded (other ranks) . . . . . Situation quiet. Two other ranks killed & 7 wounded . . . . . 1 killed, 4 wounded.'* Enemy aircraft bombing the transport lines was something new, and the attack was recorded as *'killing 13 horses & wounding 7 horses.'* When considering the carnage amongst the men we forget how the animals suffered. Despite the new mechanised transport available, the horse was still the mainstay of the supply route, especially in the mud, and in the Great War some 8,000,000 horses werc killed.

On September 20th the 2/7th Battalion, London Regiment managed a small advance and under intense artillery fire the 2/11th moved to take up their original position. The Germans counter

attacked and although beaten off 10 men were killed and 38 wounded. Later that month while out of the line they received a draft to replace their depleted ranks; 5 officers and 279 other ranks for a Battalion whose full strength would normally be about a 1,000 men.

In January 1918 orders were received for the Battalion to be disbanded. Some officers and men were transferred to the 1/20th Battalion, London Regiment and others to the 1/21st. On the 30th the remainder, 8 officers and 240 other ranks, left for the 1/22nd Battalion, London Regiment and it is almost certain that this was when George moved to his new Regiment in France. They were also battle hardened and had also suffered terrible losses. On January 22nd their recorded trench strength was down to 20 officers and 359 other ranks. Another 149 men were on ration strength - men who had to be fed, but not available to fight. That brought the total to 529 - it should have been around 1,000. They clearly needed reinforcements so when George and the other men arrived on February 3rd they would have been welcome and although numbers had dropped in transit they added another 189 men to the Battalion's strength. When they arrived the 1/22nd had just got to Bertincourt, they were quickly absorbed and the Battalion moved on to Trescault and back into the trenches. Soon afterwards about 70 men were working in the front line, and although there was no obvious cause, one man felt his throat swelling and reported that he thought that he had been gassed. Within a few hours seventy percent of the Company were casualties *'some being so bad that they acted as though they had temporarily lost their reason.'*

Little things meant a lot to the men and they must have gained much pleasure from the gifts which arrived from Queen Alexandra's Field Force Fund. The parcels contained towels or handkerchiefs, soap or candles, stationery, chocolate or sweets and cigarettes. There were also mittens and footballs. The Germans rather spoiled the fun because they sent over about 200 shells. The horrors of war continued as 'normal', broken by rest spells, when they sometimes managed to enjoy baths and an opportunity to try to remove the grime and lice that lived on the men. They also enjoyed cinema evenings and occasionally the Battalion troupe of Follies known as the Bermondsey Butterflies would perform - each an opportunity of a few hours of distraction from the war, a chance to forget.

The massive German Spring Offensive, code named Operation Michael or Kaiserschlacht, commenced on March 21st and has been mentioned in previous chapters. George and his Battalion were in camp, but were immediately ordered forward, passing through a heavy gas shell barrage on the way. They did not come under direct attack until the 24th when they were forced back, regrouped, forced back, regrouped and then forced back yet again. Sometimes this was through pressure from the enemy and sometimes because German success on the left or right put them at risk of being outflanked and cut off. The situation along the front was chaotic, but the retirement of the 1/22nd was orderly. On March 24th they were back to High Wood, a location that had cost them dearly to capture in September 1916 and they were still retreating. By April they had retired to the area around Martinsart, but the fighting was still fierce: *'This line was* (to be) *consolidated & prepared to hold at all costs.'* On the 7th they were relieved.

The situation, which was desperate for the Allied forces, eased as the German losses increased and their supply lines became over-extended. The initial high level of success could not be maintained, but it had cost all sides dearly, the allies total was over 250,000 men and the Germans nearly 240,000, including many of their specialist 'shock troops'. Operation Michael is officially recorded as ending on the 5th. At the end of April the 1/22nd found time to record their casualties for March and April; 2 officers and 24 other ranks killed in action, 6 officers and 156 other ranks wounded. These numbers included 6 who were gassed and 2 who were wounded, but remained at their post. 1 officer and 30 other ranks were missing – a total of 219 men. George was lucky,

he was not one of them.

Over the next couple of months, trench warfare returned, albeit with the British lines some distance back from where they had been. In June a large trench night raid was planned for the 17th with 3 officers and 60 other ranks participating. George is recorded as killed in action on the 17th. There were certainly casualties on the raid and while it remains uncertain (he could have been killed before the raid, for example), it does seem likely that he died on that raid.

The British casualties for the raid were 1 officer wounded, 13 other ranks wounded and 5 men were recorded as missing. The official report suggests that the missing fell and died in No Man's Land. The bodies of these men were probably not recovered and, as George's body was never found, it seems likely that he was one of them.

Whatever the facts, George's name is recorded with others from his Battalion, on the panels at Pozieres Memorial. They record some 14,300 names of the missing from United Kingdom and South African Forces who died on the Somme between March 21st and August 7th 1918. The memorial is in countryside, a little distance from the village of Pozieres, and alongside the main road from Albert to Pozieres. The walls of the Memorial stand smartly to attention and face inwards protecting the names and the 2,755, mainly Australian, burials within.

Another memorial in Old Jamaica Road, Bermondsey, names the men of the 22nd Battalion, London Regiment (Queen's), who died in the Great War and records over 800 names.

Pozieres Memorial, Somme, France.

Private 698133, George Thomas Charlick.
Commemorated on Pozieres Memorial,
Somme, France. Panel 89.

FRED ANDERSON
PRIVATE 84038, 141ST COMPANY, LABOUR CORPS.
(FORMERLY PRIVATE 34418 3RD INFANTRY COMPANY, NORTHAMPTONSHIRE REGIMENT AND
18618, 8TH BATTALION, BEDFORDSHIRE REGIMENT).
DIED: MONDAY, JULY 8TH 1918, AGED 35.
BURIED: AUBIGNY COMMUNAL CEMETERY EXTENSION, AUBIGNY-EN-ARTOIS,
PAS DE CALAIS, FRANCE. REF. IV. J. 41.
BORN IN NORTON, HERTFORDSHIRE, LIVED IN PIRTON AND ENLISTED IN HITCHIN.

Fred's connection to Pirton began only a few years before the war and for most of his life he lived in Norton, Hertfordshire. His parents, John Hagger Anderson and Elizabeth (Fanny in 1881 census) (née Grummitt), were both born in Norton. They seem to have started their married life living there, in Elizabeth's parents' home on Wilbury Farm, with their first born, Martha. By 1891 John had risen from farm labourer to bailiff on Wilbury Farm and was still living there, but now in their own home. Their family had grown and now included Fred, aged eight and born around 1893 and Minnie aged three.

In the 1901 census Fred was eighteen and was boarding with the Hooper family in 9 Lordship Cottages, Willian, while earning his living as an agricultural worker. By 1911 he was married to Lilian Lizzie, they had a young daughter Winifred and were living in one of the Highdown Cottages, Pirton. Fred's service records confirm that they married on December 23rd 1906 and his wife's maiden name was Worbey. Interestingly, a family with surname Worbey lived at number 11 Lordship Cottages, when Fred was lodging in Willian. Although there was no Lilian present in 1901, a look at the 1891 census confirms that one of the daughters was called Lilian and so it seems they met in Willian.

The October issue of the Parish Magazine in 1911 confirms he was working for Thomas Franklin on Highdown Farm. It reports the harvest supper, chaired by Mr Franklin and attended by his employees. They included Harry Crawley, who also served and died. It seems that a good time was had by all, with 'loyal toasts', 'old-fashioned English songs' and 'The health of the Chairman . . . . . most heartily drunk by all.'

In 1914 he was the stockman on Highdown Farm and although a family man, like many others he felt that it was his duty to serve. On January 2nd 1915 he travelled to Hitchin and enlisted in the Bedfordshire Regiment for the duration of the war.

He went for training and remained in England until May 18th 1916 when he embarked for France. His Battalion, the 8th Bedfords, was already in Belgium and having a tough time fighting in the defence of Ypres. Their war diary records the losses for April as 54 men killed, 3 wounded, 95 missing believed killed, 91 sick to hospital and 20 evacuated to base. Fred was probably one of the thirty-four other ranks that joined the Battalion in Belgium on May 24th - not nearly enough to replace the losses. He probably found himself in a working party almost immediately, sandbagging dugouts and generally trying to improve conditions; 310 men worked on the night of the 25th, 300 on the 26th and 27th and 400 on the 28th. On the 29th they moved back into the front line, relieving the King's Shropshire Light Infantry, and remained there until the night of June 5th. The casualties were averaging one or two a day. They rested until the 11th, then returned to the trenches the next day and saw the terrifying continuous artillery bombardment on the nearby Canadians, before they attacked to recapture earlier lost ground. This action appears to have been a complete success with no casualties and the capture of 'about one hundred prisoners' – a rare thing at this stage of the war. They stayed in the trenches until the 17th and, although the enemy was sometimes described as 'quiet' or 'non-aggressive', that must be

Harvest Home Supper.
MASTER AND MEN SPEND A HAPPY EVENING.

On Friday, Sept. 8th, Mr. T. Franklin generously entertained his employees to a supper in the Church School. The repast was admirably served by Mr. Cooper, of the Angel Vaults, Hitchin, and amply done justice to by the Company. The tables having been cleared, Mr. Franklin took the chair. The usual loyal toasts were heartily responded to, some old-fashioned English songs followed, in which Messrs. H. Crawley, D. Titmuss, E. Males, Geo. Males, F. Anderson and others, distinguished themselves. The health of the Chairman and his family was proposed by an old servant on the farm and most heartily drunk by all.

The Chairman thanked them for their good wishes, and hoped the cordial relations at present existing between himself and the men would always continue. "God save the King" finished a most enjoyable evening.

judged against their experience of 'normality' and during this period they experienced artillery bombardments and machine gun fire. To the soldiers' relief the latter half of June and the first half of July was spent resting and training, although large working parties were still sent out at night, which was a very dangerous duty.

In early August they moved to France. Their first stop was near Doullens, then Pichevillers and Louvencourt. Much of the movement, if not all, was by route march. They trained in bayonet fighting and attacking trenches until the middle of August, when they moved into the trenches around Beaumont Hamel and into the Battle of the Somme (1916). The Germans used heavy trench mortars on them and the British replied with artillery. The next day the enemy tried shrapnel and trench mortars. On the 18th the Bedfordshires carried out a dummy raid '*to worry the enemy*'. The Germans retaliated '*slightly damaging our trenches in places.*'

None of this seems out of the ordinary for the time; casualties were relatively low and it is easy to make light of the experience, as the war diaries always seem to, but it is difficult to understand what individual soldiers may have seen or experienced. Most if not all of these men would have seen comrades fall, either badly injured or killed by shell, sniper or in raids or attacks.

The Battalion diary gives the Field State of the 8th Bedfords for the month of August. '*Killed 8 Wounded 27 Sick to Hospital 72 Sick from Hospital 17 Evacuated from F.A.*(Field Ambulance) *46 "A" Coy Strength 16 officers 202 other ranks "B" Coy Strength 6 officers 214 other ranks "C" Coy Strength 8 officers 230 other ranks "D" Coy Strength 8 officers 212 other ranks - Total 38 officers 858 other ranks.*'

Fred was one of those listed as '*sick to hospital*' and the doctors decided that he was ill enough to be returned to England and so he left France on September 5th 1916. He had been in France for 110 days. His service records show that he was admitted to Norfolk War Hospital at Thorpe, Norwich with Myalgia. This is muscle pain and can be caused by overstraining the muscle, injury, allergic reaction, or disease, but this hospital had been a mental asylum, so it is possible that his sickness was actually related to shellshock. He left hospital on September 16th and went to RGH Downham – the writing is unclear - perhaps another hospital, where he stayed until

Norfolk War Hospital at Thorpe, Norwich.

October 12th.

Unfortunately, but understandable considering their age, some parts of his service records are difficult to read. They show that he was transferred on December 14th to the 2/4th Battalion of the Suffolk or Norfolk Regiment. Then, on March 14th 1917, to the 3rd Infantry Company, Northamptonshire Regiment and then to the 141st Company of the Labour Corps on May 14th 1917 and they left Folkestone for Boulogne on the 23rd. His transfer to the Labour Corps suggests that Fred had not recovered sufficiently to be regarded as fighting fit.

The Labour Corps was formed to solve a problem. The manual labour required to support the fighting troops in the building and maintaining roads, railways and other infrastructure was poorly organised and often diverted fighting men from the front line. So in January 1917 the Labour Corps was formed. It took men who were not classed as 'A1'. They could be men who enlisted and were not of the highest physical fitness or men like Fred, who through injury or illness were no longer considered fit enough for the front line. That did not mean that they were out of danger; on the contrary they often worked for prolonged periods within the range of enemy guns.

It is often more difficult to establish the movements of a Labour Corps than a Battalion in the front line, simply because there seem to be no war diaries for the former. A new reference book 'No Labour, No Battle' by J Starling and Ivor Lee *[1], is dedicated to the men who provided a labour service for the war. Their work is often misunderstood and its value underestimated and the book seeks to correct this. It also provides a few clues to Fred's service. His number, 84038, confirms the approximate date of his transfer and that his

Company was formed out of the 3rd Infantry Company, Northamptonshire Regiment. Fred's Labour Company, like the others, consisted of about 500 men, their work included digging in communication cables, mending breaks caused by shelling and making and maintaining forward roads. The range of these locations was often known to the enemy artillery and the Labour Corps suffered accordingly.

Whether he had fully recovered from his earlier illness is not known, but in August 1917 he became ill again and was hospitalised again, this time with influenza. He moved between several hospitals, before being discharged back to his unit in the field on September 8th and so he continued with his work duties for the next few months.

The only specific information for the 141st that has been found to date is that at the launch of the German Spring Offensive on March 21st 1918, they were at an ammunition dump at Flavy-Le-Martel and they were not withdrawn until it was shelled and under machine gun fire.

His poor health continued and was hospitalised again on June 29th 1918. His service record shows

that he died of broncho-pneumonia*2 on July 8th 1918 aged thirty-five.

He was buried in Aubigny Communal Cemetery Extension, which is an extension to the village cemetery and contains 2,771 Commonwealth burials of the First World War. Many of those that died were treated in the 42nd Casualty Clearing Station, so it is probable that he was taken there before he died.

The communal cemetery is quite large and sits on a raised plateau. To find Fred you must enter the raised cemetery by climbing a small set of stone steps and pass through the village cemetery to where these men lie.

Aubigny-en-Artois is a village approximately nine miles north-west of Arras on the road to St. Pol. The village cemetery lies to the south, on a road leading from the centre of the village, and the Extension lies behind it.

His headstone does not read Labour Corps, but Bedfordshire Regiment, his original Regiment, which apparently was the normal practice for men who died while serving in the Labour Corps, but who had first served in another Regiment.

By September 1918 his widow Lilian had moved to Walnut Tree Cottage, Fishponds Road, Hitchin, which is where his effects were delivered; a disc, two badges, a photograph, his wallet, a watch and chain and a few buttons – not much to remember him by. She later moved to 5 Periwinkle Lane, Hitchin.

*1 *Published by Spellmount, ISBN 978-0-7524-4975-3.*
*2 *Pneumonia is an inflammation of the lung tissue usually caused by infection. Bronchitis is an inflammation or infection of the large airways. Together they are known as broncho-pneumonia.*

Private 84038, Fred Anderson,
Aubigny Communal Cemetery Extension, Aubigny-en-Artois,
Pas de Calais, France. Ref. IV. J. 41.

ALBERT REYNOLDS

DRIVER 90497, 139TH HEAVY BATTERY, ROYAL GARRISON ARTILLERY.
DIED OF WOUNDS: FRIDAY, AUGUST 9TH 1918, AGED 35.
BURIED: PERNOIS BRITISH CEMETERY, HALLOY-LES-PERNOIS, SOMME,
FRANCE. REF. III. B. 14.
BORN IN PIRTON, LIVED IN WINDLESHAM, SURREY AND ENLISTED
CAMBERLEY, SURREY.

The Reynolds family, headed by Lewis and Mary Ann Reynolds (née Catterell), had fifteen children. More complete details of the family are given in the chapter on Albert's brother Walter, who died in 1917.

Albert was baptised on December 25th 1884 and presumably he was born earlier that year. Like Walter and many of his other siblings he attended the Pirton School.

He grew up around Little Green, now part of the High Street near the pond. By 1901 his parents were living in 3 Wesley Cottages, which are the group of cottages behind the terrace which contains the village shop. Albert was sixteen and had moved to Lane House Cottages, Kings Walden, where he was living with his brother, Jacob, Jacob's wife and their young daughter. Albert was working as a domestic groom probably at the same house as his brother who was a domestic coachman.

In 1904 he was back in Pirton and a witness at his brother William's marriage to Margaret Baines (possibly Barnes). A few years later, on May 9th 1907, Albert also married. His wife's name was Caroline Bashford from Croydon and later that year Alfred John Louis, who was their only child, was born there.

The 1911 census shows them living at Foxhills, Chertsey, Surrey and Albert was a gamekeeper. The entry looks like 'Gamekeeper on Esdale', but perhaps could be 'estate' as no explanation of Esdale has been found. However, Foxhills was a nineteenth century mansion, in a 400 acre estate, so, as that is where he was living, it is likely he was working on that estate. During the war Foxhills played its own part and served as a convalescent home for wounded Officers. This was not Albert's first job as a gamekeeper, as a later newspaper article confirmed that Albert had previously been a gamekeeper in Shillington for Mr Payne and that was there he had met his wife, who had been the cook. He had then gone on to be a gamekeeper on an estate in Yorkshire, before

Driver Albert Reynolds

moving to Surrey. The newspaper does not mention Foxhills or Esdale, but does say that he was keeper and stockman on a large estate in Windlesham when he joined the army. That was in 1915. His enlistment papers are dated December 11th and were signed in Camberley and they confirm his address as Laurel Cottage, Windlesham. Albert became Driver 90497 in the Royal Garrison Artillery and the papers describe him as thirty-two years old, 5' 9", with fresh hazel hair.

It was six months before he was mobilised (June 1st 1916) and on July 6th he was posted to the 203rd Heavy Battery. After training and home service he left Southampton for France on January 17th 1917 and on the 22nd was posted to the 127th Heavy (Battery) *'in the field'*.

The Royal Garrison Artillery (RGA) had evolved from the fortress-based artillery used to defend strategic locations on the British coastline. It came into its own from 1914 when the war required heavy guns and the RGA grew into a very large part of the army's artillery capacity. They were usually armed with 5 inch guns also known as '60 pounders', which were long range guns – sending high explosive shells accurately up to about 10,400 yards (just short of six miles) and potentially at a rate of up to two shells a minute. They were usually towed to position by teams of horses and Albert was one of their drivers, but had other duties once the guns were in position. These large, heavy guns were difficult to move so they tended to remain fairly static if the fighting permitted. Their main purpose was to destroy key enemy targets such as artillery positions, roads and railways, but they were also used in preparation for, and in support of, infantry attacks. They had immense destructive power and were largely responsible for the wholesale destruction of land and property along the Western Front. It is accurate to say that these guns changed the landscape in France and Belgium.

On July 19th 1917, still serving with the 127th Heavy Battery RGA, Albert was injured and suffered a contusion of the ankle. It happened when a horse slipped and pinned him underneath. His ankle was quite badly hurt and he was admitted to the 59th General Hospital St. Omer and then invalided to England on H.M.T.*[1] St. George on July 29th. The incident was reported and one witness statement, from Driver A Hansford, was recorded as *"we were returning with rations to wagon lines while crossing railway lines the wheel ride horse stumbled owing to defective state of crossing pinning Dvr. Reynolds left leg under him."* No blame was attached to Albert.

While in hospital, presumably to stave off boredom, he became adept at making items to sell in support of the Red Cross. The local paper notes that he '*was quickly a favourite of the local ladies for his readiness and cheerfulness to help in any way he could.*' He remained there until November when he was sent to Ireland, but he did manage to visit his family in Pirton on the way, but this was to be the last time they saw him.

Apart from Albert and Walter (mentioned above) two other brothers were also serving; William in the Kings Shropshire Light Infantry and Harry in the Royal Horse Artillery – Harry had also been in hospital around the same time as Albert having been gassed in France. Both William and Harry survived the war.

It is not clear what Albert did immediately after his recovery, his service records read '*Clg Office*' (possibly clearing office), but on November 25th 1917 he was posted to the Command Depot based at Ballyvonare Camp in Buttevant, County Cork. Then on February 5th 1918 he was posted to the 1st Reserve Brigade, Heavy Batteries and then back to France on April 13th, where, on the 22nd, he joined the 139th Heavy Battery.

One local newspaper reported that Albert had returned to France in April 1918 and was '*taking part in the gallant actions to stem the German onslaught*' – this was the German major Spring Offensive of March and April that year.

From February 18th the 139th Heavy Battery had been in the area around Peronne; their situation had been stable up to March 21st when the Germans launched their offensive. Although this was before Albert arrived and the main thrust of the offensive was over by the time he did, it is relevant to describe their circumstances and that of the front line in the period before he arrived.

The German attack did not come as a surprise, in fact the war diary records a warning of impending attacks as early as March 12th, but its determination and ferocity might have and the rapid success of the Germans certainly was. The attack is recorded as starting at 4:55am and the batteries came under fairly heavy gas attack and had to operate in respirators. It was obviously a major attack and the heavy guns were brought into full action to try to assist in repelling it. On the first day the cumulative fire from the batteries was recorded as 6,330 rounds fired by 4:00pm; that was an average of 1,557 round per battery and nearly 42 tons of shells carried and fired per battery.

The situation in the front line was chaotic and in places bordering on panic. The Germans forced the British back and the big guns, although some distance behind the lines, had to keep far enough back to operate and remain safe. On the 22nd, with little prior information on what was happening, they were ordered to fall back for the first time - an action not to be undertaken lightly given the size and weight of the guns. Having fallen back once, they received orders to do so again, but were then able to recommence firing. The next day they withdrew again, this time to a position near Maurepas and about 6,000 yards behind a line from Rancourt to

Sailley Sailisel. On the 24th they were ordered to fire until all the ammunition was gone and then retire towards Maricourt. They ended up beyond Fricourt where, once again, they commenced firing. That evening they were machine gunned by enemy planes. On the 25th they moved forward slightly and fired all day before the withdrawal continued; on the 26th to a line between Bresle and Lavievielle and on the 27th to Warloy. This was too far and on the 28th they were ordered forward and were attached to the 3rd Australian Division (one diary entry suggests that it might have been the 4th).

By early April the situation was stabilising. The German attack had been very successful. In fact too successful; their troops were exhausted, their supply lines were stretched to almost breaking point and they had to stop, which gave the British time to re-establish a proper defensive line. That did not mean that the fighting had stopped or that it was any less dangerous for the Batteries. Although they were behind the front line, they were the target of the enemy's batteries of similar guns and many impersonal artillery duels were over great distances. On April the 5th the enemy gained ground again and the Batteries again came under fire. Their casualties were recorded as *'fairly heavy'* with 2 officers wounded, 3 men killed, 43 men wounded plus several horses killed or wounded and on the 9th the 139th were gassed.

These losses may explain why Albert was needed in the 139th, and he joined them on April 22nd. Two days later the Battery suffered a direct hit on one of the guns. On May 5th they lost 2 officers, 1 killed and 1 wounded. Later in the month they assisted the troops to retake part of a trench known as Hairpin; they engaged five enemy tanks and took on the German batteries in yet another long distance duel. On the 20th a giant 8" enemy howitzer got their range and they lost a gun. There were no casualties in the 139th but a nearby battery, the 120th, had 1 man killed and 4 wounded. May ended with an aircraft attack and a gas attack and June commenced with four men being wounded, one of whom later died.

By the middle of June 1918 an epidemic of influenza hit the batteries. Although a number of men fell sick and some were hospitalised, it does not appear to have been the strain that started in1918 and which later became the worldwide pandemic. Between the 27th and 30th they took part in the wire cutting and the destruction of trench mortars prior to an attack. It seems that they did their work well because the following day the troops captured the German front line trench north-west of Albert. The Germans counter attacked twice and the batteries helped repulse them, but the Germans did not give up. They opened up a heavy bombardment along the whole of the Corps line and recaptured their trench, but two days later the tough Australians advanced one and half miles along a four mile front – a huge success, and in the following days the Batteries supported a number of other successful raids.

The entry for July 27th 1918 records interesting statistics and perhaps helps us understand the ferocity of the fight and the sheer hard work done by the guns and their crews. Between dawn on March 21st to 9:20pm on July 27th the 89th Brigade, of which the 139th were part, fired 129,377 rounds; 2 S. Battery 29,507, 3 S. Battery 34,682, 120th Heavy Battery 34,986 and Albert's Battery 30,202 rounds.

The British had finally stopped the Germans and were beginning to gain the advantage. At the beginning of August the enemy was reported to have abandoned his trenches and as a parting shot blew up Albert Cathedral. At 11:50pm on the 3rd the 139th were ordered forward with four guns and 400 rounds per gun. With growing confidence they scouted for more forward positions and then moved again. Something big was being planned by the Allies for the 8th, zero hour was 4:20am, the 139th's six guns were allocated their targets and began firing. At 11:20am the enemy were reported as massing and they were targeted by some of the Batteries.

Many argue that the 8th was the start of the allies' final offensive on the Somme – it was for Albert. On that day, probably in the exchange of artillery fire, he was badly wounded - *'abdomen penetrated'*. He was quickly taken to hospital, probably No. 4 Casualty Clearing Station, and he survived the night, but a newspaper reported that he knew the end was near and that he wrote to his wife that (his death) *'would be her loss and his gain.'* – strange words perhaps, but so brave.

He is buried in the Pernois British Cemetery, which served the No. 4 Casualty Clearing Station. A small, open cemetery lying in peaceful, green countryside near the villages of Pernois and Halloy, it only contains the bodies of 403 British soldiers, all identified, and 17 German soldiers share their rest.

Still living in Laurel Cottage, Caroline received his personal possessions in January 1919, and his death plaque in June. One hopes they were not all that she had to remember him by - a pierced shilling, disc (probably his identity tag), pipe, belt, silver ring, purse, pocket knife, cigarette holder, match box cover, two letters, badge swivel and ring (possibly ring farthing – the writing is unclear) Caroline signed the receipt, but noted that she had not received his original Will, his watch or his gold ring.

Albert is also remembered on the Windlesham War Memorial and both he and his brother Walter are remembered on their parents' grave in St. Mary's churchyard.

*1 *H.M.T. = His Majesty's Troopship.*

A PIRTON GUNNER.

The photograph is that of the late Gunner A. Reynolds (34), R.G.A., whose death in action on August 9 we announced last week. His wife lives at Windlesham, Surrey. Gunner Reynolds was a son of Mr. and Mrs. Lewis Reynolds, of 3, Wesley-cottages, Pirton. For several years he was a gamekeeper at Shillington Manor, his wife having formerly been the cook at the Manor.

Gunner Reynolds enlisted in the Army in 1916, and went to France in January the following year. The whole of Mr. and Mrs. Reynolds' six surviving sons have served in the Army.

Driver 90497, Albert Reynolds, Pernois British Cemetery, Halloy-Les-Pernois, Somme, France. Ref. III. B. 14.

FRANCIS JOHN PEARCE *1
RIFLEMAN O/127, 1/8TH BATTALION, LONDON REGIMENT
(POST OFFICE RIFLES).
KILLED IN ACTION: MONDAY, SEPTEMBER 9TH 1918, AGED 19.
BURIED: EPEHY WOOD FARM CEMETERY, EPEHY, SOMME,
FRANCE. REF. V. I. 2.
BORN AND LIVED PIRTON, ENLISTED IN HITCHIN.

*1 *He was also known as Jack and appears as John in 1901 and 1911 census, but appears as Francis on the Village Memorial and, as that is how they wished him to be remembered, that is how he appears here.*

Francis was the son of George and Ellen Pearce (nee Burton) and was the half-brother of Edward Charles Burton, who also served and died. The sibling relationships were complicated and they are described more fully in the chapter on Edward. However, in brief, George married Ellen some time around 1898 or 1899 and Ellen already had a son, Edward Charles Burton. So Francis was Ellen's second son, but the first child from the marriage. He was born on December 19th 1898 and they lived in one of the Holwell Cottages – the row of twelve terraced houses on the Holwell Road, also known as the 'Twelve Apostles'. Francis went to the village school and in the 1911 census he was still recorded as a scholar and aged twelve.

After leaving school he went to work for Innes' Sons and King, Hitchin, and was working there when he joined the army. According to the Parish Magazine, that was some time after March 2nd 1917 and then in June 1917 it recorded him as being in the Training Reserve Battalion, but gives no further details. His elder brother or half-brother Edward Charles Burton was killed in December 1916 and one wonders if that influenced Francis to enlist or whether he was conscripted – conscription began on January 27th 1916.

His Battalion is one of those known as the 'Post Office Rifles', the full Battalion name is almost certainly the 1/8th (City of London) Battalion (Post Office Rifles) and, as the name suggests, was one of the Battalions substantially made up of volunteers from amongst the Post Office workers. This was not unique to the First World War as there was a long tradition of Post Office workers joining and serving in the army at the time of war. 1914 saw this tradition continue and they went on to serve with distinction at Ypres, at Passchendaele and elsewhere. During September 1917 they lost more than half their strength in the Battle of Wurst Farm Ridge and

Rifleman Francis John Pearce

so the number of Post Office workers in the battalions was diluted by new recruits such as Francis.

He went to France on January 10th 1918, but whether that is when he joined Post Office Rifles is not yet known. If it was, then he joined them after their part in the Battle of Passchendaele or the Third Battle of Ypres, where they suffered more heavy losses.

In the early part of January they were ordered to France, first to Villers-Bretonneux by train, then Moreuil and then, at the beginning of February, to Pierremande where they took over the southernmost part of the British line with the French to the south. They were there until March 19th when they had been moved out of the line to rest, but at 4:30am on the 21st the Germans launched a major offensive, this part of which was later called the Battle St. Quentin. At 5:00pm they were ordered forward and then at 10:30pm were ordered to protect the Crozat Canal crossing. The enemy were advancing and it did not look good; secret papers were removed from Battalion HQ and the British began blowing up bridges to stop the Germans. On the 22nd it was foggy, visibility was difficult and stragglers were still finding their way back from what had been the front line. At about midday Germans dressed in British uniforms, taken from dead or captured troops, came across on the Battalion's left flank. That flank fell, largely because of these Germans, but "C" and "D" Companies held the right flank for 36 hours until the enemy were attacking them on three sides. It was recorded that very few escaped. The Germans began to pour forward; the British hit them with field artillery and massed machine gun fire. The fighting was desperate, but the hastily formed new defence lines held.

Between the 21st and the 25th the casualties in Francis' Battalion were terrible: 13 officers, 4 killed, 8 more were missing. In the other ranks 300 were killed, wounded or missing. It is known that Francis had been wounded and by April 13th 1918, had been returned to England to Eastleigh Hospital in Hampshire. Francis himself made light of the injury writing to his family saying he was '*slightly wounded*'.

It seems very likely that his injuries were received in the above battle.

He would have been out of the line for some time recovering and we do not know when he returned to the Battalion, but if it was by July 25th then he may have taken part in a large daylight raid - 300 men went over the top and attacked the German trenches. In the advance they met little resistance, except for one small section. They killed some Germans, captured a few prisoners and '*many more in attempting escape had to be shot.*' However, on the return journey the Germans reorganised and opened up with machine guns on both flanks. Two Officers were killed, 4 wounded and the casualties in the other ranks were counted as 113. Their war diary notes '*On the whole, it seems that the casualties on both sides were about equal.*' It was also noted, because it was unusual, that '*the enemy allowed the wounded to be got in without interference.*'

In early August they were withdrawn for a long period of rest and training in preparation for the next big offensive on the Somme. However, that was not to be and on the 6th they began the relief of the 2nd Bedfords near Sailly-Laurette. At dawn on the following day, still trying to complete the relief, they were attacked. Although the Germans pushed sections of the line back 400 yards they failed to break it. As the infantry attack petered out, the

Rifleman Francis John Pearce (middle row left) and his pals in the Post Office Rifles.

British front line continued to be pounded by large shells, gas shells and trench mortars. The British were planning their own offensive to begin on the 8th, which it did and began with success. The 1/8th London Battalion was held in reserve until the next day and so it was on the 9th that they went into the attack. They were joined by an American Regiment – from August 1918 the Americans were fully participating in the war. They record that the Battalion casualties were far lighter than the number of unwounded prisoners taken, but 4 officers were killed, 7 were wounded and 290 other ranks were listed as killed, wounded or missing. They were relieved two days later when they finally got some rest and yet more training. On August 22nd they moved back to the Front to support another attack, which took place during a violent thunderstorm. They had gone forward without water or rations and remained without either until the night of the 27th and then on the following day the attack was resumed.

Between the 22nd and the 28th they took 150 prisoners, captured three field guns, lots of machine guns and *'forty enemy pigeons.'* Two officers were killed, 4 wounded and 186 other ranks were killed or wounded – they were given a day's rest before the next attack. During this one, they lost 2 more officers, 5 more were wounded and 105 other ranks became casualties.

They were relieved on September 1st, but despite their horrendous losses were only allowed to remain out of the line until the 6th when they again moved forward for an attack on the 8th. Francis and his comrades must have wondered if it would ever end. They attacked on the 8th as planned, advancing an unbelievable 1,000 yards, but then came under heavy machine gun fire. The Royal Field Artillery, who had advanced behind them, poured shells onto the enemy. The Battalion was ordered to hold the gains at all costs; they did and Francis paid the ultimate price, being killed on the 9th. He was among

another 141 other ranks killed or wounded.

Although Francis was killed in action on the September 9th, the family did not know. In November the Parish Magazine published what the family had been told, which was that he had been wounded and was missing. They must have prayed that he was a prisoner and being well treated, but those hopes were dashed when the news of his death finally came.

Perhaps his body was found quickly and the news just took time to reach Pirton, but it is possible that his body was found much later when land was retaken and was identified by his identity tags or other personal belongings. Perhaps some clues come from the history of Epehy, where he is buried. It is in the area known as the Somme and between Cambrai and Peronne. It was captured by the British in April 1917, but lost to the Germans in March 1918 only to be retaken in September 18th – nine days after Francis died. Clearly there was a lot of fighting, much confusion and many casualties as the control of areas of land moved between opposing forces.

Francis is buried in Epehy Wood Farm Cemetery, but he was first buried either on the battlefield, in Deelish Valley Cemetery, which originally contained 158 burials from September 1918, or in Epehy New British Cemetery, which also contained men who died in September 1918. The latter locations were

close by and they were amalgamated into Epehy Wood Farm Cemetery after the Armistice.

The cemetery has an unusual entrance, constructed in stone and raised from the road. It is not the largest of cemeteries, containing only 997 burials, but once inside its appearance is striking and it is surrounded by views over miles of open, flat countryside. The Stone of Remembrance is placed at one end and at the other the Cross of Sacrifice is made even more poignant by the effect of two poplars rising like giant flames either side.

The losses of this Battalion are truly staggering; remembering that a Battalion is about 1,000 men in the 1/8th, Francis' Battalion to January 31st 1918, the losses were killed 565, wounded 1,598 missing or killed 189, and from February 1st 1918, when they combined with the 2/8th forming the 8th, another 288 were killed 1,214, wounded, missing or killed 327. It seems that Francis was lucky to have survived so long.

'. . . an unusual entrance, constructed in stone and raised from the road.'

Rifleman O/127, Francis John Pearce, Epehy Wood Farm Cemetery, Epehy, Somme, France. Ref. V. I. 2.
'. . . the Cross of Sacrifice is made even more poignant by the affect of two poplars rising like giant flames on either side."

FREDERICK BAINES *1

PRIVATE G/15609, 8TH BATTALION, ROYAL SUSSEX REGIMENT.
(FORMERLY PRIVATE 2365, 1ST BATTALION, HERTFORDSHIRE REGIMENT).
KILLED IN ACTION: WEDNESDAY, OCTOBER 23RD 1918, AGED 24.
BURIED: HIGHLAND CEMETERY, LE CATEAU, NORD, FRANCE.
REF. IV. C. 9.
BORN, LIVED AND ENLISTED IN PIRTON.

*1 *It seems that he was known as Fred, but he appears as Frederick on the Village memorial and, as that is how they wished him to be remembered, that is how he appears here.*

Frederick's mother was Ruth Baines, the daughter of Edward and Annice Baines (although she appears as Annis and Anice in censuses before 1911). In 1891, aged sixteen, she was working as a general domestic servant in Hornsey, Middlesex. The date that she returned to Pirton is not known, but unmarried she gave birth to Frederick on August 12th 1894 and he was christened in Pirton. Four years later she married Charles Cooper of Pirton and Herbert Clarke, who features in the chapter 'Should These Men be on Our Memorial', and his wife Martha were witnesses. As there were four years between the two events it seems unlikely that Charles was Frederick's father.

In 1901 they were living around Great Green with their three children; Frederick, who the census incorrectly records as Frederick Cooper, and half-siblings Arthur Charles and Dorothy May. By 1911 there were four more children, bringing the total to seven, but in fact one more, who is unnamed, had died*2.

Frederick went to school in Pirton and when he left he first went to work on local farms before going to Bowman's corn mill, which is still operating in Ickleford, near Hitchin.

Workers at Bowman's Mill.

Before the war he, like many of Pirton's young men,

joined the Hitchin Territorials. That was in February 1914 and when war came in August, like the rest of the Pirton Terriers he was keen to fight and enlisted as Private 2365 in the 1st Battalion, Hertfordshire Regiment. As the Territorials were already partially trained they would have gone over to France earlier than most other recruits, so it is likely that he saw service with the Hertfordshires, probably in the defence of Ypres. At some later date, as yet unknown, he was transferred to the 8th Battalion, Royal Sussex Regiment, who were one of the pioneer battalions. They were responsible for building many of the trenches along the Western Front, effectively part labour battalion, part fighting force. They supplemented the work of the Royal Engineers, but often operating in very dangerous areas close to the front line. They were trained and equipped as infantry and were required to down tools to fight when necessary.

Although the date when Frederick was transferred is not known, the report of John Parsell's death in September 1916 confirms that it must have been before that date. That report quotes from the letter to John Parsell's mother, which brought the news of his death, and which was written by Ted Goldsmith at the request of Corporal Harry Smith, both Pirton men. Harry seems to have been too affected by the death to write himself. Ted wrote that just before his death, John had been '*very cheerful having seen Fred Baines and Arthur Odell of the Royal Sussex* (although different battalions) *and George Thompson of the ASC* (Army Service Corps)' - all Pirton men. It goes on to confirm that John was killed by a shell and that literally at the time of his death he had been with yet another two Pirton men, George Roberts and Arthur Walker. Both were wounded by the same shell, Arthur later died from his injuries. Frederick was elsewhere by this time, but clearly was close to the action.

The Battalion war diary helps establish Fred's likely experience of the war and, because we know that he was definitely with the 8th Royal Sussex in September 1916, the diary was examined from the beginning of that month.

Over the first three days they moved from Doullen to Acheaux by bus. They received orders to move to Forceville and then Aveluy Wood, where they bivouacked. The next day they began their manual labour, with various platoons working on Ovillers Road, a tramway extension at Ovillers and the sidings and light railway at Aveluy. Their work included general repairs, maintenance and new build and they remained in this area working in these and other locations until the 22nd. Their experience reads as just hard work until the casualties are listed and awards are mentioned; for example on the 10th, the day that John Parsell died, 1 man was killed and 3 were wounded and on the next day the Corps Commander awarded Military Medals to ten men from the Battalion for '*gallantry and devotion to duty between the 1st and 14th July 1916*' – that would have been for more than just repairing roads and relaying railway lines!

There were three more medals awarded later in the month and up to the 22nd, when they moved to Headauville, twenty-eight more casualties. Some were due to premature shell explosions, but most were while the men were at rest on the night of the 20th when their camp was shelled; 1 man died and 18 were wounded. They were located at Pioneer Road and their work included cleaning up and repairing the trenches and communications across No Man's Land.

While the Royal Sussex worked hard, the war diary

records that their Division, the 18th, attacked and took Thiepval. This was their intermediate objective, the final one being the German fortified stronghold of the Schwaben Redoubt. This period lasted until October 7th. The orders to the 8th Royal Sussex were: 1) to make cart tracks from Crucifix Corner to Thiepval, 2) maintain the communication trench from Thiepval Avenue to Kilman Street and extend it across No Man's Land, 3) repair the Authuille to Thiepval Road, and 4) maintain the tram-lines. In the remaining six days of the month another 32 men became casualties, 3 of whom died. The total from September 20th to October 15th was 77, of whom 5 died. They were mostly from shelling but some were from gas attacks.

They then moved to Usna Valley where they stayed until December 20th. Their work was concentrated more on the maintenance and construction of trenches and in this period the number of casualties was 82 men, including 4 killed. They received a large draft of 147 recruits, replacing those lost, and moved on to Le Plessiel where they were billeted, rested and could bathe. There was no work on Christmas Day and a Divisional sports day was organised on Boxing Day.

In 1917, they moved to huts near Aveluy and from there, between January 16th and March 13th they supported operations on the Ancre – the sector near the River Ancre. This was a relatively safe period for the men with only twenty-nine casualties. The more notable events included supporting the attack launched from near Miraumont on Boom Ravine in mid-February, the capture of Irles on March 10th and, between March 14th and 20th, they worked to support the advance as the Germans began their strategic withdrawal to the Hindenburg Line.

In the middle of April they marched to Bully Grenay - the name of the railway station near Grenay village, not far from Lens. Here they worked repairing roads and suffered relatively few casualties until April 24th when, in one incident, 1 man was killed and 15 were wounded. Having noted in the diary that the roads were now in good order, between the 26th and 29th they marched about twenty miles to Pernes, then another twenty-one miles to Lattre St. Quentin - noting that the roads were dusty and the weather hot, and then about twelve miles to a camp south east of Beaurains. They spent a day resting and improvising a camp before starting day shifts on more road repairs.

On May 3rd the 18th Division attacked as part of the Second Battle of Arras. The role of 8th Royal Sussex was to provide and maintain the infrastructure, but the Germans counter attacked so fiercely that they could not work and were ordered to take up positions to prevent the counter-attack spreading. The diary is not clear whether, or how much, they fought, and certainly by the 4th they were back working on roads and digging trenches. This period was hectic and dangerous and it was several days before they could detail the casualties; May 3rd, 6 men wounded, 4th, 1 man wounded, 5th, 4 men killed and 20 wounded, 6th, 9 men wounded and on the 7th, 2 men wounded – a total of 42. Later in the month they moved to a position just South of Mercatel and then to Henin sur Cojeul. They stayed in this general area until June 17th and then marched to Couin, where they rested until the 21st before beginning their journey to Belgium. They moved from Saulty Labret to Hopoutre Station which is south of Poperinge and began work moving Nissen huts, repairing roads and digging trenches and again they were relatively safe with few casualties until the 29th, when 1 man was killed and 11 wounded.

Their diary rapidly becomes a list of names of names where they continued their physically demanding and often dangerous work. Some, such as Yser Canal Bank, which was north of Ypres, are well-known names and can be found on modern maps. Others, such as Virginia Water, Pioneer Farm, Wellington Crescent were named by the army for convenience and security and yet more, such as Shrapnel Corner, were named for self-evident reasons. Generally the casualties are recorded in twos and threes, but the entries are occasionally punctuated with more depressing numbers; July 31st 45 casualties, including 2 killed and 2 more who died of their wounds; August 8th, 7 casualties, with 1 killed and 1 dying later of his wounds; August 12th, 9 wounded and so it continued.

Sometimes, even when resting, they were not free of danger. In September they were given rest in Poperinge, which was well behind the front lines, but the shelling reached even there, and when a shell exploded, 5 men were wounded and another was recorded as missing - there may have been no remains left to find. They moved to Nortkerque where they were given a prolonged period of rest and training - presumably required due to the intense work and the conditions in which they had been operating. When reading the war diaries,

especially when the casualties are named, which in unusual, it seems wrong not to record the men, but the purpose of this book is to document the men of Pirton, not the history and detail of their Battalion. Given the numbers of casualties named it would be impossible for Frederick not to have known at least some of them – he probably knew many of them. Although there is no evidence, he surely must have seen horrific injuries and death and probably he too experienced 'close calls'.

Their experience in Belgium to November 1917 was as part of the Third Battle of Ypres, when the British Army tried to break out of the salient which they had been defending since 1914. The Royal Sussex and Frederick were operating to support that bloody action. What is missing from the description given in the war diaries are details of the conditions in which they had to work. The fact that the soldiers knew this as the Battle of Mud speaks volumes. In early August, the worst rainfall for thirty years came, it turned the soil into a quagmire and eventually the mud was so deep that men and horses drowned and were lost. The simple descriptions of Frederick's work, such as repairing roads, digging trenches or simply erecting huts is completely inadequate.

They remained in Belgium operating from Murat Camp, Turco Huts and Cambridge Camps, all for fairly extended periods. This ended on February 5th 1918 when they, and the entire 18th Division, moved back to France to the area around Noyon, Oise and then, later in the month, to Autreville, where they began general works on the defensive line. On the 28th the Battalion were warned to 'Prepare for an attack'. The 8th Royal Sussex Companies were ordered into various reserves, but later that day the word came 'Practice over – resume normal condition'. It is not clear whether this was a routine practice (no previous examples were seen in the diary), but around this time it was becoming clear to the British Army that the Germans were planning an offensive.

In March they moved to Vieville Wood near Remigny and began routine work, improving camps and shelters, digging infantry posts and cable trenches. This continued until the 20th when they were ordered to prepare to take up battle positions. The next day the Germans launched their Spring Offensive. The Royal Sussex were moved around the area to positions where they might be needed and, but for the odd note, such as 'repulsed attack at dusk,' the ferocity and success of the German attack might go unnoticed, at least until the list of casualties is found; between the 21st and the 28th, 98 men were wounded, 8 killed and 9 missing. Four of those wounded died of their wounds within this period. Toughened through their experiences and shear hard work they also proved themselves in battle.

In April, while the chaos caused by the Spring Offensive continued, the 8th Royal Sussex were moved back to repair roads and keep the men and supplies moving. The Germans over-reached their supply lines and the attack, although initially hugely successful, petered out. As it did so the casualty rate in Frederick's Battalion eased and what was considered normality returned. They spent most of May around Baisieux, June and half of July at Hénencourt and Warley and then they moved to Crouy. On July 31st they moved again, to the area around Heilly, then Contay and back to Hénencourt around mid-August. At the end of the month the diary records them working in the areas of Mametz Wood and Trones Wood, both the subject of terrible and famous battles earlier in the war, which the British lost. But now the Allied forces were planning their own offensive, one which would eventually, lead to the end of the war.

The war diary and its appendices reflect the effort and planning which was going in to the preparations for the offensive, with pages and pages of secret orders. The 8th Royal Sussex had their own role; one Company was to build tracks 'suitable for horse transport, as soon after ZERO as possible.'; two Companies were in the Divisional Reserve to 'reconnoitre, and repair, main traffic lines through ALBERT and ALBERT – La-BOISELLE – CONTALMAISON, and the ALBERT – BECORDEL roads, as ordered.'

The offensive was launched as planned on August 8th and Frederick's Battalion did what they were called upon to do. Following a frantic start, they settled to a hard slog: sometimes working to improve trenches and shelters, but more commonly filling in shell holes, clearing roads of debris (and probably worse) and generally repairing, maintaining and constructing roads and tracks to keep the supplies and men moving. In September, while the work was much the same, the workload appeared to have eased. However, the handwriting changes so it is possible that the new writer was just being a bit more circumspect. There are some more routine items mentioned, such as inspections of clothing,

rifles, box respirators (gas masks) and also foot inspections, which would be indicative of very damp conditions. Other more unpleasant duties were also recorded; six hours spent digging graves and collecting and burying the dead men and dead horses on the 10th and the same again for the following four days. Between the 11th and 14th they collected and buried 33 British soldiers, 26 Germans and 24 horses or what was left of them - some may have been lying dead for weeks if not months.

At the end of September the Battalion moved to Combles and to what again seems to be a quiet time. Elsewhere the army was fighting and in September and October the Germans were pushed back and the battles of the Hindenburg Line, the German's last line of defence, were fought. After their period away from the front line, Frederick's Battalion returned to the forward area. On the October 8th by bus and route march, they moved from Vandencourt to St. Emilie and were soon back to normal duties.

The final advance was getting close and the front line troops advanced in Picardy between the October 17th and the 25th 1918, in the Battle of the Selle. Meanwhile the 8th Battalion was working in companies in the area around Le Cateau. On the 23rd, the date of Frederick's death "A" and "B" Companies were clearing and repairing roads and "C" Company was clearing mud from roads and filling in a mine crater. There is no mention of shelling or any other event during their work, but the diary records the names of the casualties on that day; 8 men were wounded and 10 men died, one of them being 15609. PTE Baines F.

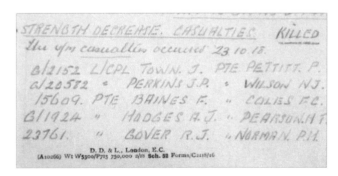

According to the Hertfordshire Express report on December 28th 1918, Second Lieutenant G Bannell wrote to Mr and Mrs Cooper, telling them of Frederick's death 'he was killed in his sleep by a direct shell' . . . 'with several of his chums'. There was a night battle going on at the time so whether they were asleep is perhaps debatable, but at least in this case death was probably instant and not just kind words written to give comfort to the men's nearest and dearest.

'Direct hit' or not, his body was found and buried close to where he died. Later, after the war, he was moved the Highland Cemetery, which is half a mile or so from Le Cateau and that is where his body now lies. It is both poignant and appropriate that the men whose names are listed next to his in the war diary lie either side of him; two of the 'chums' he died with.

The Highland Cemetery lies at the top of a gentle rising hill alongside a busy 'B' road. The town can be seen in the distance at the bottom of the hill and fields lie on three sides. It contains the bodies of 624 men, 560 of whom are named.

*2 *Frederick Cooper (b 1894). Half-siblings; Arthur Charles (b 1898), Dorothy May (b 1900), Ernest (b 1903), George (b 1905), Annie (b 1908) and Frank (b 1910).*

Private G/15609, Frederick Baines, Highland Cemetery, Le Cateau, Nord, France. Ref. IV. C. 9.

102

SIDNEY ARTHUR LAKE *1
GUNNER 60473, 138TH HEAVY BATTERY, ROYAL GARRISON ARTILLERY.
DIED: THURSDAY, NOVEMBER 28TH 1918, AGED 27.
BURIED: LE CATEAU COMMUNAL CEMETERY, LE CATEAU, FRANCE. REF. 1, 24.
BORN IN PIRTON, LIVED IN FINCHLEY.

*1 *He was baptised and enlisted as Sidney Arthur, but he appears as Arthur S on the Village Memorial and, as that is how they wished him to be remembered, that is how he appears here.*

Arthur's parents were Arthur and Julina Lake (née Bunker) and he was born on August 28th 1891. Establishing his brothers and sisters was more complicated than usual because, although Julina appears in all the relevant censuses, her name appears differently in other records. The five children, who are believed to be hers, are detailed below*2 and they include Sidney Arthur, but another child, currently unnamed, is confirmed by the 1911 census, which records six children and also records that three had died.

Like most of the men on the memorial Arthur went to the Pirton school and then left to work on local farms. However he is listed as cowman on a farm rather than just the more common description of farm or agricultural labourer.

By 1915 he had moved away from Pirton and was living at 7 Queens Cottages, Squires Lane, Church End, Finchley. He had married Dorothy Kate Worbey (possibly Wisbey?) in Finchley on June 15th and was working as a groundsman. Perhaps he decided to marry before enlisting, which he did on October 18th 1915, four months later.

Many World War One service records were destroyed by bombing during the Second World War; however in Arthur's case, his records survived, but they are badly faded and sometimes impossible to read. Frustratingly, this includes the dates of his movements and the details of his postings, so to try to make too much of them would be guess work. He reported for training at Dover with the Royal Garrison Artillery on October 25th 1915. He qualified as a cold shoer of horses on August 18th 1916 and appears to have finished his training in late November or early December 1916. Presumably his farrier training was to help make the gun team more self-sufficient, but he would also have had other duties as part of the gun team. The other information

that can be read in his records appears below, but many of the details of his service are not yet known. For instance, we know that Arthur joined the 138th Heavy Battery, but we do not know when. This Battery was also known as the 'Hampstead Heavies' due to the number of men from the London Borough of Hampstead who volunteered in late 1915. To add to the frustration, the war diary for the Battery held in the National Archives stops abruptly on January 23rd 1918, ten months before his death, and so even the movements of the 138th in the weeks before Arthur's death have to be sought elsewhere. As is it has not been possible to properly detail Arthur's movements, it seems appropriate to try give an overview of the operations of a Heavy Battery and, in particular and where possible, the movements of the 138th.

The heavy batteries fired the 'big guns', the 60 pounders. These were large guns, weighing four tons, had a six mile range and required a team of twelve horses to move them. Because of their long range they were usually remote from the battlefield.

The 'Hampstead Heavies' in training.

Their immense destructive power was usually employed against strategic targets; key enemy strongholds, stores, ammunition dumps, railways and their opposite enemy's batteries, but they also played a supporting role, targeting trenches prior to attacks or providing covering fire during an attack. They fired with the simple purpose of obliterating their targets. Some historians estimate that fifty-nine percent of all casualties during the war were caused by artillery and three times as many men were killed by shells than bullets.

Supplying the guns could be a logistical nightmare and firing them was hard work – the term 60 pounder refers to the weight of each shell. They were difficult to move because of their weight and often remained reasonably static for long periods; for instance the war diary for the 138th records that they were in the area around Bully in France from April 1916 to February 19th 1917 and then at Aix Noulette until April 16th. The 138th served predominantly in France, except for a period between May 18th 1917 and late 1917 when they served in Belgium, with some weeks spent in the area around Ypres. By the time the diary ends, however, in January 1918 they had moved back into France.

Work with a Battery was physically demanding with each shell having to be manhandled to the guns and loaded by hand and they could be required to keep up a steady rate of fire of up to two rounds per minute. Life was hard work, tiring, deafening, often monotonous and not without danger, although it would be fair to say that life in the trenches was much more dangerous and the big guns were usually a long way behind those. Duels between opposing batteries over great distances were not uncommon and they were also the target of bombing by enemy aircraft - although the latter was a very crude method of delivering death and the shells were usually far more dangerous.

The following is a fairly typical extract from the war diary and describes a period in May 1916:

May 1st - *Right section fired 10 rounds Lyddite*3. Left section fired 10 rounds Lyddite, both counter battery attack.*
May 2nd - *Right section fired 10 rounds Lyddite, counter battery attack. Left section fired 6 rounds Shrapnel*4, working parties.*
May 3rd - *Right section fired 14 rounds Lyddite on hostile battery and 16 rounds Lyddite in evening, counter battery work. Left section 4 rounds Lyddite in evening, counter battery work.*
May 4th - *Right section fired 26 rounds Lyddite and Shrapnel, counter battery attack and working parties. Left section fired 45 rounds Lyddite, hostile batteries.*
May 5th - *Right section fired 35 rounds Lyddite and Shrapnel, counter battery attack. Left section fired 6 rounds Shrapnel, counter battery attack.*
May 6th - *Right section fired 34 rounds Lyddite and Shrapnel, hostile battery and working parties (the latter dispersed by our fire). Left section fired 11 rounds Lyddite.*
May 7th - *Right section fired 12 rounds Lyddite. Left section fired 6 rounds Lyddite.*
May 8th - *Right section fired 19 rounds Shrapnel and Lyddite, hostile battery and working parties. Left section fired 4 rounds Shrapnel. Party of enemy dispersed on 2nd round.*
May 9th - *Right section fired 8 rounds Lyddite against hostile battery – 3 rounds OK. Left section fired 4 rounds Shrapnel. Working Party dispersed.*
May 10th - *Right section quiet day – no firing. Dismantling Battery and transporting baggage etc to new position at Bully. Left section fired 2 rounds Lyddite – estimate party of 50 men dispersed.*
May 11th - *Right section. Very busy day firing - Battery and Counter battery attack from 4:45am until 4:40pm – 66 rounds. 10.5. Silenced enemy battery & 2:50pm 8" Gun on Armoured tram driven away. 4:40pm until 1:55pm (sic) 117 rounds Lyddite & Shrapnel fired against enemy attack line.*

The summary of the action for May 1916 was, rounds fired 1703, casualties: killed 3, wounded 1.

Before the infantry attacked, it was commonplace for all the artillery to work together, targeting the enemy trenches and strongholds for prolonged periods. These could be anything from a few hours to days. Someone came up with a grading system for defining barrages; fewer than ten shells in ten minutes would be 'light', thirty per minute 'moderate' and fifty per minute and above, 'heavy'.

Another form of barrage, invented in the Great War, and which also became commonplace, was the creeping barrage. The artillery would lay down a curtain of fire, which in theory moved forward just ahead of the advancing troops and was intended to keep the enemy from firing. When the advance was over good ground, and particularly later in the war when lessons had been learnt, it was successful, but early on there were many problems. If it moved too quickly, it passed over the enemy while the troops were advancing, and had little effect. If it moved to slowly the advancing troops caught up with the barrage and could be hit by their own shells. It seems likely that Arthur experienced action in all types of artillery fire at some point in his service.

During the German Spring Offensive of late March 1918 the 138th was positioned near Remigny. The German's success drove back the front line and the Heavy Batteries were also forced to withdraw to positions which were less at risk. For eight days from the 21st they were more or less in constant retreat. The movements were forced, arduous and rations for men and horses short. In one thirty hour period between the 26th and 27th the men and horses marched twenty-five miles, dragging the guns behind them. The 60 pounders were heavy guns and at one point the hill was so steep that it required the combined efforts of three teams of horses to move each gun to the top and, when they had succeeded, they were ordered back down. In the previous months the guns had worked hard and they were badly in need of maintenance work, so at the end of March they were ordered to refit in the Poix area of France. To get there they had to march eighty miles, which they did over six days. After a two day refit they began their move to Amiens, which took until April 13th.

On the 14th they were ready once again to join the battle. First the centre section took up position in Gentilles Wood, where they stayed for two weeks. They were shelled and suffered a number of casualties before being withdrawn. Then the remainder of the Battery took up position about 1 ½ miles to the north-west and were also heavily shelled. After about six weeks of heavy activity they were given an opportunity to rest and to re-equip before returning to take up position. On July 13th they moved forward to Bonnay-sur-Ancre and then moved again on August 4th to Vaux-on-Somme in preparation for the imminent Allied attack.

The Allied Offensive of August 1918 was the start of the final push to win the war and it began on the 8th. The 138th were still at Vaux-on-Somme, but by the end of the first day they had moved forward almost two miles and apparently had seen hundreds of German prisoners. Over the next four weeks they continued to move forward, following the success of the front line troops. Periodically they would stop, set up position for a period of firing, before moving on again. The fighting was fierce and they again saw large numbers of German prisoners. By September 2nd they had reached Clery, just north-west of Peronne. They moved to Courcelles where they were given a few days rest, but were back in action again by the 12th, firing from Hamelot and then Hesbecourt about sixteen miles north-west of Peronne.

Following the ultimate failure of the German Spring Offensive, the Germans retreated once again to the Hindenburg Line, their 'impenetrable' last line of defence. The Allies were gaining momentum and by the end of September they had breeched it. The German Army was beginning to crumble, but that was not helping the Heavy Batteries, because the Germans artillery's resistance became more and more desperate and caused a significant number of casualties amongst the Batteries.

On October 4th the Germans asked for an armistice based on the American President Woodrow Wilson's fourteen points, which he had previously proposed in January 1918, but the Allies were not prepared to consider that. The fighting continued and the Germans were forced back and back, with the 138th Battery continuing to advance to the north-west.

The Germans were handed the Allies' terms for an armistice on November 8th and, given no choice, they finally signed it on the 11th. By then the 138th had reached St. Soupel, which was two miles south of Le Cateau and sixteen miles north-west of St Quentin.

The war was over, but Arthur died seventeen days later. His service records have been carefully inspected and one can almost imagine that the words next to his date of death read 'trenches', 'France', and 'gas', but in truth they are not clear enough to read. It could be that he was gassed or wounded in the last days of the war and sadly died a lingering death. It is perhaps more likely that he caught Spanish influenza and died as a result of the world pandemic that was gathering pace. It is known that the 138th were billeted in mid-November, when the influenza epidemic hit them. About forty men were sent to hospital and a number of those died.

Perhaps, if a more complete copy of the Battery's war diary can be found, then the cause of Arthur's death can be properly established, but nevertheless it seems almost certain that it was Spanish influenza that caused it. Arthur was taken to a hospital in or around the town of Le Cateau, where he hung on, fighting his personal battle for life, but on November 28th he lost and died.

He is buried in the communal cemetery in Le Cateau. It is surrounded by a 15 foot wall and to find Arthur's grave you must walk through a typical French cemetery – rather gothic and macabre for British tastes. His grave is typical of the style adopted by the Commonwealth War Graves Commission and a stark contrast to the rest of the cemetery - a formal straight line of headstones for Arthur and his comrades stands at the back of a long thin almost perfect rectangle of grass. A very striking piece of nature among the hard landscape of the town's graves.

Some time after the war his widow moved, not far, just to 119 Squires Lane, Church End, Finchley and that is where, on June 1919, she received a letter asking her to confirm her relationship to Arthur, so that his plaque, commonly known as the death penny, and scroll could be sent to her. Not long after this she remarried and became Mrs Foxlock and moved to 29 North Road, Lower Edmonton, London.

*2 *Augusta Nellie (b 1879), Lizzie Florence (often called Florence, bapt 1884, d 1911 aged twenty-seven), Larry (b 1886, d 1888 aged two), Frank Lindsey (b 1889, d 1889 aged seven months) and Sidney Arthur (b 1891). The 1911 census records six children and that three had died. As Lizzie Florence is named the census must have been taken before her death and a sixth child, who is unnamed, must also have died.*
*3 *Lyddite was a form of high explosive.*
*4 *A shrapnel shell contained many pellets the size of bullets which were distributed at high velocity by the explosion.*

*Gunner 60473, Sidney Arthur Lake,
Le Cateau Communal Cemetery,
Le Cateau, France. Ref. 1. 24.*

FRANK ABBISS
PRIVATE 201339, 1/4TH NORFOLK REGIMENT.
DIED: WEDNESDAY, DECEMBER 25TH 1918, AGED 38.
BURIED: ALEXANDRIA (HADRA) WAR MEMORIAL CEMETERY,
EGYPT. REF. H. 65.
BORN AND LIVED IN PIRTON.

Frank was born on November 13th 1880 to George and Ann Abbiss. The 1911 census records that they had seven children, but that three had died. Four remain unnamed to us. Apart from Frank, the two who are identified are Elizabeth, Mary (known as Polly, b c1882) and Harry (b-1890, who served and survived. Although born ten years apart both Frank and Harry went to the Pirton School and, when they left, both went on to work on local farms.

The 1911 census shows that Frank was still living in Pirton, but when he enlisted he joined the 1/4th Battalion, Norfolk Regiment. This was another regiment formed in August 1914 out of local Territorial soldiers, which could mean that he had moved from Pirton. Frank's enlistment is not recorded in the Parish Magazine, although another man of the same name is, and his service record appears to have been destroyed in the Second World War, so the date of his enlistment and home address are not known.

Obviously Frank's experience of the war would have been much the same as his Battalion's for the duration of his service, but without any more information we cannot know when that began. For that reason the experience of the 1/4th Battalion from its first campaign is given as Frank's. The campaign he is least likely to have served in would be the Gallipoli Campaign in 1915, but if he enlisted in 1914 his training would have finished around the time that the Battalion left for the Dardanelles, so it is possible that he was with them.

On July 29th 1915 the 1/4th Battalion boarded the H.M.T.*1 Aquitania. The next day they set sail to join the 163rd Infantry Brigade in the 54th Division as part of the Mediterranean Expeditionary Force and to reinforce the Gallipoli Campaign which had started in February. On August 9th they disembarked at the Isle of Lemnos, just off the western coast of Turkey, and transferred to the S.S. Osmanieh to continue. They landed at Suvla Bay, Gallipoli, on the 10th. They were very lucky, as they appear to have landed

without interference; in other landings thousands were slaughtered on the beaches. The next day they entered the reserve trenches and then went into action against the Turks. Shelling of the base camp began on the 14th and in the following days "A" and "B" companies and "C" and "D" companies took turns between the reserve and the front line trenches. The war diary provides no detail of their action, but between the September 2nd and 30th they suffered 81 casualties. In October there were 24 casualties and only 6 in November. Then between December 7th and 8th they embarked for Mudros – a port on the small Greek Island of Lemnos and on the 16th, on board the H.M.T. Victorian, they headed to Alexandria, Egypt, leaving the Gallipoli campaign behind them.

The Gallipoli Campaign was a disaster. Originally it was the idea of Winston Churchill, then the First Sea Lord of the Admiralty. The intention was to open another front and ultimately pull some of the Germans forces away from Europe. The British, Australian and New Zealand forces landed with thousands killed in the process. They fought hard to get off the beaches, but the war quickly reached a stalemate. Supplying the army was extremely difficult; water was scarce and dysentery rife. There were over 200,000 allied casualties from the fighting and dysentery. The one real 'success' was the amazing evacuation of 105,000 men and 300 guns from Anzac Cove and Suvla Bay. The withdrawal officially began after Frank's Battalion had left and it took place over several weeks. During the last phase elaborate ruses were used to make the Turks believe the Allied forces were still in the trenches and they withdrew without a man being killed. Apparently the Turks were still firing on the empty trenches some hours after the withdrawal was complete.

In Egypt, where the Norfolks went, the enemy was the Ottoman Empire (the Turks) who were helped and advised by the Germans. The Norfolks spent the whole of January 1916 in the Sidi Bishr area of Alexandria (sometimes written as Bishi), receiving training and then moving to Mena Camp, which was near Cairo and within sight of the Pyramids. This would have been an exotic experience for a villager from Pirton, although during February and March they were kept busy training and integrating replacement men into their ranks. At the end of March they moved to Shallufa just a few miles north of the Suez Canal. War was getting closer again and the enemy was reported as attacking another part of the line on April 24th. They stood to arms and were asked to maintain great vigilance, but nothing occurred. They continued their general defence work until May 28th when they entrained for Serapeum, some 38 miles south, at the other end of the Bitter lakes and near the Suez Canal. Here they were positioned to defend the Canal.

During June the enemy dropped five bombs, but there were no casualties and there was no fighting, but the war diary records 2 casualties; 1 man died '*wounds self-inflicted*' and 1 drowned while on duty. The Battalion continued with its duty of '*Guards, Outposts, Patrols, Fatigues and Training.*'

In late July they moved 20 miles north by train to El Ferdan. Then in August they moved back to Serapeum, where they stayed until January 1917, then moving first to Serapeum West and then Moascar. The war diary notes no significant events just more '*Guards, Outposts, Patrols, Fatigues and Training.*' The most exciting experience, at least for some of the men, was a trip to the seaside camp at Sidi Bishr during September and October. On the whole it sounds boring and monotonous and probably was, just one long round of routine, undertaken in the sun and heat.

In February they were once again on the move, but this time on foot. Between the 1st and the 28th they marched from Moascar (Al Isma'iliyah, Egypt) to El 'Arish and then to Khan Yunis (Khan Yunus) just 160 miles or so in 28 days and in scorching heat. They remained in that area before marching another 25 miles in late March to In Seirat (south of Gaza and in Palestine). They were about to enter the First Battle of Gaza, which commenced on March 26th. It was a two-day battle and the British almost won. In fact they came so close that the German commander, Major Tiller, destroyed his wireless set and prepared to surrender. Unfortunately, through lack of efficient communications, the British did not know this. Turkish reinforcements were spotted and it was thought that there was a danger of the British troops being cut off. The troops were ordered to new positions causing confusion. The Norfolks entered the trenches on the 27th with orders to prepare to repel an attack. They were shelled and 2 men were killed and 13 wounded. Eventually the British had to pull back and consolidate. The British suffered over 4,000 casualties during the battle; 523 dead, 2,932 wounded and 512 missing. It is estimated that the Turkish casualties were only 2,450.

A second battle was planned to start on April 17th. By this time the Norfolks were at Sharta. They moved into a position to provide support to the 1/8th Hants and the 1/3rd Suffolks. On the 19th the Norfolks moved forward into the attack. That is all that the war diary records; it adds no detail about the battle other than the Battalion casualties; 42 killed, 12 died of wounds, 317 wounded, 2 wounded and missing, 92 missing, 6 taken prisoner of war and 6 slightly wounded. Of around 1,000 men, 17 officers and 460 other ranks were recorded as casualties; it must have been horrendous. At 6:00am the next day they withdrew. The losses were so great that they had to join with the 1/8th Hants to form a composite battalion.

A report on the action was added later. The attack commenced at 7:30am and the Battalion went forward in two lines over a ridge. The first line was immediately met with shrapnel shells and machine gun fire. They spread out to reduce casualties, as did the second line and got about 100 yards before being forced down. They rose up and moved forward, covering about 500 yards and getting to within 150 yards of the Turkish redoubt, but they had lost a lot of men. The 1/8th Hants came up to reinforce the attack and, with the help of the 1/5th Norfolks, reached the redoubt at about 9:00am. By then '*the Battalion were not strong enough to attack the* trenches' but they held position awaiting reinforcements. '*No reinforcements arrived and after about three hours owing to ammunition being nearly expended superiority of fire could no longer be maintained*' - they suffered more heavy casualties during this stage. Believing that an order to withdraw had been issued they began to retire, but realised that the line was still being held to their right. This could have left those soldiers desperately exposed, so with amazing discipline and incredible bravery they checked the withdrawal and tried to re-establish the line. The Commanding Officer became a casualty. The only unwounded officer 2nd Lt J H Jewson took command and, waiting until dusk, completed the withdrawal trying to bring the wounded with them. Seven medals were won but hundreds of men were lost.

The British attack was defeated and in this, the Second Battle of Gaza, the British received another 6,444 casualties. Turkish casualties were estimated as only 2,000. The Army withdrew, dug in and consolidated again. It was a heavy defeat and they remained in defensive positions, undertaking working parties or training and awaiting new men to bring them back up to strength. The Norfolks were out of action and behind the lines until early September. Even so they were not completely out of danger and occasionally their bivouacs were shelled. They returned to the front line trenches but without much in the way of incident. By the end of the month they were back to within 200 or so of full strength.

They saw some action in November between the 1st and 7th when, following an artillery barrage, they attacked the Turkish lines; there were a few casualties, but nothing compared to the early scale. They experienced some success and the Turks responded with gas while the Norfolks tried to consolidate. During November their casualty list was 21 men killed, 4 died of wounds, 106 were wounded but remained at their posts, 5 were missing, including 1 believed wounded, and 1 believed killed – another 136 men and, very unusually all, including the 'other ranks', are named in the diary. Frank was lucky not to be among them.

Despite the major set backs earlier, from October 1917 the British were beginning to win the war in the Middle-East. The tide was turning and on December 11th 1917 Jerusalem fell – a major success for the British.

In December the 1/4th Norfolks moved from Haditheh to Deir Turief and to Yehu Diyeh (believed to be Tell eh-Yehu-diyeh, Egypt) and relieved the 5th Bedfords and the 1/10th Londons. Another quiet time, but in an attack by the Turks on the 11th and the preceding shelling, there were another 55 casualties. On the 15th the Norfolks returned the compliment but suffered another 80 casualties. The official report adds that '*out of a total of 6 officers and 219 other ranks who carried out the attack, nearly all these casualties being from M.G, fire during the advance.*' Again at the end of the month the casualties were summarised including the above, and again all were named; 30 men killed, 89 wounded, 22 others were wounded and had since died – 141 men.

They had fought long and hard, suffered high numbers of casualties and deserved some respite. The war diary for the next few months indicates that is what they got and, although there were occasional enemy actions, it was mostly training, fatigues, patrols and the inevitable working parties. Effectively they were out of the 'real' action until the middle of June 1918 and at the end of the month they moved to Surafend in Palestine.

August and September 1918 were mostly quiet with more training and the standard working parties and patrols, but they did move on several occasions to new camps and positions. On September 19th and 20th one and a half companies were detailed to attack the Turks at Sirisia, but the Turks withdrew before the attack. The Norfolks pursued them to the village of Bidieh. They paused and then the next day moved forward only to find that the Turks had withdrawn again, this time in even more haste, leaving an enormous amount of artillery ammunition, a gun and several wagons behind. Casualties were nil. The Norfolks moved from Bidieh to JilJulish for a few days' cleaning and training before moving to Kakon, then Kakkur, Zimmarin and then at the beginning of October to Athlitt and the port of Haifa - about sixty miles through Palestine and the area that is now Israel. There then followed more training, fatigues and working parties plus guard duties. But in late October they moved yet again to Acre on the 24th, then in the following days to, Musheirefeh, Ras El Ain, Nahr El Kasimyreh,, Ain Barak, Saida and finally to Ed Damur.

Although the war diary provides no explanation, something was amiss with the Battalion numbers;

at the end of September its strength was given as 33 Officers and 863 other ranks and then at the end of October, although difficult to read, it appears to be 27 Officers and 693 other ranks. Only 1 officer and 29 other ranks were recorded as casualties of the recent march, some of whom had gone to hospital. In November they moved again ending up in Beirut; interestingly there is no mention of the armistice in Europe on the 11th. From here the Battalion, now consisting of only 19 officers and 441 other ranks, boarded two ships, the H.T. Ellenga and the H.T. Hunslet, and left Beirut bound for Kantara in Egypt. Two days later, on November 30th 1918, the Turkish army surrendered to the British. Amazingly this event is also given no comment in the diary.

From the numbers given above the Battalion strength seems to have dropped from 896 to 460 without much in the way of comment. Perhaps some men had gone ahead to Kantara, which might explain a substantial proportion, but the numbers still do not seem right. From Kantara they moved to a camp at Halmieh and on December 7th, 8 Officers and 247 reinforcements 'rejoined' from Kantara. The grammar used does not make it clear whether all or just some of these men were rejoining from hospital, but on the 9th 5 Officers and 41 other ranks rejoined, on the 10th 41 more other ranks and on the 11th, 32 more other ranks rejoined and all were rejoining from hospital. Although no detail of why the men were hospitalised appears, it is clear that there must have been major illness within the Battalion. The illness could have been any of a number of diseases that were rife such as dysentery, but it could also be the Spanish influenza pandemic, which had been gathering pace during 1918. Lyn MacDonald's excellent book, *The Roses of No Man's Land*[2], confirms that there were many cases in the hospitals at Alexandria around that time. She quotes the fact that VAD Nurse Kit Dodsworth of No. 19 General Hospital in Alexandria, Egypt, heard about the Armistice being signed *'after a busy day caring for victims of an influenza outbreak that cost many lives.'*

We will probably never know for certain, but it seems very likely that it was Spanish influenza that killed Frank. He had survived past the end of the war in Europe and in the Middle-East. He had survived the horrendous numbers of casualties that his Battalion had suffered, only to die on Christmas Day 1918.

He is buried far from Pirton, in the Alexandria (Hadra) War Memorial Cemetery, Egypt - Hadra is a district on the eastern side of Alexandria, Egypt. The cemetery contains 1,700 First World War burials and, as most were from the hospitals, almost all are identified.

Interestingly, the original information papers from the Cemetery Record Office were found in the summer of 2010 in the Rectory Manor House. They were presumably because one of his sisters married into the Weeden family who owned the house.

*1 *H.M.T. = His Majesty's Troopship.*
*2 *Published by Michael Joseph Ltd, ISBN 0-7181-1785-9.*

> *Private 201339, Frank Abbiss,*
> *Alexandria (Hadra) War Memorial Cemetery,*
> *Alexandra, Egypt. Ref. H. 65.*

FREDERICK ODELL
PRIVATE G/82152, 26TH BATTALION, ROYAL FUSILIERS.
DIED: WEDNESDAY, APRIL 23RD 1919, AGED 19.
BURIED: ST. MARY'S CHURCHYARD, PIRTON,
HERTFORDSHIRE. REF. 1156.
BORN AND LIVED IN PIRTON.

In many ways Frederick's is the saddest story of all the Pirton men who died.

He was born on July 4th 1899 to John and Mary Odell (née Dawson) and baptism and census records reveal eleven children in the family*1. Like two of his older brothers, James and Arthur, who also served, he went to Pirton School and when war came he had only recently left. He probably went straight to work on the local farms and that is certainly what he was doing when he enlisted. The family home was in Dead Horse Lane - later renamed as Royal Oak Lane and their house was number two.

He saw his brothers James and Arthur enlist in 1914; James in the Navy and Arthur in the Army. Frederick, of course, was too young to follow them at that stage, but on June 16th 1917 he enlisted or was conscripted for the duration of the war and started active service two months later, when he was posted to the 107th Training Reserve Battalion. As his training continued the Battalion changed its name and he was transferred accordingly to the 265th Infantry Battalion, the 62nd Graduated Battalion and then the 52nd Graduated Battalion Royal Fusiliers

While in training he would have heard of the death of his brother Arthur in France on February 26th 1918. Frederick's training was completed about a month later and he left Folkestone on April 2nd 1918 and arrived in Boulogne on the same day. On the 3rd he was temporarily posted to the 15th Royal Fusiliers – a reserve battalion and then, the next day, to the 26th. Events were moving fast for Frederick as he joined his unit on the 5th.

The Battalion had originally served in France, but had moved to Italy in November 1917. By March 1918 they were returning to France and they arrived on the 7th. Up to the 20th they were in training. On the 21st they were to march to Saulty Station and then were to move to the Baizeaux area; however at 4:30am on the 21st the Germans launched their

major Spring Offensive and so they were ordered to the forward zone instead, where the fighting was fierce. They detrained at Achiet le Grand on the 22nd and then marched to Favreuil, arriving at about 5:30am. From this location they were immediately engaged in operations on the River Somme. Their losses between March 22nd and the 31st were 41 men killed, 146 wounded and 103 missing and they were forced back. On the night of April 1st they were relieved.

On the 2nd they marched to Bienvilliers, where they boarded buses to Halloy and rested there for the night. The next day at 6:30am they marched the eight or nine miles to Mondicourt, then a bus to Bonniéres, some fourteen miles and where they stopped for the night. On the next day, the 4th, they marched to Frévent, 3 ½ miles and took the train to Hopoutre rail head at Poperinge (Belgium), about fifty-three miles and then went by bus to Winnizeele. Here they rested, refitted and reorganised and here

Frederick and 419 other reinforcements joined the Battalion.

On the 7th they marched towards the front line. They were resting on the 8th, but at 6:30pm received orders to entrain for Brandhoek. When they arrived, at 8:00pm, they were ordered straight to the front line around Passchendaele. To Frederick, who was just eighteen, new to the Battalion, Belgium and to the war, it must have been exciting and terrifying. On the 9th they had been in battle for about twenty-four hours. Disappointingly the war diary makes no mention of any special events, just 'Two *Companies in the front line, one in support and one in reserve*', but Frederick was hit and it was a terrible wound.

His medical notes from France read '*Hit in chest just below left of scapula (shoulder blades). Entry wo*' (wound) *left side penetrating kidney and lodging in Rt* (right?) *chest. Wound involving spinal cord almost complete paralysis.*' He clearly was not going to fight again, so when his condition was stable enough he was returned to England and left France on April 17th 1918. The next day he was admitted to the King George Hospital in Stamford Street, London. They gave more details of his condition; '*Slight sensation in feet . . . General condition poor . . . Troublesome cough . . . flaccid paralysis of the legs . . . . no reflexes . . . bowel incontinence . . . bladder incontinence . . . has a good deal of pain*'.

By December he was descried as '*General condition fairly good . . . marked wasting of lower limbs with a fair amount of movement present . . . incontinent*'. Unsurprisingly, they recommended that he be discharged as '*permanently unfit.*'

His official discharge from the army came through on December 11th 1918 – the day that he was discharged from hospital. He was too ill to return home and instead he went to the Star and Garter Home*2 in Richmond. The Star and Garter had been founded in 1916 following concern from Queen Mary as to how the severely disabled young men returning from the battlegrounds of the war could be cared for on a permanent basis.

They would have done their best for him and despite his serious condition it was said that he maintained a very cheerful spirit and although, quite a distance from Pirton, his mother paid him a number of visits. On April 23rd 1919, one year and fourteen days after he was wounded and five months

and twelve days after the war had ended, he lost his personal war and died. His body was returned to Pirton and his burial took place on April 28th.

He was just nineteen and had joined the Army when he was seventeen. He went to France when he was eighteen, spent just one day at the Front and died at nineteen – terribly tragic. The funeral took place amongst the worst snowstorm for years, somehow sadly appropriate, and Frederick was laid to rest in St. Mary's churchyard.

The Hertfordshire Express dated May 24th 1919 reported his funeral and the events that led to it. It was to be the last death of a Pirton man which was directly attributable to the war. '*Six Pirton soldiers officiated as bearers, and in addition about twenty ex-Service men joined the cortege. Besides the family wreaths, several other floral tributes were received, including one from the Star and Garter, and also one from the lady whose generosity maintained the bed which the deceased had occupied there. There was also a wreath from the Pirton Glove Factory, where the deceased's sister was employed.*'

The paper added details about his death. '*He was taking water up to firing line, when a German aeroplane swooped down over the line, and began to machine gun the British. While in the act of taking shelter, Pte Odell was shot in the spine.*'

Both Frederick and Arthur are listed on the Village War Memorial. Frederick's headstone in St. Mary's churchyard remembers Frederick and his brother Arthur:

IN LOVING MEMORY OF
OUR DEAR BOYS
PTE FREDERICK ODELL
WHO DIED OF WOUNDS
APRIL 23RD 1919
AGED 19 YEARS
ALSO OF
LCE-CPL ARTHUR ODELL
KILLED IN ACTION IN FRANCE
FEB 26TH 1918
AGED 21 YEARS
GONE BUT NOT FORGOTTEN

A terrible end, with perhaps the only consolation being that unlike a million or so other families, Frederick did not lie in a foreign field, but a quiet, traditional, English country churchyard, where family and friends could at least visit at any time they wished.

*1 *Jane (bapt 1881), James (b 1883), Martha (bapt 1885), Robert (b 1886), Nellie (b 1888), Frank (b 1890), William (1894), Arthur (b 1896), John (b 1898, died at seventeen), Frederick (b 1899) and Marjorie (b 1902).*
*2 *The Star and Garter Home received its Royal Charter in 1979 and became The Royal Star and Garter Home.*

Private G/82152, Frederick Odell, St. Mary's Churchyard, Pirton, Hertfordshire. Ref. 1156.

Frederick would have received a certificate of honourable discharge after being wounded - like this one.

St. Mary's Church, Pirton, Hertfordshire.

Should These Names Be On Our War Memorial?

It is not always obvious why some names appear on a village or town memorial and others do not. Sometimes a name seems to have a tenuous connection, yet in other cases a man with a strong connection is missing. One common explanation for the latter is that when the memorial was erected, the man had no family living in the village and therefore the name was not put forward.

It is also quite common for a name to appear on memorials in more than one village or town. The man may have been born in one place, but then moved away leaving family behind. When a memorial was erected, his name would be added by the family left behind and also by family or friends in the place he had moved to. It is also not uncommon for soldiers who had been decorated to be recorded in several locations, each of which was particularly proud to acknowledge its connection to the man.

During the research for this book a Pirton connection was identified for many men. A few, those identified here, died but do not appear on our Village War Memorial. Sometimes the connection appears strong and sometimes relatively weak, but it should be remembered that the strength of the Pirton connection for the names that do appear on the memorials varies considerably. The strongest connections are obviously the men born and bred in Pirton and who were still living here at the time of the war. At the opposite end of the scale are men like William Hill and George Charlick, who both appear on the war memorials. William's only Pirton connection seems to be that he married a Pirton girl in September 1914. In George's case, his parents moved to Pirton sometime after 1901 and before 1914, but no other direct personal connection for George himself has been found.

It is certainly not up to us to question those names that are listed. Their connection was recognised as sufficient at the time, however perhaps we can ask whether any men who do not appear have a case for inclusion. The purpose of this chapter of the book is therefore to document the connection of these men to Pirton.

Herbert appears in a report contained in the period scrapbook of newspaper cuttings from the war, handed down through the Marshall family. The cuttings seem to fall into two categories. Those that relate directly to Pirton men and general articles about the local regiments in which they served. So it seems possible that this man had a Pirton connection.

One cutting highlighted concern for Herbert, for although no official information had been sent, letters from Offley and Pirton friends at the Front in Flanders were received in Pirton and they indicated grave fears for his safety. One read *'Poor Tricky Clark, I am sorry to say he has gone under.'* They also contain information helpful in identifying Herbert. He was thirty-nine. Before the war he worked for Mr Allingham at White Hill Farm and he lived, with his wife and ten children, in a cottage opposite the church in Lilley.

An investigation of Pirton records, and the help of Patti Salter, revealed that Herbert was the son of Alfred George Clark and Emily Day and that he had married Martha Baines in February 1897. For the marriage both Herbert and Martha were recorded as *'from Pirton'*, indicating that both were living in Pirton. Herbert's parents were from Offley and Herbert was born there, but Martha and her parents were born in Pirton.

By March 1897 a daughter was born and she was baptised Ethel Maud in St Mary's Church, Pirton. Herbert's occupation was recorded as a labourer. In January 1898 they were in Pirton and were witnesses at Martha's sister's wedding, when she (Ruth Baines) married Charles Cooper. A son Herbert 'G' was born to Herbert and Martha around 1899 and then another son, Frederick George was born in July 1900. The elder and younger children were baptised in Pirton and from this information it seemed likely that Herbert and his family were living in Pirton, but in fact the census of 1901 reveals otherwise.

Although Herbert's name is absent, the family was living in Lower Offley and they now had another child. Despite the elder and younger child being baptised in Pirton, all three children were born in Offley and so the family had been living there since at least February 1897. The newspaper cutting mentioned above tells us that Herbert fought in the Boer War (1899-1902),

Private Herbert John Clarke
(confirmed by the Bedfordshire cap badge)

and this explains his absence from the census. We know that by April 1902 he had returned, because they were once again in Pirton for another happy event, the wedding of another of Martha's sisters, Kate, to Bertram Chamberlain; Herbert was again one of the witnesses.

The 1911 census records that Herbert was working as a labourer on a local farm, that he and his family were living in Lilley and that they now had eight children, Ethel Maud (b c1897), Herbert G (b c1899), Frederick George (b c1900), Bertha M (b c1903), Emily L (b c1904), Elsie (b c1905), Stanley F (b c1907) and Violet (b 1909). They must have had two more, whose names we do not yet know, because later newspaper reports record ten.

So Herbert's military career began long before the Great War. We know that he served in the Boer War, had survived without a scratch and that he had served his time. By the start of the Great War in August 1914 he and his wife had a large family. His loyalties must have been split, but he knew where his duty lay and during October 1914 he travelled to Luton to re-enlist and became Private 3/8664 in the 2nd Battalion, Bedfordshire Regiment.

He clearly loved and missed his wife as the newspaper reported that he regularly wrote twice a week from the Front. From incidents he related to his wife we know that not only was he an experienced soldier, but also a brave and compassionate one. On one occasion he went to the rescue of wounded soldiers, helping carry two of them through a river, *'while up to his armpits in water'*. On another occasion, during heavy fighting, he and his comrades were going over the dead strewn German trenches, when one of the wounded Germans appealed for help - Herbert dragged him back to the British lines for attention.

Around the time of his death his Battalion was in Northern France. On September 25th they moved from Noyelles to Vermelles and were preparing for an attack on Vermelles and Cit-St-Elie. This was part of the Battle of Loos. At 11:30am they moved to attack. The Battalion war diary records that they went across no-man's land and over the first line of German trenches, practically without casualties, but as they began to advance further they came under very heavy rifle fire and suffered severe losses. Even so they managed to reach the second line (or gun trench). It was estimated that between two and three hundred 'other ranks' became casualties*1. When they tried to advance from the gun trench, numbers reduced further, to the point where they had to fall back to it.

Some time later they were strategically withdrawn and began digging a new support trench on the British side of the gun trench. At about midnight the Germans attacked, bombing the gun trench and forcing the remaining men to again withdraw, this time to the new trench. This line held. The men regrouped and charged the Germans and they were so successful that practically all the Germans, then in the gun trench, were killed or taken prisoners.

On September 26th they held the 'new' front line until relieved and then withdrew to what was the old German front line, now behind the support trench. They stayed there for September 27th and 28th and at night working parties went out, but no casualties were recorded. On the 29th they relieved Cameron Highlanders in the gun trench, but again there was little action. Then on the 30th the Germans, who were armed with bombs, which were fairly crude hand grenades, attacked on three sides and in the face of *'bombing with great violence'*, they began to lose ground. No losses were recorded in the other ranks, but at least one officer was wounded.

So from this information we know that Herbert died in France in the Battle of Loos, but the exact date is unclear. Officially he was killed in action on September 27th 1915, but his wife Martha received a letter from him on October 6th, dated September 30th and postmarked October 2nd. So the family believed that he died on September 30th and that is the date they had printed on Herbert's memorial card. Indeed from the information in the war diary it seems unlikely that he died on the 27th and much more likely that he died in the action of the 30th. The fact that he is commemorated on the Loos Memorial means that his body was never found, or at least never identified, which also suggests that he was killed on the 30th and his body left behind on the ground recaptured by the Germans.

The Loos Memorial commemorates 20,582 officers and men, who like Herbert, have no known grave. It is situated about half a mile west of the village of Loos-en-Gohelle. Herbert's name appears on panel 41 and it also appears on the Lilley Village War Memorial.

*1 Men were Officers or Other Ranks.

The records of the Commonwealth War Graves Commission list him as Private 31838 of the 6th Battalion York and Lancaster Regiment. Other information suggests that he was formerly Private 25643 in the Northamptonshire Regiment and that he enlisted in Hitchin.

Bertram was born around 1889 in Tilsworth, Bedfordshire and his parents were Frederick Arthur and Elizabeth Cooper. In 1891 the family of three were living in Stanbridge, Bedfordshire and then in 1901 at Bush Farm, Little Berkhamstead, Hertfordshire. Bertram now had a sister, Elsie M, aged eight. A niece, Lily Tompkins, was also living with them. Sometime after the 1911 census and before the war, the family moved to 16 Fishponds Road, Hitchin. Bertram was making his own way in the world and working as a railway porter while lodging with the Bent family in New Mill End, near Luton, Bedfordshire.

Thanks to the research of David Baines we know more; Bertram was a quiet man seeking little in the way of excitement and he kept pigeons as a hobby. He enlisted with the first 'Derby' Group – this was a scheme brought in by Lord Derby, which predated conscription. Men attested their willingness to serve, but would only be called up if needed. Bertram signed these papers on November 22nd 1915, when he was twenty-seven, working as a horse keeper and living in West Mill. He was subsequently mobilised to the 8th Battalion, Northampton Regiment on June 5th 1916.

His address is his connection to Pirton; West Mill lies near Ickleford and is adjacent to Oughtonhead Common and the River Oughton, which at the time lay within the Pirton parish boundary. In fact this connection is virtually identical to that of Frank Cannon, the first man listed on the Pirton Village Memorial.

As part of the Northampton Regiment, Bertram left for France on the September 1st 1916 and remained in the base depot until September 29th when he was posted to the 2nd Battalion before joining the 6th Battalion, York and Lancaster Regiment on October 14th 1916 and then served in "B" Company. Bertram was reported missing after an action at Beaumont Hamel in the Somme sector. Company Serjeant Major Bessant wrote that Bert was wounded and had set off for a dressing station, but he did not arrive. He is recorded as killed in action on January 17th 1917.

He is commemorated on Thiepval Memorial, which is built on the skyline above the village of the same name and which dominates the surrounding countryside. It lies off the main Bapaume to Albert road and commemorates 72,092 officers and men of the United Kingdom and South Africa who died on the Somme and who have no known grave. As you approach the memorial, its scale and meaning threaten to become overwhelming. Bertram's name appears on pier 14, panel 14B and also on the Hitchin Town War Memorial.

The Parish Magazine of June 1917 acknowledges Bertram's connection to Pirton, listing him under the heading '*Pirton Men in His Majesty's Service*' and having been called up since March 2nd 1916 and serving in the Yorkshire and Lancashire Regiment (this should be York and Lancaster). It also lists him as missing when in fact he had been killed.

FREDERICK COX
PRIVATE 266835, HERTFORDSHIRE REGIMENT.
DIED: TUESDAY, JULY 31ST 1917, AGED ABOUT 19.
COMMEMORATED: YPRES (MENIN GATE) MEMORIAL, YPRES (IEPER), WEST-VLAANDEREN,
BELGIUM. PANEL 54 AND 56.
BORN IN HITCHIN, LIVED IN LETCHWORTH AND ENLISTED IN HERTFORD.

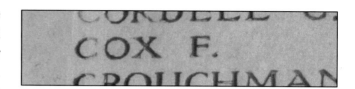

While researching Sidney Cox, who appears in the Pirton scrapbook owned by the Marshall family, and is included as one of Pirton's survivors, his brother Frederick was identified. The Hitchin census of 1901 identifies their parents as William and Ruth Cox who were living at 6 Taylors Cottages, Old Park Road, Hitchin. William was born in Hitchin and Ruth in Pirton. They had four children; Sidney William (b c1894), Lilian (b c1896), Frederick (b c1898) and Arthur (b c1900). All the children were born in Hitchin, although Sidney was baptised in Pirton.

By 1911 his mother, Ruth, had died. The household now included Frederick's grandmother Sarah, another brother, Cecil (b c 1903) and another sister, Nellie (b c1906). They were living at 47 Green Lane, Letchworth. Fred was being educated at the local school. Both Cecil and Nellie were born in Hitchin.

At first the Pirton connection, just through his mother's place of birth, seems weak, but it was strengthened with more research. Their father, William, was born in Hitchin, and was thirty-one at the time of the 1901 census. So he would have been born around 1870. Pirton records identify a William Cox as born in Hitchin and baptised in Pirton on October 2nd 1870, so he could be the same man. His parents were William and Sarah Cox (née Males) and they were both from Pirton. Returning to the Hitchin 1901 census, they show that a Sarah Cox was living next door to William and Ruth and she is the right age to be his mother, so it seems likely that Frederick's father and the son of William and Sarah are the same man. This means that Frederick's mother was born and his father was baptised in Pirton. They had lived in Pirton, as did his grandparents on his father's side. Although the evidence is less conclusive, it is likely that his grandparents on his mother's side also lived in Pirton. It is probably because of the family's strong connection with Pirton that Sidney, Frederick's older brother, was baptised here.

Frederick served as Private 266835 in the Hertfordshire Regiment. He enlisted in Hertford while living in Letchworth. He served in France and

Flanders and, as he is commemorated on the Menin Gate Memorial in Ypres (Belgium), we know that he died in Belgium. The date of his death is recorded as July 31st 1917. From the location, the date and Battalion war diary it looks very likely that he served with the 1st Battalion, of the Hertfordshire Regiment.

The war diary gives the following information for the date of his death:

'31-7-17. About 3.50am the Battalion moved forward in 4 lines behind the 116th & 117th Infantry Brigades east of the river Steenbeek. Up till this time the casualties had been very slight indeed but as the Battalion advanced from the Steenbeek toward the Langemarck line (the Battalion objective) casualties grew heavier from sniper and machine gun fire. However the Battalion continued advancing. About half way to the objective some of No. 3 Company came upon a German strong point which they gallantly charged, capturing or killing most of the garrison and sending the remainder back as prisoners. On reaching the enemy wire this was found to be practically undamaged (except in one place) & very thick. 2/Lieut Marchington & a handful of men of No. 3 Company got through the only gap and got into the enemy trench & killed a lot of Germans. The remainder of the Battalion, being unable to get through the wire and suffering severe casualties from enfilade machine gun fire & the Germans making a strong counter attack from our left flank about this time, had to fall back having suffered exceptionally heavy casualties. The remnants of the Battalion subsequently dug themselves in line with the 1st Cambs Regiment on the west side of the Steenbeek.'

This action was part of the Battle of Passchendaele, also known as the Third Battle of Ypres. The soldiers called it the 'Battle of Mud', which describes the conditions in which they fought. Although estimated figures were higher, casualties for the battalion on

July 31st were recorded as 8 men died of wounds, 129 were listed as missing and 188 more were listed as wounded. The fact that Frederick is commemorated on the Ypres (Menin Gate) Memorial means that his body was never found or at least never identified, so he would have been one of the 129 missing men.

The impressive memorial in Ypres commemorates 54,322 officers and men with no known grave and is situated a few hundred yards from the beautiful town square of Ypres. Frederick's name appears on Panel 56 and he is also recorded on the Letchworth War Memorial.

Interestingly, Corporal 265408 Harry Smith from Pirton, who does appear on the Village War Memorial, was killed on the same day, fighting with the 1st Hertfordshire Regiment. His body lies in Tyne Cot Cemetery a few miles away and so they would have been fighting in the same battle, in the same Battalion and perhaps even together.

EDMUND CHARLES PEARCE

This name appears on the School War Memorial as an ex-pupil who gave his life, so a strong connection is indicated. However, although the Commonwealth War Graves Commission's records contain a number of similar names, none is identifiable as this man. Detailed investigation of the parish and census records was needed to solve this puzzle. An '*Edward*' Charles 'Burton' exists in the records and he was born on December 25th 1896 to Ellen Burton, daughter of Goliath and Mary Ann Burton. Sometime later, and before 1901, Ellen married George Pearce in Woolwich. In the 1901 census Edward appears as *their* son Edward Burton, with other, younger children, having Pearce as their surname. One of these, Francis John, appearing as John, but who was apparently often known as Jack, also served and related newspaper cuttings mention that his eldest brother Charles (Edward Charles?) had served and was killed in 1916. A Parish Magazine also mentions Charles Pearce as serving.

There are errors on the School War Memorial, so it is perhaps not a surprising that Edward may appear as Edmund and with everyone else in the family carrying the surname of Pearce, his surname may also have been confused. Indeed it could even be that George Pearce was his father.

From all of the above, and with no confirming evidence to the contrary, it is reasonable to assume that Edmund Charles Pearce is in fact Edward Charles Burton, who died and is listed on the village memorials.

FREDERICK SKEYS

The Commonwealth War Graves Commission, and other databases, currently record Frederick William Skeys as being born in Pirton, Hertfordshire. This is not correct. No evidence has been found to support this and, in fact Frederick William Skeys aged eight appears in the 1901 census for Pirton, *Worcestershire*. His name also appears on that village's memorial in their church St Peter's. That Pirton is now listed as being in Herefordshire, so it is easy to see how this error has occurred. Frederick Skeys is listed here, in order to provide the information to other researchers who may be confused by the official records. We are seeking to get the official records changed as soon as possible.

E SOUT...

SERJE... OF THE ASSISTANT DIRECTOR OF MEDICAL SERVICES
TOR... DIED: 1917.
P... T SOUTHGATE - 9TH MI...UGA HORSE.
... TORONTO (ST. JOHN'S NORWAY).
... W 8, GRAVE 84.

Serjeant Major E Southgate came to light in a report from the Hertfordshire Express dated January 19th 1918 and entitled *'Old Pirtonian's Death at Toronto'*. So the newspaper certainly believed there to be a Pirton connection. A similar report also appeared in the North Hertfordshire Mail dated January 17th 1918. From these papers we know that he had kept The White Horse public house (where The Motte and Bailey now stands), but a more substantial connection than that has yet to be found, as he does not appear in the parish and census records.

He had worked at the Toronto Mobilisation Centre, but at the time of his death he was working for the Department of the Assistant Director of Medical Services in the Toronto Military District. He fell ill with nephritis, which is an inflammation of one or both of the kidneys that can lead to kidney failure. He was admitted to hospital on June 9th 1917, but his condition deteriorated and he later died.

We don't know what his responsibilities were, but he seems to have been very well thought of as several senior military staff attended his funeral as well as *'all members of the Toronto Mobilisation Centre staff who were there during Southgate's time.'*

All the other men listed in this book were considered to be on active service, but is that the case for this man? He was not fighting, but it can be argued that he was still doing his military duty. In the mobilisation centre he would have been involved in the provision of men for military service, but research has not yet provided any further information about this organisation and very little about the medical history of the Medical Services

in the Toronto Military District. However, they were responsible for all the medical services provided by the military in that area and that certainly involved treating the soldiers who had returned due to illness or injury. One extract from the war diary for Davisville Military Hospital in Toronto, for April 1918, gives the following statistics for the month and they are probably typical:

'Patients admitted 469, discharged 423, remaining from the previous month 712 and the number of amputation cases 433. Other statistics show that 84 operations, 4774 dressings and 55 artificial limbs were supplied.'

Can his service, especially with the Toronto Military District's medical services, be considered as war service?

[1] During the research for E Southgate no other information was found in Canadian or British records until it was discovered that Ernest Southgate had been added to the Commonwealth War Grave Commission's records in 2009. We are trying to obtain further information to confirm whether they could be the same man.

OLD PIRTONIAN'S DEATH AT TORONTO.

Sergeant-Major E. Southgate, of the Department of the Assistant Director of Medical Services in the Toronto Military District, who formerly kept the White Horse publichouse, Pirton, has died at the Base Hospital, from nephritis. He was admitted to hospital on July 9. He was formerly employed at the Toronto Mobilisation Centre. The deceased was accorded a military funeral, the service being conducted by Canon (Major) Dixon. Attending the funeral were Major R. J. Christie, O.C., Lieutenant James, second in command, Lieutenant Guy Rutter, and all members of Toronto Mobilisation Centre staff who were there during Southgate's time.

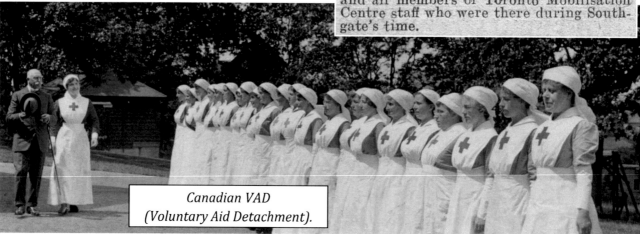

Canadian VAD
(Voluntary Aid Detachment).

This name appears on the School War Memorial, which confirms that Francis was a pupil and that he gave his life, so there is a strong Pirton connection. An initial investigation of the Pirton parish and census records did not provide any further information, but fortunately the Hitchin census did. That information, and a subsequent revisit to the Pirton records, revealed a family headed by William Tarrier and his wife Emma (née Jarvis). They were born in Holwell and Pirton respectively. In 1911 they were living at 4 Diamond Jubilee Terrace, Highbury Road, Hitchin and then later at 40 Highbury Road, Hitchin. Their children were Ida (b c1877), Walter William (b c1879), Frederick Edward (b c1885), Archie (b 1892), Francis Ralph (b c1898) and Winnie (b c1904). All the children were born in Pirton except Ida and Walter who were born in Ickleford and Winnie who was born in Hitchin. In 1891 the family were living near Little Green and William was working as a carpenter. All the sons served; Walter, Frederick and Archibald survived the war, but Francis was killed.

Private Francis Ralph Tarrier

His death was simply recorded in the Hitchin Express of June 2nd 1917 as *'Died of Wounds'* - *'Private F. R. Tarrier, Hitchin, Beds Regiment'* and then more fully in the June 19th edition and this report provides the photograph appearing here. It also gives his parents' address as 40 Highbury Road, Hitchin and that he had been apprenticed to Mr J Cain, a coach-builder of Queen Street. Bertie Dawson, another Pirton man who survived, was also apprenticed there, so they would have known each other.

Commonwealth War Grave Commission's records show that Francis had enlisted in Ampthill on November 15th 1915, that he served as Private 23269 in the 2nd Battalion of the Bedfordshire Regiment and that he died on April 9th 1917. He was just nineteen.

The Battalion's war diary, for the date of his death April 9th 1917, records that at 1:30am they were near St-Martin-sur-Cojeul in France and that they were to launch an attack on that village. "D" Company attacked, with "C" Company pushing forward on

their flanks. They were successful, and lucky, with only one officer and two other ranks wounded. They then withdrew, having captured several Germans, and rested until 2:00pm, when they were used as the support for the general attack that their Brigade had started at about 5:30am. The enemy fought back with a *'fairly strong barrage in Henin'* and the British attack was held up by wire and machine gun fire, which forced them to dig in.

The action between the April 8th and the 12th resulted in 8 officers becoming wounded or sick and in the other ranks, 13 were killed, 4 died of wounds, 2 were listed as missing, 68 were wounded and 2 suffered shell shock - a total of 89. This action was part of the Arras offensive of April to May 1917. Francis was almost certainly killed by shell or machine gun fire. It was reported that he died of his wounds, which means that he did not die instantly and usually means that the body would be buried. Perhaps Francis was seen to be wounded, but had to be left behind in the attack or perhaps he was recovered back to the British lines and his body was lost or destroyed in later action. In either case his body was another not recovered or if it was, then not

121

identified. His name is commemorated on the magnificent memorial at Arras.

This memorial is located off the Boulevard du General de Gaulle in the western part of Arras and, as well as containing a cemetery and the Arras Flying Services Memorial, it commemorates 34,750 service men from the United Kingdom, South Africa and New Zealand with no known grave. Francis Ralph Tarrier's name can be found in Bay 5, and he is also listed on the Hitchin Town Memorial.

TARRIER F. R.

FREDERICK JOHN THOMPSON
PRIVATE 2312, 1ST BATTALION, HERTFORDSHIRE REGIMENT.
DIED: THURSDAY, AUGUST 3RD 1916, AGED 20.
BURIED: BROWN'S ROAD MILITARY CEMETERY, FESTUBERT, PAS-DE-CALAIS,
FRANCE. REF. II. C. 16.
BORN IN PIRTON.

Frederick was brought to our attention by the late Lynda Smith who was deeply involved with the website project www.roll-of-honour.com. Once identified other information quickly came to light, initially from Allan Grant of Pirton and then from the research of David Baines.

The parish records show that Fred was the son of Elijah and Polly (Mary Ann) Thompson (née Stapleton), both of whom were born in Holwell. In 1901 they were living in Holwell Road with their five children, Elizabeth (b c1887), Eveline (b c1890), Ida Mary (b c1893), Frederick John (b June 7th 1896) and Hubert Charles (b 1900 or 1901). The family had moved between Holwell, Shillington and Pirton, presumably following the farm work that employed Elijah. Both Fred and Hubert were born in Pirton and both served in the war. Hubert was in the navy and he survived.

Allan Grant, who is married to Liz Thompson, confirmed that Hubert was his wife's father, and therefore Fred was her uncle. He also confirmed that the family lived at the Holwell end of the row of twelve terraced cottages in Holwell Road. These cottages were also known as the 'Twelve Apostles' and, more informally, as 'Merry Arse Row' – apparently due to the amount of children with no nappies!

By 1911 the family was living in Holwell and now had a sixth child, Constance Mary, born in Holwell around 1909. Fred, although only fourteen was already earning a wage as a farm labourer.

Before the war, in January 1914, like many local men, Fred joined Hitchin Territorials, probably attracted by the mix of soldiering, socialising and the summer break away in a training camp. From his service records we know that he was then seventeen and seven months old and at 5' 11 ½" was a tall lad, but very thin. At the outbreak of war Fred was living in Hitchin in 3 Barker's Cottages, Hitchin Hill (also called Sunnyside) and he was employed as a polisher of horse drawn hearses at Ralph Saunders Coach Builders on the Walsworth Road. When war was declared, as a Territorial he was mobilised, but he was only required to defend home soil and could not be ordered to undertake overseas duty. Fred was then eighteen and keen to fight so he volunteered, signing his overseas service papers on August 31st 1914. As a Territorial he would normally have received a shorter period of training than most, but officially the rule was that no man under nineteen should be sent overseas to fight and although that was not always adhered to, it seems to have been with Fred. To his dismay he had to watch his friends and comrades go when the 1st Hertfords were ordered overseas on November 1st 1914. With the older, trained soldiers departing, Fred would have been senior to the raw recruits arriving and that probably explains his promotion to Lance Corporal on December 22nd.

He finally left for France on July 10th 1915, embarking at Southampton, but he did not join the Hertfords immediately as he was attached to the 4th Entrenching Battalion in Rouen on July 20th 1915. He seems to have finally re-joined his own Regiment on November 9th and, for his own reasons, asked to revert to the rank of Private. He was still very young and had no battle experience, perhaps he felt uncomfortable being in charge of older, more experienced fighting men. Apart from a sprained knee in June 1916 he seems to have remained unscathed until his death on August 3rd 1916 when he was just twenty.

He must have died in an isolated incident because according to the Battalion history in the spring and summer of 1916 they were not involved in any major engagements and mainly acted as relief for other regiments. The Battalion war diary confirms that they relieved the 13th Royal Sussex Regiment in the area of Festubert on August 1st and then stayed in the line until the 7th. The diary does not record Fred's death,

but does mention that Company Serjeant Major Langford was killed by a shell during this period. Fred is recorded elsewhere as being killed instantly, when he was shot in the head while in the trenches. The family believe this was a bullet fired by a sniper in a church tower who was in turn killed shortly afterwards. His mother's death quickly followed, perhaps the shock of losing one of her sons contributed. Nothing more is known, because, as was common in many families, after the tragedy Fred was rarely spoken about. However, Liz's brother, who lives in Holwell, was named after him.

Fred was buried near where he fell and rests in the Browns Road Military Cemetery, Festubert, France, plot II. C. 16. He is also recorded on the Hitchin Town War Memorial and on the TA Memorial at the Drill Hall on Bedford Road, Hitchin, but not on the Pirton or Holwell Memorials.

JOSEPH WALKER
PRIVATE 16092, 8TH BATTALION, BEDFORDSHIRE REGIMENT.
DIED: WEDNESDAY, NOVEMBER 17TH 1915, AGED 22.
BURIED: FLUSHING (VLISSINGEN) NORTHERN CEMETERY, ZEELAND,
NETHERLANDS. REF. I. 9.
BORN IN PIRTON, LIVED IN OFFLEY, ENLISTED IN HITCHIN.

As with Fred Thompson, Lynda Smith provided the initial information and again, once identified, more information quickly came to light. The School Memorial lists him, confirming that he attended Pirton School, but he is incorrectly shown as surviving.

Joseph was the son of Stephen and Emma Walker (née Weeden) and he was born in Pirton on December 11th 1890. Parish and census records show the family to be Charles (b 1880), Albert (b 1882), Frederick (bapt 1884), Ellen (b 1887) and Joseph (b 1890). The census of 1881, 1891 and 1901 confirm that the family was living in Pirton during

this period and all, parents and children alike, were born in Pirton. Stephen earned his living from agriculture and then, later, non-domestic gardening. Emma earned extra money for the family by straw plaiting - a common source of income in the village. Interestingly Albert and Frederick's connection to Pirton seems to be confirmed by their inclusion on the lists of Pirton men serving in the Parish Magazine, but Joseph appears to have been missed.

Sometime after 1901, but before the war, at least some of the family including both parents and Joseph moved to Offley and lived in one of the Claypit Cottages. By 1914 Joseph was working for a farmer called Mr Miller, presumably in or around Offley. Whether he was living in Pirton is not known, but he was certainly visiting Pirton and was active in village life, as the Hitchin Express of July 11th mentions him as a steward at the Pirton Transept Fete. Apart from this and the fact that he was single, little else is known of his life before the war, but in early September 1914, just over a month after war was declared, he went to Hitchin and joined up for the duration. He became Private 16092 of the 8th Battalion, Bedfordshire Regiment. As mentioned, his brothers Albert and Frederick also served, but they survived.

Joseph's death is recorded as November 17th 1915. He did not die as a result of injuries received on that date, but died as a consequence of the conditions in which he had been fighting.

Channel and at 12:30pm, just one mile east of Folkestone Gate they struck one. Within fifteen minutes the ship had sunk and despite another ship racing to her aid, the estimated loss of life was between 120 and 164 including 25 crew and sadly, Joseph Walker. As a 'cot case', one of two hundred on board, he would have stood little chance of survival.

The Hospital Ship Anglia sinking off the coast of Dover.

His Regiment was formed in October 1914 and they spent a lot of time training, mostly in Bedford, but with additional training in Surrey. They were finally mobilised to fight at 11pm on August 28th 1915 and by September were fighting in France in the Battle of Loos. By the end of September conditions were awful and then got worse and wetter as the year progressed. In November the Regimental War diary makes references to the conditions; *'Wet weather. Pumping and draining trenches, many trenches falling in. Garden Street* (a trench) *full of water.' 'Trenches very muddy and in bad condition.' 'Trenches very full of water it rained heavily during the day'.* Joseph had written home on November 7th *'I am going in the trenches again tonight (Sunday) for six days, and then we are starting our holidays when we come out.'* So he was expecting leave and he added that he was looking forward to his visit home.

In excessively wet conditions men could suffer from an infection known as trench foot - a very painful condition. This could turn gangrenous and, if so, amputations were necessary. This seems to have been the case for poor Joseph as Luton papers reported that he had lost both legs though trench foot. He must have suffered terribly, but was considered strong enough to be returned to England, but to what future? On November 17th 1915 he joined 390 injured officers and soldiers, together with doctors, nurses and crew of 56 on the hospital ship the HMHS Anglia and headed back to England. Unfortunately they could not know that the German submarine UC-5 had been laying mines in the English

The news of his death came as a terrible shock to his parents and the Hertfordshire Express of December 4th 1915 reported that they had not been aware that he was incapacitated and was on his way to England. In fact they were under the impression that he was with his Battalion in the trenches. The same report refers to Joseph as *'the first old boy of Pirton School to lose his life in the present war.'* The Dover local paper, incorrectly, reported that the ship had been sunk by a torpedo.

Captain Manning, who was in command of the ship, had no doubts that it was a deliberate act to target the hospital ships. The mines had been laid near one of the buoys placed on the route for the hospital ships. These ships were clearly marked and no other ships were allowed to follow their route.

Interestingly the German submarine UC-5 later came to grief after she became stranded on a sandbank and was captured by the Royal Navy. She was later put on display at Temple Pier on the Thames and then transported to the U.S.A. to be displayed.

Joseph's life ended on that day and he was within a mile of being buried in England, but sadly his body was washed out to sea and was not recovered until January 11th 1916, when, complete with his 'dog tags', he was washed up on the beach at West Capelle, in the Netherlands. Unsurprisingly, after two months in the water, the paper reported that his burial was to take place immediately. His burial and the associated ceremony caused quite a stir and were reported in the Amsterdam papers and the war time magazine, Land and Water. The reports were accompanied by the drawing, which is reproduced here, by the distinguished war artist Louis Raemaeker.

For his funeral his white wooden coffin rested on a bier in the church. The service was undertaken by an English clergyman, the Rev. Mr Fraser and the Vice-Consul from Flushing attended the service. He laid the Union Flag over the coffin, which was then carried to the grave by four local men. The following words were read:

'Who is Walker, No. 16092, Pte. Joseph Walker Bedfordshire Regiment? Who in loving thoughts, thinks of him with hope even now when we strangers to them, stand near to him in death? Where is home? We know not, but in our inmost hearts we pray for a message of comfort and consolation for his people.'

Some time after the war his body was exhumed and laid to permanent rest in one of the Commonwealth War Graves of the town cemetery, Flushing (Vlissingen). Ref I. 9. Northern Cemetery. He is also commemorated on the Offley memorial.

Then and now.

Louis Raemaeker's drawing of Joseph's funeral and the same location as it is now.

Private 16092, Joseph Walker's final resting place Flushing (Vlissingen) Northern Cemetery, Zeeland, Netherlands. Ref. I. 9.

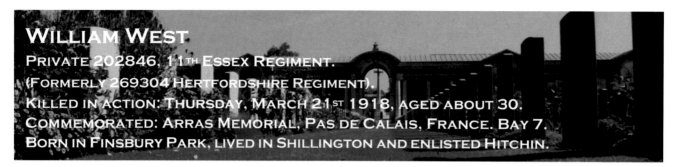

WILLIAM WEST

PRIVATE 202846, 11TH ESSEX REGIMENT.
(FORMERLY 269304 HERTFORDSHIRE REGIMENT).
KILLED IN ACTION: THURSDAY, MARCH 21ST 1918, AGED ABOUT 30.
COMMEMORATED: ARRAS MEMORIAL, PAS DE CALAIS, FRANCE. BAY 7.
BORN IN FINSBURY PARK, LIVED IN SHILLINGTON AND ENLISTED HITCHIN.

William's name appears on the School War Memorial, confirming that he was a pupil and that he gave his life.

The Shillington census of 1901 identifies William and records his family living on Church Hill. His parents were James and Louisa West and her maiden name is believed to have been Arnold. They were born in Shillington and Pirton respectively and Louisa's parents were born in Pirton.

In 1901 they had three children, Ethel (b c1896), William (b c1898) and Emma (b c1900). All the children were born in Finsbury Park, London, so they must have lived there for quite a while. James was listed as a general labourer. That and the location might well indicate that he worked on the railway - Pirton had a strong enclave of families living in the Finsbury Park area doing just that. The family must have also lived in Pirton in the early 1900s because William attended Pirton School.

In 1911 they were living in Pirton and then had seven children. The additional four were Walter George (b c1903), Christopher Frederick (b c1905), Ada Mary (b c1908) and Leonard Arthur (b c1910). The family had obviously moved around, probably following work, as the locations of the children's birth included Finsbury Park, Shillington and Pirton. By the time William enlisted he was again living in Shillington. He enlisted in Hitchin and was originally Private 269304 of the Hertfordshire regiment, but was transferred to the 11th Essex Regiment, becoming Private 202846.

The date of his transfer has not yet been discovered so his war service leading up to his death on Thursday March 21st 1918 is not known. However, from the date, he must have died in the major German attack in the spring of that year. This was a desperate action by the Germans who saw an urgent need for victory before significant numbers of Americans, who had just joined the war, could be mobilised into action. They were nearly successful with the allied forces being pushed back considerably before they were able to rally and the advance was halted. It seems likely that poor William's body was left behind in the British retreat and was lost or buried before he could be recovered and identified. His name is commemorated on the Arras Memorial, one of the 34,750 men from the United Kingdom, South Africa and New Zealand who have no known grave.

The Arras Memorial is located off the Boulevard du General de Gaulle in the western part of Arras and, as well as the names of the missing, it contains a cemetery for 2,651 Commonwealth burials and the Arras Flying Services Memorial. William West's name can be found in Bay 7 and he is also listed on the Shillington War Memorial.

The Pirton War Memorials
- We Will Remember Them

WHY MEMORIALS?

The government's decision not to repatriate the fallen was controversial. Many, understandably and desperately, wanted the remains of their sons, brothers, husbands and sweethearts returned, but with vast numbers of dead, the government knew that this would have been an immense and costly task to undertake. It was not just about cost; manpower was needed for the war, the ships and other transport were needed to move troops, supplies and equipment in one direction and the wounded in the other, so it simply was not practical. With hindsight, for many, this decision could even have been considered a kindness. Once the war had

They shall not grow old,
As we that are left grow old:
Age shall not weary them,
Nor the years condemn,
At the going down of the sun
And in the morning
We will remember them
(From 'For the Fallen'
by Laurence Binyon)

stagnated into trench warfare and the machine guns and shelling became the biggest killers, the men's remains, if they existed at all, were often incomplete or unidentified. Back home, few had any idea of the conditions in which the men were fighting, nor the implications to their loved ones' remains. If incomplete bodies had been returned or no body could be found, how heart-wrenching would that have been for the families and what of the huge number of unidentified bodies?

It is an easy thing to say, especially if you have no relative buried overseas, but the laying of comrades together, near where they fell, seems a tremendously respectful thing to do.

At the end of the war, with travelling abroad difficult and expensive and especially if there was no grave to visit, it was natural that the distressed family and friends of those who fell felt an overwhelming need to record the sacrifice and remember their men. Not just in Pirton, but right across the country, thoughts turned to raising suitable memorials.

Initially in Pirton a public subscription was organised and this was first used for the wooden Church War Memorial Shrine, and then to commission a Village War Memorial to be carved in stone. Most villagers will know of these, but there are three others, which are less well known: the School War Memorial and two Pirton British Legion memorials.

THE CHURCH WAR MEMORIAL SHRINE

In Pirton, the need for a memorial was talked about early in 1918, long before the war's end. The Parish Magazine for the month of March recorded that a memorial service would be held on 17th, and that the proceeds of the collection would form the commencement of the memorial fund. The memorial itself was not described, but sentiments were very clear and the bible was quoted, '*The righteous shall be had in everlasting remembrance*'. The service delivered a good start with £1 0s 8 ½d*1 collected.

By the following month's magazine, and before all the money had been collected, the first Pirton memorial was made. It was a beautifully carved oak

shrine. The carving was by Miss Maria Pollard of Highdown and it must have been a labour of love. The construction of the shrine was undertaken by Mr Frank Newton of Hitchin, who was a local builder and the cost recorded as six guineas*2. No one needed to have worried about any shortfall however as, by April 18th the full amount had been raised.

Although with some months of war left to run and with the names to be included not yet complete, this memorial was unveiled and dedicated in a ceremony performed by Mr W H Hanscombe on Whit Monday 1918, with the words '*In memory of the Pirton men whose lives have been sacrificed in the righteous cause of truth and justice, honour and liberty, I unveil this war shrine'*.

This memorial sits in a prominent position in St Mary's Church. The main panel must have been replaced or altered several times; initially to add more names of the fallen in the Great War and then again, following the Second World War, to include the names of the Pirton men who fell in that war.

THE VILLAGE WAR MEMORIAL

The amount raised by public subscription for the Church War Memorial was soon up to £8 9s 8½d, which exceeded the cost. Many sad relatives, friends and local wealthy families had given generously. Thoughts soon turned to a second memorial. Initially, in the words of the Vicar, Rev E W Langmore, ideas were for something "*of a practical rather than of a sentimental nature*" and an oak hand-bier for transporting coffins to the church was suggested. Other suggestions soon followed, including using the money to restore the mullions of the church windows, a stained-glass window for the church, and the erection of another memorial on Great Green, or in the Churchyard. A further £13 0s 4d was soon available and, although well short of the final amount that would be needed, it was a good start, and it was decided that another memorial, this time in stone, was most appropriate.

> Enough money has now (April 18th) been subscribed towards the War Shrine. Any further sums sent to the Vicar will be kept in hand, after the payment of all expenses, towards another Memorial. Suggestions have been made to erect one (1) in the Churchyard ; (2) on the Great Green, towards which a parishioner has said that he would give £5 ; (3) another proposal made some time ago was to restore the mullions of the Church Windows which are much decayed through the action of the weather. This is a practical matter of some urgency. (4) A Stained Glass Window in the Church. (5) A Bier. This is an important matter, and subscriptions are already coming in for it. We shall have to discuss these proposals later on : for the present all our efforts must be bent towards helping our Country to win victory whatever personal sacrifice we are asked to make. Nothing is so important from a patriotic point of view as the winning of the War, and the establishment of a just, a righteous, and a lasting peace under the Blessing of Almighty God.

Michael Newbery undertook some excellent research for his article, which appeared in the Pirton Magazine in October 2006 and so we know that the second memorial was commissioned from '*Cornish Granite Sculptors*' G Maile and Son of 376, Euston Road, London. The original cost was £105, which included a '*Rough Hewn Grey Granite Obelisk on die and plinth, with a step in hard stone, engraved with twenty-five names cut in and blacked, fully erected, for the sum of £105'*. A further four names, Albert Raymond Jenkins, William Baines, Charles Wilshere and George Charlick were added to the memorial before delivery and, from correspondence, we know that Fred Odell, who died as a result of wounds in 1919, was added later by the

The dedication ceremony on April 25th 1920.

stone masons. As a result of changes in design and carving requirements, the cost rose and was disputed, probably unreasonably. Following much correspondence between the Pirton committee and the stone masons, the cost was finally agreed at £120.

It is presumed that the original carved names from the Great War still exist and lie below the current metal plates which include the names added after the Second World War.

The Village War Memorial was dedicated at a service held at 3:00pm on the April 25th

1920, at which two army chaplains were present, and of course, every year, it is the scene of Pirton's act of remembrance.

In recent years the Memorial has not looked at its best, so the War Memorial Group was formed in 2009 to put that right. Thanks to them, and the eleven sponsored volunteers who walked the 42 miles from Pirton to the cenotaph in London over two days, enough money was raised to refurbish and maintain the Village War Memorial. The overgrown yew trees have been pollarded, new fencing and gates erected, a yew hedge has been planted and new steps constructed. It is already looking better and over the next few years, as the hedge becomes established, it will once again be a Memorial that the village can be truly proud of.

The Village War Memorial in 2010 following the work done by the War Memorial Group.

Eleven sponsored walkers arrived at the London Cenotaph having raised £4,500 to refurbish and maintain the Pirton Village War Memorial.

THE SCHOOL WAR MEMORIAL

The School Memorial is made of solid wood with the centre panel, below a carved laurel wreath, portraying the patriotic figure of St. George overcoming the dragon. It names the Pirton men who had been to the school and then served in the Great War. The upper left hand panel lists the men who died and the remainder of that panel and the right hand panel list the men who survived. The whole school used to gather around it for a Remembrance Service every November.

The School Memorial back. in its proper place.

The memorial on the classroom wall, in its original position.

For many years the memorial hung on a classroom wall in the school, certainly up to the mid-1950s, but it went missing, probably in the 1970s, when the head teacher removed it. Fortunately, this was traced to Joe Titmuss, who had saved it for the village. It was restored in 2006/07 and, at a service of re-dedication in May 2007, was returned to its rightful place in the Pirton School.

Note: Research has shown that there are a number of errors on this memorial; the corrections are given at the end of this chapter.

Remembrance Day
Top - 1950
Centre - 1984
Bottom - 2009

THE METHODIST CHURCH WAR MEMORIAL (THE BRITISH LEGION WAR MEMORIAL (1))

Pirton's branch of the British Legion was active up until the early 1990s, with monthly meetings and many other social events. Their regular meetings were held in The Fox until the death of the landlady, May Cook, in 1978; afterwards they were held in the Sports and Social Club or The Motte and Bailey.

This simple oak memorial duplicates the names on the above memorials,

130

and is mounted on the wall in the Methodist Chapel, to the right hand side as you face the pulpit. It was made during the late 1950s or early 1960s, because as St Mary's Church had a memorial inside, it was felt appropriate that the Chapel should also have one. The woodwork was beautifully crafted by Ron Burton and the lettering by Claude Farey.

The Pirton British Legion flag and standard are displayed in St Mary's Church and their Union Flag, somewhat moth-eaten now, is held by Jonty Wild, and was taken on the WW1 Project's group visit to Belgium and France in 2007.

THE BRITISH LEGION WAR MEMORIAL (2)

Little is known of this memorial, which again duplicates the names from both wars as they appear on the Church Memorial Shrine and Village War Memorial. It is fairly modern and sits behind glass in a picture frame. From the style it would seem likely that it was painted by the late Joe Titmuss, but the writing is not his. The reason for its creation is a mystery, and whether it was displayed in public is not known. It is currently held by Jonty Wild for safe keeping until a suitable home can be found.

*1 *£1.035 in today's money.*
*2 *20 shillings = £1 and 21 shillings = 1 guinea.*

CORRECTIONS TO THE SCHOOL MEMORIAL LISTINGS

The following are corrections to the names appearing on the School Memorial identified during the research for this book. Also listed are the two ex-pupils who died, but who do not appear on the other village memorials.

There seem to be several Fred Baines; the two men of the same name who survived are correctly listed, but one who died is not listed amongst the war dead. However, it is believed that he did attend the school.

William Baines is listed, but is incorrectly shown as surviving.

Edward (Charles) Burton is listed, but is incorrectly shown as surviving.

Charles James Devereaux is listed, but should read Charles **Joseph** Devereaux or possibly Devereux.

Leonard Charles Jenkins is listed and should read Leonard **Cyril** Jenkins.

Edmund Charles Pearce is listed amongst the dead, but is not listed on the other memorials for reasons explained in the chapter *'Should These Men Be On Our War Memorial?'*. This man is actually Edward Charles Burton, who is listed on the other village memorials.

Francis Tarrier is recorded amongst the dead, but is not listed on the other memorials; however, in this case the School Memorial is correct.

The Albert James Titmuss, listed amongst the dead, should read Albert John Titmuss.

Joseph Walker is listed, but is incorrectly shown as surviving.

William West is recorded among the dead, but is not on the other memorials; however, in this case the School Memorial is correct.

> *"Memorials are the way we make promises to the future from the past."*

Remembrance in Perpetuity

A first visit to the war cemeteries and memorials abroad is an astonishing experience; ninety years on from the end of the War, you might think that these men have been forgotten, their bodies languishing in some forgotten corner of a cemetery, perhaps overgrown and unkempt? But not at all; these men continue to be treated with the most moving respect and tenderness. For those whose relatives fell and those with a respect for our history, this is important.

Thanks to the Commonwealth War Graves Commission they are always immaculately kept; bowling green grass, edges cut with military precision, headstones clean, upright and lined up in perfect formation in remembrance of the brave soldiers that they represent. Importantly, by clever, considerate design and quiet unobtrusive care, they are not places of great sadness, but rather peaceful oases of quiet and dutiful respect. Of course, the experience of visiting them is sombre, thought-provoking and can be emotional, but never one to be regretted.

We should be grateful to the Commonwealth War Graves Commission who undertake and organise the work, and it is very interesting to see that some of the people who have dedicated their working lives to this organisation chose to be buried alongside the soldiers they have served - so much more than just another job of work.

To fully understand and appreciate how these men are served, it is necessary to understand the history of this organisation and how it could all have been so very different.

The Commonwealth War Graves Commission started life as the Imperial War Graves Commission, which was established by Royal Charter in May 1917. The word 'Imperial' was dropped in the 1960s, as it was felt to not be in tune with the individual countries' own national identities. But the need for the Commission was identified much earlier, in fact in 1914 by the man who would later be credited as its founder, Fabian Ware. He realised that no-one was taking responsibility for recording the location of graves and, consequently, there was a great risk that they would be lost, so he started to record this information himself. By 1915 this need was recognised by others, his work became 'official', and the department he formed became the 'Graves Registration Commission'.

Following the war, a huge amount of work was required; bodies had to be found, recovered and, wherever possible, identified. As explained elsewhere, the government had decided that it was not practical to repatriate the fallen; the grateful French and Belgian people recognised the sacrifice of these men, and freely gave land in perpetuity as resting places for these heroes. The Commission began organising proper and fitting resting places for the men. In some cases, scattered graves were brought together into more manageable cemeteries. In other locations, the temporary resting places were converted to the cemeteries that now exist, and the wooden crosses were replaced by carved headstones.

The Commission is now responsible for thousands of cemeteries, from tiny examples such as Berles Position Military Cemetery, quite literally in the middle of a field, and where Pirton's Edward Charles Burton lies, to huge cemeteries such as Tyne Cot, where thousands of men are buried and thousands more remembered, including Pirton's Harry Smith and William Thomas Hill. They are also responsible for graves and some memorials in the UK, including the single war grave in Holwell Church cemetery.

The extremes of the Commonwealth War Grave Commission's responsibilities; from the 11,956 graves at Tyne Cot to the single grave in the Holwell cemetery.

By the end of the Great War, 580,000 identified graves and 180,000 unidentified graves had been marked and recorded. The names of those with no known grave were later commemorated on memorials, often impressive architectural works in towns, sometimes dominating features in the countryside.

Many men have no known grave. With an understanding of the war, the reasons are not difficult to explain; an exploding shell could completely destroy men's bodies or bury them in their trenches. A failed attack would leave the dead in 'no man's land', sometimes for months and then, when finally recovered they could be unidentifiable. Many bodies were simply submerged in the mud or were buried by shell explosions. It is shocking to know that this includes nearly 530,000 Commonwealth men, which accounts for nearly forty-eight percent of those who died in the British Army. These men are not forgotten and have been commemorated on memorials. Some are grand and impressive, such as the Menin Gate in Ypres, with nearly 55,000 names and where, at 8:00pm every night of the year, a ceremony remembers the fallen. Some are massive, such as Thiepval, which dominates the local countryside and records nearly 72,000 casualties of the Somme.

In the cemeteries, contrary to first impressions, the headstones are also surprisingly individual. In fact, there are many variations. The 'standard' ones bear the name of the man, his rank, his regiment, a regimental motif, a date of death and, if a Christian, a cross. Sometimes there is an additional message such as '*Rest in Peace*'. These simple messages were optional and free of charge. Longer or more complicated messages could be paid for by the family and some are very poignant, but none more so than '*Shot at dawn, one of the first to enlist, a worthy son to his father*'. Jewish headstones carry the Star of David and you will often see small stones placed on the top by a visiting relative or in fact any visitor, as a traditional mark of respect. If the man had been decorated, then the initials of the medal are added. Interestingly, and almost without exception, the only decoration displayed as an emblem is the Victoria Cross.

133

A Jewish headstone with examples of the traditional mark of respect.

Different nationalities who served with or in the British Army, such as the Chinese or Indians, have variations in the engraving and the shape of the stones. Belgian, French and even German soldiers can sometimes be found sharing Commonwealth resting places, and they have a headstone of their own nationality's design.

There are many headstones inscribed with '*A Soldier of the Great War*', '*Known unto God*', clearly marking where men whose identity is unknown are laid to rest. Sometimes named headstones are around the boundary of the cemetery, which indicates that the man is known to be buried in the cemetery, but not exactly where. If named headstones have little or no gap between them, then this denotes a communal grave; often the names of the men being known, but sadly not necessarily which body is which.

Different countries' cemeteries can have a very different feel. The French are similar to ours, open, airy and respectful, but are not so well kept. The German ones are completely different: dark, cold, sombre and often feel enclosed. Understandably the French and Belgians were not quite so keen to give land to the 'invaders', and there are many examples of cramped German cemeteries or mass graves. Visitors from Britain, who compare the Commonwealth, French, Belgium and German cemeteries, can proudly say that ours are the best.

A RECOMMENDED VISIT

There is a short itinerary, which is highly recommended and can be done on a day trip to Ypres, but an overnight stay is better.

Visit the memorial at Menin Gate, which is easily found and just a few hundred yards off the town square. Look for Pirton's William Baines. Then visit Tyne Cot, which is only a few miles outside Ypres. Wander among the graves and the memorial names, look for the Pirton men, Harry Smith and William Thomas Hill, buried and commemorated respectively. Return to Menin Gate for the moving ceremony, which takes place at 8pm prompt every night of the year, but get there early as although sometimes there may only be a few people on most nights there are a few hundred. Probably the best place to stand is on the kerb at the far end, away from the town square, left hand side. There are plenty of local hotels of all standards and excellent places to eat after the ceremony.

The ceremony at Menin Gate.

Was it Worth it?

By the end of the war on the 11th hour of the 11th day of the 11th month of 1918 at least 230 men with a Pirton connection had joined the armed forces. Of the thirty men appearing on the village memorial twenty-seven had been killed, three more were yet to die, and at least one of them suffered from terrible and ultimately fatal wounds.

Dozens of Pirton men had been wounded or had been desperately ill at some point during their service. After what they had seen and experienced, almost all of those returning must have carried scars, but for many they may not have been visible.

The tragedy of the Great War in human life was huge; the casualties for the armed forces of all nations is estimated at 8.5 million men dead and 21 million wounded - many left crippled in body, mind or spirit. The financial cost was estimated at an incomprehensible 125,000,000,000 dollars for the allies (1918 value) and about half as much again for the Germans and the other central powers. As a result the economies were depressed, and in Britain, far from returning to 'a land fit for heroes', many faced a depressing and uncertain future.

The infrastructure damage to Europe was colossal; much of Belgium and a huge swage of France had been reduced to rubble. 11,000 public buildings, 750,000 French homes and 28,500 miles of roads were destroyed. 10,000 square miles of farmland and 2,300 square miles of building land had to be reclaimed and 233,000 miles of barbed wire had to be cleared. And, about 350,000 men from Britain and the Commonwealth countries still lie there, lost under French and Belgian soil.

Although the rate has slowed considerably, there are still deaths attributable to the war - farm equipment raises First World War munitions to the surface when ploughing and, occasionally they still bring death. When touring the French and Belgian countryside it is not uncommon to see small piles of rusting shells waiting to be collected and safely disposed of. Indeed in 2007, during the minibus trip organised by the book team to visit some of the Pirton men and the battlefields, whilst walking between the Thiepval museum and the Memorial, one of the party spotted this hand grenade, just off the road and lying on an adjacent field.

Millions had given their lives as volunteers or as conscripts, but France and Belgium were saved from the Germans. The regions of Alsace and Lorraine, lost in earlier wars, were returned to France. Germany was forced to make reparations. Some of their land was given to Belgium, Denmark, Czechoslovakia, Poland and Russia, and Germany was required to pay £6,600 million to repair the damage of the war. Arguably the German resentment of this helped bring Hitler to power and would eventually lead to another war.

Women experienced working in what had been 'a man's world'. Many earned wages for the first time when they took over men's jobs to release them to fight. They gained a measure of freedom, a leap in confidence and a new perspective on their position in the world and this helped enormously towards their emancipation, getting restricted rights to vote in 1918 and then finally getting full rights in 1928.

But, in Pirton alone there were 57 grieving parents. 164 siblings or half-siblings had lost a brother and there were 9 widows and 18 fatherless children.

The popular view is that it was a waste of human life. Inevitably that must be true, but it was not *just* that and many of the returning men would have been insulted by the simplicity of that argument. Many believed that they had indeed fought for Freedom, Honour and Justice.

Perhaps the biggest tragedy of all was that the Great War, was supposed to be '*the war to end all wars*' and, despite all the sacrifice, we know that was not to be.

Poignant statues at the German cemetery of Langemark.

'*Yesterday I visited the battlefield of last year. The place was scarcely recognisable. Instead of a wilderness of ground torn up by shell, a perfect desolation of earth without a sign of vegetation, the ground was a garden of wild flowers and tall grasses. ..... Most remarkable of all was the appearance of many thousands of white butterflies which fluttered round this solitary grave. You can have no conception of the strange sensation that this host of little fluttering creatures gave me. It was as if the souls of the dead soldiers had come to haunt the spot where so many fell. It was so eerie to see them, the only living things in that wilderness of flowers. And the silence! Not a sound, not even the rustling of a breeze through the grass. It was so still that it seemed as if one could almost hear the beat of the butterflies' wings.'*

Originally written by a British officer at the Front – borrowed from the excellent book:
1914-1918 Voices and Images of the Great War by Lyn MacDonald (ISBN 0-09188-8879) - read it!

The trenches today.

THESE MEN — THE SURVIVORS

In this chapter there are details for 194 Pirton men who served during the war. Not all would have been resident in Pirton at the time, but all had a connection. It is a large number, but even so it is probably incomplete.

Many of the men volunteered, the rest were conscripted - increasingly the case as the war progressed. Quite a few had previously emigrated to Canada, but still felt a strong sense of loyalty and returned to help their King and Country. All did their duty and often their contribution was significant; three Military Medal winners are listed here and there are other stories of bravery, but how many more remain lost to us?

Reading through the men's details, it is astonishing to realise how many were wounded, often several times. The death toll of thirty men, as listed on our memorials, could so easily have been much higher.

Many of these men knew fear, exhaustion, comradeship, heartbreak and would have experienced terrible conditions in the trenches. Many saw friends and comrades die. As with men right across Great Britain and indeed the world, many of Pirton's men were scarred by their experience and not all those scars were visible.

What stories they could have told of their experiences, but all too often little was said, even to family and friends. British reserve? Stiff upper lip? Or perhaps just best forgotten?

British War Medal and
Victory Medal.

RESEARCH NOTES BY JONTY WILD

More complete details of the research for this book are given in the reference section and at www.pirton.org.uk. For a more comprehensive understanding of the following pages and of potential errors, it would be wise to read those notes before continuing.

Where available, the names and basic information of parents and siblings have been included. They are intended to help 'paint a picture' of the man's family life and to help people confirm relatives. It is also hoped that this information will enable relatives and researchers of family histories to add information or perhaps correct errors. It is quite possible that the list of siblings may not be complete as many children died young and, if children were born or baptised away from Pirton, or if they were not in their parents' house at the time of a census, they may not appear in the records.

Last, it is perhaps wise to mention age. Some men listed may appear to be too old to have served and, where it appears so it is probably the case, but not always. During the early stages of the war, providing they had a reasonable level of fitness, men between nineteen and thirty-eight were accepted for service and this age was extended to forty-five if the volunteers had previously served. Later in the war, after so many had died and when conscription had been brought in, the age for call up was eighteen to forty-one, then, by April 1918, it became eighteen to fifty-one, although very few of the older men were actually called up.

ABBREVIATIONS USED IN THE TEXT

Serjeant, rather than sergeant, is the spelling used because it reflects the use by the Commonwealth War Graves Commission on the headstones and memorials.

Abbreviations commonly used in the following text include: b = born, bapt = baptised, c = circa and d = died, MM = Military Medal, OR = Other Ranks (i.e. all men other than commissioned officers).

ABBISS, FRANK

Frank was one of two men of that name who were born in Pirton and who fought in the war. One died and is recorded on the Village War Memorial and one survived.

Frank Abbiss, ready for war. His wife and son, Stanley appear in the top left hand corner. That photograph was in Frank's locket which he carried throughout the war.

This Frank was born on March 2nd 1880 to George and Ellen (née Clark). Baptism and census records list eight children: Ruth (bapt 1873), Frederick George (b 1875), Alice (bapt 1878), Frank (b 1880), Harry (b 1888), Margaret Lizzie (b 1892), Violet (b 1895) and Nellie Ivy (b 1899).

By 1911, Frank's father had died leaving his mother Ellen a widow, then fifty-six, living with her daughters, Violet and Nellie. She was illiterate – the enumerator signed the census on her behalf and her opportunity to earn money limited. Frank had left home, probably to earn a living and could have been helping his mother who was surviving on Parish relief.

It is not clear exactly when he enlisted. Possibly in 1915, as the Parish Magazine of September 1915 records Frank Abbiss as enlisting during 1915, but before August, and serving in the 1st Bedfordshire Regiment. However, photographs seem to show that he served in the Queens (Royal West Surrey Regiment). He would have been thirty-four at the outbreak of war.

Thanks to Stanley Abbiss (his son, now deceased) and Gladys Tullett (née Abbiss, his granddaughter) it has been possible to add a lot more information for the Frank that survived.

In 1902, on March 31st, when his profession was recorded as a labourer, aged twenty-two, he married Ruth Titmuss, aged twenty-eight in St. Mary's Church. They had four children, including George (Gladys' father), Elsie, Eva and Stanley, and then six grandchildren.

Gladys remembers that Frank worked in the building trade and lived in Finsbury Park where he spent the rest of his life. In 1929 they were living in Charteris Road before moving to Lorne Road. He died on March 1st 1951, aged seventy.

Frank's Locket.

Stanley remembered the following information. Frank was born in Pirton around 1880 and his mother was Ellen. She lived all her life in Cromwell Terrace and, in fact, died there. Stanley remembers walking with his father at her funeral. They followed the funeral bier, pictured in the Pirton book 'A Foot on Three Daisies' (page 105). He confirmed the marriage to Ruth Titmuss, that by the time of the war they were living at 39 Charteris Road, Finsbury Park, London, and that he worked as a builder. He was also able to add that he was involved in the construction of the old Arsenal football ground and later worked on the Golders Green Crematorium.

Stanley was born just before the start of the war and kept the birthday cards sent by his father from the Front. Copies can be seen in the Pirton 'Archive*1.

Little is known about his war service; like a lot of the men, he didn't speak much about his experience. However, Stanley remembers that, while he was waiting to join up for service in World War Two, his dad told him that he had been wounded in the arm and, during one of the retreats, *"when he was carrying an anvil in a wheelbarrow, he couldn't keep up with the rest of his unit, so he tipped the lot into a ditch beside the road."* *"Perhaps an experience in the Great War was responsible for the fact that Frank would never go into the shelter during the Second World War?"*

*1 The Pirton Historic Photograph and Document Archive at www.pirton.org.uk.

ABBISS, HARRY

By 1918 he was Private 106070, 1st Company, 1st Battalion, Hertfordshire Yeomanry Regiment. Home was recorded as 'near Burge End', a name then given to a much larger area than the current road. It was probably one of the cottages known as 'Ten Steps'. These were a row of four small cottages, built in the mid 18th century and demolished in 1980 to make way for the new development near 13 Shillington Road.

Harry was born on April 17th 1890 to George and Ann Abbiss. The 1911 census records that they had seven children, but three had died and to us remain unnamed. The surviving children were: Harry, two sisters, Elizabeth (b c1882) and Mary (known as Polly, b 1886) and an elder brother, Frank (b 1881), who sadly died in the war and appears on the War Memorial. Harry appears on the School War Memorial, confirming that he attended the school. In the years before the war he worked on the local farms.

He is recorded in the Parish Magazine of July 1916 as enlisting between October 21st 1915 and March 2nd 1916 and serving in the Hertfordshire Yeomanry. He would have been twenty-five.

His grandson, Richard Abbiss, has helped provide some details of Harry's life; he married Kate Ethel (possibly née Titmuss) and they had a son, Frank, probably named after Harry's brother. Kate died on August 12th 1934, aged forty-one. Four years later, on November 11th 1938, Harry was killed in an accident on Henlow airfield. He had been working in one of the buildings and was putting tools away with a workmate when a plane crashed into the building, killing him. He was forty-eight. The pilot survived and later visited Harry's sister Polly to apologise.

Interestingly, and only very recently, a letter has been discovered written by R W Ellis, First Lieutenant Adjutant, No 4 (T) Wing, RAF Henlow Camp, to Harry's sister, Mrs Weeden. In it he expresses his *'deepest sympathy'* and offers the comfort that *'we do know that his death was instantaneous, and that he suffered no pain.'*

Harry Abbiss

Harry Abbiss is on the right, the other two men are also believed to be family members, but have not been identified. They all seem to be in the same Regiment - the Hertfords.

ABBISS, THOMAS WILLIAM

Richard Abbiss has helped provide details of Tom's life.

Tom was born on November 10th 1893 and was the son of Frank and Elizabeth Abbiss of Great Green, Pirton. He had three older siblings: Annie (bapt 1884), Albert*1 (b 1887), who was killed in the war and is listed on the Village War Memorial, an elder sister, Rose (b 1891) and a younger sister, Alice (b 1896). He appears on the School War Memorial, confirming that he attended the school.

By 1911, Tom, then seventeen, was working as a farm labourer. Edna Lake from Canada, informs us that five Pirton men, including Tom, emigrated to Canada together in 1912. The others were Albert William (Toby) Buckett, Edward Lake, Charlie Stapleton and one of the Walkers, possibly Arthur Robert Walker. However, there is conflicting information for the emigration dates, including a North Herts Mail report, which suggests 1909 or 1910 for Toby. Tom was following in his brothers' footsteps, as Albert had gone to Canada some years before.

An unidentified man believed to be one of the local Abbiss family and probably in the Bedfordshire Regiment.

He enlisted during June 1915, joining the 47th Battalion, Canadian Regiment in New Westminster, British Columbia. He was not married and would have been twenty-four. Tom, Toby, Edward, and Arthur all joined the Canadian Expeditionary Force, returning to Europe to fight; their allegiance to Great Britain was still very strong.

Tom's attestation papers give some details of his appearance; at 5' 10" he was a tall man, had light brown hair and grey eyes. He is also recorded as not having any previous military service, but perhaps confusingly, had been a member of the Canadian Militia.

The North Herts Mail of November 18th 1915 reported that he had returned from Canada to fight and that he was home (in Pirton) from training camp. In March 1916 his brother Albert was killed. The October 12th 1916 edition later recorded that he had been in France for about six weeks, had already been wounded, but not by the Germans: *'We were in No Mans Land and a mate stuck me with a bayonet.'* The injury was to his right thigh. He again returned to England and was in a VAD*2 Hospital in Church Stretton, Shropshire. He got some leave in November and managed to get back to Pirton. This must have been a little comfort to his parents following the death of his brother.

The North Herts Mail, December 14th 1916 edition also recorded that after emigrating to Canada he worked for Philip Trussell, the son of the Pirton post office man who had also emigrated and was an engineer on a boat. The same paper in a report on the Military Medal-winning Pirton man Arthur Robert Walker contained a part of a letter from him dated September 29th, which mentioned Tom; '*I heard about Tom Abbiss being wounded. I saw him and was speaking to him the day before he went out on a raiding party (the same night that I was), and he was unfortunate enough to get wounded.*' So it was in September that Tom was wounded for the second time.

*1 A newspaper article refers to Alfred Abbiss, however this is believed to be a misprint.

*2 Voluntary Aid Detachments (VADS) were formed in 1909 by the War Office. Under this scheme, the British Red Cross Society was given the role of providing supplementary aid to the Territorial Forces Medical Service in the event of war. By the summer of 1914 there were over 2,500 VADs in Britain. Of the 74,000 VADs in 1914, two-thirds were women.

ASHTON, FRANK

Frank is recorded in the Parish Magazine of July 1916 as enlisting between March 2nd and July 1916 and serving in the Army Veterinary Corps. He also appears on the School War Memorial, confirming that he attended the school.

Stan Ashton, Frank's son, confirms that Frank was the son of Arthur and Emma Ashton and that he had two siblings, one who died at a very young age and Harry. The 1911 census records that he was born in Shillington around 1894, so he would have about twenty when war was declared. Before the war he had worked in the family bakery business, which was in the Knoll at 1 Burge End, (now 17 Shillington Rd), but by 1911 was recorded as a farm labourer.

His brother Harry also served and survived, as did their cousin Jack Ashton. Frank joined up at the same time as John Kingsley (another survivor) and underwent training at Wardown Park in Luton. By 1918 he was Lance

Bombardier 196695, 1st Battery, Royal Horse Artillery, with his home address as near Burge End, a name then given to a much larger area than the current road. He returned to Pirton after the war and continued to work in the bakery, which he later took over from his father and ran until 1958 when he in turn retired.

He married Edith Bertha Kingsley and they had three sons, including Stan. Both Frank and Edith are buried in St. Mary's churchyard. Frank died in 1974 and Edith in 1984.

Intriguingly, Stan is convinced that there was a photograph of his father, in uniform, in St. Mary's Church. It was in a frame, but behind a copy of some records relating to the bell ringing of quarter peals. Unfortunately this has yet to be found, but hopefully it will be, in the future.

The Ashton family baker's cart.

ASHTON, HARRY

Harry is recorded in the Parish Magazine of September 1915 as enlisting sometime during 1914, but after July, and serving in the 4th Hussars. In all it would appear that two brothers served and survived - refer to Frank Ashton for more family details.

Harry was one of the original 'Old Contemptibles', so called because the British Expeditionary Force (BEF) was so small that Kaiser Wilhelm II called it '*General French's contemptible little army*'.

In August 1914, the BEF was tiny in comparison to the German Army, just 70,000 men facing 160,000, but they fought incredibly bravely and with immense discipline. They were continually forced back by what should have been overwhelming numbers, but fought so well that the Germans believed they were a larger force with substantial reserves. Eventually, east of Ypres, they were able to dig in and hold the Germans, while the British, French and Belgians re-grouped, recruited and gathered strength. By the end of November 1914, of the original BEF men, perhaps 120,000, casualties numbered around 90,000, and these were the most experienced soldiers in the British Army.

Harry is believed to have been in the army before the war, serving in Ireland and then, after the war, went on to serve in India.

ASHTON, JACK

Stan Ashton, son of Frank Ashton, confirms that Jack was the cousin of brothers Frank and Harry Ashton and that, before and after the war, he lived in the Croft, Shillington Rd. No birth or baptism records have been found for Jack, but his parents were Thomas and Phoebe Ashton (née Pearce). Baptism records list four siblings, Alice (bapt 1863), George Thomas (bapt 1864), Lizzy (bapt 1866) and Hedley (bapt 1879).

The Parish Magazine of June 1917 records him as serving in the Training Reserve and then, in September 1918, notes that he had recently received a slight wound, so by then he must have been on active service.

Sometime after the war Jack took a smallholding near Baldock.

Bertram Baines

BAINES, BERTRAM

Bertram appears on the School War Memorial, confirming that he attended the school.

Muriel Timbury, his niece, confirms that his parents were George and Emma Baines (née Cooper), who lived in one of Allen's Cottages, the row of cottages opposite the pond, built by Sam Allen, but later, after being bought by Mr Palmer, known as Palmer's Row. He had a younger brother Leonard George (b 1908) and two sisters, Alice (b 1890) and Gladys Ethel (b c1903). From this information records can be found that show that Bertram was born on October 28th 1892.

Before 1911 he worked as a farm labourer on the local farms, and is recorded in the Parish Magazine of July 1916 as enlisting in 1916 after March 2nd and serving in the Army Service Corps. He would have been about twenty-three. By 1918 he was recorded as Driver 196016, 38th Divisional Artillery Column, with his home address as '*near Burge End*', a name then given to a much larger area of Pirton rather than just the current road.

After the war he became a bus conductor and lived in London with his wife Dinah. He died early in the nineteen sixties.

BAINES, ERNEST FRANK, (ERNIE)

The photographs and much of the following information was provided by Roger Baines, Ernest's son and Jean Keane (née Baines) his daughter.

Ernest Frank Baines or 'Ernie' was a Pirton lad, born in Pirton on August 28th 1895, the son of Frank and Pamela Baines (née Dawson), who lived in Ivy House, Crabtree Lane, opposite the entrance to St. Mary's Church and now known as Ivy Cottage. He appears on the School War Memorial, confirming that he attended the school. Baptism and census records list five children: Arthur (b 1886), Edith Minnie (b 1888), Alice (b 1891), Ernest Frank (b 1895) and Gertrude Mary (b c1904).

Ernest Baines

By 1911, Ernest, then aged fifteen, was already earning a living as a cart boy. Four years later, the Parish Magazine of September 1915 records him as enlisting during 1915, before August and serving in the North Staffordshire Regiment. His training was undertaken in St. Albans, which is where the photographs, appearing here, were taken. At this time, he was in the 59th Signals Company, "B" Detachment, Royal Engineers, and training on horseback. The family believe that he was a despatch rider in France/Belgium and that he also served in Ireland at some point, possibly about the time of the Easter uprising in 1916. Pamela died in February 1916 not long after Ernie joined up, when he would have been about nineteen years old.

Ernest Baines (sixth from right) with his pals.

By 1918 he was recorded as Driver 492373 in the 59th Division Signals Corps , Royal Engineers, with his home address as the cottage 'near the Church', now Ivy Cottage.

His service medals are held by his son, Roger, and are complete with box and the envelope in which they were sent. The envelope is addressed to Ivy House, Pirton and the box inside has '*B WAR and VICTORY*' stamped in red, the numbers 43608 and 492373 and DVR. E. BAINES R.E. typed in black. Apparently Ernie was not impressed by what he and others went through and dismissed the medals as an insult.

After the war, during the nineteen twenties, he played for the Pirton football team 'The Robins'. It must have been a successful era for them, because Roger has several of his father's silver medals dating from 1923-1925. His wife was Lilian McNaughton Baines.

Sadly, Ernie was killed on December 11th 1953, in an accident which happened while he was working for Wilmotts, building the telephone exchange in Hitchin. He was fifty-eight. Lilian died November 8th 1982, aged eighty-six. They are both buried in St. Mary's churchyard.

BAINES, FRED

One Frederick Baines died and is recorded on the Village War Memorial. The School War Memorial records two more; Frederick and Frederick John Baines, so both attended the school and the memorial records that both survived the war.

The Parish Magazine of September 1915 records one of them as enlisting sometime during 1914, but after July, and serving in the 1st Hertfordshire Regiment, but which Fred this refers to is not known.

Frederick (not Frederick John) was the second son of Mr and Mrs A Baines - confirmed by parish records as Albert and Emma Elizabeth Baines (née Weeden) and he was born March 7th 1890, so at the outbreak of war he was twenty-four years old. Baptism and census records list ten children: Charlie (bapt 1885), Mary (b 1886), Ida (b 1888 and who died in infancy), Fred (b 1890), Sidney (b 1891), Rose (b 1895), Edward (b 1897), Lily (b 1900), Harry (b 1902) and Hilda (b 1906). Sidney also served, but sadly died. He is recorded on the Village War Memorial. In 1911, Fred was recorded as a coach builder and wheelright.

The Hertfordshire Express of April 21st, 1917 reports the wartime wedding on April 4th, in St Nicholas Church, Stroud, between Fred and Miss Kathleen Chambers from Stroud (granddaughter of Pirton man Thomas Ashton). The article records that one of their presents was from Private N Newberry, another Pirton survivor. Fred must have had a fairly decent period of leave, because the article reports that he and his new bride left by car for a honeymoon in Southend.

BAINES, FREDERICK JOHN

One Frederick Baines died and is recorded on the Village War Memorial. The School War Memorial records two more: Frederick and Frederick John Baines, so both attended the school and the memorial records that both survived the war.

Frederick John Baines, was the son of Thomas and Mary Baines (née Hodson) married in Pirton, but they were living in Pegsdon when Frederick John was born on August 4th 1893. The census reveals that they had returned to Pirton by 1901 and lists no other siblings. At the outbreak of war (his birthday) he was twenty-one years old.

BAINES, JAMES

James appears on the School War Memorial, confirming that he attended the school. Parish records suggest only one man of this name who could have served, and he was baptised on June 1st 1879, the son of Charles and Martha Elizabeth Baines (née Weeden). He would have been thirty-five at the outbreak of war. Baptism records list eight children: Emma (bapt 1870), Thomas (bapt 1872), Elizabeth (bapt 1875), Ann (bapt 1877), James (b 1879), Peggy (b 1883), Frederick (b 1885, died aged two) and Mary (b 1889).

BAINES, SIDNEY

One Sidney Baines is recorded on the Village War Memorial. However, the Parish Magazine of July 1916 records two Sidney Baines, indicating that one survived. The survivor is believed to have enlisted between October 21st 1915 and March 2nd 1916 and served in the Bedfordshire Regiment.

The Sidney who died was the son of Albert and Emma Elizabeth, but sadly the parish and census records do not provide any information that could identify the Sidney who survived, so this could be an error in the Parish Magazine.

BAINES, WALTER JAMES

Parish records suggest only one man of this name who could have served, and he was born on May 13th, 1894 and was the son of Samuel and Louisa Mary Baines (née Weeden). He would have been about twenty at the outbreak of war.

Baptism and census records list eight children: William (b 1877), John (b c1879) Emma (b 1881), Eleanor Jane (Ellen? b 1883), Nelly (b c1884), Bertha (b 1886), Emily Ida (b 1888) and Walter James (bapt 1894). It is possible that Walter's brother was the William Baines who also served and survived.

The research of David Baines' shows that Walter was a private in the Cheshire Regiment, having volunteered in June 1915, when he would have been twenty-one. He was drafted to Egypt in 1915, served with General Allenby in Palestine and was involved in the Battle of Gaza and the capture of Jerusalem. By the end of 1917 he had been sent to India and then to various garrison outposts. He returned home and then in August 1918, he was discharged as medically unfit for further service. Walter held the 1914-15 Star, British War and Victory medals and his address at the end of the war was given as Lea Green, Kings Walden, Herts.

BAINES, WILLIAM

One William Baines is recorded on the Village War Memorial. However, the Parish Magazine of October 1915 records another, who was serving in the Bedfordshire Regiment and *'indirectly connected to Pirton'*. Parish records reveal one possible man, the son of Samuel and Louisa Mary Baines (née Weeden), but if they were his parents then he is more likely to be recorded as having a direct connection to Pirton. If he is our man, then he was baptised on May 20th 1877, and so he would have been about thirty-seven at the outbreak of war. In all it is possible that two brothers served and survived - refer to Walter James Baines for more family details. However, as explained, the reference to an indirect connection leaves doubt as to whether the correct man has been identified. Perhaps William was not this man, but part of an extended family living outside of Pirton.

BARKER, GEORGE

George is recorded in the Parish Magazine of September 1915 as enlisting in the 63rd Rifles, Nova Scotia (Canadian Regiment) during 1915 and before August. A newspaper article dated October 27th 1917 reveals that he was the only son of Mrs Barker, who lived on Great Green, and that he had previously emigrated to Canada, sometime around 1902.

Parish records suggest only one man of this name who could have served, and he was baptised on March 6th 1878, the son of Samuel and Elizabeth Barker (née Smith). As George's attestation papers give his next of kin as his mother, Elizabeth, he certainly appears to be the right man. Baptism records list eight children: Joseph (bapt 1875), Elizabeth (bapt 1876), George (bapt 1878), Emma (b 1879), Clara (b 1883), Minnie (b 1888), Daisie (b 1893) and Alice (b 1896). In 1911, his parents were living near the Blacksmiths Arms, which was in the High Street, opposite where the Blacksmith's pond remains to this day.

His attestation papers provide other useful information; he was born July 7th 1874 and he was not married. The oath was taken on January 20th 1916 and so he was forty-one (albeit that the form records forty years and seven months). This age would normally have been too old to serve; however he was almost certainly accepted because of his previous service record, five years in the Royal Garrison Regiment and five years in the Bedfordshire Regiment. He was a well built man, 5' 9" tall with a chest just short of 40", with a fresh complexion, blue eyes and dark hair.

By October 27th 1917, having been in France for over twelve months, the Hertfordshire Express reported that he was in a London hospital suffering with ague (shell shock).

BEDALE, JOHN LEIGH

The Parish Magazine of October 1915 records John, who was serving as a Lieutenant on H.M.S. Bacchante and as *'indirectly connected to Pirton'*. Michael Newbery suggests that John was related to the Rev. Frederick Bedale who was vicar of Pirton between 1896 and 1903. The North Herts Mail of August 12th 1915 states that the vicar's brother had been shot through the thigh and was in hospital in Rouen. It was his third wound, but that does not seem likely to be John.

H.M.S. Bacchante. A First Class Armoured Cruiser, Cressy Class, built in 1906.

H.M.S. Bacchante was an armoured cruiser captained by Eric Wheler. In the early days of the war she was part of the 7th Cruiser Squadron North Sea, Cruiser Force C and was involved in the Battle of Heligoland Bight on August 28th 1914 and then, in October, was part of the escort for a convoy to Gibraltar. From January to March 1915 she helped defend the Suez Canal and, from April 1915 to 1916, was in the Dardanelles as part of the Gallipoli campaign. Most notably during this period, she was involved in the landing at Anzac Cove and, when the infantry came under fire from Turkish artillery at Gaba Tepe, she bravely approached close to the shore and fired directly on the gun emplacements, in an attempt to silence them, and in the process demolished the Turkish barracks. In 1917 she became part of the 9th Cruiser Squadron, West Africa.

The date that John joined the ship's company is not known, but he presumably had been involved in some, if not all, of these actions.

BELL, WILLIAM

William appears on the School War Memorial, confirming that he attended the school. Parish records suggest only one man of this name who could have served, and he was born on January 31st 1891 to Ellen Bell. His father's details are not provided. However, records show that Ellen (née Males) married Philip Bell in 1877. Philip's occupation is recorded as a gentleman's steward. Perhaps this is a clue to his absence but, in any case he is not listed in subsequent census records. Baptism records name them as parents to William's elder brother, Charles (bapt 1878), and census records reveal another older brother Frederick (b c1876), who became the village blacksmith, and that they were the grandsons of Eliza Males. The 1911 census still fails to record the father, but confirms that Ellen was still married and all three children are listed. They are recorded as tenants of a property on Great Green. Intriguingly, William's occupation appears to have been listed as a solider (soldier?), but this has been crossed out.

William is recorded in the Parish Magazine of September 1915 as enlisting in 1914 after July, and serving in the 75th Battery of the Royal Field Artillery, and so he would have been twenty-four years old.

The North Herts Mail of February 15th 1917 reported that he had been on leave from Salonika, but contradicts the earlier Parish Magazine by suggesting that he had been in the army for six years.

Royal Field Artillery cap badge.

By 1918 he was recorded as Corporal 66474, 75th Battery 263rd Brigade Royal Field Artillery with his home address as '*around Great Green*'.

BOTTOMS, SIDNEY ALFRED

Parish records suggest only one man of this name who could have served, and he was born on August 13th 1899 to Arthur and Rose Bottoms. He would have been about fourteen when war was declared; therefore, although not impossible, it is unlikely that he served until much later in the war. Baptism and census records list five children. However, the 1911 census gives the number as six, but one had died and remains unnamed at this time. The surviving children were Gertrude (b 1881), Samuel (b c1884), Emma (b c1890), Elizabeth (bapt 1896) and Sidney Alfred (b 1899).

BRERETON, CLEMENT S

The Parish Magazine of October 1915 records Clement, who was serving as a Second Lieutenant in the Hawke Battalion, as '*indirectly connected to Pirton*'. Michael Newbery suggests that Clement was related to the Rev. Erskine William Langmore's housekeeper, Miss Brereton.

Although the Hawke Battalion was part of a Royal Naval Division, at the start of the war there were too many naval reservists for the ships available, so they were formed into land fighting divisions. It is likely that Clement fought in some of the battles on the Western Front.

BROOKS, FREDERICK WILLIAM

Frederick married Annie Priscilla Carter of Pirton on December 27th 1915, the same day as Jack Lawrence (another soldier) married Violet Abbiss. The North Herts Mail of January 6th explained that Frederick was from Cole Green, Hertingfordbury. His best man was his brother, William Brooks, who was already serving. Annie's brother, Walter Edward Carter, also served and survived and attended the wedding wearing his 'hospital blue' uniform, so he had already been wounded.

The Parish Magazine of June 1917 records Frederick as serving in the Buffs (Royal East Kent or Royal West Surrey Regiment). In fact, he originally enlisted in the 3rd Bedfords in Hitchin on February 26th 1916. His service record shows that he was thirty years old, working as a motor car builder and living in the Carter family home, Burge End House (now known as Burge End Farm House). He was not mobilised until April 21st 1917, by which time Annie was pregnant. He went for training and on September 10th 1917 his son, Charles Frederick William was born. Charles was the name of Annie's father; he had been the village policeman and then the school attendance officer. He died in May 1914.

At one point Frederick was Private G/22237, 3rd Battalion, 'The Buffs' and then became Private M/324284, 1023rd Mechanical Transport, Army Service Corps , probably in a posting on November 14th 1917. He passed his Army driving test a month later and served 'at home' until January 6th 1918, when he boarded a ship and headed to Mesopotamia, arriving on February 21st. He was there until April and then he moved on to India and served there until September 1919. In June 1919, he caught Spanish Flu in the pandemic, which started in 1918, and was in the 34th Gent Hospital in Deolali, between June 27th and August 14th 1919. Even without knowing how close he came to action, he may well have been in his greatest danger during this period. The 1918 flu pandemic spread right across the world; estimates of the number of deaths vary considerably, some as low as twenty to forty million and others between fifty and one hundred million - many more than were killed in the war. After recovering, he headed home, arriving in England on September 27th and was demobilised on November 16th 1919.

BUCK, ARTHUR

The Parish Magazine of October 1915 records Arthur, who was serving in the 5th East Surrey Regiment, as '*indirectly connected to Pirton*'. Unfortunately parish and census records provide no further information.

BUCKETT, ALBERT WILLIAM, (TOBY)

The Hertfordshire Express of May 19th 1917 reports that Albert was also known as 'Toby' and that he was with the Canadians. He was the grandson of Mrs D Buckett (probably Dinah), who lived on Great Green. No photograph has been found of Toby, but his attestation papers reveal that he was 5' 7 3/4", had brown eyes and dark brown hair.

Unfortunately there is the possibility of some confusion over Albert's parents. The 1891 census records indicate that he was the son of George and Dinah Buckett and that his siblings were Harry, Alice, Ellen and Frederick. However, the 1901 census suggest that he was in fact their grandson. The latter is confirmed by a newspaper cutting and other parish and census records, so it would indicate that Albert was the man baptised on August 4th 1889 and the son of Mary, who was the daughter of George and Dinah Buckett. The latter is also confirmed in the 1901 census, which records that he was living with Dinah and aged eleven. He would have been about twenty-five at the outbreak of war.

Edna Lake, from Canada, informs us that five Pirton men, including Toby, emigrated to Canada together in 1912. The others were Tom Abbiss, Edward Lake, Charlie Stapleton and one of the Walkers, possibly Arthur Robert Walker. However, there is conflicting information for the emigration dates, including from the North Herts Mail, which suggests 1909 or 1910 for Toby. He then lived in New Westminster. Toby, Tom, Edward, and Arthur all joined the Canadian Expeditionary Force returning to Europe to fight – their allegiance to Great Britain still being strong.

In November 1916, he was given leave and returned to Pirton *'His many friends found a hearty welcome for him and were pleased to see him looking so well.'* Then on May 19th 1917, the Hertfordshire Express informs us that, before the war, Toby had worked for *'Messers. Lucas, of the brewery, Hitchin'*, confirms his emigration to Canada in about 1912, that he was married and that he had been wounded by a shell splinter to the face, and as result was back in England. The Parish Magazine of June 1917 records him as serving in the 47th Battery and wounded.

His attestation papers record him as born May 5th 1889, a labourer and married. He was in the 104th Regiment of the Active Militia. The oath was taken in New Westminster on February 28th 1916, when he would have been twenty-six.

BUCKETT, ARTHUR FREDERICK

Arthur appears on the School War Memorial, confirming that he attended the school. Parish records suggest only one man of this name who could have served, and he was born on November 10th 1897 to Charles and Laura Emily Buckett of 109 Moray Road, Finsbury Park. In the 1901 census, Arthur is listed in the household of his grandfather, William Titmuss. So he was living there and attending Pirton School. There was a similar arrangement recorded in the 1911 census, but he had now been joined by his brother Leonard Charles. His mother Emily, more probably Laura Emily, was the daughter of William and was born in Pirton. Their mother died on May 13th 1910, when Arthur would have been just twelve years old.

Arthur would have been seventeen at the outbreak of war, and it seems likely that his brother Leonard also served and survived the war.

BUCKETT, BERTRAM

Bertram appears on the School War Memorial, confirming that he attended the school. The 1911 census adds some information: he was the grandson of Frederick and Eliza Buckett and he and two siblings Lizzie and George appear to be living with them. All three were born in Finsbury Park, London, George (b c1894), Lizzie (b c1893) and Bertram (b c1900). Bertram would have been about fourteen at the outbreak of war, so he is unlikely to have served until the very late stages. It appears that his brother George also served and survived.

BUCKETT, 'DICK'

The North Herts Mail of February 15th 1917 reported that 'Dick' Buckett of Pirton was in France. Parish and census records have so far failed to provide any further corroboration for this man, but he seems to have been a compassionate man. He had found a photograph on the battle field and returned it to the man's mother. She wrote the following letter, which had been passed to the paper;

'52 Garmoyle Road
Sefton Park, Liverpool

'Dear Private Buckett, I feel I would like to write a few lines to thank you for a photograph which was found on the battlefield by you on the 4th July, and recognised as belonging to me.

It is a photograph of my dear son of the (Liverpool Scottish) who was killed in that terrible charge at Hooge, June 16, 1915, and was in the pocket of his friend J F Arrowsmith (Liverpool Pals) who was killed on the 1st July. The photo of the little girl, also found by you at the same time (which I have given into the hands of her parents), was his cousin. I am very grateful to you, though it came as a great shock when the Sunday paper of the beginning of November was shown to me.

This is a very terrible war, and I am one who has known the greatest sorrow that anyone was ever called upon to bear, I have lost two dear sons, within three months of each other, two of the best on earth. The eldest, twenty-three years of age, was in the City of London Yeomanry – killed at Gallipoli, on 23rd Sept 1915. The second whose photograph you found was twenty-one. Both were clever men, with fine prospects and careers before them. I have still another son (my only child left now) aged nineteen, who is exempt till January 31st and I am afraid he will have to go then. It is too dreadful, and will not bear thinking of. I intended writing you when I first received the photo, but have had such a breakdown in health through my awful sorrow and loss, that I have been unable to collect my thoughts. If this letter reaches you kindly reply and send your full regimental address. I would like to send you a parcel; also, I should like to know if you are a Liverpool man, or anything else about yourself you may care to tell me. Again thanking you and wishing you a safe return home, I am yours faithfully, Mrs F Rimmer.'

A later report dated April 4th 1917 shows him to also be a man of strong opinions and reports *'Private Dick Buckett, Bedfords says that tribunals are too easy in letting off men, declaring that a bomb ought to drop on some of the tribunals to teach them the seriousness of war.'*

BUCKETT, FREDERICK

Frederick appears on the School War Memorial, confirming that he attended the school. Parish records suggest only one man of this name who could have served, and he was baptised on December 25th 1884 and was the son of George and Dinah Buckett (née Mabbet). He would have been thirty at the outbreak of war. Baptism records list eight children: Mary (bapt 1869), Henry (bapt 1872), Alice (bapt 1875), Anne (bapt 1877), Ellen (bapt 1878), Frederick (bapt 1884), Rose (b 1886) and Charles (b 1890). Frederick would have been the uncle of Albert William Buckett, who also served and survived.

In 1911, Frederick was twenty-six and earning a living as a farm labourer, but still living with his mother near the Baptist Chapel on Great Green or Bury End.

He is recorded in the Parish Magazine of September 1915 as enlisting during 1914, but after July, and serving in a Mortar Battery. It would have been late in 1914 as the Hertfordshire Express of October 17th 1914 reports a Frederick Buckett as being involved in an *'infamous fracas'* in Pirton on October 3rd. The paper headlines this event as *'War Against Special Constables'* *1. Frederick was summoned for assaulting Bertram Walker (a special constable, who also served in the war), was found guilty and ordered to pay two pounds or go to prison for one month. The case against him for using foul language during the same incident was dismissed. Perhaps by joining up he avoided the prison sentence?

By 1918 he was recorded as Private 191555, 2nd Battalion, Bedfordshire Regiment with his home address as *'around Great Green'*.

*1 The full report is included in the reference section of this book.

BUCKETT, GEORGE

George appears on the School War Memorial, confirming that he attended the school. School records indicate that he was admitted in 1899 and that his father was Albert Buckett. The 1911 census adds that he was the grandson of Frederick and Eliza Buckett, and that he and two siblings, Lizzie and Bertram, were to be living with them. All three children: George (b c1894), Lizzie (b c1893) and Bertram (b c1900), were born in Finsbury Park, London. It appears that his brother Bertram also served and survived. Before the war George worked as a farm labourer.

He married Eva Rose Bunyan on September 23rd 1914 and they had a son, Francis George who was born in February 1915. On June 7th 1916, when George was twenty-two years old he went to Hitchin and enlisted in the Royal Engineers, Railway and Canal Troops. His service record shows that he was living near The Fox and working as a platelayer for the GNR (Great Northern Railway) at the time. He was mobilised in December 1916 and left for France as Sapper 218018, 119th Rly. Co. (Railway Company), Royal Engineers on January 18th 1917. He would have been working to maintain the railway lines to keep the troops and supplies moving. On March 25th 1917 he was admitted to hospital, although the reason is unclear. A copy of a death certificate held in George's records confirms that his son died from a 'convulsion' on March 23rd 1917, aged two - just two days before George was admitted to hospital. One wonders if he had been told and whether this was connected in some way. He rejoined his unit on April 1st only to be admitted again on the 24th for four days. Later that year on October 2nd he was back in hospital for the third time and remained in one hospital or another until November 28th. In 1918 between July 9th and 17th he was in hospital yet again. All these dates are recorded in the 'Date of Casualty' column of his records, but it is not clear whether these admissions were through illness, injury or being wounded.

He was awarded a good conduct badge in December 1918, dispatched to England late in October 1919 and was granted twenty-eight days furlough. So he must have been demobilised after that date.

BUCKETT, LEONARD CHARLES

Leonard appears on the School War Memorial, confirming that he attended the school. Parish records suggest only one man of this name who could have served, and he was born October 3rd 1899 to Charles and Laura Emily Buckett, then of 57 Clinton Road, West Green, South Tottenham. In the 1911 census, Leonard had joined his brother Arthur Frederick and was listed in the household of his grandfather, William Titmuss. So he was living there and attending Pirton School. His mother Emily, more probably Laura Emily, was the daughter of William and was born in Pirton. Their mother died on May 13th 1910, when he would have been just nine years old.

Leonard was very young at the start of the war, so it is likely that he only served in the later stages. His brother Arthur also served and survived the war.

BUNYAN, EDWARD

Edward appears on the School War Memorial, confirming that he attended the school, but unfortunately parish and census records provide no further information, other than to confirm that the surname was present in Pirton at the time.

School entrants' records show that a Teddy Bunyan, born in 1893 and the son of Susan Bunyan, was registered in 1893. However other records would suggest that this would be Hedley Bunyan and, therefore, contradicts the name appearing on the School War Memorial.

BUNYAN, GEORGE

The name of George Bunyan appears in the Hertfordshire Express of July 11th 1914, which reports him as a member of the organising committee for the Pirton Transept Fête.

George appears on the School War Memorial, confirming that he attended the school. Parish records suggest only one man of this name who could have served, and he was born August 12th 1888 to Alfred and Ann Bunyan (née Pitts). The number of children they had is confusing as the 1911 census records that there were seven, who all survived, but from various census records there appears to be eight, George and Albert (b 1888 - twins), Alice (b 1892), Eva Rose (b 1896), Clara (b 1898), Lilian (b 1900), Arthur Charles (b c1905) and Gladys Anne (b c1909).

Baptism records indicate another four, Alfred John (bapt 1883), Gertrude Kate (b 1886), Rosetta Kate (b 1891) and Frederick John (b 1894), but Gertrude's parents are recorded as Alfred and Amy, but as no corresponding records were found corroborating this, it was assumed that Amy should have read as Ann. However, it is possible that there was another couple, Alfred and Amy, in Pirton at the same time and if so there is a possibility that some records have become confused.

School entrants' records suggest that he was probably born in Palmer's Row (the row of cottages opposite the pond, built by Sam Allen, but later, after being bought by Mr Palmer, known as Palmer's Row).

The Parish Magazine of February 1917 records George as being 'called up' and in June 1917 as serving in the Royal Naval Air Service. He would have been twenty-eight and was married. He had married Alice Louisa Smith on November 14th 1908 and they had at least one child, a fact revealed by their headstone in St. Mary's churchyard, which records George as a father. George and Alice are both buried in the churchyard, so it is likely that they lived in Pirton for the rest of their lives. George died on April 6th 1956, aged sixty-seven and Alice on July 4th 1961, aged seventy-one.

BURTON, ALFRED FRANK

Alfred appears on the School War Memorial, confirming that he attended the school. He is recorded in the Parish Magazine of September 1915 as enlisting during 1914 and serving in the 1st Hertfordshire Regiment.

A search of the parish and census records is not conclusive; only one Alfred Frank Burton is found and he was born in 1900, which would appear to make him too young to have enlisted during 1914. Although it was not unknown for boys of fourteen to enlist, it would be very unusual and illegal.

Alfred married Emily and both are recorded in St. Mary's Church Garden of Rest. Arthur died in 1966 and Emily in 1985.

BURTON, BERT

Bert is recorded in the Parish Magazine of November 1918 as serving in the US Army. Parish and census records suggest three possible men:

The first, Herbert David was born on August 13th 1881 to Goliath and Mary Ann Burton (née Halfpenny), and so he would have been thirty-two at the outbreak of war.

Baptism records reveal nine children: Frederick (bapt 1864), Martha Elizabeth (bapt 1867), Joseph (bapt 1869), Rose (bapt 1872), Ellen (bapt 1874), John (bapt 1875), Charles (bapt 1879), Herbert David (b 1881) and Lilian Mary (bapt 1884). Mary died in 1902 and subsequently Goliath married again, this time to a Charlotte Weeden.

This Herbert married Isabella Jane Titmuss in 1907. In 1911 he was twenty-nine, recorded as a farmer, his wife's name confirmed as Jane and they now had two children: Jack (b c1908) and Frederick (b c1900).

The second Herbert William was born on June 22nd 1891 to William and Jane Burton (née Walker) and so he would have been twenty-three at the outbreak of war.

Baptism and census records for this man also reveal nine children: Peggy (bapt 1878), John (b 1880), James (b 1883), Charles (b 1886), Anne (b 1888), Herbert William (b 1891), Nellie (b c1894), Albert Edward (b 1897) and Emily May (b 1900). A John Burton also served, possibly this man's brother.

The third possible man is Bertram Charles Burton, son of Alfred and Selina Burton and baptised in April 5th 1885. He died on January 5th 1972, aged eighty-seven and was married to Mabel Burton who died on December 27th 1966, aged eighty-seven. If this is the same man, then perhaps he left America after the war and returned to settle in Pirton?

Unfortunately, at this time, it is not known which, if any of these men, is the man that served.

BURTON, FRANK

The Parish Magazine of September 1918 records Frank as being *'called to service'*. Parish and census records suggest the following possible men:

The first was baptised on March 2nd 1873, and was the son of George and Emma Burton. He would have been about forty at the outbreak of war. This Frank married Esther Kate and they are buried in St. Mary's churchyard. Frank died in 1950 aged seventy-seven and Esther in 1958 aged sixty-nine.

The second was baptised May 16th 1875 and was the son of Amos and Sarah Burton and so he would have been about thirty-eight at the outbreak of war. By 1911, he had left his parents' home and does not appear elsewhere in the Pirton census. The census also confirms that Amos and Sarah had eleven children, of whom seven had died, so this Frank had three living siblings.

Unfortunately, at this time, it is not known which, if either, is the Frank Burton who served, but unless the older man had previous military experience and if the enlistment rules were applied, then it is only the younger man who could have served.

BURTON, JOHN

John appears on the School War Memorial, confirming that he attended the school. The Parish Magazine of June 1917 records John as serving in the Royal Flying Corps (RFC). Parish and census records suggest the following possible men:

The first was baptised December 25th 1875, and was the son of Goliath and Mary Ann Burton (née Halfpenny). He would have been about thirty-eight at the outbreak of war, perhaps a little old to be in the RFC. Baptism records reveal nine children: Frederick (bapt 1864), Martha Elizabeth (bapt 1867), Joseph (bapt 1869), Rose (bapt 1872), Ellen (bapt 1874), John (bapt 1875), Charles (bapt 1879), Herbert David (b 1881) and Lilian Mary (bapt 1884). Mary died in 1902 and subsequently Goliath married again this time to Charlotte Weeden. If this is the correct man then it is possible that his brother Herbert is the Bert Burton who served and also survived.

The second man was born on November 7th 1880 to William and Jane Burton (née Walker), and so he would have been about thirty-three at the outbreak of war.

Baptism and census records for this man also reveal nine children: Peggy (bapt 1878), John (b 1880), James (b 1883), Charles (b 1886), Anne (b 1888), Herbert William (b 1891), Ellen (called Nellie, b c1894), Albert Edward (b 1897) and Emily May (b 1900).

The 1901 census records his occupation as an apprentice engineer, perhaps an occupation which would mean that he is the most likely of the two to have served in the RFC.

By 1911, this man had married Clara Titmuss and they were living with her parents, Frank and Elizabeth, near, or possibly in, the Blacksmith's Arms, which was in the High Street, opposite the Blacksmith's pond. John was recorded as a general engineer.

It is not certain which is the John Burton who served, but by 1918, he was recorded as A.M. (Air Mechanic) 53425, 1st A.R.S. (Advanced Regulating Station), S.A.R.D. (Southern Aircraft Repair Depot), Royal Air Force and his home was in Little Green. The latter man, with his engineering background, would seem most likely to be serving in the Royal Air Force.

An active airfield like the one John Burton would have been stationed at.

BURTON, SIDNEY CHARLES, (POSSIBLY SIDNEY JAMES)

Parish and census records suggest that there were two Sidney Burtons; Sidney Charles (census records) and Sidney James (baptism records). However, despite the difference in middle names, they are both recorded as the son of David and Rose Fanny Burton (née Walker)*1 and the same age. So they must be one and the same person. The listings of Sidney Charles outnumber the listings of Sidney James (and Sydney), so the former is likely to be correct and is therefore used here.

Sidney appears on the School War Memorial, confirming that he attended the school and was born on October 25th 1883, so he would have been thirty at the outbreak of war. When he was born, his parents were running The Red

Lion PH in Crabtree Lane, near the entrance to the church. Later the family moved to Great Green, where they had a smallholding. The 1901 census records Sidney as seventeen and a stable helper groom, presumably on his father's smallholding. He had three siblings, Fred (b 1888), Thomas (b 1886) and Beatrice Ruth (b 1881). By 1911, he had left the family home and does not appear in the Pirton census.

His father died on February 28th 1916, aged fifty-eight, followed by his brother, Serjeant Fred Burton of the 2/4th Royal Berkshire Regiment, who is recorded on the Village War Memorial, and was killed in France on December 2nd 1917. To complete a sad triple tragedy, their mother died on December 22nd 1917. This was only a few days after learning of her son Fred's death. She was only fifty-eight and perhaps she was another, indirect, victim of the war.

The Hertfordshire Express of December 22nd 1917 reports Sidney as 'in hospital in Bristol with a broken ankle sustained at the Front through falling down a disused trench.' The Parish Magazine of November 1918 records Sidney as being a casualty, suffering from a 'trench accident to the foot'. The difference in dates suggests a second accident.

*1 Recorded as Rose Mary on Sidney's baptism record, but Rose Fanny in the 1901 census and on the family headstone in St. Mary's churchyard.

CARTER, ALFRED

A search of the parish and census records does not identify any obvious men. However, a report about William Edward Carter (another survivor) in the North Herts Mail reveals that Alfred was his brother, and also identifies another brother, Charles. This enabled their parents to be identified as Charles and Eliza Carter. Charles (senior) had been the village policeman and then the school attendance officer. Baptism and census records confirm that they had thirteen children, but by 1911 three had died. Baptism, school and census records only reveal eleven names, Elizabeth A (b c1871), Henry A (b c1872), George (b c1874), Alice E (b c1877, d 1897), Ellen L (b c1879), Ernest F (b c1880), Annie Priscilla (b c1883), Walter Edward (b c1885), Daisy (b c1886), Florence Rachel (b 1886) and Esther Kate (b 1888) and then Alfred and Charles (b c1869) were identified from the newspaper. Alfred, Charles, Ernest and Walter all served and survived.

The 1901 census shows that the family home was Burge End House, now known as Burge End Farmhouse. Alfred's father died on May 18th 1914 and his sister, Florence Rachel, married William Thomas Hill on September 16th 1914. William was later killed in the war and appears on the Village War Memorial. It is presumed that the family continued to live in the same house, as the Parish Magazine of January 1916 records that Frederick Brooks (another soldier) married Annie Priscilla Carter in 1915, and in 1918 his home address was given as Burge End House.

The Hertfordshire Express of November 11th 1914 lists Alfred as serving in the Royal Marine Light Infantry and in the Parish Magazine of September 1915 as enlisting during 1914, but after July, and serving in the Royal Marine Transport. The North Herts Mail of November 19th 1914 reported that he had been wounded on October 30th. That would have been twenty days after his brother Walter was wounded.

The North Herts Mail of February 4th 1915 confirms his Regiment and that he had been in Antwerp when a small contingent of the British Army had supported the Belgian Army in the defence of that key city. Antwerp fell, but Alfred had managed to get away with some of the Belgian Army. He had been back to Pirton, probably recovering from his wound, but at the time of the report was back with his Company.

CARTER, CHARLES WILLIAM

Charles William Carter was a witness to the marriage of George Alfred Flack of Camberwell to Elizabeth Ann Carter of Pirton in 1895 and this could be the same man who served.

The Charles Carter who served appears on the School War Memorial, confirming that he attended the school. A search of the parish and census records does not identify any obvious man. However, a report about William Edward Carter (another survivor) in the North Herts Mail reveals that Walter Edward was his brother and also identifies another brother, Alfred. This enabled their parents to be identified as Charles and Eliza Carter. Charles (senior) had been the village policeman and then the school attendance officer. In all it would appear that four brothers served and survived - refer to Alfred Carter for more family details.

By 1897 Charles had married Eliza Bailey - Eliza was also his mother's name.

His father died on May 18th 1914 and his sister, Florence Rachel, married William Thomas Hill on September 16th 1914. William was later killed in the war and appears on the Village War Memorial.

The North Herts Mail of February 4th 1915 confirmed that Charles (junior) had previously completed twenty-one years service in the 3rd Dragoon Guards and had reached the rank of Serjeant Major, before retiring with a pension - this would have been before the war. When war came, he and his wife were living in Kent at 11 Rock Road, Borough Green. Charles was then forty-four and working as a farrier. Like many 'old soldiers', he felt the urge to do his bit for King and Country, so on October 12th 1914, then aged forty-five, he went to Maidstone and enlisted for home service.

He was posted to Canterbury as a Private 11148 and then, presumably because of his previous service and rank, was promoted almost immediately to Staff Serjeant Farrier in the Corps of Dragoons, Special Reserve. Quite how fit for service he was is unclear, because he was discharged from service on July 16th 1915, less than a year later *'His services no longer required'* and rather unkindly, especially for an old soldier, they add the note, *'This NCO re-enlisted as a Staff Serjeant Farrier, and is quite incapable of carrying out the duties of his rank, and is useless in any other capacity.'*

CARTER, ERNEST F

Ernest appears on the School War Memorial, confirming that he attended the school. He is recorded twice: in the Parish Magazine of September 1914 as being in the Army Reserve, and then in the Parish Magazine of 1915, as enlisting during September 1915 before August and serving in the 3rd Grenadier Guards.

Parish and census records suggest two:

The first man was born on May 5th 1900 to George and Kate Ethel Carter and so he would have been fourteen at the outbreak of war, and only fifteen at the date of enlistment. He is therefore unlikely to be the right man. Baptism records list two children: Ernest (b 1900) and Arthur George (b 1898).

The second was the son of Charles and Eliza Carter. Charles had been the village policeman and then the School Attendance Officer. Ernest was born circa 1880, and so he would have been about thirty-four at the outbreak of war. He was born in Datchworth, Hertfordshire and census records show that he is the elder brother of a Walter Carter who also served and survived. This is likely to be the correct man. In all it would appear that four brothers served and survived - refer to Alfred Carter for more family details.

CARTER, WALTER EDWARD

Walter appears on the School War Memorial, confirming that he attended the school. Parish records suggest only one man of this name who could have served, and he was born circa 1885 to Charles and Eliza Carter. Charles had been the village policeman and then the School Attendance Officer. Walter was born in Datchworth, Hertfordshire and would have been about twenty-nine at the outbreak of war. In all it would appear that four brothers served and survived - refer to Alfred Carter for more family details.

Walter was found in several reports; in the Parish Magazine of September 1914 and recorded as being in the Army Reserve; in the Hertfordshire Express of November 11th 1914 and serving in the Royal Horse Guards (this entry also reports him as wounded on the October 30th) and in the Parish Magazine of September 1915 as enlisting during 1914, but after July, and in the North Herts Mail of February 4th 1915. The latter provides most of the following information.

He had been a policeman, but had been invalided out eleven years earlier - he would have only been about nineteen so perhaps the paper has confused this fact with Walter's father who had been the village policeman. When war broke out he was working as a clerk at Lacre in Letchworth and immediately volunteered for service, becoming Trooper W E Carter 1647, Royal Horse Guards. The report suggests that he had served with them before. The Regiment went to Belgium in September and the details were reported as *'being among the last contingent that were able to land at Zeebrugge, which place was shortly afterwards knocked to pieces by the Germans, who overran that district. Needless to say it was hot work, for they were in the thick of the artillery fire, the Guards covering the retreat of the Belgians from Antwerp. After that the Guards went to Ypres district, and held the line for the British to advance again after the memorable retreat from Mons. Thus, this crack regiment of the Household cavalry was among the units that helped to bring about the turning point of the battle, namely the advance from near Paris. When his contingent of the Guards, the second to go out, arrived, the Uhlans were scattered all over the North of Belgium, and it was their job to chase them and lay them by the heels. We know how gallantly the Guards did this. Afterwards the Guards had to go in the trenches – probably the first time in history that English cavalry have had to do this. It was a noble part they played, because at that time England was rather short of infantry at the Front.*

It continues and explains the wound he received on October 30th 1914 *'They had been relieved from the trenches that morning, and his squadron were with the first line of baggage columns behind the firing line. The Germans were shelling the transport, and some men of the 11th Hussars got knocked over. He had gone to the assistance of a wounded Hussar when he was laid out by a portion of bursting shrapnel which went between the two bones of his right leg, near the shin. So severe was the artillery fire that he had to lay nearly seven hours before the ambulance could attend to him. The following morning the Germans began to shell the hospital at Ypres, and the whole of the patients had to be moved to a convent, including himself. The day after he and other wounded left for Boulogne the railway line was being shelled by the Germans. He was in hospital at Boulogne till November 9th, when he was brought to England, having since been in hospital (Northern) at Leeds.'* By February 4th he had been home from hospital recovering for two or three weeks. He was making steady progress and hoped *'to be quite fit and well enough to have another smack at the Germans.'*

In December 1915 he was back in Pirton for his sister's wedding on the 27th, when Annie Priscilla Carter married Frederick William Brooks. Frederick also served and survived. Walter was wearing hospital blue so presumably he had been wounded again.

Walter Carter is mentioned in the Kelly trade directory of 1926 as a builder and carpenter, located in The Old Post Office, Little Green, so this seems to have been his work after the war.

CASTLE, ARTHUR

Arthur was not born in Pirton, but married Annie French (Brenda Dawson's mother) in 1915. It is thought that they lived in Pirton after marriage and before Arthur went to war. Annie was the sister of Joseph French, who was killed in the war and is recorded on the Village War Memorial. Arthur and Joseph joined up together. Arthur served in the Hertfordshire Regiment and was gassed, but recovered enough to continue serving. In 1919 he returned to Pirton and established himself as a 'Pirtonian'. In 1920, he started the Men's Social Club, acting as secretary until 1924, when he took over as the secretary of the Pirton Benefit Society, a post he held until 1943. In the pre-National Health Service days members paid into these 'Friendly' societies and received financial help in times of need. He was also involved in the Parish Council and Village Hall and, for his effort and personality, he was well thought of. He died in 1943, aged fifty-five. Perhaps the gassing during the war contributed to his early death.

Parish and census records provide no further information, but by 1918 he was recorded as Private 291080, 7th Suffolkshire Regiment, British Expeditionary Force and his home was 'around' Little Green.

CHAMBERLAIN, THOMAS

Thomas appears on the School War Memorial, confirming that he attended the school. Parish and census records suggest only one possible man and in the 1891 census he is recorded as eleven and illegitimate. The census also reveals that he was living near Little Green with Ann Chamberlain, his mother, and Arthur Titmuss whom she had married in 1879. It also records three half-siblings, Lydia (b 1880), Charles (b 1883) and Albert Hezekiah (bapt 1885). He would have been about thirty-four at the outbreak of war.

CHAMBERLAIN, WILLIAM

William appears on the School War Memorial, confirming that he attended the school. From the information supplied by Tracey Chamberlain, William must have been her Great-Grandfather. If this is the case, William was born on December 21st 1888 to Charles and Martha Chamberlain (née Martin), who lived in one of the Holwell Cottages (second from the village end). These are the twelve terraced cottages in Holwell Road also known as the 'Twelve Apostles'. He would have been twenty-five at the outbreak of war. Baptism and census records reveal six children: Bertram Frank (b c1878), Jane (b 1880), Anne (b 1882), Emily (bapt 1885), William (b 1888) and Ellen Rebecca (b 1891).

By 1911, he was twenty-two, earning his living as a farm labourer and had been married for a year to Annie. They had a son, Phillip Edwin (b 1910), and were living near the Blacksmith's Arms, which was in the High Street opposite the Blacksmith's pond. They had two more sons, Alfred (b 1912) and Jack. Alfred was the father of Frederick William Walter Chamberlain, Tracey's father, who was perhaps, at least in part, named after William.

So, William was married and had children before he went to war. His family believe that he served in the artillery and that he was gassed. He died on October 8th 1924, aged thirty-eight, and is buried in St. Mary's churchyard with Charles and Martha. It is believed by the family that his early death was at least part due to the mustard gas poisoning he suffered during the war.

CHERRY, OSCAR CHARLES

Oscar appears on the School War Memorial, confirming that he attended the school.

Grace Tomlin (née Cherry) informs us that his parents were William Henry Cherry (sometimes recorded as Henry William Cherry) and Susannah (née Thrussell or possibly Trussell). He was born August 17th 1888, and so he would have been twenty-six at the outbreak of the war. Baptism and census records and Grace's family tree reveal eight children: Ann Maria (bapt 1873), Harry (bapt 1875), Ellen (bapt 1878), Gertrude (b 1879), Emily (b 1882), Agatha Grace (b 1883), Tobias (b 1885) and Oscar Charles (b 1888), but the 1911 census reveals that William and Susannah had a total of twelve children of whom five had died. At that date, they were living at 10 Holwell Road.

Family records show that Oscar was confirmed in Pirton Church on March 20th 1903 by the Bishop of Colchester, presumably along with many others. His brother Tobias emigrated to Canada in April of that year and returned in December 1906. The reason for

Oscar (left), Emily and Tobias, just before their emigration.

his return is not known, but other records suggest he then went back to Canada in June of 1907. He must have sent back good reports of life there because Oscar then followed. He left Pirton on March 22nd 1911, sailing on the S.S Corsican, and landed at St. John's on April 3rd. From there, he travelled to Calcarry arriving on April 7th. Canada was a popular destination for the young men and women of Pirton that year, for family documents record that Oscar's sister, Emily, also emigrated along with at least one other woman (Kate Trussell) and six other Pirton men.

Surprisingly, travelling to and from Canada seems not to be as uncommon as might be expected, for Oscar returned in 1913, landing on November 30th - strange timing as his brother Tobias got married on November 22nd. Perhaps he was delayed at sea. He may have returned for good as, on July 5th 1915, in Holwell, he married a girl called Bertha Jane (surname unknown), perhaps a marriage before going to war. It is not clear where they lived, probably Holwell, but certainly by 1921 they were living in Holwell and had a son Kenneth Charles in December of that year.

CHRISTMAS, WALTER FOSTER

David Doorne, who researches the Bedford Yeomanry, informed us that Walter served with them. It was for a short period and he did not serve abroad, as he was discharged as medically unfit on November 2nd 1914.

The Kelly Trade Directories list him in 1926, 1929, 1935 and 1937, initially as a builder and carpenter and then adding portable building manufacturer before, in the last two entries, reverting to carpenter. In all listings he was living in the Old Post Office, Little Green.

Walter married Helena Jane Trussell, a fact confirmed, along with the date of her death on May 5th 1923, aged forty-one, by a monumental inscription in the churchyard. The marriage was certainly after 1911, but probably before the war.

An interesting article on glove-making in Pirton, first produced in the Pirton Magazine in June 1996, which can be read on the village website (www.pirton.org.uk) adds some information. Helena is believed to have been commonly known as Nellie, and seems to have started a glove-making business before the war. The war meant that the demand for gloves accelerated, and the business moved to bigger premises in December 1915. It is not clear whether it remained in her ownership, but she certainly remained in charge, and then later, when she died, Walter took over.

COOPER, ARTHUR

Arthur appears on the School War Memorial, confirming that he attended the school.

Parish and census records suggest three possible men:

The first was baptised on April 13th 1873 and was the son of James and Ann Cooper (née Shepherd). He would have been about forty-one at the outbreak of war. They had five children: Arthur (b 1873), John (bapt 1875), Harry (b c1878), Jane (b 1880) and Charles (b 1881).

The second, Arthur William, was born on July 25th 1881 to William and Mary Cooper (née Odell) and he would have been thirty-three at the outbreak of war. They had nine children: Clara (b c1866), Emma (b c1870), Mary Ann (bapt 1872), Charles (bapt 1875), Martha (bapt 1878), Arthur William (b 1881), Harry (b 1884), Ethel (b 1886) and Alice (b c1888). The North Herts Mail of November 19th 1914 reported that a Charles Cooper, likely to be Arthur's brother, had offered himself as a recruit, but at thirty-nine was just one year too old to be accepted as a volunteer.

Arthur William Cooper married Rose Weeden of Pirton on October 5th 1901. By 1911, Arthur was a horse keeper on a local farm and they had two children: Violet May (b c1905) Hilda Rose (b c1906), but sadly two other children had died.

This Arthur died in 1967, aged eighty-six, and is buried in St. Mary's churchyard.

The third man, Arthur Charles, was born on May 31st 1898 to Charles and Ruth Cooper (née Baines), and so he would have been sixteen at the outbreak of war. Baptism and census records, including 1911, identify eight children,

The Royal Norfolk Regiment cap badge.

one of whom had died. It is not entirely clear if Frederick Baines, a son to Ruth before her marriage, is included in the count, but is seems probable. The children who have been identified are Frederick (Baines, b c1895) and those born after their marriage, Arthur Charles (b 1898), Dorothy May (b 1900), Ernest (b c1903), George (b c1905), Annie (b c1906) and Frank (b 1910). Frederick was killed in the war and appears on the village memorial.

The North Herts Mail of November 19th 1914 reported that Charles Cooper, who would have been this man's father, and the brother of Arthur William listed above, had offered himself as a recruit, but at thirty-nine was just one year too old to be accepted as a volunteer.

Unfortunately, at this time, it is not known which is the Arthur Cooper who served. The man who did serve is recorded twice, once in the Parish Magazine of September 1918 as being 'called to service', and then in the Parish Magazine of November 1918 as 'enlisting recently' and serving in the 4th Norfolk Regiment. As he was called up late in the war, it perhaps suggests he was the youngest of the three men, the third of those mentioned above, who would have then been twenty.

COX, SIDNEY, (MM)

Sidney is recorded in two undated cuttings in the village scrapbook of the war. Nothing in the cuttings actually records a connection with Pirton. However, with the exception of some general newspaper cuttings about the local regiments, the scrapbook seems to only record information about Pirton-related men. For this reason, and because this appears to be supported by the following baptism record, which does relate to Pirton, he is included.

Baptism records show a Sidney William Cox, the son of William and Ruth Cox of Hitchin, was baptised in Pirton on May 13th 1894. So he would have been about twenty at the outbreak of war. 1901 census records for Hitchin show that he was actually born in Hitchin - he was probably baptised in Pirton because of his family's association with the village. The same census shows that his father, William, was also born in Hitchin, but that his mother, Ruth, was born in Pirton. Pirton records show that William was also baptised in Pirton and his parents, Sidney's grandparents, were William and Sarah Cox (née Males) both born in Pirton.

William and Ruth Cox had four children: Sidney William (b c1894), Lilian (b c1896), Frederick (b c1898) and Arthur (b c1900). It is almost certain that it is his brother, Frederick, who also served. He was killed and is recorded on the Letchworth War Memorial.

The assumptions about Sidney are supported by other information; one of the cuttings from the village scrapbook reports that Sidney enlisted in August 1914, so he was one of the first to do so, and served in the Bedfordshire Regiment. At the time of the report, he had been out at the Front for 'one year and eight months' and 'is twenty-two years of age'. This would seem to tie in with the baptism record above and so it is certainly possible that he is the right man and has a Pirton connection. The cuttings also confirm him as a native of Hitchin (confirmed by the baptism records above) and that he had been living with his grandmother at 47 Green Lane, Letchworth.

Sidney had been in the thick of the fighting and had been wounded. As a result, he was hospitalized in Felixstowe. He was a hero. During the war both sides often attempted to tunnel under their enemies' lines, packed the end with explosives and attempted to blow up the front line of the opposite side. This was usually followed by soldiers rushing forward to take the position before the confusion had died down and reinforcements could be deployed. Sidney and his comrades suffered such an attack, probably many of his comrades were killed and certainly many were buried alive. Sidney was responsible for digging out, unaided, seventeen men, saving the lives of fourteen of them. For this 'conspicuous act of bravery and life-saving' he was awarded the Military Medal. The cutting records that 'Letchworth is proud of this hero' and so are we.

Note: Four men with a Pirton connection were to be awarded a medal. Military Medals were awarded to Sidney Cox (baptised in Pirton), Lieutenant Arthur Robert Walker (born in Pirton, but who had been living in Canada before the war) and Charles Furr (born in Pirton) and a Distinguished Conduct Medal to Henry George Chamberlain (born in Pirton and who was killed in the war).

COXALL, CHARLES FREDERICK

The Parish Magazine of October 1915 records Charles, who was serving in the Royal Horse Artillery, as 'indirectly connected to Pirton'. Parish records suggest only one man of this name who could have served, and he was born February 5th 1898, the son of Frederick William and Grace Coxall, and so he would have been sixteen at the outbreak of war. If this is the right man then he had an elder sister Margery Jane (b 1893); however the reference of 'indirectly connected to Pirton' means that perhaps this is a false trail.

CRAWLEY, FRANK

Frank appears on the School War Memorial, confirming that he attended the school. Parish records suggest only one man of this name who could have served, and he was born on September 5th 1896 to Henry Charles (Charlie) and Minnie Crawley (née Cherry) of Middle Farm, Crabtree Lane (roughly where 16 Crabtree Lane is today). The 1911 census confirms that they had ten children, one of whom had died. The children were: Harry (b 1881 or 1882), Annie Jane (bapt 1885), Albert Vincent (b 1886), Florence Rose (b 1888), Alice (b 1891), Helen (possibly Ellen, b c1893), Milly (b 1892 or 1893), Katie (b 1895), Frank (b 1896) and Phillip (b 1902). Which child died is not yet known. The youngest, Phil, was baptised at St. Mary's in 1902. Harry, Frank's older brother, was killed in the war and is listed on the Village War Memorial.

Before the war, he worked for Mr Franklin of Walnut Tree Farm. Frank's father died in 1915, aged fifty-six, just a few months before Frank joined up. He joined the 10th Bedfordshire Regiment on June 16th 1916 and would have been nineteen. Three months later he was drafted to France. Sometime in 1917, probably September, he was wounded, gassed and returned to England. Later, he was transferred to the South Staffordshire Regiment and was wounded again in late 1917, badly enough to be returned to a hospital in Rochdale. However, by November 17th he had recovered sufficiently to be able to return home on hospital leave.

DAVIS, HARRY

Harry Davis was born in Shillington and married Ellen Weeden from Pirton sometime around 1908. In 1911, he was a butcher and they were living in Pirton and the newly weds, Will and Mary Weeden, were lodging with them. By this time, Harry and Ellen had one child, Lily Margaretta (b 1909), although oddly she is not listed in the census.

Another child, Milner Lawrence, followed in 1912, so by the outbreak of war, Harry was married with at least two children.

The Hertfordshire Express of October 26th 1918 reports Harry as serving as a private in the Sherwood Foresters and having been in France for about six months. He had just suffered internal injuries which were sustained in action (on his birthday). They were serious enough for him to be hospitalised in Huddersfield. It also reports that, before the war, Harry was a grocer. In fact, he had worked for Palmers, a butchery business in Shillington. In the 1911 census, Harry is recorded as a butcher.

Harry Davis outside his shop.

After the war, he returned to Pirton and had another daughter, Vera Betty (b 1921). Sometime in the early 1920s, Harry and Ellen bought Peartree Cottage from Jim Throssell. This was situated to the right of the village pond, now 28 High Street. It had been a general store in which Ellen had worked. They worked hard and extended the business (and the property). The left side served as the grocers and the right as the butchers. This part of the business seems to have started in 1926 and was announced the Parish Magazine of 1927. The butchery took place in a large outbuilding, some of which remains today and still has the grooves in the concrete floor to channel the blood away and into the village pond. It appears that he and Ellen lived in Pirton for the rest of their lives; Harry died on February 28th 1951, aged sixty-seven, and Ellen on March 19th 1961, aged seventy-eight. Both are buried in St. Mary's churchyard. Their son, Milner, continued to run the business after Harry's death until 1970.

DAVIS, HENRY

The Hertfordshire Express of November 17th 1917 reports Henry as joining up in the week before. Prior to the war, Henry was a pork butcher and grocer. No further corroboration of Henry has been found, and the mention of him being a pork butcher and grocer suggests that perhaps the paper had mistakenly recorded Harry Davis as Henry. So it is likely that this is a false trail and that 'Henry' is, in fact, the Harry Davis above.

DAWSON, ALBERT

Albert appears on the School War Memorial, confirming that he attended the school. Parish records suggest only one man of this name who could have served, and he was born on November 21st 1887 to Samuel and Lavinia Dawson (née Pitts). He would have been twenty-six at the outbreak of war. Baptism records list four children: Herbert Charles (b 1880), Emily (b 1881), George (b 1885) and Albert (b 1887), but the 1911 census records that they had six, of whom one had died. At that time, Albert was still living with his parents near the Blacksmith's Arms, which was in the High Street, opposite where the Blacksmith's pond remains to this day. He was twenty-three and like his father was working as an agricultural labourer on one of the local farms.

DAWSON, BERTIE

Bertie appears on the School War Memorial, confirming that he attended the school. He was the son of Edgar and Elizabeth Jane Dawson (née Reynolds), and in 1901 they lived in Ann Reynold's house (Elizabeth's mother), which was 2 Holly Cottages, Little Green - now in Hambridge Way.

Baptism and census records list seven children. However, the 1911 census notes that they had eight, of whom two had died. At this time only seven can be identified; they are Reginald (b 1889), Ethel Annie (b 1890), Emily Almond (b 1891), Charlie (b c1895), Bertie (b c1899), Kate (b 1901) and Harry (b c1905). Sadly Emily only survived for six weeks, so she was one of the two who died.

In 1911, Bertie was eighteen and recorded as the third son of the family, an apprentice to John Cain coachbuilder of Hitchin, and was still living with his mother in 2 Holly Cottages. His brother, Charlie, also served and survived. His other brother, Reginald, did not serve for the reasons given below.

The Parish Magazine of June 1917 records that Bertie had been '*called up*' to the Training Reserve since March 1916, but tragic family circumstances meant that he was not called to service immediately. In fact, the family was hit by two tragedies and other unfortunate circumstances. These are described below or under the section for Bertie's uncle, Harry, and they must have affected the direct and extended Dawson family, including two serving soldiers - Bertie's brother, Charlie, and their Uncle Harry.

On January 22nd 1917, at the age of seventeen years and eleven months, Bertie went to Hitchin to enlist. At that date, he was living with his parents and working as a motor body builder. Tragically, within a few days (January 31st), Bertie's father Edgar, who was fifty-four, died in an accident. He was leading a horse pulling a manure cart when the horse was startled. It bolted and at least one wheel ran over Edgar, crushing his ribs terribly. He must have died almost immediately.

The request for compensation by Elizabeth was reported in the Hertfordshire Express of April 14th 1917, which confirmed that they had six children, including one daughter working in the Pirton glove factory, another as a pupil teacher, a son in the army (Charles), and another as an apprentice coachbuilder (Bertie). Compensation of £13 19s 2d and an allowance of 12 shillings a week was recommended. It was because of Edgar's sad death that Elizabeth sought a postponement of Bertie's call up - *'for a few weeks so that her son could get a garden and some land into cultivation'*. It was agreed that Bertie should not be called before May 1st 1917.

Later that year, and now a widow, Elizabeth received a second blow; Reginald, another son, died. He did not serve in the forces, but worked in a TNT factory, which would have been a reserved occupation. While working there, on November 9th 1917, he died from illness, aged twenty-seven. Many men and women who worked in the explosives factories became ill, and many died from over exposure to TNT. Perhaps Reginald was one of them. He is buried in St. Mary's churchyard. Her sons who served as soldiers survived the war, but perhaps Reginald should also be recognised as giving his life for the war effort. This is the case in some other villages where such names appear on memorials.

The family headstone which includes Reginald Dawson.

Returning to Bertie, following his successful appeal, he was not called upon to commence his service until May 2nd 1917, when he was mobilised as Private A/205302 2nd Battalion, Kings Royal Rifles Corps and, after training, went to France in the early part of 1918. The Hertfordshire Express of April 13th 1918 reported that he had been seriously wounded by a gun shot to the chest and returned to a hospital in Birmingham. The date reported for the injury was March 21st. However, this seems to conflict with his service records, which give the date as April 3rd. He was given leave in May, presumably for further recuperation. Having already suffered the double tragedies described above, his mother must have been constantly in fear of the worst. Her concern was further justified when again, later in the year, after he had recuperated and returned to the Front, the Parish Magazine of November 1918 recorded him as then being wounded for a second time. This time he was shot in the left shoulder. Strangely, despite this being given as the reason for his discharge, he was not discharged until May 8th 1919. His mother had written from Thatched Cottage, Holwell, to query the dates that he was wounded for British Legion records, but by July 14th 1919 they had moved back to Pirton. Bertie was recorded as thirty percent disabled and awarded a pension with a further assessment after twelve months. He married Evelyn Ada Baines of Holwell on October 1st 1927.

DAWSON, CHARLIE

Note: Read Bertie Dawson (Charlie's brother) for more details of the family's tragedies relating to their father and their brother Reginald. Read Harry Dawson (1) (Charlie's uncle) for other difficult family circumstances.

Charlie appears on the School War Memorial, confirming that he attended the school. He was the son of Edgar and Elizabeth Jane Dawson (née Reynolds) and, in 1901, they lived in Ann Reynolds' house (Elizabeth's mother), which was 2 Holly Cottages, Little Green - now in Hambridge Way. In all it would appear that two brothers served and survived - refer to Bertie Dawson for more family details.

Charlie enlisted in 1916 and the Hertfordshire Express of April 13th 1918 reports him as convalescing in the Maples Hospital, Hitchin, having been wounded in the arms and leg during July 1917, while serving in the Royal Engineers in France.

By 1918 he was recorded as Sapper 524546, 237th Field Company, Royal Engineers with his home address as *'around'* Little Lane.

DAWSON, HARRY (1)

Note: Read Bertie Dawson (Harry's nephew) for details of the tragedies affecting the extended family of Harry.

The School War Memorial lists two Harry Dawsons who served and confirms that both attended the school and survived.

This Harry Dawson was born on October 6th 1879 to William and Emma Dawson, and so he would have been about thirty-four at the outbreak of war. Baptism records list nine children: Edgar (bapt 1863), Christopher (bapt 1864), Pamela (bapt 1867), Ralph (bapt 1869), Arthur (bapt 1871), Percy (bapt 1872), Minnie (bapt 1874), Reginald (bapt 1876) and Harry (b 1879). In the 1901 census, along with his brother Percy, he is listed as the farmer's son; presumably both were working on their father's farm.

The Parish Magazine of June 1917 records him being *'called up'* since March 2nd 1916 and serving in the Royal Inniskilling Fusiliers. This article also reports him as wounded.

More information for Harry was obtained from the family's unfortunate situation, which was reported in the local newspaper. Harry's father, William, died on June 24th 1912, leaving his wife, Emma (née Bottoms) as a widow. The Hertfordshire Express of July 7th and August 4th 1917 provide further information; Percy and Harry, two of the brothers, were executors of William's will. The article mentions that Harry was serving with the Royal Inniskilling Fusiliers in Salonika, confirming that he is the right man. The house was occupied by Harry's wife and five children and possibly his mother, but was mortgaged to Mr Franklin (Walnut Tree Farm). Apparently the interest had not been paid for thirty months and the property was falling into a state of poor repair. It is not clear whether Harry was in attendance; after all, he was serving King and Country, but he had been wounded recently so it is possible that he was on leave. Either way, it must have been a terrible worry for him knowing that his family was struggling financially. Mr Franklin must have been sympathetic because he stated that '*he did not wish to be hard on people and didn't want to action*', '*but payments had not been paid and he had to protect his interest*'. Bertie Dawson (probably the brother, rather than the nephew who served) offered to pay the year's interest and some of the arrears, and the outcome seems to have been reasonable with time being given to pay.

DAWSON, HARRY (2)

The School War Memorial lists two Harry Dawsons who served and confirms that both attended the school and survived.

One is definitely identified as the son of William and Emma Dawson (see above). Parish records suggest only one other man of this name who could have served, and he was born on June 20th 1880. His mother was Martha Dawson and he would have been thirty-four at the outbreak of war. Martha was the daughter of Charles Dawson and married George Handscombe on August 12th 1883, possibly his second wife.

DEAR, HORACE PERCY, (PERCY)

Little is known of Percy Dear; the source of the only information is an undated newspaper cutting from a village scrapbook. His only connection to Pirton may be that he married one of Lewis and Mary Reynolds' daughters. If that is correct, it would mean that he was the brother-in-law of the six Reynolds brothers who served; George, George's twin Harry, Walter and Albert (sadly both died and are listed on the Village War Memorial), William and Jacob. It is known that Percy was serving in the Hertfordshire Regiment. He was wounded in the right wrist on July 31st 1917, and was recorded following his injury as '*at Crowborough*' - probably the military hospital at Crowborough Camp, Sussex.

Parish and census records provide no further information, but by 1918 he was recorded as Private 269386, 5th Reserve Battalion, Bedfordshire Regiment, but attached to the 1st Hertfordshire Regiment. His home address was near Cromwell Terrace - the terraced houses where the village store is today.

DEVEREAUX, CHARLES JAMES

Charles James Devereaux appears on the School War Memorial, confirming that he attended the school. Parish and census records suggest only one man of this name who could have served. They identify a Charles **Joseph Devereux** (note the different spelling of Devereux and the different middle name). However, there are errors on the School War Memorial, so it is possible that this is another and that they are the same man. If so, then he was born June 27th 1900 and the son of Joseph, a grocer and cowman born in Shefford, and Jane Devereaux (née Chamberlain) born in Pirton, but lately of 91 Dunham Rd, Finsbury Park (in 1900). Charles would have only been fourteen at the outbreak of war, so if he is the right man, he is unlikely to have served until late in the war. Baptism and census records list five children: Charles James (b 1900), Annie (b c1903), Maisie (b c1907) and Constance (b c 1909) and Constance Mildred (b 1908). It is believed that another daughter, Cosa Megan was born on October after the 1911 census.

FRANKLIN, LAURENCE THOMAS

Laurence was the son of Thomas and Annie Catherine, born in Whitwell and Shenley respectively. Thomas moved to Pirton, taking on Walnut Tree Farm before the war and later Highdown farm.

The 1911 census lists two children: Laurence Thomas (b c 1894) and Kathleen Mary (b c 1898), both born in Whitwell. The census lists three others at the address, Thomas Hearle, a boarder, and Gladys Bales and Alice Barker, both servants.

Laurence is recorded in the Parish Magazine of July 1916 as enlisting since March 2nd 1916 and serving in the Army Veterinary Corps. The North Herts Mail of May 11th 1916 reported that he was stationed in Luton at that date. He was born in 1883

Laurence Thomas Franklin

or 1884 and was Dick Franklin's father. Dick died in 2008, but he confirmed that Laurence was called up in 1916, and that he only served for a short time because, as Laurence's father was ill, he had to return to run Walnut Tree Farm.

He was married to Clara Cassandra Franklin and they had two children: Dick and Joy (the benefactor of Pirton JoyCare). Laurence and Clara are buried in St. Mary's churchyard. Laurence died on April 26th 1975, aged eighty-one and Clara on June 26th 1980, aged ninety-one.

FRENCH, GEORGE

George appears on the School War Memorial, confirming that he attended the school. A search of the parish and census records suggests four possible men:

The first was born on September 24th 1882 to Eliza Sarah French. So if this is the right man he would have been thirty-one at the outbreak of war. Two years later, on May 24th 1884, Eliza married Charles Furr and it would seem that she was then commonly known as Sarah. A family tree provided by Bob Lawrence lists nine children: George (French, b 1882) and then his siblings or half-siblings named Furr; Charles (b 1884), Ethel (b 1886), Ellen Louisa (b 1888), Winifred (b 1898), Albert (b 1895), Frederick (b 1900), Zillah (b 1903) and Harry (b 1906).

If this is the George who served, then he and his brothers or half-brothers, Charles, Albert and Fred all served and, remarkably, all survived the war. Charles was awarded the Military Medal.

The second possibility is the George French, born on February 3rd 1897 to Thomas and Alice French. This George would have been seventeen at the outbreak of war.

A third possibility was born circa 1883 to Emma Fanny French. The 1901 census records them living with her mother Frances French. He would have been about thirty-three at the outbreak of war.

This George married Cordelia and they are buried in St. Mary's churchyard. George died in 1953, aged seventy and Cordelia in 1968, aged eighty-three.

There seemed to be a forth possibility; he was born around 1895 and was the son of William and Mary Ann Maria French (née Reynolds). So he would have been about nineteen at the outbreak of war, but it is likely that this George died in 1901, at the age of six.

Unfortunately, at this time, it is not known which of the first three is the man who served.

FURR, ALBERT

Albert appears on the School War Memorial, confirming that he attended the school. Parish records suggest only one man of this name who could have served, and he was born on March 15th 1895 to Charles and Eliza Sarah Furr (née French), who seems to have been commonly known as Sarah.

A family tree, provided by Bob Lawrence, lists nine children: George (with the surname French, b 1882) and then his siblings or half-siblings named Furr; Charles (b 1884), Ethel (b 1886), Ellen Louisa (b 1888), Albert (b 1895), Winifred (b 1898), Frederick (b 1900), Zillah (b 1903) and Harry (b 1906), but by 1911 one had died. George and his brothers or half-brothers, Charles, Albert and Fred, all served and, remarkably, all survived the war. Charles was awarded the Military Medal.

The Parish Magazine of September 1915 records him as enlisting during 1915, but before August. Albert would have been nineteen. It also records that he was serving in the Royal Navy on H.M.S. Lark – a fact repeated in the Parish Magazine of June 1917. H.M.S. Lark was a modern destroyer launched in 1913. She served with the 3rd Destroyer Flotilla upon completion and then transferred to escort duties after 1917. However, this may be an error, or he may have changed ships, because in 1916 the North Herts Mail of June 15th reported that, as an Able Seaman, he was serving on the H.M.S Balmoral (it is possible that this should read H.M.S Balmoral Castle or H.M. Paddle Minesweeper 'Balmoral Castle') and that he had taken part in a naval battle (possibly the Battle of Jutland). He *'took part in the recent naval battle in the North Sea and fortunately escaped injury. His boat was in the midst of the fighting, and he had the pleasure of seeing several shells from their guns hit the enemy vessels. His boat sustained some damage, but the men behaved splendidly, and were in their element when the danger was the greatest. He has been about four years in the Navy and this is not the first time he has been under fire. On previous occasions he has been wounded lightly twice. He agrees with the others that the Germans sustained heavy losses in the recent battle. He saw an enemy boat of the Kaiser class sink, and others were also in a sad plight towards the end of the action. He is a keen sailor and formerly was in the merchant service.'*

By 1918, he was recorded as S.D. (possibly Special Duties) 1118 Deck Hand, Royal Naval Reserve on H.M.S. Balmoral, with his home address as Dead Horse Lane (now Royal Oak Lane).

FURR, CHARLES, (MM)

Charles appears on the School War Memorial, confirming that he attended the school. Parish records suggest only one man of this name who could have served, and he was baptised on September 7th 1884, the son of Charles and Eliza Sarah Furr (née French), who seems to have commonly been known as Sarah. In all it would appear that four

Charles Furr Military Medal winner.

brothers or half-brothers served and survived - refer to George French and Albert Furr for more family details.

It seems that George and his brothers (or half-brothers), Charles, Albert and Fred, all served and, remarkably, all survived the war.

Charles is recorded in the Parish Magazine of September 1915 as enlisting sometime during 1914, but after July, and serving in the 2nd Bedfordshire Regiment. He would have been about thirty. He lived with his wife, Clara (née Males), and the three children they had before the war, in one of the Holwell Cottages, - they are the twelve terraced cottages in Holwell Road also known as the 'Twelve Apostles'. His wife's brother, Harry Males, also served and survived.

He had been a navvy, working in Letchworth, but, prior to enlisting, he was employed in the building of a new house in Hitchin for a Mr Lance Wright. He is first recorded in the Hertfordshire Express of January 8th 1917, when he wrote a sad letter, conveying news of the death of Charles Burton to his wife. Charles was also known as Edward Charles and is listed on the Village War Memorial. The letter was written after December 21st 1916, and the article reports Charles as being a stretcher-bearer. He was wounded several times, possibly while performing this work. He certainly went on to be decorated for doing it.

It is complicated to piece together the chronological order of events and the number of times he was wounded but, from a mixture of Parish Magazine and newspaper reports, the following is believed to be correct:

Charles went to France in June 1915 and was recorded as being in hospital in September 1915. He managed to get home on leave around November 16th 1916. On May 12th 1917, the Regiment's War Diary records a Brigade ceremonial parade in Buire-au-Bois, during which Charles, and others were awarded their medal ribbons by G.O.C. (General Officer Commanding) XIX Corps, Lt. General H.E.Watts, C.B., C.M.G. The London Gazette confirmed this on June 18th 1917: *'His Majesty the KING has been graciously pleased to award the Military Medal for bravery in the field to 19157 Private Charles Furr of the Bedfordshire Regiment.'* The newspapers were more specific *'courageous stretcher-bearing under shell fire'* - it was common for stretcher bearers to go into no man's land, unarmed to recover the wounded. He must have been a very brave man. By April 1918, he had been wounded for the second time (Parish Magazine report), this time in the hand which resulted in him being hospitalized to Stoke-on-Trent. The Hertfordshire Express confirmed this as occurring about March 20th. The Hertfordshire Express of September 28th 1918 reports Charles as being wounded again, for the third time. This time it was a severe bullet wound to the left shoulder and he went to Trouville Hospital in France.

Charles Furr photographed on a pub outing from The Red Lion in the early 1930s.

By 1918, he was recorded as Private 19157 (the war diary transcription suggests 19167, but is probably an error) 2nd Battalion of the Bedfordshire Regiment and his home address confirmed as 5 Holwell Road.

After the war, Charles and Clara went on to have another seven children, bringing the total to ten: Frederick C Males (b 1910), Clarence, Betty, Dan, Molly, Charlotte, Lilian, John, Sheila and Laura. Charles died on April 19th 1952,

Charles Furr's Military Medal and service medals.

aged sixty-seven and Clara died on January 5th 1980, aged ninety.

Note: Four men with a Pirton connection were awarded a medal. Military Medals were awarded to Charles Furr (born in Pirton), Sidney Cox (baptised in Pirton) and Lieutenant Arthur Robert Walker (born in Pirton, but who had been living in Canada before the war) and a Distinguished Conduct Medal to Henry George Chamberlain (born in Pirton and who was killed in the war).

FURR, FREDERICK

Fred appears on the School War Memorial, confirming that he attended the school. Parish records suggest only one man of this name who could have served, and he was born on March 20th 1900 to Charles and Eliza Sarah Furr (née French) who seems to have commonly been known as Sarah. In all it would appear that four brothers or half-brothers served and survived - refer to George French and Albert Furr for more family details.

He is recorded in the Parish Magazine of November 1918 as 'enlisting recently' and serving in the Queen's, so Frederick would have been eighteen years old when he enlisted.

FURR, HAROLD

The Parish Magazine of September 1918 records Harold as being 'called to service'. A family tree, provided by Bob Lawrence, shows that Harold was born in 1887 to Frederick and Emma Furr and that they had seven children: Amelia G (b 1883), George (b 1886), Harold (b 1887), Miriam (b 1890), William (b 1892), Augustus (b 1893) and Victor (b 1898). He does not appear to have been living in Pirton at the time of the 1901 or 1911 census. He would have been about twenty when he was called up.

GILBERT, H. JAMES

The Parish Magazine of October 1915 records James as 'indirectly connected to Pirton'.

A search of the parish and census records does not identify any possible men. However, marriage records do show that members of the Gilbert family were in Pirton in 1908, i.e. William Henry Gilbert of Maidstone married Kate French of Pirton. William's father is recorded as Henry John Gilbert. Perhaps William settled in Pirton and James was related to him. However, this theory seems to be unlikely to be correct as William Gilbert was Brenda Dawson's uncle. Brenda (now deceased) had a detailed knowledge of her family history and she was unaware of James.

GOLDSMITH, ARTHUR

Arthur appears on the School War Memorial, confirming that he attended the school. Parish records suggest only one man of this name who could have served, and he was born on December 11th 1880 to Henry and Ann Goldsmith (née Baynes or perhaps Baines). He would have been thirty-four at the outbreak of war. Baptism records list fourteen children: Elizabeth (bapt 1864), Frederick (bapt 1865), Abigail (bapt 1867), Martha (bapt 1868), Alice (bapt 1870), Peggy (bapt 1871), Albert (bapt 1873), James (bapt 1874), Frank (bapt 1875), Charles (bapt 1876), John (bapt 1878), Arthur (b 1880), Peter William (b 1882) and Rosetta (bapt 1891). The 1911 census records them living at 11 Cromwell Terrace - the terraced row, which now contains the village stores – and adds Gwendolin Clara (b c1909). Peter died, aged sixteen months, so Arthur was the youngest member of the family who could have served. A John Goldsmith also served and survived, but it is unclear whether it was Arthur's brother or the brother of Edward Goldsmith.

The Parish Magazine of June 1917 records him as serving in the 3rd Essex Regiment, but the 1918 Absent Voters' List records him as Private 38281, 1st Company, 4th Battalion, Gloucestershire Regiment, with his home address given as 11 Cromwell Terrace.

GOLDSMITH, EDWARD, (TED)

Edward appears on the School War Memorial, confirming that he attended the school. Parish records suggest only one man of this name who could have served, and he was born on September 28th, 1896 to William and Emma Goldsmith (née Walker). Baptism and census records list twelve children, but by 1911 two had died. At this time, only ten can be identified with certainty; they are Frederick Goldsmith Walker (b July 1879 – William and Emma married in October 1879), George (b 1881, d 1883 aged two), Mary Jane (b 1883, Jane Mary in the 1901 census), William Charles (b 1885, d 1912), John (b 1887), Bertie (b 1890), Susan (b 1892), Sidney (b 1894), Edward (b 1896), Alice Mabel (b 1898) and Emily Elizabeth (b 1901). One of the unknown children could be Harry (b1904, died at two months), which would leave one unnamed. Sidney, Ted's brother, served and survived and it is also possible that the John Goldsmith who also served and survived was Sidney's brother, but there appear to be two possibilities, with Ted's brother being one.

In the 1911 census, Edward, although only fourteen, was listed as a surgeon's assistant. However, the assistant was subsequently crossed out and the correction is unclear.

Ted is recorded in the Parish Magazine of October 1914 as enlisting during 1914, but after July, and serving in the 1st Hertfordshire Regiment. He would have been about eighteen years old.

The Hertfordshire Express of April 13th 1914 reports his parents as living around Little Green - in fact they had done so since at least 1901. It also confirms that he also had an older brother serving (believed to be Sidney). Both his brother and Ted had been wounded, Ted in the leg.

A letter from Norman Newbery, dated December 1914, thanks Mr Franklin for the gift of jerseys for him, W Reynolds (could be Walter or William) and Edward Goldsmith. It also confirms that all three were in "G" Company and at Thurston in Suffolk, near Bury St. Edmunds.

He went to France in January 1915 and in May 1915 he was reported as killed. His family must have been distraught, but the North Herts Mail of May 20th 1915 confirms, from information provided by a cousin Private Vine from Henlow, that the earlier report was a mistake.

A local paper from 1916 reported that on September 11th, at the request of Corporal Harry Smith, Ted performed the sad duty of writing to inform the mother of John Parsell that he had died the day before. All three were Pirton men. It seems likely that Edward was also injured in this explosion as the North Herts Mail reports, shortly afterwards, that one of the Goldmiths had been slightly wounded (for the second time), near his ear by a bit of shell. In the letter, she is told that, just before his death, John (Parsell) of the Hertfords had been *'very cheerful having seen Fred Baines and Arthur Odell of the Royal Sussex and George Thompson of the ASC'* - again all Pirton men. Sadly the same shell resulted in the injury of George Roberts and the death of Arthur.

Patti Salter, whose family tree includes many Pirton people, believes that it is possible that Ted was John's cousin. Corporal Harry Smith, who died later in the war, was his fourth cousin and Arthur Walker was Ted's second cousin. Perhaps this sad incident amply demonstrates the interrelationship of the families of Pirton and the widespread impact a death could have.

The North Herts Mail of November 9th 1916 adds to the information: the family lived in Franklin's Lane, (now Walnut Tree Road), and Ted had been employed in Dr Grellett's surgery in Hitchin - Dr Grellett was a popular doctor in Pirton. By that date, he also held the rank of Lance Corporal. He had been wounded again (third time), but was *'making good progress'* in Boulogne Hospital, where he had been admitted on October 15th. His injury, if taken at face value, seems relatively minor - *'A piece of barbed wire being in his foot'*, but perhaps it had been lodged there by explosion because he was moved from Boulogne Hospital to the G N Hospital in Leeds and then The Red Cross Hospital at Malton, Yorkshire, where he was operated on. At the time that he was wounded, the 1st Hertfordshire Battalion was fighting on the Somme, in a battle for the Schwaben Redoubt*1, which was finally taken on October 14th. The North Herts Mail of April 11th 1918 confirms that he had healed and he certainly carried on fighting because he was wounded again, for the fourth time, during the massive German offensive during the spring of that year – the Germans were desperate to break the Allies before the Americans could join them in full force.

*1 *A redoubt is a fortified stronghold.*

GOLDSMITH, GEORGE

George appears on the School War Memorial, confirming that he attended the school. Parish records suggest only one man of this name who could have served, and he was baptised on September 1st 1895, the son of Frederick and Prudence Elizabeth Goldsmith (née Titmuss). Baptism and census records list eight children: Grace (b 1888 or 1889), Frank (bapt 1891), Elsie (b 1893), George (b 1895), Lilian Ruth (b 1898), Effie (b 1900), Lennard (sic) (b c1905) and Charly (sic) (b c1908). In 1911, George was working as a general labourer.

He is recorded in the Parish Magazine of July 1916 as enlisting between October 21st 1915 and March 2nd 1916 and serving in the Royal Field Artillery, so he would have been twenty years old when he enlisted. The 1918 Absent Voters' List records him as Private 110823, confirming that he was with the Royal Field Artillery, and his home address as Little Green.

Evidenced by the birth date, George seems to have married Maud Isabella (surname unknown) and both are recorded in St. Mary's Church's Garden of Rest, Maud died in 1967, aged seventy and George in 1973, aged seventy-eight.

GOLDSMITH, JACK

Jack appears on the School War Memorial, confirming that he attended the school. Parish and census records provide no further information, other than to confirm that the surname was present in Pirton at the time.

GOLDSMITH, JOHN

The Parish Magazine of June 1917 records John Goldsmith (Senior) as enlisting after August 1915 and before March 2nd 1916, serving in the 3rd London Royal Fusiliers.

Parish and census records suggest two possible men:

The first was baptised on October 6th 1878, the son of Henry and Ann Goldsmith (née Baynes or perhaps Baines), so he would have been about thirty-seven at the time of his enlistment. Baptism records list fourteen children: Elizabeth (bapt 1864), Frederick (bapt 1865), Abigail (bapt 1867), Martha (bapt 1868), Alice Elizabeth (bapt 1870), Peggy (bapt 1871), Albert (bapt 1973), James (bapt 1874), Frank (bapt 1875), Charles (bapt 1876), John (bapt 1878), Arthur (b 1880), Peter William (b 1882) and Rosetta Mary (bapt 1891).

If this is the John who served then he was married and a father when he went to war. His brother Arthur also served and survived the war.

The second was born on December 20th 1887 to William and Emma Goldsmith (née Walker), so he would have been about twenty-eight at the time of his enlistment. Baptism and census records list twelve children, but by 1911 two had died. At this time, only ten can be identified with certainty; they are Frederick Goldsmith Walker (b July

1879 – William and Emma married in October 1879), George (b 1881, d 1883 aged two), Mary Jane (b 1883, Jane Mary in the 1901 census), William Charles (b 1885, d 1912), John (b 1887), Bertie (b 1890), Susan (b 1892), Sidney (b 1894), Edward (b 1896), Alice Mabel (b 1898) and Emily Elizabeth (b 1901). One of the unknown children could be Harry (b1904, died at two months), which would leave one unnamed. If this John is our man then his brothers, Sidney and Edward, both served and survived.

By 1911, John had been married to Mary for a year. Her maiden name may have been Baines, as the census records Rose and Lily Baines as relatives and being in the house. However, another possibility, perhaps more likely, is that they were cousins, as John's mother's maiden name was Baines. They had a daughter, Doris Mary (b c1900), and were living near Little Green. In 1911 John was working as a railway labourer.

Ordinarily, it would seem more likely that the latter would be the man who served. However, because the Parish Magazine refers to John Goldsmith 'senior', perhaps the former is more likely. Unfortunately, at this time, it is not known which, if either, is the relevant John Goldsmith.

GOLDSMITH, SIDNEY

Sidney appears on the School War Memorial, confirming that he attended the school. Parish records suggest only one man of this name who could have served, and he was born on July 23rd 1894 to William and Emma Goldsmith (née Walker). Baptism and census records list twelve children, but by 1911 two had died. At this time, only ten can be identified with certainty. They are Frederick Goldsmith Walker (b July 1879 – William and Emma married in October 1879), George (b 1881, d 1883 aged two), Mary Jane (b 1883, Jane Mary in the 1901 census), William Charles (b 1885, d 1912), John (b 1887), Bertie (b 1890), Susan (b 1892), Sidney (b 1894), Edward (b 1896), Alice Mabel (b 1898) and Emily Elizabeth (b 1901). One of the unknown children could be Harry (b1904, died at two months), which would leave one unnamed. Edward, Ted's brother, served and survived. It is also possible that the John Goldsmith, who also served and survived, was Sidney's brother, but there appear to be two possibilities with Ted's brother being one.

By 1911, Sidney was sixteen and working as a farm labourer on one of the local farms. The Parish Magazine of September 1915 records him as enlisting during 1915, but before August, and serving in the Royal Engineers. He would have been about twenty years old.

The Hertfordshire Express of April 13th 1914 reports Sidney's parents as living around Little Green - in fact they had done so since at least 1901. It also confirms the fact that his younger brother, Ted, was also serving and that both men had been wounded.

HANDSCOMBE OR HANSCOMBE?

There is potential for confusion arising from the different spelling of this name and which spelling applies to the following men. Different families, probably connected, use different spellings and parish and census records also vary, so which spelling should be used is unclear. As the Commonwealth War Grave Commission has used Handscombe for the two men who died, this spelling is used for all. We apologise if this is incorrect.

HANDSCOMBE, CHARLES

Parish and census records suggest two possible men; however the Hertfordshire Express of May 19th 1917 reports Charles as being the brother of Frank and Joseph. From this information, it is clear that Charles was the son of George and Martha Handscombe (née Dawson) and baptised on August 3rd 1884. He would have been twenty at the outbreak of war.

Charles lived with his parents and siblings in a thatched cottage set back from Shillington Road, which was near to the present number fifteen. Baptism and census records list ten children including Bertie (b c1879), Frisby (b c1881), Charles (bapt 1884), Jane (b 1885), Frederick (b 1888), Emma (b 1890), Sidney (b 1891), Frank (b 1893), Joseph (b 1896) and Hedley (b 1900). At least four sons served; Charles, Hedley and Frank and Joseph. Both Frank and Joseph were killed.

The Hertfordshire Express of May 19th, 1917 reports Charles as being discharged from training due to illness.

HANDSCOMBE, GEORGE

George appears on the School War Memorial, confirming that he attended the school. Parish and census records suggest only one man of this name who could have served, and he was born on June 3rd 1880 to John and Caroline (née Burton). He would have been thirty-four at the outbreak of war. Baptism records list five children: George (b 1880), Ruth (b 1882), Fred (b c1885), Harry (b 1886) and Mary Rose (b 1898). Although of an age to have served, it is unlikely that Harry followed his brother into the army as the Hertfordshire Express dated April 28th 1917 reports that he had applied to the Hertfordshire Appeal Tribunal for exemption, presumably because of his work as a farmer and this was conditionally granted.

George married Alice Arnold in 1906, with his sister Ruth, and brother Harry, as witnesses. By 1911, he was thirty and had been married to Alice for five years and was a carpenter by trade. They were living in Woodbine cottage (still in the High Street by The Fox) and they had two children of their own: Dorothy Ruth (b c1908) and Edward

George (b 1910). So, when George went to war, he was married and a father.

The Parish Magazine of June 1917 records George as serving in the Royal Naval Air Service. As a carpenter, he would probably have been involved in the maintaining and repairing of those fragile aircraft of the time. The 1918 Absent Voters' List clarifies this further, recording him as 212616 1st A.M. (Air Mechanic) Air Service Construction Corps, and confirms his home address as Woodbine Cottage in the High Street.

George and Alice are both recorded in the St. Mary's Church's cemetery records; George died in 1951, aged seventy, and Alice in 1968, aged eighty-six. The headstone also records Leslie William Handscombe, who was presumably another son.

HANDSCOMBE, HEDLEY

Hedley appears on the School War Memorial, confirming that he attended the school. Parish and census records suggest only one man of this name who could have served, and he was born on January 19th 1900 to George and Martha Handscombe (née Dawson). In all it would appear that four brothers served. Charles and Hedley survived, Frank and Joseph were killed - refer to Charles Handscombe for more family details.

Hedley lived with his parents and siblings in a thatched cottage set back from Shillington Road, which was near to the present number fifteen. Baptism and census records list ten children, including Bertie (b c1879), Frisby (b c1881), Charles (bapt 1884), Jane (b 1885), Frederick (b 1888), Emma (b 1890), Sidney (b 1891), Frank (b 1893), Joseph (b 1896) and Hedley (b 1900). At least four sons served; Hedley, Charles, Frank and Joseph. Both Frank and Joseph were killed.

Hedley is recorded in the Parish Magazine of November 1918 as recently enlisting; he would have been about eighteen.

It appears that, after the war, he married and his wife was called Zilah. Together they had at least one child, Frances Rose, who was born April 23rd 1925. A photograph taken during the Second World War shows Hedley serving in the Pirton and Holwell Homeguard.

HANDSCOMBE, HORACE WILLIAM

Margaret Handscombe identified Horace. Although it is not known if he was living in Pirton at the time of the war, there are definitely some strong Pirton connections.

Hedley Handscombe, photographed serving in the Homeguard during WW2.

Horace was Margaret's grandfather and she believes that his father, William, was born in Pirton circa 1863 and that his son Horace was born in Luton on November 7th 1886. In the 1901 census he is recorded as living in Emma Handscombe's house (his aunt) with his cousins Clara and Alice Maud. She knows that he spoke a little of the war to her father and certainly told him about the horrendous punishments meted out to soldiers, such as being tied to a wheel.*1

1 This particular punishment was known as 'Field Punishment No. 1' and consisted of the man being tied or shackled to a gun wheel or similar for up to two hours in twenty-four, but apparently not for more than three days in four or more than twenty-one days in his sentence.

HARE, FRANK

Frank appears on the School War Memorial, confirming that he attended the school. Parish records suggest only one man of this name who could have served, and he was born in 1888 or 1889 to William and Jane Hare (née Hall). So he would have been about twenty-five at the outbreak of war. Baptism and census records list ten children: Anne (bapt 1879), Arthur (b c1881), Fred (b 1883), Henry (bapt 1884), Nellie (b 1887), Aleaner (perhaps Eleanor? b c1887), Frank (b 1889), Edith (b 1892), Bessie (b c1895) and Ruth (b c1899).

Horace Handscombe

HEAD, ALBERT HAROLD

Albert appears on the School War Memorial, confirming that he attended the school. Parish and census records suggest only one man of this name who could have served and they show that Albert was born on September 15th 1891 to David and Elizabeth Head. Baptism and census records list eleven children, but by 1911 four had died. At this time, only nine can be identified with certainty, and they are William (b 1878, possibly died 1910), Frederick (b 1881), Fanny (b 1884), Alfred (b 1887), Arthur (b 1889, d 1889, aged three months), Albert Harold (b 1891), Charles (b 1893), Alice Kate (b 1896) and Arthur Sidney (b 1897). It is possible that another of the children who died was Frank (b c1882, d 1893, aged eleven). At least two brothers, Alfred and Charles, also served and survived.

His service records list him as Harold Albert, a reversal of his Christian names. He married Emily Baines on October 29th 1910 and, by the time war came, they had two children: Kathleen Emily (b 1911) and Rhoda Lilian (b 1913). They lived in Rose Cottage, Pirton and Albert was employed as a roadman. He enlisted, or more likely was called up, and joined the Bedfordshire Regiment on October 14th 1916, aged twenty-six. He remained on home service until June 5th 1917, when his Battalion left for France. He transferred to the Labour Corps on May 7th 1917 and was allocated to the 1st Battalion, Labour Corps on May 12th. This usually indicates that the man was no longer considered fit for front line duty, usually through illness, injury or as the result of wounds received, but does not mean that he was out of danger, as the Labour Corps often worked in locations exposed to shelling and snipers. Indeed his records show that he was severely wounded on September 21st 1917. He remained in France until December 29th 1917, when he returned to England. This was possibly due to further illness or injury. Whatever the reason, following treatment in a London Hospital, as Private 201412, 1st Labour Corps, he was discharged as no longer fit for war service due to bronchitis, on June 19th 1918.

Records show that, when awarded his war service medals, he and his family were still living in Rose Cottage.

HEAD, ALFRED

Alfred appears on the School War Memorial, confirming that he attended the school. Parish records suggest only one man of this name who could have served, and he was baptised on November 17th 1887, the son of David and Elizabeth Head. In all it would appear that three brothers served and survived - refer to Albert Head for more details.

Alfred married Lydia Titmuss on February 11th 1911 and, by the time he enlisted, they had three children: William George (b 1911), Frederick Arthur (b 1913) and Leonard David (b 1915). On December 12th 1915, at the age of twenty-eight years and eleven months, he went to Hitchin and enlisted in the Bedfordshire Regiment. At the time, he was working as a labourer and his home address was Holwell Road - probably one of the terraced cottages also known as the 'Twelve Apostles'.

On August 1st 1916, Alfred was 'Called to Colours' and was first posted to the Bedfords, then, in November, to the Machine Gun Corps, 5th Battalion and to the 220th Company on December 16th 1916. They went to France on March 17th 1917 and then Italy on November 19th 1917. He was given UK leave and left his Regiment on August 22nd 1918, rejoining them in Italy on September 18th. The remainder of the war was spent there and he finally left for the UK in March 1919 with the Cadre*1 of the Battalion. He was not demobilised straight away, but was stationed at Dreghorn Camp, Edinburgh, until finally demobilised on September 9th 1919.

Alfred and his wife Lydia seem to have spent the rest of their lives in Pirton as they are buried in St. Mary's churchyard. Lydia died in 1969 and Alfred in 1976.

*1 A small military unit capable of expanding.

HEAD, CHARLES

Charles appears on the School War Memorial, confirming that he attended the school. Parish records suggest only one man of this name who could have served, and he was born on March 8th 1893 to David and Elizabeth Head. In all it would appear that three brothers served and survived - refer to Albert Head for more family details.

He is recorded twice in the Parish Magazine: in October 1914 as being in the 1st Hertfordshire Territorials, and in September 1915 as enlisting in 1914 after July, and serving in the 9th Middlesex Regiment. He would have been about twenty-one when he joined up. The Hertfordshire Express of November 11th 1914 also suggests that he was serving in the Middlesex Territorials, so his exact regiment may be uncertain. However, by 1918, he was Private 94395, 222nd Company of the Machine Gun Corps, with his home address as 3 Andrew's Cottages (the three cottages at the bottom of the High Street). His father, David, died in 1915, while he was serving.

HILL, WILLIAM ALBERT

William is recorded in the Parish Magazine of February 1917 as enlisting and serving in the 5th Suffolk Regiment, while the Parish Magazine of June 1917 records him as serving in the 8th Lancashire Fusiliers. Unfortunately, parish and census records provide no further information.

HODSON, HARRY, (POSSIBLY HODGSON)

The Parish Magazine of October 1915 records Harry, who was serving in the Royal Engineers, as 'indirectly connected to Pirton'.

Parish records suggest only one man of this name who could have served, and he was born on October 29th 1879 to William and Asenath Hodson (née Crouch and possibly Aisena or Asinath), so would have been thirty-four at the outbreak of war. Baptism records list five children: Charles (bapt 1863), Emma (bapt 1871), Lois (bapt 1875), Joseph (bapt 1876) and Harry (b 1879). It seems likely that this is the correct man. However, the above information would normally be sufficient to confirm this man's Pirton connection, so the reference of 'indirectly connected to Pirton' means that perhaps this is a false trail.

HOYE, ALBERT

Albert appears on the School War Memorial, confirming that he attended the school. Parish records suggest only one man of this name who could have served, and he was born on February 14th 1877 to Elijah and Eliza Taylor Hoye (née Holes). He would have been thirty-nine when he enlisted. Baptism and census records list twelve children, but by 1911 one had died: Emma (bapt 1866), James (bapt 1867), Ann (bapt 1869), Harry (bapt 1871), Charles (bapt 1875), Albert (b 1877), Arthur (b 1873, d 1881, aged eight), Ellen (b 1880), William (b c1883), Lois (b 1884), Arthur (b 1888) and Elizabeth (b 1891). The Hertfordshire Express of May 19th 1917 reports that three brothers with the surname Hoye were serving; Albert and Arthur were two of them, but the third is uncertain. James at forty-seven would have been too old, but it could have been Harry at forty-three, Charles at thirty-nine or William thirty-one; the latter obviously is the most likely.

In 1911, Elijah and Emily were retired and living, with their son William and grandson Peter Sexton in Workhouse Yard (somewhere near the junction of the High Street and Walnut Tree Road).

Albert had married Emily Dawson in 1899 and, in 1911 they were living near his parents, also in Workhouse Yard. They had five children: Annie (b c1900), James (b c1902), Ethel (b c1905), Grace (b c1907) and Cyril (b c1910). Albert earned his living as a farm labourer on one of the local farms.

When he went to war he was married and a family man. The Parish Magazine of July 1916 records him as having enlisted since March 2nd 1916 and serving in the 10th Suffolks. By 1918, he is recorded as Private 5075, 6th Battalion, Prince of Wales Leinster Regiment, with his home address as around Little Green.

HOYE, ARTHUR

Arthur appears on the School War Memorial, confirming that he attended the school. Parish records suggest only one man of this name who could have served, and he was born on April 5th 1888 to Elijah and Eliza Taylor Hoye (née Holes). He would have been twenty-six when he enlisted. In all it would appear that three brothers served - refer to Albert Hoye for more family details.

In 1911, Elijah and Emily were retired and living with their son, William and grandson Peter Sexton in Workhouse Yard (somewhere near the junction of the High Street and Walnut Tree Road), and his brother Albert lived close by. Arthur is missing from the census, so presumably living or working away from Pirton.

He is recorded in the Parish Magazine of October 1914 as enlisting and serving in the Royal Army Medical Corps – which may be an error as the Parish Magazine of September 1915 lists the 1st Bedfordshire Regiment and in the June 1917 Magazine the 7th Bedfordshire Regiment. The latter two both record wounds. The North Herts Mail of July 15th 1915 explains the wounds, reporting that he had been home from Nottingham Hospital, where he had been recovering from bullet wound to his jaw and that, just a month earlier, he had been wounded in the groin. Intriguingly in the North Herts Mail of July 13th 1916, it is reported that he was in St Albans and stole a bicycle from outside the Queen's Hotel. He had entered, had a drink, left hurriedly and stolen a bicycle belonging to Joseph Hawes. He was caught and agreed to go to the police station, but then darted down Victoria Street. He was caught again, but again escaped by running down St Peter's Street. He was caught yet again, and this time arrested. Two weeks later he had been charged and was in court. He said '*I admit I stole the bicycle and I am very sorry. I did it because I did not want to go back to France. I am a deserter and have been wounded twice.*' That carried no weight and he was committed for trial.

Given that he had already been wounded twice, his fear of going back was very understandable. Although committed for trial, he appears, perhaps after some sort of punishment, to have been allowed to return to service. If he had deserted in France, he may well have been shot. His fears were not unfounded, and were perhaps a premonition, as the North Herts Mail of May 17th 1917 reported that he had been wounded again, the third time, but on this occasion just a slight wound in the arm.

The Hertfordshire Express of May 19th 1917 reports that three brothers with the surname Hoye were serving; Albert and Arthur were two of them, but the third is uncertain. James at forty-seven would have been too old, but it could have been Harry at forty-three, Charles at thirty-nine or William thirty-one; the latter is obviously the most likely.

By 1918, Arthur is recorded as Private 8550, 2nd Battalion, Bedfordshire Regiment, with his home address as Little Green.

HOYE - EITHER JAMES, HARRY, CHARLES OR WILLIAM

The Hertfordshire Express of May 19th 1917 reveals that three sons of Elijah and Eliza Taylor Hoye (née Holes) served. Baptism and census records list twelve children, but by 1911, one had died; Emma (bapt 1866), James (bapt 1867), Ann (bapt 1869), Harry (bapt 1871), Charles (bapt 1875), Albert (b 1877), Arthur (b 1873, d 1881, aged eight), Ellen (b 1880), William (b c1883), Lois (b 1884), Arthur (b 1888) and Elizabeth (b 1891). Albert and Arthur were two who served, but the third is uncertain. James at forty-seven would almost certainly have been too old, but depending on the date of enlistment it could have been Harry at forty-three, Charles at thirty-nine or William thirty-one. The latter, as the youngest man, is the most likely to have served.

HUBBARD, ELDRED RICHARD, (RICHARD)

The 1911 census reveals the Hubbard family as husband and wife, Eldred and Eleanor, who had been married for fourteen years, and their children: Richard (b c1897), Eleanor (b c1898) and John (b c1907). Only the latter two were born in Pirton, so the family must have moved to Pirton around 1906/07. Richard was born in Hertford. In 1911, at fourteen, he was working as a gardener's boy, probably with his father who was a domestic gardener.

E. Richard is recorded in the Hertfordshire Express November 20th 1914 as serving on the ship the Gloucester Castle (Transport). From the age of his father - thirty-eight in 1911, it is much more likely to be his son Richard who served.

The Gloucester Castle was commissioned in September 1914 and served as a hospital ship with 410 beds. By April 1915 she was taking part in the Dardanelles campaign, carrying Royal Marines and in 1917, although clearly identified as a hospital ship, was torpedoed by the German submarine UB-32 but did not sink. It is not clear whether Richard was on board this ship at this time, because the Parish Magazines of June and September 1915 records Eldred Rich as enlisting during 1915, before August and serving in the Royal Fleet Auxiliary 'Reliance'. H.M.S. Reliance spent a large part of her war service at Mudros (Gallipoli) and in the Mediterranean, but by January 1916 had been transferred to the Royal Field Artillery as a store support ship.

Obviously the information from the Parish Magazines is contradictory in respect of when he enlisted and his service history. Another possibility is that they could perhaps refer to two different men or perhaps his father did serve, although that seems unlikely. A Richard Edward Hubbard appears on the School War Memorial. It is possible that they are the same man, or perhaps two men with similar names. Unfortunately parish and census records do not clarify this situation.

The Gloucester Castle

HUBBARD, RICHARD EDWARD

Richard Edward Hubbard appears on the School War Memorial, confirming that he attended the school. However, it could be that this is a mistake and perhaps this is the Eldred Richard Hubbard listed above. If not, then perhaps some of the details for these two men have become confused. - see Eldred Richard Hubbard for possible information. Unfortunately, parish and census records do not clarify this situation.

JACKSON, ARTHUR CHARLES

Arthur appears on the School War Memorial, confirming that he attended the school. Parish records suggest only one man of this name who could have served, and he was born on April 29th 1892 to Nathan and Ellen Jackson (née Odell). He would have been twenty-two at the outbreak of war. Baptism records list two children: Arthur (b 1892) and George William Jackson (b 1898). His younger brother George also served and survived.

JACKSON, GEORGE WILLIAM

George appears on the School War Memorial, confirming that he attended the school. Parish records suggest only one man of this name who could have served, and he was born on May 16th 1898 to Nathan and Ellen (née Odell). He would have been sixteen at the outbreak of war. Baptism records list two children: Arthur Charles (b 1892) and George (b 1898). His elder brother Arthur also served and survived.

JARVIS, FREDERICK, (FRED)

Frederick appears on the School War Memorial, confirming that he attended the school. He was working for Frank Burton before the war and lived in Andrew's Cottages (the three cottages at the bottom of the High Street). Parish and census records listed three Frederick Jarvis', although cross-referencing these with burial records originally suggested only one entry that could be correct. However, the release of the 1911 census revealed another possibility.

The first man was born on April 3rd 1886 to Edith Jarvis and his father is not named. He appears to have a brother or half-brother, Sidney John (b 1892), who died aged twenty months. Edith later married Herbert Butterfield, in 1898. Then in the 1901 census, Fred is recorded as living with his widowed grandfather William and working as a ploughboy and then in 1911, as still living with his grandfather and a farm labourer. Edith Butterfield is not recorded so had possibly moved away with her husband.

The second man identified was Fred Jarvis from Croydon, Surrey, fifteen in 1911. He was working as a farm labourer and boarding with Joseph Waldock in West Mill Cottage.

In the 1911 census, both men are recorded as Fred, so there is no clue from his name usage. It is therefore not possible to say with certainty which man served. The Fred that did is recorded in the Parish Magazine of September 1915 as enlisting during 1915 and serving in the 1st Bedfordshire Regiment (number 20165). The men identified above would have been twenty-nine and nineteen respectively, so it could be either. A newspaper cutting from July 1916 confirms his enlistment date as April 1915 and that he went to the Front in October. It also reports that Fred had recently been severely wounded in the head. The North Herts Mail of August 31st 1916 recorded that he was home on leave after convalescing in Hospital. He must have recovered reasonably well from that wound, since by 1918 he was recorded as Lance Corporal 135120, "W" Company, Army Service Corps (ASC). This may however indicate that he was no longer considered fit for the front line. His home address was given as 4 Andrew's Cottages, the three cottages at the bottom of the High Street.

JENKINS, ARTHUR GEOFFREY, (GEOFFREY)

Arthur appears on the School War Memorial, confirming that he attended the school, however little more can be confirmed. Initial investigation only reveals an Arthur *Alfred* Jenkins born on May 26th 1893 to Alfred and Elvina Elizabeth Jenkins (née Carter and sometimes recorded as 'Edwina Elizabeth', 'Albina Elizabeth' and 'Elvira Elizabeth', but believed to be the same person). However, this Arthur Jenkins died aged ten months and was buried in 1894, so he could not be our man. The 1911 census reveals a Geoffrey Jenkins (b c1899), so the only evidence points to him being our man. Analysis of all the baptism and census records identifies eleven children, but by 1911 two had died. The children were; Ethel (b c1886), Alice Elma (b 1887, d 1890, aged two years and three months), Montague Harold (b 1889), Arthur Alfred (b 1893, d 1894), Alfred Raymond (b 1895), Edward Victor (b 1897), Leonard Cyril (b 1899), Geoffrey (b c1900), John (b c1902), Norman (b c1905) and Emma (b c1909). Four other brothers - Montague, Edward, Leonard and Arthur (Geoffrey) - are believed to have served and survived. Alfred Raymond (known as Raymond) sadly died in the war and he is listed on the Village War Memorial.

JENKINS, EDWARD

Edward appears on the School War Memorial, confirming that he attended the school. Baptism and census records suggest only one man of this name who could have served. Edward Victor Jenkins was born on May 10th 1897 to Alfred and Elvina Elizabeth Jenkins (née Carter and sometimes recorded as 'Edwina Elizabeth', 'Albina Elizabeth' and 'Elvira Elizabeth', but believed to be the same person). He would have only been sixteen at the outbreak of war. In all it would appear that five brothers served and four survived – refer to Arthur Jenkins for more family details.

JENKINS, LEONARD CHARLES

Leonard Charles appears on the School War Memorial, confirming that he attended the school. Parish and census records suggest only one man who could be correct, but baptism records show him as Leonard *Cyril* Jenkins. However, there are errors on the School War Memorial so, in the absence of any other information, it is assumed that he is the correct man. He was born on March 6th 1899 to Alfred and Elvina Elizabeth Jenkins (née Carter and sometimes recorded as 'Edwina Elizabeth', 'Albina Elizabeth' and 'Elvira Elizabeth', but believed to be the same person). He would have only been fifteen at the outbreak of war, so it is likely that he served in the latter stages. In all it would appear that five brothers served and four survived – refer to Arthur Jenkins for more family details.

JENKINS, MONTAGUE HAROLD

Montague appears on the School War Memorial, confirming that he attended the school. Baptism and census records suggest only one man of this name who could have served, and he was born on August 20th 1889 to Alfred and Elvina Elizabeth Jenkins (née Carter and sometimes recorded as 'Edwina Elizabeth', 'Albina Elizabeth' and 'Elvira Elizabeth', but believed to be the same person). He would have only been sixteen at the outbreak of war. In all it would appear that five brothers served and four survived – refer to Arthur Jenkins for more family details.

JENKINS, RAYMOND

The Parish Magazine of October 1915 records Raymond as serving in the Grenadier Guards and as *'indirectly connected to Pirton'*. An Alfred Raymond Jenkins from Pirton served, died and is recorded on the Village War Memorial. He also served in the Grenadier Guards, but he has strong connections with Pirton, so the reference to an indirect connection would not seem to apply to this man. No other information has been found to substantiate the existence of a second man with a similar name, but if he existed and was only *'indirectly connected to Pirton'*, then this would not be entirely unexpected. So, at this time, it is not known if two men with similar names existed or whether they are one and the same man.

KINGSLEY, OLIVER JOHN NEWTON, (JOHN)

John appears on the School War Memorial, confirming that he attended the school. Census records suggest only one man of this name who could have served. He was born late 1895 or early 1896, the son of George and Sarah Ann Kingsley. Census records list four children but by 1911 one had died. At this time only three can be identified with certainty and they are James Griffin (b c1889), Edward George (b c1891) and Oliver John Newton.

In 1911, the family was living in Rose Cottage, possibly in Royal Oak Lane, formerly Dead Horse Lane. This must have been a divided property, as three other people lived there in what appear to be separated dwellings. He was still living there in March 1st 1916 when, aged twenty, he went to Hitchin to enlist. On January 15th 1917, he was posted to the 8th Reserve Brigade, Royal Horse Artillery and then to the Army Veterinary Corps, 126th Brigade on May 23rd 1917. He went to France on June 21st and was very fortunate to receive two weeks home leave on July 12th 1918.

Stan Ashton, Frank Ashton's son, believes that John joined up at the same time as Frank – who also survived, and that, after the war, John worked at Elm Tree Farm for Alan Walker. A monument inscription in St. Mary's churchyard, which also records his parents as George and Sarah, records that John died October 4th 1963, aged sixty-eight.

Lake, Albert George, (George)

Albert George Lake appears on the School War Memorial, confirming that he attended the school. Parish records suggest only one man of this name who could have served, and he was born on February 21st 1898 to Charles James (James) and Susan Lake (née Catterill). Baptism records list six children: twins - Edward and Ernest (b 1886), Ethel Emma (b 1888), Gertrude Jane (bapt 1891), Thomas (b 1895) and Albert George (b 1898). However, a family tree held by Norah Lake adds Harry to the list but fails to include the two daughters. The 1911 census records that they had nine children, of whom four had died, so there are two siblings who remain unnamed at this time.

The Hertfordshire Express of August 10th 1918 reports Albert George's brother Tom as the third son and confirms that one of his brothers was H. Lake (Harry). So it is clear that Edward, Thomas and Albert George all served and survived.

The Parish Magazine of September 1918 records George Lake as 'called to service'. The parish, census and school entrance records do not reveal any obvious candidate and therefore it is likely that Albert George and George were the same man. He would have been twenty when called up.

Lake, Charles

Charles appears on the School War Memorial, confirming that he attended the school. Parish records suggest only one man of this name who could have served, and he was born on May 17th 1882 to George and Emma Lake (née Parkins). He would have been thirty-two at the outbreak of war. Baptism and census records list nine children but by 1911 one had died. The children were; Herbert Lindsay (b 1880), Charles (b 1882), Alice Emma (b 1883), Leonard (b 1885), Anne Elizabeth (b 1888), Ralph Joseph (b 1889), Frank (b 1893), Reginald (1895) and Philip (b c1904). His brothers Herbert, Joseph (Ralph) and Reginald also served and survived.

Lake, Edward

Edward appears on the School War Memorial, confirming that he attended the school. Parish records suggest only one man of this name who could have served, and he was born on July 24th 1886 (although his Canadian attestation papers record 1887) to Charles James (James) and Susan Lake (née Catterill). He would have been about eighteen at the outbreak of war. In all it would appear that three brothers served and survived – refer to Albert Lake for more family details.

Edward is absent from the 1911 Pirton census, so presumably he had already gone to Canada by this date. It is recorded that, before his emigration, he worked for Mr Davis which would have been at Rectory Farm.

Edna Lake, from Victoria Canada, is Edward's daughter and she adds to our information. She confirms that Edward and Ernest were twins and that Edward emigrated to Canada in 1912 or thereabouts leaving his twin, Ernest, behind. Ernest had married Ellen Rose Titmuss in 1909 and he seemingly spent the rest of his life in Pirton. It is believed that Edward emigrated with four other Pirton men, Toby (Albert William) Buckett, Tom Abbiss, Charlie Stapleton and one of the Walkers, possibly Arthur Robert Walker. However, there is conflicting information for the emigration dates, including a North Herts Mail report which suggests 1909 or 1910 for Toby.

He arrived in New Westminster, British Columbia with his friends and, very shortly afterwards, started work as a labourer in the construction of the new main road, Columbia Street. He met Ethel Birch (b 1891 in London), who had also emigrated there. They were married on April 28th 1915.

The Parish Magazine of August 1916 records Edward as serving in the

Edward Lake

131st Overseas Regiment. The North Herts Mail of November 30th 1916 tells us that he had been home to Pirton on leave before rejoining his Regiment.

The Parish Magazine of June 1917 records his Regiment as the Canadian Forester's Corps - Edna confirms this to be the case, and his attestation papers confirm that he enlisted on February 28th 1916. He served in France and was demobilised on April 5th 1919. Edward, Toby, Tom and Arthur all joined the Canadian Expeditionary Force returning to Europe to fight – their allegiance to Great Britain still being strong.

After the war he returned to New Westminster and then, a few years later, moved to Victoria, where he worked on the roads for the Municipality of Saanich. He lived there for the rest of his life. *'Dad kept in touch with the Pirton boys and I remember them in my younger days.'* - Edna Lake (b 1923).

LAKE, HERBERT

Herbert appears on the School War Memorial, confirming that he attended the school. Parish records suggest only one man of this name who could have served, and he was born on April 8th 1880 to George and Emma Lake (née Parkins). He would have been thirty-four at the outbreak of war. In all it would appear that four brothers served and survived – refer to Charles Lake for more family details.

LAKE, RALPH JOSEPH, (JOSEPH)

Joseph appears on the School War Memorial, confirming that he attended the school. Parish records suggest only one man of this name who could have served, and he was born on November 17th 1889 to George and Emma Lake (née Parkins). He would have been twenty-three at the outbreak of war. Ralph is recorded as Joseph in the 1891 and 1901 census and then as Ralph Joseph in 1911, so he is the right man. In all it would appear that four brothers served and survived – refer to Charles Lake for more family details.

In 1911 he was still living in the family home near Burge End and working as a carpenter. By 1918 he was recorded as 85419 A.M. (Aircraft Mechanic), Royal Air Force with his home address the same as his brother Reginald's, West View, which is believed to be 15 Shillington Road. As a carpenter, he would probably have been involved in the maintaining and repairing of those fragile aircraft of the time.

He died on November 25th 1962, aged seventy-three, and his ashes are interred in St. Mary's Church's Garden of Rest.

LAKE, REGINALD

Reginald appears on the School War Memorial, confirming that he attended the school. Parish records suggest only one man of this name who could have served, and he was born on June 22nd 1895 to George and Emma Lake (née Parkins). He would have been nineteen at the outbreak of war. In all it would appear that four brothers served and survived – refer to Charles Lake for more family details.

Reginald Lake

In 1911, Reginald was still living in the family home near Burge End and working as a farm labourer on one of the local farms. The Hertfordshire Express of October 17th, 1914 reports him as being present, on October 3rd, when the *'infamous fracas'* took place in Pirton, which led to the headline *'War Against Special Constables.'* *[1]

He enlisted in Hitchin on December 19th 1915, aged twenty. At that time he was working as a blacksmith's stoker and unmarried. He was not mobilised until almost a year later, December 2nd 1916 and, during March 1917, he was transferred to the Machine Gun Corps (MGC) as Private 88190.

Reginald had leave, probably embarkation leave, in August 1917; he was a day late returning and lost a day's pay as punishment. He left Southampton for Salonika on September 13th 1917, arriving on October 11th and then joined the 78th MGC. He remained in Salonika for the rest of the war, transferring to the 77th MGC just before leaving for home on April 21st 1919, and was demobilised in December 1919. His address, when discharged, was given as West View, Pirton, which is believed to now be 15 Shillington Road. The Absent Voters' List of 1918 confirms this to be the same home address as his brother Joseph.

He married and his wife's name was Lilian Grace. They are both buried in the churchyard, so it is likely that they lived in Pirton for the rest of their lives. Reginald died on November 28th 1960, aged sixty-five and his wife Lilian died on February 3rd 1961, aged sixty-one.

[1] The full report is included in the reference section of this book.

LAKE, TOM

The name Tom Lake appears in the Hertfordshire Express of July 11th 1914, which reports him as a member of the organising committee for the Pirton Transept Fête.

He appears on the School War Memorial, confirming that he attended the school. Parish records suggest only one man of this name who could have served and he was born on March 10th 1895 to Charles James (James) and Susan Lake (née Catterill), so he would have been sixteen at the outbreak of war. In all it would appear that three brothers served and survived – refer to Albert George Lake for more family details.

In 1911, he was still living in the family home near Burge End (a name then given to a much larger area than the current road) and was an apprentice coach and motor body builder.

By October 1918, he was serving as a driver in the Mechanical Transport, Army Service Corps. The Hertfordshire Express of October 10th 1918 reports him as being on leave from France for his wedding to Miss Alice Miriam Weeden, with his brother Harry acting as best man. Alice's only brother Leonard Stanley

Tom Lake after the war.

Weeden was also serving at the Front. After the war, Tom went on to be the Pirton dairyman.

Tom Lake and his new wife Alice Weeden in 1918.

The 1918 Absent Voters' List confirms the above information and clarifies his address as one of Handscombe's Cottages (the terraced row now at the beginning of Shillington Road).

Tom and his wife are buried the St. Mary's churchyard. Tom died in 1943, aged forty-eight and Alice in 1965 aged sixty-eight. The monument inscription also names Bernard Wilfred Lake, died 1993, aged seventy. Bernard was their son (b 1923).

LANGMORE, LESLIE GASPARD

The Parish Magazine of October 1915 records Leslie, who was serving as a Captain in the 11th King's Liverpool Regiment, as *'indirectly connected to Pirton'*. Michael Newbery believes that Leslie was probably related to the Rev Erskine William Langmore, who was vicar of Pirton between 1903 and 1922.

Parish and census records provide no further information. However, one possible clue comes from the Parish Magazine of August 1915, which records that the Vicar's brother had been shot through the thigh, having already been wounded twice before, and was in a hospital in Rouen, France. Perhaps Leslie was Rev Langmore's brother.

LAWRENCE, JACK, (JOHN)

Jack's great niece, Rose Agnew, provided much of the following information and confirmed that Jack Lawrence was sometimes known as John.

Jack was born in Hitchin and baptised at St. Mary's Church (Hitchin) on August 10th 1893. He was the second of eight children born to George and Kate Lawrence (née Hill), four of whom were Lucy (b c1892), Jack (b c1894), George (b c1897) and William (b c1900). He grew up at 9 Russell Slip in Hitchin. His sister (Lucy?) died at about eleven years old, having contracted lockjaw (tetanus) while picking blackberries.

Jack married Violet Abbiss, a Pirton girl, on December 27th 1915, the same day as Frederick William Brooks (another Pirton Soldier) married Annie Priscilla Carter. Violet was a younger sister of the Frank Abbiss who died in the war, and who is listed on the Village War Memorial. Jack's brothers George and William also fought. George, the grandfather of Rose, lost a lung after being gassed with mustard-gas in the trenches at Ypres, and she remembers the hacking cough it left him with for the rest of his life. William died just two weeks before the Armistice, in what must have been one of the last battles of the war, during the taking of Heestert in Belgium. Neither man had a direct connection to Pirton.

Jack was wounded in the leg during the war, which resulted in its amputation. Following the war, as with so many injured men, he was given training as a cobbler. He trained at the Bedfordshire Disability Centre, and then repaired boots and shoes from his tin shed on Village Green, also known as Chipping Green and situated near to Great Green. His skills not only earned a living, but when Rose's father was born with rickets, which could well have crippled him

Jack Lawrence outside his business on Chipping Green.

for life, Uncle Jack fashioned the leg irons that enabled him to walk. He went on to work as a postman for many years.

Jack and Violet had two sons Brian and Geoff.

Jack also features in Joy Franklin's book – Memories of Old Joys. Joy wrote; *'Jack Lawrence, the local shoe mender, lost a leg in the First World War and rode a bicycle with one fixed pedal which intrigued me very much, but he sometimes walked to his little tin shop situated on the village green. People used to congregate in this little shop for a chat and the children were just as welcome as were their elders, providing they behaved themselves. He would hammer nails into heels and soles with a mouthful of nails for supply. I always hoped he would not swallow any of them and I never heard that he did. He used the expression 'Oh! Lor'.' a lot and because of that some of us used to refer to him as 'Oh! Lor'.'*

Parish and census records provide no further information, except that he and his wife's ashes are interred in the Garden of Rest of St. Mary's Church.

LAWRENCE, JOHN

The Parish Magazine of June 1917 records John as being a Sapper in the Royal Engineers, joining up sometime after August 1915 and before March 2nd 1916.

Parish and census records provide no further information and, given that Jack Lawrence (above) was sometimes known as John, it would seem quite likely that they are one and the same man.

MALES, HARRY

Harry appears on the School War Memorial, confirming that he attended the school. Parish and census records suggest only one man of this name who could have served and he was born on June 13th 1892 to Ernest Ephraim and Mary Males (née Males (sic) - marriage records). Baptism and census records list nine children: William (b c1876), Rhoda (bapt 1879), James (b 1881), Jane (b 1883), Anne (b 1886), Clara (bapt 1889), Harry (b 1892), Mary (bapt 1895) and Frederick Charles (b 1910).

He is recorded in the Parish Magazine of November 1918 as enlisting '*recently*' and serving in the West Yorkshire Regiment. He would have been twenty-six years old.

MALES, JOHN

John appears on the School War Memorial, confirming that he attended the school. Parish records suggest only one man of this name who could have served and he was born on February 11th 1895 to Charles and Sarah Ann Males (née Chamberlain). He would have been nineteen at the outbreak of war. The 1901 census records him as the nephew of Lucy Durham. Baptism and census records list eleven children, but by 1911 four had died. At this time, only ten can be identified with certainty; Rachel (b 1879), Clara Amelia (b 1882, d 1884, aged two years and eight months), Isabella Rose (b 1884), Ellen Elizabeth (b 1885), Alice (b 1887), Sarah (b 1888), Florence (b 1890, d 1891, aged twenty-one months), Michael George (b 1892), Arthur (b 1893) and John (b 1895). His older brother, Michael, also served and survived.

John Males in the Homeguard during WW2.

In 1911, his parents were living with two of their children, Michael and Arthur, in 3 Holwell Road, and another, John, was a few doors away at number seven - the house of his brother in law John Baines and his sister Alice (now Baines). John's profession was given only as an iron foundry moulder, probably in Hitchin.

The Parish Magazine of June 1917 records John as serving in the Royal Engineers and in 1918 he was recorded as Sapper 193539, 96th Field Company, Royal Engineers, with his home address the same as his brother Michael's, 3 Holwell Road. A photograph taken during the Second World War shows a John Males as serving in Pirton and Holwell Homeguard, possibly the same man.

MALES, MICHAEL GEORGE

Michael appears on the School War Memorial, confirming that he attended the school. Parish records suggest only one man of this name who could have served and he was born on June 23rd 1892 to Charles and Sarah Ann Males (née Chamberlain). So he would have been nineteen at the outbreak of war. In all it would appear that two brothers served and survived – refer to John Males for more family details.

In 1911, Michael was eighteen, still living in the family home at number 3 Holwell Road and earning a living as a boot repairer.

He is recorded in the September Parish Magazine of 1915 as enlisting during 1914, but after July, and serving in the 11th Middlesex Regiment. However, the Parish Magazine of June 1917 records him as serving in the East Surrey Regiment. In fact, both are true and this is confirmed by his certificate of discharge, which was provided by his grandson Alan Males. This also confirms that he enlisted on August 15th 1914 and that he served overseas, although confusingly gives a different date of birth (1894). At some point, he was transferred to the 386 HS (Home Service) Labour Corps and then, as Private 626743, he was discharged on March 28th 1919 as medical category B II. This medical category might have been the reason for his transfer and means that he was not deemed suitable for combatant service - probably due to a war injury or sickness.

In a letter home in December 1914, he confirmed his Regiment as the 11th Middlesex and lets his family know '*I am getting on all right and hope to be at the Front soon with the boys.*'

By 1918, he was recorded as Private 203318, 12th Battalion, East Surrey Regiment, with his home address the same as his brother John's, 3 Holwell Road.

Michael George Males

Alan also provides other information. Within three months of his discharge, Michael married Elizabeth Maud Bethell at Marylebone Registry Office. Interestingly, Maud's brother Thomas married Michael's sister Sarah. After their marriage, Michael and Maud lived in Henlow, where he set up a business as a boot and shoe maker/repairer. Sadly, Michael died in 1926 and is buried in Henlow churchyard. Maud continued to live in Henlow until her death in 1964, aged seventy-three.

MILES, ELYSTAN

The Parish Magazine of October 1915 records Captain Elystan as '*indirectly connected to Pirton*'. Unfortunately, parish and census records provide no further information.

MORRISON, RIDDLE

The Parish Magazine of October 1915 records Captain Riddle as '*indirectly connected to Pirton*'.

Parish and census records provide no further information for this man. The only reference found is to a Robert James Alexander Morrison of Richmond, who married Gertrude Pollard of Highdown in 1900. Perhaps he was a relative of James.

MOSSMAN, WILLIAM

William was only revealed during a search for soldiers' service records. His shows that, when he enlisted, he was living in Pirton.

He was born in Pirton on August 31st 1882 and married Jennie Ada Ashpool in Luton on March 29th 1904. William's mother was Miriam Mossman and by then his father had died and William's family was living in his mother's house in Luton. All three were connected with the straw hat trade and perhaps that is how William met his wife. Miriam and Jennie were listed as straw hat finishers, and William as a straw hat stiffener. At that date William and Jennie had two children, Miriam Leah (b 1904) and George Charles (b 1908), both born in Luton. He enlisted there on September 5th 1914, aged thirty-two, just a month after the war began. He became Private 16436, "D" company, 7th Battalion, Bedfordshire Regiment. His home address is now given more fully as 196 Wellington Street, Luton. His service did not last long, as on January 25th 1915, having not left the country, he was discharged as medically unfit due to deficient teeth and gastric pain.

MURRAY, JOHN H.

The Parish Magazine of October 1915 records John, who was serving in the Canadian Field Artillery, as '*indirectly connected to Pirton*'. Unfortunately parish and census records provide no further information, and there is insufficient information to locate him in the Canadian database and to find his attestation papers.

NEWBERY, JOHN NORMAN, (NORMAN)

There appear to be several spellings of the surname, i.e. Newbery, Newberry and Newbury, but Newbery is believed to be the correct spelling for John Norman.

In a number of newspaper reports it seems that John was commonly known as Norman, and the name Norman Newbery appears in the Hertfordshire Express of July 11th 1914, which reports the Pirton Transept Fête. He was listed as a judge or official for the sports and as a member of the organising committee.

Norman appears on the School War Memorial, confirming that he attended the school, although he appears as Norman John. Parish records suggest only one man of this name who could have served and he was born on September 22nd 1892 to William and Ellen Newbery. William, his father, was the village blacksmith operating from Great Green and a church warden for twenty-six years. Norman would have been twenty-one at the outbreak of war. Baptism and census records list three children, but by 1911 one had died; Ellen (bapt 1891, d 1891, aged two months), John Norman (b 1892) and William Alexander (b 1889). William also served and survived.

Norman is recorded twice in the Parish Magazine; in September 1914 as being in the Territorials and in September 1915 as enlisting in 1914 after July, and serving in the 1st Hertfordshire Regiment. The Hertfordshire Express of November 11th 1914 reports that he was serving in the Middlesex Territorials, so his exact Regiment is uncertain and it could be that all the reports may be correct.

A letter from Norman, dated December 1914, thanks Mr Franklin for the gift of jerseys for him, W Reynolds (could be Walter or William) and Edward Goldsmith. It also confirms that all three were in "G" Company and in Thurston in Suffolk, near Bury St. Edmunds.

He was a good friend of Fred Baines, who also served, and provided a gift of a case of carvers at Fred's wedding to Kathleen Chambers in April 1917.

By 1918 he was recorded as Private 2367, 1st Hertfordshire Regiment, with his home address as Great Green.

NEWBERY, WILLIAM ALEXANDER

There appear to be several spellings of the surname, i.e. Newbery, Newberry and Newbury, but Newbery is believed to be the correct spelling for William.

William appears on the School War Memorial, confirming that he attended the school. Parish records suggest only one man of this name who could have served, and he was born on October 15th 1889 to William and Ellen Newbery. William his father was the village blacksmith operating from Great Green and had been a church warden for twenty-six years. William would have been twenty-four at the outbreak of war. Baptism records list three children: Ellen (bapt 1891), William Alexander (b 1889) and John Norman (b 1892). William's younger brother, John (Norman), also served and survived.

The Hertfordshire Express of October 27th 1917 reports that before the war William held 'an important position as teacher, in the Licensed Victuallers School, London.' He must have already enlisted by this date as it adds that he had 'come home preparatory to joining the Forces'. The Hertfordshire Express of November 17th 1917, just three issues later, reports him 'has(sic) Dover Castle' (presumably stationed at Dover Castle) – this could be the H.M.H.S (Hospital Ship) Dover Castle.

By 1918, he was recorded as Private 178526, Royal Garrison Artillery, with his home address as Great Green.

NIGHTINGALE, ALFRED

All that is known of Alfred comes from the 1918 Absent Voters' List. He was Private 202815 in the York and Lancaster Regiment and his home address was given as The White Horse Inn, which was where The Motte and Bailey now stands on Great Green. This is the same address as given for Percival Harry Wright and James William Wright, both of whom also served and survived. Unfortunately, parish and census records currently provide no further information.

ODELL, JAMES

James appears on the School War Memorial, confirming that he attended the school. Parish records suggest only one man of this name who could have served, and he was born on September 18th 1883 to John and Mary Odell (née Dawson). He would have been thirty at the outbreak of war. Baptism records list eleven children: Jane (bapt 1881), James (b 1883), Martha (bapt 1885), Robert (b 1886), Nellie (b 1888), Frank (b 1890), William (1894), Arthur (b 1896), John (b 1898, died at seventeen days), Frederick (b 1899) and Marjorie (b 1902). His brothers Arthur and Frederick served and died in the war and are listed on the Village War Memorial.

For most of John and Mary's married life, the family lived at number 2 Silver Street, which was part of what is now number 10 or 12 Royal Oak Lane.

The family is shown in the various censuses of 1891, 1901 and 1911 as living near Little Lane, or in Dead Horse Lane - later renamed as Royal Oak Lane. In fact, these could have all been the same house. His brother's official war records give the address as number two.

The Parish Magazine of September 1915 records that Frank enlisted in the Royal Navy during 1914 and served on the H.M.S. Galatea. This ship was a light cruiser and, at the time, brand new, having been completed in December 1914. In January 1915, the Parish Magazine records that Miss Helen Davis from Hitchin arranged for the Pirton men who were serving to receive a booklet called 'The Happy Warrior', which contained bible thoughts for each day of 1915 and some of the last words of Lord Roberts as the preface. James had written saying, '*I am very glad that they all think of us at sea.*'

The North Herts Mail of June 15th 1916 reported that '*Able Seaman J Odell of H.M.S. Galatea sent a wire home saying he went through the recent battle in the North Sea The news is very comforting to his relatives and we trust that should there be another scrap he will pull through alright without any injury.*'

His ship is recorded as firing the first salvoes at the Battle of Jutland on May 31st 1916, when she attacked the German light cruiser Elbing.

H.M.S. Galatea

OLNEY, JAMES

James appears on the School War Memorial, confirming that he attended the school. Unfortunately, parish and census records provide no further information other than to confirm that the surname was present in Pirton at the time.

OLNEY, JOSEPH FRANK, (FRANK)

Joseph appears on the School War Memorial, confirming that he attended the school. Parish records suggest only one man of this name who could have served, and he was born in Highgate, Middlesex in about 1890. He was the son of Sarah Olney and he appears as Frank in the 1911 census. This information is derived from census records before 1911. He would have been about twenty-four at the outbreak of war. Other records show that Sarah was married to Thomas Olney, who was a railway labourer; as such he would have worked away from Pirton and this could explain his absence from some census records. Baptism and census records list eleven children, but, by 1911, one had died. At this time, only ten can be identified with certainty: they are Alice (b 1896), Annie Eliza (b c1886), Rose (b 1889), Joseph Frank (b 1890), Sidney (b c1894), Lily (b 1896) and Frederick Charles (b 1900), Charles (b c1901}, Leonard (b c1905) and Reginald (b 1910). His brother Sidney also served and survived.

In 1911, Frank was living in the family home and working as a farm labourer on one of the local farms.

The Parish Magazine of February 1917 records Frank as being '*called up*' and serving in the Royal Field Artillery. A newspaper article, believed to be from spring 1918, confirms that he was the brother of Sidney and the eldest son of Mr and Mrs Thomas Olney of Andrew's Cottages (the three cottages at the bottom of the High Street). It also informs us that Joseph or *Frank* was serving in India at that time.

By 1918, he was recorded as Driver 182823, 79th Battery Royal Field Artillery, with his home address the same as his brother Sidney's, 2 Andrew's Cottages.

Baptism records show a Ruth Elizabeth as born to Joseph and Alice, so it would seem that Joseph married, probably after the war, continued to live in Pirton and that they had at least one child.

OLNEY, SIDNEY

Sidney appears on the School War Memorial, confirming that he attended the school. Parish records suggest only one man of this name who could have served, and he was born in Finsbury Park in about 1894, and was the son of Sarah Olney. This information is derived from census records before 1911. He would have been about twenty at the outbreak of war. Other records show that Sarah was married to Thomas Olney, who was a railway labourer; as such he would have worked away from Pirton and this could explain his absence from some census records. In all it would appear that two brothers served and survived – refer to Joseph Frank Olney for more family details.

Before the war, Sidney used to work for Thomas Franklin as a ploughman. He enlisted in November 1914 and served as Private 19156 in the "A" Section of the 2nd Battalion, Bedfordshire Regiment. He went to France in June 1915 and, within a month had been wounded in the right arm and was in hospital. His parents received the news by letter on July 12th. Following hospital treatment, recovery and leave, he went to Salonika.

The North Herts Mail of October 12th 1916 reported that he had transferred to the Royal Irish Fusiliers and had written to his mother saying that they '*wish to be remembered to all*'. He had written from St Paul's Hospital in Malta, where he was recovering from enteric fever; a tropical infection, enteric fevers include typhoid and paratyphoid fevers and gastroenteritis. It is not surprising that he became ill as, in the Salonika campaign, for every casualty of battle three died of malaria, influenza or other diseases. He must have then gone to Egypt, as newspaper reports in April 1918 mention another wound, received there on March 10th. One of those reports confirms that Sidney was the younger brother of Joseph Frank and the second son of Mr and Mrs Thomas Olney of Andrew's Cottages (the three cottages at the bottom of the High Street).

By 1918, he was recorded as Private 22449, 5th Battalion, Royal Irish Fusiliers, with his home address the same as his brother Joseph Frank's, 2 Andrew's Cottages.

PEARCE, ARTHUR

Arthur appears on the School War Memorial, confirming that he attended the school. Parish records suggest only one man of this name who could have served, and he was baptised on January 1st 1896, the son of Charles and Naomi Pearce (née Hare). Baptism and census records list six children but, by 1911, two had died and so had their mother Naomi (d 1906). The children were; Jane (b 1888), John (b 1890), Albert (b 1892), Arthur (b 1896), Alfred (b 1898, d 1899, aged one year) and Frederick Charles (b c1904). Arthur's elder brother John also served and survived.

In 1911, Arthur was fifteen, still living in the family home, which was one of the Handscombe Cottages, Burge End - the row of terraced cottages in Shillington Road - and was earning a living as a farm labourer on one of the local farms.

Arthur is recorded in the Parish Magazine of September 1915 as enlisting sometime during 1915, but before August, and serving in the 2nd Battalion, Bedfordshire Regiment as Private 20819. He would have been nineteen years old. The North Herts Mail confirms that, before the war, he worked for Thomas Franklin and that he went to the Front in February 1916. He was reported missing on April 19th, but subsequently on May 9th, to his family's great relief, he was confirmed as a prisoner of war and in Germany. What a worrying five weeks that must have been for those that knew him. In August he was in Gresham Camp and had written that he is all right, and sends no complaint and that he receives parcels from home and the Regiment.

The North Herts Mail of October 20th 1917 reports that 'Lance Corporal Arthur Pearce had sent home to Mrs Joan Burton of Burge End a photograph of the memorial to the Irish who died at Limbury.' This must have been while he was a prisoner of war. One theory, which might explain the photograph, is that as there was a prison camp at Limburg an der Lahn, which sometimes appears as Limbury an der Lahn, he may have spent time in that camp - although it seems that it predominantly held Irish prisoners of war. Perhaps the prisoners themselves erected some sort of memorial to men who died, either in the camp or in the battles in which they were captured. If this is correct, then his time there may have overlapped with Charles Titmuss, who also appears to have spent time there.

The Hertfordshire Express of December 1st 1917 confirms that he was still a prisoner of war, but now in Giesson, presumably having been transferred there from Limbury.

Pirton resident Ron Burton recalled being told that at one time 'the POWs were so hungry that they ate grass'; he also confirmed that Arthur was the brother of John Pearce who also served and survived.

By 1918, he was recorded as 20819 (should be Lance Corporal), 8th Battalion, Bedfordshire Regiment with his home address as Handscombe's Cottages, Burge End.

PEARCE, JOHN*1

John appears on the School War Memorial, confirming that he attended the school. Parish and census records suggest two entries that could be correct. However, the information provided by Ron Burton confirms that the man who served was Arthur's brother and therefore this John was born on June 9th 1890 and was the son of Charles and Naomi Pearce (née Hare). In all it would appear that two brothers served and survived – refer to Arthur Pearce for more family details.

The Parish Magazine of June 1917 records him as serving in the Training Reserve Battalion.

The identity of John is confirmed by the 1918 Absent Voters' List, which identifies this John Pearce as Private 59779, 100th Labour Corps and gives his address as the same as his brother Arthur's, Handscombe's Cottages, Burge End, (the row of terraced cottages now at the start of Shillington Road). Ron died in 2009, but always kept the shell fuse, which was brought back as a souvenir of the war by John, in a prominent position.

The shell fuse brought back from the war by John Pearce as a souvenir.

*1 This is a different person to Francis John Pearce (known as Jack) who he is recorded separately on the School War Memorial.

PITTS, JAMES

James appears on the School War Memorial, confirming that he attended the school.

Adrian Pitts, who is researching the Pitt family, thinks that James may be the son born in 1883 to George and Ann

Pitts. This could indeed be correct, but parish and census records also suggest another possibility.

Adrian's suggestion is also supported by parish records, which record a James born on January 16th 1883 to George and Ann Pitts (née Hare). He would have been thirty-one at the outbreak of war. Baptism records list six children: Elizabeth (bapt 1877), Emma (bapt 1879), William (b 1881), James (b 1883), Ruth (b 1886) and Ellen (b 1889).

The other possibility was baptised in 1875, the son of Elizabeth Pitts. Baptism records identify two children: James (bapt 1875) and Alice (b 1880), but no father is named. The 1881 census confirms these children and lists another sister, Ann (b c1872). James would have been about thirty-six at the outbreak of war.

Elizabeth's surname changed when she married George Trussell in 1885. They had three children together; Ellen (bapt 1885), Emily (b 1886) and George Thomas (b 1888). Sadly, they only had three years of marriage as George died in 1888.

In summary, it seems this James had two siblings and three possible half-siblings and, if this is the correct James, then it was his half-brother George who served and was killed, and he is recorded on the Village War Memorial.

Unfortunately, it is not certain which is the correct man. However, he is recorded in the Parish Magazine of September 1915 as enlisting sometime during 1915, but before August, and serving in the Royal Engineers.

PITTS, WALTER JAMES

Walter appears on the School War Memorial, confirming that he attended the school. Parish records suggest only one man of this name who could have served, and he was born on March 13th 1899 to William Josiah and Abigail Pitts (née Goldsmith). He would only have been fifteen at the outbreak of war and so it is likely that he served in the latter stages of the war. Census records confirm Walter James (b 1899) and Martha (b 1901) as children and Adrian Pitts, who is researching the Pitts family, was able to add Ethel Annie (b 1904) and Zilla Rose (b 1905).

Walter married Elizabeth Florence Tansley, the daughter of Alfred Sharp and Florence Emily Tansley, on September 15th 1923 in St. Johns Church, Hitchin. Elizabeth was born in 1901 in Pirton and they had two children: Raymond Wally and Derrick William Pitts. Walter and Elizabeth are both buried in Holwell, Walter passed away on July 20th 1974.

Adrian consulted his father about Walter, and he produced Walter's war medals inscribed on the edge with '46160 Pte W J Pitts Rif Brig', confirming that he served in the Rifle Brigade. He also confirmed that Walter had been wounded, receiving a shrapnel wound to the nose. It is thought that this required a plate to be inserted.

POCOCK, EDWIN

All that is known of Edwin comes from the 1918 Absent Voters' List. He was Private 48097 in "B" Company, 1st Battalion, H.C.B. and his home address given as Holly Cottage, Hambridge Way. C.B. indicates Cyclist Battalion. Research shows that a number of men serving in the Hertfordshire Regiment transferred to the Huntingdonshire Cyclist Battalion. Perhaps this is the battalion in which Edwin served. Unfortunately, parish and census records currently provide no further information.

POLLARD, HUGH B. C.

The Parish Magazine of October 1915 records Lieutenant Hugh as 'indirectly connected to Pirton'. Michael Newbery informs us that Hugh's connection to Pirton was that he was the grandson of Joseph Pollard of Highdown, and this is confirmed by census records. These also record him as being born in Marylebone, London, and aged two in the 1891 census. This means that he would have been about twenty-five at the outbreak of war.

POULTER, F.

The Parish Magazine of October 1915 records Mr Poulter, who was serving in the 18th Battalion, Royal Fusiliers, as 'indirectly connected to Pirton'. Unfortunately, parish and census records provide no further information.

REYNOLDS, ARTHUR (1)

The name Arthur Reynolds appears twice in the Parish Magazine, once in February 1917, recording one Arthur Reynolds as being 'called up' since the last list, and then in November 1918, recording another Arthur Reynolds as 'joined up lately' and serving in the Army Service Corps (ASC). This suggests that there were two men with the same name and it is possible to identify two possible men from baptism records. One Arthur appears on the School War Memorial, confirming that at least one of the men attended the school.

As there is a considerable difference in age between the two men, it was originally assumed that the early entry would refer to the older man and vice versa. However, the discovery of the official service record for one of the men contradicts this and raises questions as to whether there were in fact two men. This is because the latter Parish Magazine entry refers to the ASC, but the service record confirms that the younger man was in the ASC and that he was called to service in October 1916. This would seem to reflect the earlier Parish Magazine report. This could simply mean that the later Parish Magazine is wrong, but as it is still possible that both men served and both served in the ASC, they are included here.

This Arthur was born on April 5th 1897 to Frank and Elizabeth Reynolds. Baptism and census records list six children, but by 1911 two had died. At this time only five can be identified with certainty; they are Lillian (b 1881), Annie (bapt 1885), Charles (b 1887), Frederick (b 1894) and Arthur (b 1897). Frederick also served and survived.

Arthur was working as a coach builder when he enlisted and, at nineteen, was called to service on October 11th 1916, becoming Private 231762 in the Army Service Corps (ASC). He was given the opportunity to learn to drive and passed his test on January 21st 1917, becoming a lorry driver in the Motor Transport Corps (MTC) of the ASC. It appears that he served entirely on home service.

Between January and March 1917 he drove lorries in the 12th Company, then to August 1918 was listed as an MTC driver in the 804 MTC ASC Darlington.

The Hertfordshire Express of April 13th 1918 reports that Arthur was serving in the 'Transports' in Wiltshire. The report confirms his parents as Mr and Mrs Frank Reynolds, who lived in Handscombe Cottages, Burge End - the row of terraced cottages in Shillington Road and that his elder brother, Frederick, was also serving. In the Absent Voters' List of 1918 his home address was confirmed as the same as his brother Frederick's, 1 Handscombe's Cottages, Burge End.

He spent a brief period to the middle of September 1918 with the 7th Company, before moving to the 728th MTC, which conveniently for Arthur operated out of Hitchin until April 1919. After a short gap, presumably leave, he moved to the 373rd MTC and remained with them until he was demobilised on December 25th 1919 as Private 231762, 373rd Motor Transport Company, RASC (Royal Army Service Corps). At that time he was recorded as having a thirty percent disablement, due to DAH (Disordered Action of the Heart), and received a provisional award of 12s 0d per week.

REYNOLDS, ARTHUR (2)

The information given above explains the possibility that two Arthur Reynolds served. The first is identified above. If a second man served, then the only other possibility identified is an older man, who was baptised on April 1st 1877 and was the son of Oswald and Emily Reynolds (née Larman) (m-1874). He would have been about thirty-seven at the outbreak of war. Baptism records list four children: Clara (bapt 1874), Arthur (bapt 1877), Alice (bapt 1879) and Nellie (bapt 1884).

REYNOLDS, FREDERICK (1)

The name Frederick or Fred Reynolds appears twice in the Parish Magazine, once as Fred in September 1915 as enlisting during 1915 and before August, and serving in the Westminster Dragoons. Then in the November 1918 Parish Magazine, a Frederick Reynolds is recorded as 'joined up lately' and serving in the Lancashire and Yorkshire Regiment (should be York and Lancaster). This suggests that there were two men with the same name and it is possible to identify two possible men from baptism records. One Frederick appears on the School War Memorial, confirming that at least one of the men attended the school.

The discovery of the service record for one of the men provides information which questions whether there were actually two men of this name who served. The man appearing here definitely served and, because of his enlistment date, he would be the former mentioned above but he did not serve in the Westminster Dragoons as reported. He served in the York and Lancs Regiment, which the Parish Magazine attributes to the latter man. Other possible men have been identified from official records. So it is still possible that two men of the same name did serve, but that the Parish Magazine confused their information.

The Hertfordshire Express of April 13th 1918 provides information on the Frederick Reynolds, who served in the York and Lancs Regiment. The newspaper reports that, before the war, this Frederick was a footman in private service in Scotland. His parents were Mr and Mrs Frank Reynolds, who lived in Handscombe Cottages, Burge End - the row of terraced cottages in Shillington Road, and that his younger brother Arthur was also serving. It also reports that Private Frederick had written from the General Hospital in Etaples, France, to say he had been wounded on the 21st (March?). The official report said 'gun-shot, shoulder and knee, severe.'

This confirms that he is the man for whom a service record exists and that he was the son of Frank and Elizabeth Reynolds, baptised on May 13th 1894. In all it would appear that two brothers may have served and survived – refer to Arthur Reynolds(1) for more family details.

Frederick was a postman when he signed his attestation papers on August 23rd 1915. He joined the Territorial Force, 2nd Battalion, County of London Regiment, at the age of twenty-one and became Private 2749. His service records show that he remained on home service until April 25th 1916, and then he left for France. He remained there until August 19th 1917 when he returned to the UK, transferring to the Tank Corps the next day, probably as Private 300765. He then joined the York and Lancaster Regiment on August 28th, as Private 205415 and then, presumably, had a period of training. He returned to France on November 29th 1917 and joined the 12th Battalion, York and Lancaster Regiment, in the field on December 8th.

The Absent Voters' List of 1918 recorded him as Private 205415, York and Lancaster Regiment with his home address the same as his brother Arthur's, 1 Handscombe's Cottages, Burge End - one of the row of terraced cottages in Shillington Road.

In March 1918, he was in the area of Bayeaux, when the Germans launched their massive Spring Offensive, and he received a gun shot wound to the shoulder on the 22nd. As a result, he was moved back to a hospital in the area of Etaples. Following his recovery, he was transferred to the 31st Prisoner of War Company, Labour Corps as Private 564436. Perhaps he was unhappy about this because, on June 6th, before joining them, he broke out of camp after roll call and was caught returning to camp at 6am the next day. He forfeited a day's pay and was deprived of a further seven days' pay. He joined his new Regiment as Private 564436 on June 19th 1918. Later that year, in December, he was give UK leave, but was again a day late returning and received more punishment, this time being confined to barracks for seven days.

Frederick remained in France until May 5th 1919 and was demobilised on June 3rd 1919.

REYNOLDS, FREDERICK (2)

As explained above, the information available suggests that there were two Fred or Frederick Reynolds who served. Much of the information is confirmed as being for the Frederick listed above, so it is more difficult to identify the Frederick who may have served with the Westminster Dragoons. Discounting the above Frederick Reynolds then, the parish and census records suggest two possible men.

The first was five in the 1891 census, so he was born in about 1886 or 1887. He was the grandson of Ann Reynolds, and would have been about twenty-three at the outbreak of war. The records are confusing, but Edgar Dawson married Elizabeth Jane Reynolds*1 in 1888 and the 1891 census records list them as living in the house belonging to Elizabeth's mother, Ann. There are five grand children listed, including two Joseph Reynolds. They are Joseph Reynolds (b c1878), Joseph Reynolds (b c1881), Frederick Reynolds (b c1886), Reginald Dawson (b 1889) and Ethel Annie Dawson (b 1890).

Reginald and Ethel are confirmed as Edgar and Elizabeth's children and then baptism and the 1911 census confirm their other children as Emily Almond (b 1891, d aged six weeks), Charles (b c1896), Bertie (b c1898), Kate (b c1900) and Harry (b c1905). The census also confirmed eight children, two of whom had died.

There are no children listed as Elizabeth's in 1881, before she was married, but it is possible that Joseph Reynolds (the youngest) and Frederick Reynolds were also her children. However, this has not been proved and therefore it is not clear whether any of the children named are Frederick's siblings or half siblings, nor who his parents were.

The second possible man was baptised on August 3rd 1873, the son of William and Sarah Reynolds. Baptism and census records identify eight children: Elizabeth (bapt 1862), Amos (bapt 1864), Fanny (b c1866), Mary Ann (b c1868), Alice (b 1870), Frederick (bapt 1873), Ruth (bapt 1876) and Charles (b c1885). Frederick would have been forty-one at the outbreak of war, which is only just young enough to have served. In 1898, he was listed as from Shilley Green, (near Hitchin, not far from Rush Green) when he married Ellen Catterill from Pirton.

Unfortunately it is not certain which, if either, of the above is the second Frederick Reynolds who served, if indeed one did, but the former is certainly the most likely.

*1 *This was her maiden name. She is not the Elizabeth Reynolds identified as the mother of the first Frederick Reynolds as she and her husband are still listed in the 1911 census; therefore there are two Elizabeth Reynolds.*

REYNOLDS, GEORGE THOMAS

George appears on the School War Memorial, confirming that he attended the school. Parish records suggest only one man of this name who could have served, and he was born on March 21st 1890 to Lewis and Mary Ann Reynolds (née Catterell). He would have been twenty-four at the outbreak of war. Baptism and census records list fifteen children, but by 1911, five had died: James (bapt 1870, d 1871, aged seven months), Clara (bapt 1872, d 1874, aged two years), Maria (bapt 1874), Jacob (bapt 1876), Peggy (bapt 1877), Daisy Emma (b 1879, possibly d 1900, aged twenty), Mary (b 1881), William (b 1883), Albert (bapt 1884), Abigail (b 1886), Sarah (b 1888), George Thomas (b 1890), Harry (b 1890 and George's twin), Emily Agnes (b 1893) and Walter (b 1894).

By 1911, all but Walter appear to have left the family home, which was 3 Wesley Cottages - the group of cottages behind the terrace which now contains the village shop. George does not appear in the Pirton census, so must have been working or living away from Pirton at the time.

A newspaper cutting from very late 1917, or perhaps early 1918, provides confirmation that George's parents were Mr and Mrs Lewis Reynolds of 3 Wesley Cottages. His father had a small-holding and his mother had been an invalid for several years. George was one of six brothers serving; the others were Walter and Albert, who both died and are listed on the Village War Memorial, and Jacob, William and Harry who survived. It is also recorded that they had at least one sister, whose husband was also serving. At the time of the report, George was serving as a private in the Suffolk Regiment, but had not yet gone to war, as he was helping his father.

A monument inscription in St. Mary's churchyard records that George died on June 10th 1946, aged fifty-six. It also lists Mabel Florence Cook died April 27th 1988, aged ninety.

REYNOLDS, HARRY

Harry appears on the School War Memorial, confirming that he attended the school. Parish records suggest only one man of this name who could have served, and he was born on March 21st 1890 to Lewis and Mary Ann Reynolds (née Catterell). So he would have been twenty-four at the outbreak of war. In all it would appear that six brothers served, four survived - refer to George Thomas Reynolds for more family details.

By 1911, all but Walter appear to have left the family home, which was 3 Wesley Cottages - the group of cottages behind the terrace which now contains the village shop. Harry does not appear in the Pirton census, so must have been working or living away from Pirton at the time.

A newspaper cutting from very late 1917 or perhaps early 1918 provides confirmation that Harry's parents were Mr and Mrs Lewis Reynolds of 3 Wesley Cottages. His father had a small-holding and his mother had been an invalid for several years. Harry was one of six brothers serving; the others were Walter and Albert, who both died and are listed on the Village War Memorial, and Jacob, William and George who survived. It is also recorded that they had at least one sister, whose husband was also serving.

Harry was a driver in the Royal Horse Artillery in France, but prior to December 1917 had been badly gassed. He must have recuperated because the newspaper reports him as returning to his Regiment in Yorkshire. It also reports that he was married.

A monument inscription in St. Mary's churchyard records that Harry died on June 10th 1955, aged sixty-five. It also lists Elizabeth as his wife. She died November 26th 1959, aged seventy-four, and Francis William Reynolds, presumably their son, died in 1944 aged twenty-one.

Note: The 1911 census indicates that there is another man of this name, the son of John and Ann Reynolds; however because of the evidence from the newspaper reports he is not the Harry that served.

REYNOLDS, JACOB

Jacob appears on the School War Memorial, confirming that he attended the school. Parish records suggest only one man of this name who could have served, and he was baptised on June 4th 1876 to Lewis and Mary Ann Reynolds (née Catterell). So he would have been thirty-eight at the outbreak of war. In all it would appear that six brothers served and four survived - refer to George Thomas Reynolds for more family details.

By 1911, all but Walter appear to have left the family home, which was 3 Wesley Cottages - the group of cottages behind the terrace which now contains the village shop. Jacob does not appear in the Pirton census, so must have been working or living away from Pirton at the time.

Two newspaper cuttings, one from very late 1917, or perhaps early 1918, and the other from around August 1918 provide the following information. Before the war Jacob had been an ostler (stableman) at the Sun Hotel in Hitchin and was also a driver for Hitchin Fire Brigade. He had a wife and six children. The earlier article confirms Jacob's parents were Mr and Mrs Lewis Reynolds of 3 Wesley Cottages. His father had a small-holding and his mother had been an invalid for several years. Jacob was one of six brothers serving; the others were Walter and Albert, who both died and are listed on the Village War Memorial, and William and Harry and George who survived. It is also recorded that they had at least one sister, whose husband was also serving. At the time of the report Jacob was on home service.

REYNOLDS, PHILIP

Philip appears on the School War Memorial, confirming that he attended the school. Parish and census records initially suggest only one possible man of this name who could have served, and he was Philip Kenneth Reynolds, born on December 8th 1899 to Fanny Reynolds. The release of the 1911 census seems to reveal another possibility, Philip (b c1900) the son of John and Ann. However, this is probably a mistake as the earlier1901 census records him as their grandson and so Fanny, his mother, was John and Ann's daughter. Fanny was unmarried.

The Parish Magazine of September 1918 records Philip as *'called to service'*. He would have been eighteen when called up. Parish and census records provide no further information other than to record a Philip Reynolds, who died on March 20th 1974, aged seventy-four and is buried in St. Mary's churchyard.

REYNOLDS, WILLIAM

William appears on the School War Memorial, confirming that he attended the school. Parish records suggest only one man of this name who could have served, and he was born on January 24th 1883 to Lewis and Mary Ann Reynolds (née Catterell). He would have been twenty-four at the outbreak of war. In all it would appear that six brothers served and four survived - refer to George Thomas Reynolds for more family details.

In 1904, on March 12th, William married Margaret Barnes. His sister Abigail and brother Albert were witnesses. At that time William was a gamekeeper,

By 1911, all but Walter appear to have left the family home, which was 3 Wesley Cottages - the group of cottages behind the terrace which now contains the village shop. William does not appear in the Pirton census, so must have been working or living away from Pirton at the time.

A newspaper cutting from very late 1917 or perhaps early 1918 provides confirmation that William's parents were Mr and Mrs Lewis Reynolds of 3 Wesley Cottages. His father had a small-holding and his mother had been an invalid for several years. Harry was one of six brothers serving; the others were Walter and Albert, who both died and are listed on the Village War Memorial, and Jacob, Harry and George who survived. It is also recorded that they had at least one sister, whose husband was also serving. At the time of the report, William was a private in the King's Shropshire Light Infantry serving as an officer's servant in France. He had a wife and five children living in Edenbridge, Kent.

A letter from Norman Newbery, dated December 1914, thanks Mr Franklin for the gift of jerseys for him, W Reynolds (could be Walter or William) and Edward Goldsmith. It also confirms that all three were in "G" Company and at Thurston in Suffolk, near Bury St. Edmunds.

Grace Tullett (née Abbiss), William's Granddaughter, provided the photograph and confirms that he was born in 1883 and died in 1968.

William Reynolds

ROBERTS, GEORGE

There were two George Roberts, both listed in the Parish Magazine of September 1915. The first George Roberts enlisted during 1914, but after July, and was serving in the 1st Hertfordshire Regiment. The report also recorded that he was wounded. The second man was recorded as George Roberts (senior), who enlisted during August 1915 and served in the Army Service Corps. Len Blackburn, Sidney George's son-in-law, confirms that he was commonly known as George.

Careful analysis of the several newspaper cuttings that refer to George Roberts reveals that they all seem to relate to Sidney George (next entry), and very little information was available for George until his service record was found. They revealed that he was born in 1871. In 1915, he was working as carpenter, with his address being in Great Green. He had married Georgina Stanbridge on October 31st 1898 and they had two children: Lewis (b 1902) and Harold Joseph (b 1912). He signed his attestation papers in London on July 3rd 1915, aged forty-four, and became Private 13610 in the Army Service Corps (ASC). Labour was desperately needed in France to free up first line troops to fight, so he went to France very quickly, embarking on July 18th on the S.S. Lydid and then, within a month, had transferred to the 16th Labour Company. In November 1916 he was treated in hospital for multiple abrasions, which happened while he was loading hay on to trucks at the base supply depot. He suffered another injury and was again treated in hospital in December, this time a contusion (bruising) at the upper end of his tibia; however, this injury was not while on duty. In February 1917 the Labour Corps was formed and, in August, he was transferred to it.

By the end of the war, he was recorded as Private 305443, 126th Labour Corps, and was demobilised on March 22nd 1919, by which time his home address was 7 Dunstable Street, Ampthill.

ROBERTS, SIDNEY GEORGE, (GEORGE)

As explained above, there were two George Roberts, both listed in the Parish Magazine of September 1915. The man recorded as enlisting during 1914, but after July, and who was serving in the 1st Hertfordshire Regiment is this man. The Parish Magazine also recorded that he had been wounded. Len Blackburn, Sidney George's son-in-law, confirmed that Sidney George was commonly known as George.

George appears on the School War Memorial, confirming that he attended the school. Parish and census records confirm that he was baptised Sidney George and was born on November 21st 1893 to Charles and Isabel Reynolds (née Lake). He would have been twenty at the outbreak of war. Baptism records list three children: Alice Mary (b 1891), Sidney George (b 1893) and Rose (b 1896).

In 1911, George was seventeen and working as a farm labourer on one of the local farms, but when war came he was working as an undergroom in Wellbury for a Mrs Gosling.

Letters home from the Front reveal much about his experience; they describe the twenty-mile walk of the 1st Hertfordshire Regiment to get to the trenches, with the '*First night billeted in a town, then slept in a barn*'. Christmas Eve and Christmas Day were spent digging trenches. By Boxing Day, they were occupying them and only about 200 yards from the Germans. '*We are all tired and want to sleep. What with the rattle of the big guns and having to keep awake it soon begins to play on us.*' '*It seems as if everyone must get hit, with the shells bursting over our heads the whole time.*' '*We have seen some sights since we have been out here, what with towns and villages that have been destroyed and people being turned out of their houses. We shall all be glad when it is over.*' And in another letter '*On New Year's Eve we could hear the Germans singing, as we were only about 200 yards from their trenches. Thank God we got through it once again. You will be pleased to know that all the Pirton chaps are quite well, and we still have some lead left for the Germans!*' On this occasion, they remained in the trenches until January 20th.

He was wounded sometime in May 1915 and sent a field card home to his parents, telling them that he had been wounded in the head and legs and was in the base hospital in France – the British Army did not issue helmets until late 1915. Initially, it was thought to be not too serious, but by the 27th his parents had received a letter to say that it was more serious than had first been thought, and that he had been returned to England and was now in Walsworth Hospital in London. The North Herts Mail was reporting and ended with its good wishes 'We hope the brave young soldier will soon get convalescent.' A later report revealed that he had been with Arthur Walker and Sidney Smith also of the same Regiment. Sidney was also wounded. Arthur escaped uninjured, but was killed in a similar incident in September 1916 along with John Parsell. By cruel coincidence, George was present at both and wounded in both. In the second incident he was returned to King George's Hospital in Stanford Street London. One wonders how many other unreported near misses they had experienced.

Other newspaper cuttings from the village scrapbook provide more information. They confirm George was the son of Mr and Mrs Charles Roberts, who lived near Little Green. Cross-referencing this information with other articles recording the death of John Parsell suggest that the article is dated sometime around September 1916. This confirms that, in the second incident George was slightly wounded in the ear by a fragment of a shell and was later transferred to King George's Hospital in London. This was almost certainly the same shell that killed John Parsell and Arthur Walker.

Perhaps because of his injuries he may have transferred regiments and duties, since, in the 1918 Absent Voters' List he was recorded as Private 254547, Agricultural Corps, Labour Corps, with his home address given as Little Green.

Len Blackburn kindly provided the following information: *"George was my father in law, he had married Annie Emily Carter in the late 1920s and lived in 24 Royal Oak Lane. He was a carpenter by trade, working for a film-maker in Welwyn Garden City and then for British Rail. He was also the Chairman of the Pirton branch of the British Legion and went to the annual Remembrance Service at the Royal Albert Hall up until about 1971."* George and his wife's ashes are interred in the Garden of Rest of St. Mary's Church. George died in 1980 and Emily in 1983.

The North Herts Mail of December 17th 1914 gives information for a Private T G Roberts (*note T G not S G*) serving in "G" Company of the Hertfordshire Territorials. A search of the parish and census records does not reveal any T or a T G Roberts, so it is probable that the T G is a misprint of the S G Roberts. This is supported by the fact that the content of the letter seems to fit with letters quoted above, and that T G and S G Roberts are both listed as in "G" Company, 1st Hertfordshire Regiment.

In a letter to Mr Franklin, he wrote '*We are not up in the firing line just now, but have been there. We can hear the guns where we are and want to get up there. The French relieved us* (the) *first time we went in the trenches. All the Pirton lads in 1st Herts. are quite well and happy.*'

REYNOLDS, T. G.

See Roberts, Sidney George.

SCOTT, JAMES

The man's name was found in the 1918 Absent Voters' List. He was Private 47500, Royal Army Medical Corps and his home address was given as Great Green.

Parish and census records suggest only one possible man, a James Scott who was the father of William Foster Scott from Brompton Sw (possibly Brompton on Swale) who married Kate Weston of Pirton on December 31st 1900. Perhaps he moved with his son to live in Pirton, but surely, as the father of William, he would have been too old to have served?

SEXTON, PETER

Peter appears on the School War Memorial, confirming that he attended the school. Unfortunately, the parish and census records available provide no further information.

SHARPE, ALBERT JAMES

Albert was only revealed during the search service records for Pirton soldiers. He lived in one of the Wellbury Cottages on the Hexton Road which were in the Parish of Pirton.

He was born in West Hill, Wandsworth and had married Pirton born Louisa Weston on April 13th 1903 in Pirton. They had obviously lived in various parts of the country as their first born child Harold Albert was born in Southfields, and the next two, Dorothy Mary (b 1907) and John Edward (b 1909), were born in Tisbury, Dorset (now Wiltshire).

By 1915, he was working as a chauffeur and living in one of the Wellbury Cottages. He signed his attestation papers on April 24th 1915, aged thirty-nine. His previous work made him suitable for the Motor Transport Corps (MTC) section of the Army Service Corps (ASC) and he joined the 234th Company, MTC as Private 113396. He is listed as on home service until December 19th 1915, when he joined the 338th Company, and then served with the Mediterranean Expeditionary Force in Salonika until March 11th 1919. He arrived back in England on the 29th but was not demobilised until April 24th.

SHEPHERD, SHEPPARD OR SHEPPERD?

There is potential for confusion arising from the different spellings of this name and which applies to the following men. Different families, perhaps connected, used a different spelling and parish and census records also vary, so usage is unclear. The spelling that appears to be most common in the 1911 census has been used, even if the parent's surnames appear differently in earlier records. We apologise if this is incorrect.

SHEPPARD, HARRY

Harry appears on the School War Memorial, confirming that he attended the school. Parish and census records suggest only one possible man of this name who could have served, and he was born on June 12th 1889 to Alfred Thomas and Elizabeth Shepherd (née Walker). He would have been twenty-five at the outbreak of war. Baptism and census records list eleven children, but by 1911 one had died. The children were; Rosetta (bapt 1877), Clarence Frederick (bapt 1878), Hedley Albert (b 1880), Mabel Lizzie (b 1882), Cordelia Jane (bapt 1884), Bertie John (b 1887, d 1894, aged seven), Harry (b 1889), Alice Elizabeth (bapt 1891), Sidney William (b 1893), Violet Maud (b 1896) and Lilian Grace (b 1899). Harry's brothers Hedley and Sidney also served and survived.

In 1911, the family home was around Little Green. Harry, then twenty-one, was living with his parents and working as a machinist in a joinery works.

He is recorded in the September Parish Magazine of 1915 as enlisting sometime during 1915, but before August, and serving in the Royal Naval Flying Corps (this must be Royal Naval Air Services or Royal Flying Corps). The skills learned in his work would have been essential to keep these fragile machines repaired and in the air.

SHEPPARD, HEDLEY ALBERT, (EDDY)

Hedley Sheppard appears on the School War Memorial, confirming that he attended the school. Parish and census records suggest only one possible man of this name who could have served, and he was born on October 22nd 1880 to Alfred Thomas and Elizabeth Shepherd (née Walker). He would have been thirty-three at the outbreak of war. Baptism and census records list eleven children, but by 1911 one had died. In all it would appear that three brothers served and survived - refer to Harry Sheppard for more family details.

In 1911, the family home was around Little Green, but Hedley is absent and not listed in the Pirton census, so was presumably working or living away from Pirton.

He is recorded in the Parish Magazine of September 1915 as enlisting sometime during 1915, but before August, and serving in the King's Royal Rifle.

The North Herts Mail of December 14th 1916 reports that Sapper 'Eddy' Sheppard was married, lived around Great Green and had been in France for fifteen months. It also adds that he was currently on leave in Pirton. Although listed as Eddy, he is believed to be Hedley as no alternative man has been found in parish or census records and Clare Baines, who has a tremendous amount of knowledge about Pirton history and its inhabitants, believes Eddy and Hedley to be the same man.

By 1918, he was recorded as Private 90552, Royal Engineers, with his home address as 'near' Great Green.

SHEPPARD, SIDNEY WILLIAM

Sidney Sheppard appears on the School War Memorial, confirming that he attended the school. Parish and census records suggest only one possible man of this name who could have served, and he was born on October 13th 1893 to Alfred Thomas and Elizabeth Shepherd (née Walker). If this is the right man, then he would have been twenty at the outbreak of war. Baptism and census records list eleven children, but by 1911 one had died. In all it would appear that three brothers served and survived - refer to Harry Sheppard for more family details.

In 1911 the family home was around Little Green. Sidney, then seventeen, was living with his parents and working as an undertaker's apprentice.

SMITH, ARTHUR FREDERICK

Arthur appears on the School War Memorial, confirming that he attended the school. Parish records suggest only one man of this name who could have served, and he was born on July 21st 1899 to Frederick and Lizzie Smith (née Arnold). He would have been fifteen at the outbreak of war, and so it is likely that he served in the latter stages. Baptism and census records list three children: Arthur Frederick (b 1899), Eleanor Mary (b c1902) and Alice (b 1910).

The North Herts Mail of November 19th 1914 reports that a Fred Smith, almost certainly Arthur's father, had offered himself as a recruit, but at fifty-one, was considered too old to serve.

SMITH, CHARLES, (POSSIBLY BERTRAM CHARLES)

Charles appears on the School War Memorial, confirming that he attended the school. Parish and census records suggest two possibilities for the man that served:

The first was born on November 16th 1881 to Edwin and Emma Louise Smith (née Furr) and so he would have been thirty-two at the outbreak of war. Baptism and census records list eight children: Martha (bapt 1870), Frank (b 1871), Clara (bapt 1874), George John (bapt 1876), Lydia (b 1879), Charles (b 1881), Grace (bapt 1884) and Alice Louisa (b 1888).

By 1911 Charles was twenty-nine and working as a general labourer.

There is a second possibility, Bertram Charles born on March 25th 1894 to Clara Smith, and this man would have been twenty at the outbreak of war. Clara was the daughter of Edwin and Emma Louise Smith (née Furr) and she married William James Dawson in 1895. The 1901 census confirms that when they married Clara already had two children: Sidney Smith and Bertram Charles Smith. Subsequently all other children have Dawson as their surname. William is absent from the 1911 census, as he had died in 1909, but in 1901, when he was known as James, he was working as a navvy ground worker. The census confirms that there were six children and that Bertram Charles Smith was then known as Charles Smith.

Linda Smith, who is the daughter-in-law of the Sidney Smith who served, was able to confirm that Charles was also known as Chubb. However the family has so far not been able to confirm whether or not he was the Charles who served.

Baptism and census records list the children as Sidney (Smith, b c1892), Charles (Smith, b 1894), Lily (b c1896), Emma (b c1899) and Bertram (b c1901) and Leonard (b c1903). It is likely that his brother, Sidney Smith, was another man who served and survived.

In 1911, the family is known to be living near The Fox Inn, with Charles (Smith), Bertram and Leonard (Dawson) all present.

Charles is recorded in the Parish Magazine of July 1916 as enlisting between October 21st 1915 and March 2nd 1916 and serving in the Bedfords. By 1918, the man who served was recorded as Private Charles Smith, 30930, "A" Squadron, 1st Troop, 8th Hussars, with his home address as 'near' The Fox Inn. After the war he married Florence Bunker.

SMITH, SIDNEY

Sidney appears on the School War Memorial, confirming that he attended the school. Parish and census records revealed several possible men who could be the man who served. However Linda Smith, who is the daughter-in-law of the man who served, was able to confirm that he was the son of Clara Smith, the grandson of Edwin and Emma Louise Smith (née Furr) and that he was born on January 20th 1892. His father is unknown. Clara had been working at Knebworth Lodge Farm, Knebworth, and the family believes that the father may have been the master of the house. She was certainly absent from the Pirton 1891 census, when she would have been about seventeen.

Clara married William James Dawson in 1895 (James in later census). The 1901 census confirms that when they

Sidney Smith with his wife, Win, and son, Kenneth John.

married, Clara already had two children: Sidney Smith and Bertram Charles Smith. Subsequently all their other children have Dawson as their surname. William is absent from the 1911 census, as he had died in 1909, but in 1901, when he was known as James, he was working as a navvy ground worker. Sidney's brother, Bertram, later recorded as Charles, may also have served and survived - refer to Charles Smith for more family details.

Sidney is not present in the 1911 Pirton census, so was presumably working or living away from the village. He joined the Hertfordshire Territorials on February 10th 1914. Later the Parish Magazine of September 1915 confirms his enlistment in the 1st Hertfordshires, during 1914 and that he had volunteered for overseas service. His army medal roll index card gives that date as November 6th. Initially he was Private 2367 and then later Private 265409, probably when the Hertfordshires and Bedfords merged.

An undated newspaper cutting reports that Sidney was in "G" Company of the 1st Hertfordshire Regiment. The same report reveals glimpses of his life in the trenches, by quoting from a letter he wrote on the January 14th, (*must be 1915 or later*). He had to stand for twelve hours at a time in muddy conditions, but he makes light of that, describing how they have good fires afterwards to dry their clothing. It also records that '*When we were in the trenches we started singing, and the Germans* (only 200 yards away) *heard us, they had the cheek to get on the top of their trenches and waved their hats to us, but we soon made them get lower by putting a few bullets into them.*' He expected to go back to the trenches soon, and adds that '*The Herts. have been lucky up to the present, and hope to be lucky enough to get home safe. We are still merry, and we all keep in good heart.'*

In a separate, and also undated newspaper cutting, he optimistically, writes *'We live in hopes of being home in England soon after Christmas, as we all think that the war will be over very soon.'* He adds *'But there is one thing I should like, and that is just one shot at the Kaiser.'*

He wrote to his mother on May 21st 1915 that he had a wound to the top of his head caused by shrapnel – the British Army did not issue helmets until late 1915. At least for Sidney it was not too serious, but he was admitted to hospital in France. A later report revealed that he had been with Arthur Walker and Sidney George Roberts, also of Pirton and the same Regiment. Sidney Roberts was also wounded Arthur escaped uninjured but was killed in a similar incident in 1916.

The Parish Magazine of June 1917 records Sidney as wounded again, this time in the leg. The injury was serious enough for him to be discharged on July 27th 1917. The family story is that, upon his return to Pirton, the Lord of the Manor paid for an operation that enabled him to walk again, albeit with a stick.

After the war Sidney left Pirton and went to live in north London. He worked as a customs officer for Gilbeys and married twice, first to Elizabeth Barber, who died, and then to Winifred Waters. He died in November 1956.

STAPLETON, GEORGE HENRY

George appears on the School War Memorial, confirming that he attended the school. Parish and census records provide only limited information. The 1901 census lists Ruby, aged eight, and a George Henry, aged three, as the children of Annie Elizabeth Stapleton (with George born in Finsbury Park and Annie and Ruby in Ipswich). No marriage record was found, but school admissions record Ruby's father as William, so it is likely that George's father was William Stapleton. If he is the right man, then George was born in 1897 or 1898.

The 1911 census records Annie as living around Little Green, being married for fifteen years and having had five children, of whom two had died. Another son was born later. It has only been possible to name four of these children at this time: Ruby (b c1893), George Henry (b c1898), Cecil John (b c1902) and Alfred Edward (b 1917).

George is recorded in the Parish Magazine of February 1917 as enlisting and serving in the Transports, and the Parish Magazine of June 1917 records him as serving in the Connaught Rangers. He would have been about nineteen years old.

STAPLETON, HUBERT JOHN

There are a number of possibilities for this man, as there are several Herbert Johns and Hubert Johns appearing in the records. It is obvious that Herbert/Hubert could easily be transcription or spelling errors. Separating the men's information was difficult, but hopefully the following records are correct:

The three possibilities are Herbert John, son of John and Ann, baptised in 1891, Hubert John born in 1890 to Herbert Charles (recorded as Charles in some census records) and Ellen (née Parkins) – this man is recorded as John in the 1911 census and then Herbert John, son of Charles and Mary born May 13th 1880. However, the latter man appears as Hubert in the 1881 census and Hubert John in the 1911 census. For this reason it is believed that the baptism record is incorrectly transcribed as Herbert.

The weight of evidence is that it is one of the Hubert Johns who served. One was born in 1880 and the other in 1890, so both could have served. Evidence from various sources helps identify which is the right man. The Hertfordshire Express of March 23rd 1918 reports that H J Stapleton was on leave from the Naval Air Service and that he played the *'Dead March'* at the memorial service for those Pirton soldiers who had already given their lives. A monumental inscription inside St. Mary's Church informs us that from 1902 to 1910 Hubert was the organist at St. Mary's Church and took a leading part in the construction of this transept, which was completed and opened in 1913. It seems conclusive that the Hubert who served must have been the older man, as the other would have been too young to be the organist, and certainly too young to have had a substantive role in the re-building of the transept.

The Hubert who served appears on the School War Memorial, confirming that he attended the school. His parents were Charles and Mary Stapleton (née Hodson). The children of the family were Hubert John (b 1880), and Charles (bapt 1883).

Hubert Stapleton married Emma Stapleton (sic) on November 28th 1903, by which time his father had died. Her father is recorded as William Stapleton. In 1911, he was thirty and had been married to Emma for seven years but they had no children. Hubert was a carpenter and joiner in the building trade and so he was married when he went to war.

The Parish Magazine of February 1917 records him as serving in the Royal Naval Air Service and that is confirmed in the Hertfordshire Express of March 23rd 1918. The skills learned in his work would have been essential to keep these fragile machines repaired and in the air and seems to confirm that this is the right man. He would have been thirty-four at the outbreak of war.

STAPLETON, JESSE

Jesse appears on the School War Memorial, confirming that he attended the school. Parish records suggest only one man of this name who could have served, and he was born on August 6th 1892 to Herbert Charles (recorded as Charles in some census records) and Ellen Stapleton (née Parkins). He would have been twenty-one at the outbreak of war. Baptism and census records list seven children: Frank (Stapleton - born 1988, before their marriage), Hubert John (possibly Herbert and later listed as John, b 1890), Jesse (b 1892) and Ethel Lizzie (b 1897), Richard (b c1902), Edward (b c1909) and Kathleen (b 1910).

In 1911, Jesse was eighteen, still living in the family home and earning a living as a domestic groom.

Jesse is recorded in the Parish Magazine of September 1915 as enlisting sometime during 1914, but after July, and serving in the Lincolnshire Yeomanry. The Hertfordshire Express of November 20th 1914 reports him as serving as an officer's servant. Then an undated cutting from the village scrapbook, which must have been before September 1916, reports a J Stapleton writing from Oakley Park, Eye, Suffolk, headquarters, D Squadron (probably Hertfordshire Regiment). He says that his Regiment is going abroad any time now to join the Leicestershire Regiment, who are in action now, and *our men are filling in the gaps.*

TARRIER, ARCHIBALD

The North Herts Mail of June 7th 1917, which mainly relates to Francis Ralph Tarrier, reports that he had three brothers in the army, two in France and one in Blackpool. The School War Memorial reveals that one was Walter William. Parish and census records (including the Hitchin census) identify four sons, and from the records available it seems that all four served.

Archibald was born in1892 and was the son of William Edward and Emma Tarrier (née Jarvis) and so would have been about twenty-two at the outbreak of war. Parish and baptism records list five children: Ida (b c1877), Frederick Edward (bapt 1885), Francis Ralph (b c1888), Walter William (b c1889) and Archibald (b 1892). All the children were born in Pirton, except Ida and Walter, who were born in Ickleford. All his brothers served. Frederick and Walter survived the war and Francis was killed, but he does not appear on the Village War Memorial.

TARRIER, FREDERICK EDWARD

Frederick was baptised on July 5th 1885, the son of William Edward and Emma (née Jarvis, born Pirton), and so would have been about nineteen at the outbreak of war. In all it would appear that four brothers served and three survived - refer to Archibald Tarrier for more family details.

TARRIER, WALTER WILLIAM

Walter appears on the School War Memorial, confirming that he attended the school.

Walter was born in 1889 and was the son of William Edward and Emma (née Jarvis, born Pirton). He would have been twenty-five at the outbreak of war. In all it would appear that four brothers served and three survived - refer to Archibald Tarrier for more family details.

Les Blackburn kindly provides the following information; Len's wife's grandmother was Emily Carter (née Baines), and her sister was Walter's wife. They were both Pirton girls. After they were married Walter and Emily lived in Westmill, Hitchin.

THOMPSON, GEORGE

A newspaper cutting from late 1916 (September or later) reports information written in a letter by Private Edward Goldsmith, which informed Mrs Parsell of the death of her son, John Frederick Parsell (also from Pirton). He was killed in a shell burst, which also injured two other Pirton men, Arthur Walker and George Roberts. Arthur later died. George Thompson is referred to along with Fred Baines and Arthur Odell, all named as Pirton men whom John had met before he died.

Parish and census records provide no further information, other than to confirm that the surname was present in Pirton at the time.

THOMPSON, HUBERT CHARLES

There was originally some confusion as to whether Hubert served, but the discovery of his brother Frederick's service records confirmed that he did. On August 10th 1919 his sister signed the form requesting information on Frederick's relatives; Hubert is listed as eighteen and serving on the H.M.S. Indomitable.

The parish records show that Hubert was the son of Elijah and Polly (Mary Ann) Thompson (née Stapleton), both of whom were born in Holwell. In 1901, they were living in Holwell Road with their five children: Elizabeth (b c1887), Eveline (b c1890), Ida Mary (b c1893), Frederick John (b 1896) and Hubert Charles (b c1900 or 1901). The family had moved between Holwell, Shillington and Pirton, presumably following the farm work that employed Elijah. Later, Elijah and Polly had another daughter, Constance May (b c1909). Both Fred and Hubert were born in Pirton and both served in the war; Fred was killed but is not listed on the Village War Memorial.

Allan Grant confirmed that Hubert was his wife's father and that, at some point, the family lived in the row of twelve terraced cottages at the Holwell end of the road. These cottages were also known as the 'Twelve Apostles' and, more informally, as 'Merry Arse Row' – apparently due to the amount of children with no nappies!

Hubert served on H.M.S. Indomitable, which was a very new ship having been 'laid down' in 1906 and completed in March 1909. She was an Invincible class battlecruiser. From early August 1914 she served in the 2nd Battlecruiser Squadron in the Mediterranean and then, from November 3rd, supported the Gallipoli campaign and the bombardment of Dardanelles forts. In December 1914 she joined 1st Battlecruiser Squadron with the Grand Fleet, was refitted in January 1915 and then rejoined 2nd Battlecruiser Squadron Grand Fleet, taking part in the Battle of Dogger Bank and, in 1916, the Battle of Jutland. She was undamaged in the latter and is recorded as firing 175 12-inch shells. She had another refit in August 1916, which is probably when she had facilities for fighter aircraft added. However, Hubert was very young and would have only been involved in the later stage of her war service.

H.M.S. Indomitable at full speed.

THROSSELL, THRUSSELL OR TRUSSELL?

It should be remembered that there are several similar spellings of this surname, e.g. Throssell, Thrussell and Trussell and it is quite possible for these to be confused.

THROSSELL, PHILIP JOHN

Phillip Throssell is identified on the School War Memorial, confirming that he attended the school. Parish and census records suggest the following possible men:

The first was baptised as Philip John Trussell and born on March 21st 1889 to John and Ellen Trussell, and so he would have been twenty-two at the outbreak of war.

The second possibility is revealed by a monument inscription in the St. Mary's Church, Garden of Rest. It records a Philip Throssell as born 1898 and died in 1977, his wife being Bertha who died in 1988. He would have been sixteen at the outbreak of war but no further information has been found.

Geoffrey Colin Budd (Colin) from Port Clinton, Ohio, USA kindly provided further information. He believes that Phillip Throssell may be the son of James Throssell (b 1867) and Clara Trussell (b 1865) and therefore is perhaps a third possibility. If so, he had a brother, Edward and two sisters, May and Hilda. By 1951 he was living at Ramridge Farm, Kimpton, near Welwyn, with his son James Throssell.

Parish and census records confirm the marriage of James and Clara Throssell (née Trussell) and Hilda (bapt 1896), with May Elizabeth (b 1891) and Edward (b 1888) as their children. It does not reveal a Philip, but it is still quite possible that Philip was their son as Colin Budd believes.

Unfortunately it is still not certain which is the Philip Throssell who served.

THRUSSELL (POSSIBLY THROSSELL), JOHN EDWARD

John appears on the School War Memorial, confirming that he attended the school. Parish and census records suggest only one possible man of this name who could have served and, in fact, it is the 1891 census records which reveal a John Thrussell, aged five, as the son of William and Sarah Thrussell. He would have been about twenty-eight at the outbreak of war. Before the war he was recorded as a boot and shoemaker.

The Parish Magazine of June 1917 records him as serving in the Royal Engineers. After the war he must have returned to his original trade, as the 1926 Trade Directory records him as working as a boot maker from the Post Office, Little Green. He presumably married, as his headstone in St. Mary's churchyard reads John Edward Thrussell 1885-1966 and Ethel Alice Thrussell 1888-1966.

THE TITMUSS, CHARLES THAT SERVED

There is a question mark over the number of men called Charles Titmuss who served. There are two Charles Titmuss' listed on the School War Memorial, confirming that two men definitely served and both went to the school. Various Parish Magazines refer to one who served in the Royal Field Artillery (RFA), and the late Edna Titmuss recalled that one joined up in 1915 and served in the Transport Corps. She also thought that, at some time, he suffered from Malaria and that in 1918 he went to Ireland. So, some of this information is contradictory and appears to be transposed between the two men identified here, and some cannot definitely be attributed to either of the men. It is possible that there could be a third Charles Titmuss who served. However, the only other potential Charles Titmuss identified so far was the son of Matthew and Eliza (née Weeden). This would mean that he would have been about forty-two at the outbreak of war, and probably too old to have served unless he had previous military service. At present, the information available is not considered strong enough evidence to confirm a third man and so, at this time, the reference to the RFA is considered to be spurious.

TITMUSS, CHARLES (1)

One of the newspaper articles and the 1918 Absent Voters' List confirm that one Charles lived in Holwell Road. The 1901 census records that Arthur and Ann Titmuss (née Chamberlain) had a son, Charles, and were living in Holwell Cottages, which are the terraced cottages in Holwell Road, also known as the 'Twelve Apostles'. For this reason, it is almost certain that it is their son Charles who served, and he was born on January 7th 1883. Baptism and census records support this, including the 1911 census which lists Charles and his wife (although now living in Walkers Cottages). The only doubt is that his age on his enlistment papers does not tie in with this information. However, as his wife and children are confirmed, it must be concluded that his age on the service records is wrong.

Baptism records list three children for Arthur and Ann: Lydia (b 1880), Charles (b 1883) and Albert Hezekiah (bapt 1885) and the 1901 census records Edward as another son, born in 1884 or 1885. Edward also served in the war.

Charles married Jane Odell in Islington on June 23rd 1907, and they had two children: Hilda (b 1907) and Kathleen Annie (b 1909). In 1911 Charles was twenty-eight and the family was living in one of Walker's Cottages. Charles was working and earning a living as a farm labourer on one of the local farms. Sometime later he moved back to Holwell Road and had become a bricklayers' labourer for Mr Souster, a builder from Letchworth.

He enlisted in Bedford on December 11th 1915, joining the Bedfordshire Regiment as Private 31482. The papers show his age as one month short of thirty-four, but that should read one month short of thirty-two.

He was mobilised on September 1st 1916, and was then posted to the Machine Gun Corps (MGC) in November as Private 67956. He joined the 2nd Battalion, MGC on January 26th 1917, went to France on the 29th 1917 and transferred to the 97th Company on February 22nd 1917.

The Hertfordshire Express of April 28th 1917 reports that he had recently written to his wife, living in Holwell Road, to tell her he had been injured, 'We were asleep in the dug-out, so the shell came as a surprise. I happened to be the unlucky one to get hurt.' This was on April 13th 1917. Soon afterwards he was home on hospital leave and spent the period between May 5th and August 26th 1917 in England recovering. At least seven days in June were spent in Pirton. Charles obviously recovered as he returned to France on August 27th. On March 24th 1918, soon after the start of the major German spring offensive, he was reported as missing. That information had reached Pirton by April 5th, and Jane had a very worrying twelve weeks of not knowing what had happened to him. To what must have been her great relief, Charles managed to get a postcard to her in July telling her that he was a prisoner of war in Limburg. This is possibly the prison camp at Limburg an der Lahn, which sometimes appears as Limbury an der Lahn. If so, his time there may have overlapped with Arthur Pearce, who also appears to have been imprisoned in that camp.

He was released at the end of the war and reached England in December 1918, transferring to the 59th Company, MGC before finally being demobilised from the 11th Reserve Battalion, MGC on October 15th 1919. His records show that he was considered to have suffered a disability of forty percent due to the affects of contusion and crushing.

He died January 28th 1954, aged seventy, and is buried in St. Mary's churchyard. The headstone also records his wife Jane who died April 24th 1966 aged eighty-four.

TITMUSS, CHARLES (2)

The text to the Charles Titmuss above identifies one man who served, but as there are two Charles Titmuss' listed on the School War Memorial, two men served and both went to the school. The 1918 Absent Voters' List helped identify the second. This confirms that this Charles lived in the Blacksmith's Arms (opposite the Blacksmiths Pond in the High Street). The 1901 census records that Frank and Elizabeth Titmuss (probably Emily Elizabeth, née Chamberlain) had a son, Charles, and were living near the Blacksmith's Arms. For this reason it is fairly conclusive that their son is the second Charles Titmuss who served. He was born on May 2nd 1885 to Frank and *Emily* Elizabeth, and so he would have been nineteen at the outbreak of war. In trying to name their children, there may be some confusion as some have their parents named as Frank and Emily and others as Frank and Elizabeth. However, it is believed that they are the same couple and, if so, the baptism records list seven children: Ellen (b 1882), Charles (b 1885), Frank (b 1887), Kate Ethel (b 1893), Clara (b 1883), Frederick (b 1889) and Emily (b 1891). His brother Frederick also served and survived.

By 1918, he was recorded as acting Lance Corporal 349668, 711th A.E.C. (Army Education Corps), Labour Corps, with his home address the same as his brother Frederick's, the Blacksmith's Arms (opposite the Blacksmith's Pond).

He died May 19th 1944, aged fifty-nine, and is buried in St. Mary's churchyard. His monument records him as a husband and father, his wife being Jane Titmuss who died July 18th 1980 aged eighty-seven.

TITMUSS, EDWARD

Edward appears on the School War Memorial, confirming that he attended the school. The 1901 census records Edward as the son of Arthur Titmuss and aged sixteen, so he is likely to have been born in 1884 or 1885. His parents were Arthur and Ann Titmuss (née Chamberlain), and he would have been about twenty-nine at the outbreak of war. In all it would appear that two brothers served and survived - refer to Charles Titmuss (1) for more family details.

By 1911 Edward had been married to Jane for a year. They were living at 13 Cromwell Terrace - the terrace of houses containing the current village stores, and he was earning a living as a farm labourer on one of the local farms. So, when he went to war he was a married man.

This information concurs with a memorial inscription in St. Mary's churchyard, which confirms that he married Jane and that they had at least one child, Margaret Ruby. Jane died on May 27th 1951 and Edward on January 6th 1954, aged sixty-eight.

TITMUSS, FREDERICK, (TED)

There are two Frederick Titmuss' listed on the School War Memorial, which confirms that two went to the school, but evidence seems to suggest that three Frederick Titmusses served.

It is believed that this Frederick, or Ted as he was known, was the youngest son of Mr and Mrs Frank Titmuss, who ran the Blacksmith's Arms in the High Street. The parish and census records confirm his birth date as May 18th 1889, and his parents as Frank and Elizabeth Titmuss (probably Emily Elizabeth, née Chamberlain). He would have been twenty-five at the outbreak of war. In all it would appear that two brothers served and survived - refer to Charles Titmuss (2) for more family details.

By 1911 Frederick was twenty-one, living with his parents in or near the Blacksmith's Arms - opposite the Blacksmith's Pond. Frederick was earning a living as a domestic gardener. His sister Clara was also living in the family home but was married to John Burton. John also served and survived.

The North Herts Mail of April 19th 1917 confirms some of the above, and adds that he had been in France since July 1916 but was in Birkenhead Hospital with slight wound to his left arm. He was then reported in the Hertfordshire Express of April 21st 1917, and that report confirms his rank, injury and where he was serving, but states his Regiment as the Sherwood Foresters.

By 1918 he was recorded as Lance Corporal 202187, A.C. Co. (possibly Army Cyclist Corps), 1st Nottinghamshire and Derbyshire Regiment (also known as the Sherwood Foresters), with his home address the same as his brother Charles at the Blacksmith's Arms.

A memorial inscription in St. Mary's churchyard confirms that he married Ruth and that he was a father. Frederick died on October 14th 1956, aged seventy, and Ruth on August 23rd 1988 aged ninety-nine.

TITMUSS, FREDERICK, (DABBER)

As mentioned above, there is evidence to suggest that three Frederick Titmusses served.

This Frederick Titmuss was also known as Fred, Freddie and Dabber. He was born on February 15th 1895 to George and Emma Juliana Titmuss (née Cherry), and so he would have been nineteen at the outbreak of war. Baptism and census records list seven children: Mary (bapt 1876), Elizabeth (bapt 1878), Peggy (b 1879, d 1915), Ellen Rose (b 1882), Albert John (b 1884), Sidney (b 1888) and Frederick (b 1895), but it is possible that there was another daughter, Lily (poss-b1893). His brother Albert was killed in the war and is remembered on the Village War Memorial.

The Pirton Football Club photograph, reproduced here, resides in the Sports and Social Club and records that Fred lived at 25 Shillington Road and worked at Walnut Tree Farm. He was a keen and skilled footballer and before the war played for Pirton United (Luton Alliance League) and Hitchin Town. During the war he served with the Lancashire Fusiliers and played football for the army.

By 1911 his mother had died. Fred was still living in the family home on the Church Baulk, with his father, his sister, Lilian and two of his brothers, Sidney and Albert John – who was killed in the war. Fred was sixteen and earning a living as a general labourer.

Following the war, he went on to have a distinguished football career; he joined Southampton in 1918, playing inside left and left-back, debuting in 1919. Southampton won the Third Division (South) Championship in 1922, and he won two caps for England, one in 1922 and the other in 1923, both times playing against Wales in the Home Championship (one won and

Fred 'Dabber' Titmuss

one drawn). The Southampton FC website describes him as a *'remarkable player'.*

In 1926 he transferred to Plymouth Argyle, playing in the Third Division (South) Championship, making 166 league and seven FA Cup appearances. His playing career ended in 1932 but he later assisted St Austell FC (Cornwall).

After his playing days ended, he ran a newsagents with his wife and then a pub, both in Plymouth. He died in 1966 aged about seventy-one. His sister Rose married Ernie Lake and their grandsons (Fred's great nephews) Mick and Peter played for Pirton FC. Peter still lives in Pirton.

TITMUSS, FREDERICK JOHN

As mentioned above, there is evidence to suggest that three Frederick Titmusses served.

Frederick John was born on August 31st 1883 to William and Hannah Titmuss (née Stapleton) and so would have been thirty at the outbreak of war. Baptism records list ten children: Arthur Charles (bapt 1859), Joseph (bapt 1862), Alice Eliza (bapt 1865), Norman George (bapt 1867), Leonard Joseph (bapt 1869), Henry David (sometimes David Henry - bapt 1871), Laura Emily (bapt 1874), Isabella Jane (bapt 1877), Walter William (b 1879) and Frederick John (b 1883).

In 1911, Frederick is absent from his parents' home near Great Green and from the Pirton census, so was living or working away from Pirton. His nephews, Arthur Frederick and Leonard Charles Buckett, who were living in his parents' home, both went on to serve and survive.

The Parish Magazine of February 1917 records Frederick as *'having been called up since our last list was published'* and serving with the Army Service Corps. The later issue of June 1917 records him as serving in the Labour Battalion.

By 1918 he was recorded as Private 49024, 82nd Labour Corps, with his home address as in Church Walk - this is the path from Crabtree Lane to the Church.

TITMUSS, JESSE

Jesse appears on the School War Memorial, confirming that he attended the school. Parish records suggest only one man of this name who could have served, and he was born on July 9th 1892 to Charles and Eliza Mary Titmuss (née Weeden). He would have been twenty-two at the outbreak of war. Baptism records list eleven children: Emma (bapt 1872), Anne Maria (bapt 1874), Ellen (bapt 1876), Alice (b 1879), Lizzie (b 1882), Minnie (b c1883), Frederick (b 1886), Jesse (b 1892), Bertram (b 1889), Ethel and Mary (twins? bapt 1895).

By the 1911 census all the children had left their parents home, given as near the Baptist Chapel. Jesse is missing, so he was either living or working away from Pirton.

Jesse is recorded in the Parish Magazine of September 1915 as enlisting sometime during 1914, but after July, and serving in "D" Company, 2nd Battalion, Bedfordshire Regiment.

Two newspaper cuttings, unfortunately undated, provide further information on Jesse. The first reports a letter written by Jesse on December 22nd (another newspaper report suggests that this must be 1914). In it he says he is getting on well and hopes all the Pirton boys at the Front are likewise; he adds *'I have not seen any of them since I have been out here. I have been in the trenches many times.'* He describes the rough weather, the mud and the slush in the trenches, but adds *'But we keep sailing on. As we marched from the trenches the other day we could see the houses that had been blown to pieces by shell fire. Never seen such sights in my life. The big guns rattle out like thunder. I don't think it will last much longer. We are about 300 yards from the German trenches. We get plenty of food out here.'* and concludes with *'a happy new year to all at Pirton.'*

The second cutting confirms that he had been wounded, shot in the face, which fractured his jaw and as a result he had returned to England, landing in Southampton, and he had then gone to the Clearing Station at Eastleigh, Hants. A newspaper report confirms that this injury had been received on October 1st, and that must have been in 1915.

The North Herts Mail of April 6th 1916 reports that he had written, saying that he had to again see a doctor, was back in hospital and that there was a probability of his getting his discharge. That seemed likely, given the content of the rest of the report. He arrived home on or about the third week of March, but he must still have been suffering; *'He was shot through the jaw at Loos, the bullet going in at one side and coming out at the other. His jaw bone was splintered and he had undergone an operation for the removal of the bones. He was returning on Monday, three weeks ago, when he fainted in the train, and was taken very bad. Dr Charles, of Hitchin, was in the same train, and he examined him on arrival at King's Cross. The police brought a hand-stretcher and the soldier was removed. This gallant solder has seen a lot of fighting. He went out with the earlier contingents, coming from South Africa in August 1914 with his Regiment. After twenty-four hours leave they went off to France. He went through several big battles before Loos. He finishes his time with the Army next October.*

The Parish Magazine of June 1917 confirmed that he was discharged from the army as a result of his wounds.

At some point he married and his wife's name was Rose. A memorial in St. Mary's churchyard records that Jesse died in 1954, when he would have been about sixty-two, and that Rose died in 1972.

TRUSSELL, THROSSELL OR THRUSSELL?

It should be remembered that there are several similar spellings of this surname, e.g. Throssell, Thrussell and Trussell and it is quite possible for these to be confused.

TRUSSELL, ALBERT EDWARD

Geoffrey Colin Budd (Colin) from Port Clinton, Ohio, USA believes that Albert and Charles Trussell were brothers, born respectively on July 2nd 1882 and December 13th 1885 to Thomas and Mary Trussell (née Goldsmith). Parish records confirm Albert's date of birth and his parents, but no Charles born on the date Colin suggests has been found. However a brother, William Charles, was born on January 14th 1886.

Baptism records list five children: Lizzie (b 1879), Albert Edward (b 1882), William Charles (b 1886), Susan (b 1890) and John (b 1892). It would also seem that William Charles also served and survived - see William Charles Trussell for clarification.

Before the war Albert married a girl called Elizabeth and they had a child Richard George (b 1907) and then another, William (b 1915), born during the war but before Arthur was called up. The Parish Magazine of February 1917 records this Arthur as *'having been called up since our last list was published'*. He would have been thirty-four.

A memorial in St. Mary's Church's Garden of Rest records that Albert died in 1967, when he would have been about eighty-five. Elizabeth also died that year, aged about eighty-seven.

TRUSSELL, ARTHUR

Arthur appears on the School War Memorial, confirming that he attended the school. Parish records suggest only one man of this name who could have served, and he was born on January 10th 1884 to George and Elizabeth Trussell (née Roberts)*1. Baptism records list twelve children: Elizabeth (b c1864), Clara (bapt 1865), Emma Louisa (bapt 1866), Edward John (bapt 1869), David (bapt 1871), Charles (bapt 1873, believed died, aged fourteen days), Frederick (bapt 1874), Herbert George (bapt 1877), Albert (bapt 1878, believed died, aged five months), Thomas Charles (b 1880), Arthur (b 1884) and Ellen (bapt 1885). Arthur's brother Thomas Charles also served and survived.

Arthur married Ida Walker in 1907. His father died in 1909 so Arthur became the bread winner. By 1911 Arthur and Ida had one child, Nancy Eva (b c1910), and they were living at Hill Farm (now 25 Priors Hill). His trade was now given as pig dealer and he was supporting his own family and his mother. By 1912 he was listed as a Farmer and still living at Hill Farm. When he went to serve he was married and a father.

The Parish Magazine of July 1916 records him as enlisting between March 2nd and July 1916, when he would have been thirty-two years old. The later magazine of June 1917 records him as serving in the 3rd Army Purchasing Board.

By 1918 he was recorded as Private 74771, Central Purchase Board, with his home address as Hill Farm.

*1 *In the 1880s there were two sets of George and Elizabeth Trussells recorded in the village. One couple were Arthur's parents, the other were the parents of George Thomas Trussell who died in the war and is listed on the Village War Memorial.*

TRUSSELL, THOMAS CHARLES, (CHARLES)

Charles appears on the School War Memorial, confirming that he attended the school. When trying to identify the correct man there initially appeared to be two possibilities, both from the same family. However, it seems that the older son died at a very young age. The subsequent discovery of a service record confirmed the man who served to be Thomas Charles, the son of George and Elizabeth Trussell (née Roberts)*1. In all it would appear that two brothers served and survived - refer to Arthur Trussell for more family details.

Thomas Charles may well have been known as Charles, as it was not uncommon to be known by a middle name, particularly it seems when an older sibling of the same name had died. Census records provide evidence that this was the case here, as in later censuses Thomas is listed as Charles.

Charles married Beatrice Ruth Burton in 1907 and in 1911 was living with his wife in his parents-in-law's home and working as a postman. By the time war came in 1914 Beatrice was pregnant and in 1915 their daughter Phyllis Rose was born.

The Parish Magazine of February 1917 records Charles Trussell as *'having been called up since our last list was published'*, and the Parish Magazine of June 1917 records him as serving in the Post Office Rifles. In fact, he was *'deemed to have enlisted'* on June 24th 1916, but was not called to service until January 17th 1917. He damaged his ankle the day before, but an X-Ray confirmed that it was not broken. He was, however, unable to march for some time. Initially he was Private 374741 in the 8th London Regiment, who were also known as the Post Office Rifles – obviously because of his job this may have been his preference, but he was transferred to the Royal Engineers (RE) on April 27th 1917 and embarked for France on June 1st 1917. By the end of March 1918, he had been appointed to the rank of Lance Corporal in the 331st Company, RE in the Department of Roads. The Absent Voters' List of 1918 recorded him as Lance Corporal 24158 (should be 21155?) Royal Engineers, with his home address as *'near Great Green'*.

He was given UK leave in August 1918, then returned to France where he remained until March 1919. He was demobilised in April from the 331st RC(?) Company, RE and, under the document headed 'Trade and Special Qualifications', was recorded as *'Proficient road foreman'*.

It seems that he continued to live in Pirton after the war, as he is buried in St. Mary's Church yard. He died January 21st 1950, aged sixty-nine.

1 In the 1880's there were two sets of George and Elizabeth Trussells recorded in the village. One couple were Charles' parents, the other were the parents of George Thomas Trussell, who died in the war and is listed on the Village War Memorial.

TRUSSELL, WILLIAM CHARLES, (CHARLES)

Charles William appears on the School War Memorial, confirming that he attended the school. However, Charles William is more likely to be William Charles. Baptism records list William Charles, born on January 14th 1886, as the son of Thomas and Mary Trussell (née Goldsmith). The suggestion that the names may have been reversed is substantiated by the school admission records, which record the admission of a Charles, born in the same year, and naming his father as Thomas. For this reason it is believed that William Charles is the man appearing on the School War Memorial. In all it would appear that two brothers served and survived - refer to Albert Trussell for more family details.

WALKER, ALBERT

The detail provided by David Walker for Albert John Walker, who is detailed below, is comprehensive. For this reason, and because it conflicts with the information appearing here, it suggests that another Albert Walker served.

This Albert Walker, who served and survived, appears on the School War Memorial, confirming that he attended the school. Parish records suggest only one man of this name who could have served, and he was born on June 18th 1882 to Stephen and Emma Walker (née Weeden) and the school records confirm this man as the person who attended. Baptism records list five children: Charles (b 1880), Albert (b 1882), Frederick (bapt 1884), Ellen (b 1887) and Joseph (b 1890).

Sometime after 1901, but before the war, at least some of the family including both parents and Joseph, moved to Offley and lived in one of the Claypit Cottages. Albert, Fred and Joseph all served. Albert and Fred survived, but Joseph suffered a terrible death and appears in the chapter 'Should These Names Be On Our War Memorial?'

The Parish Magazine of September 1915 records Albert as enlisting during 1915, but before August and serving in the King's Bays. He would have been about thirty-three when he enlisted.

WALKER, ALBERT JOHN

David Walker, the grandson of Albert informs us that Albert John Walker was born on July 18th 1882 in Pirton and was the son of John Walker (also Albert John).

Albert John Walker with his prison guard, perhaps surprisingly he looks smarter than his guard.

Parish and census records confirm the birth date and that Albert was born to John and Lucy Walker (née Presland). He would have been thirty-two at the outbreak of war. Baptism records list six children: Florence Ann (b 1879), Albert John (b 1882), James (bapt 1885), Eleanor Rose (b 1888, sometimes recorded as Helena), Daisy (b 1893) and Nellie (b 1897).

David also added that Albert married Florence in 1907 and by 1908 they were living in Conford. Albert was working as a baker and they had a son, Albert Edward.

His research also provided the following information: Albert appears to have joined the 1st Battalion, Bedfordshire Regiment and according to the Imperial War Museum his regimental number was 8000. However, that would suggest that he was in the army in 1904, which does not appear to be correct. The Bedfordshire Regiment went overseas on August 15th 1914 and fought in the first battle of Mons. At some point he was captured by the Germans and became a prisoner of war, possibly the Albert Walker shown in records as arriving in the POW camp at Schiesspl on March 4th 1915. Albert received the 1914 Mons Star, confirming that he fought in France or Belgium between the outbreak of war in August 1914 and midnight on November 22nd 1914. By the time he was issued with his Victory and war service medals he was an acting Corporal.

After the war, he became a railway policeman and in 1926 he and Florence had another child, Olive (b 1926). Albert died in May 8th 1950, aged sixty-seven and Florence died in 1948.

WALKER, ARTHUR

There were three Arthur Walkers who served; one died and is listed on the Village War Memorial, a second, Arthur Robert, served with the Canadians and is detailed below and the third is the man detailed here.

This Arthur appears on the School War Memorial, confirming that he attended the school.

A newspaper cutting, mostly relating to Hubert Walker, reveals that their parents were James and Ann Walker of Little Green Farm, (now demolished, but was to the rear of Elm Tree Farm and the new development off Hambridge Way). It also confirms his elder brother as Hubert James and that another brother, who must have been either Harry or Jesse, was at home working on the farm as their father was an invalid. Arthur was born on October 2nd 1892 and would have been twenty-one at the outbreak of war. Baptism records list seven children: Abram Frank (bapt 1877), Harry (b 1879), Daisy Helen (b 1881), Hubert James (b 1883), Ida (b 1885), Jesse (b 1889) and Arthur (b 1892). His brother, Hubert James, also served and survived.

The 1911 census confirms that Arthur, like his brothers Hubert and Jesse, was living and working on his father's farm, Little Green Farm. '*A Farmer's son working on farm*'.

Another newspaper cutting, which is undated, reports that Arthur first served in the Bedfordshire Yeomanry but was transferred to the Liverpool Regiment. He had been in France for eight months when, on March 22nd 1918, he was shot in the leg and thigh. He was sent to the 4th General Hospital, but sadly, as a result of the wounds, his leg was amputated.

In the 1918 Absent Voters' List he was recorded as Private 85912, 13th Battalion, Kings Liverpool Regiment, with his home address the same as his brother Hubert's, Little Green Farm.

A memorial in St. Mary's churchyard records that Arthur was married to Gladys Jessie. They had their first daughter, Elsie, sometime around 1918 and a second daughter on July 22nd 1923, but Gladys died in child-birth at just thirty, so his daughter was christened Gladys Jessie. Arthur died in 1983, when he would have been about ninety.

WALKER, ARTHUR ROBERT, (MM)

There were three Arthur Walkers; one died and is listed on the Village War Memorial; another served with the Bedfordshire Yeomanry, and then with the Liverpool Regiment (as detailed above) and the Arthur Robert Walker who is detailed here.

This Arthur Robert appears on the School War Memorial, confirming that he attended the school.

Arthur Robert Walker, Military Medal winner.

Art Walker is Arthur Robert's son and lives in Canada,. He provided much of the following information:

Arthur Robert Walker was a 'Pirton Lad' born on March 4th 1887 the sixth of eight children born to James and Martha Walker (née Titmuss – the family think Titmys). They lived in one of the Wellbury Cottages, Hexton Road in the Parish of Pirton. His siblings were Maud (bapt 1875), Thomas (bapt 1877), Mary (b 1879, d 1882, aged two years ten months), Harry (b 1881), Bertram (b 1884), Katherine Mary (b 1895) and Edgar Sidney (b 1890). The census confirms that by 1911 Mary had died.

Arthur emigrated to Canada, aged twenty, leaving Liverpool on January 16th 1907 on the S.S. Lake Erie. For the first few years he worked as a farmhand east of Regina Saskatchewan, eventually becoming a shipping clerk for the Massey Harris Company in Regina. By 1911 all the other children except Katherine had left the family home.

The Parish Magazine of September 1915 records Arthur enlisting during 1915, but before August, and serving in the 3rd Canadian Infantry, returning to fight and help '*His King and Country to defend the right*'. His attestation papers confirm his date of birth, record him as a clerk and confirm that he was not married. The oath was taken in Regina Saskatchewan on January 23rd 1915, and he became Private 426433 in the 46th Battalion of the Canadian Infantry, South Saskatchewan Regiment. He was twenty-seven.

He sailed for England on the S.S. Lapland, arriving at Devonport on October 30th 1915. He was promoted to Corporal the next day and to Serjeant on July 1st 1916, when he was serving as a bombing instructor at Bramshott Camp, which was on Bramshott Chase, just south of Hindhead.

He went to France with his Battalion and the 15th Reserve Battalion on August 10th 1916, disembarking at Le Havre. One week later they were in the front line. He distinguished himself in battle, leading a night attack behind enemy lines. The Hertfordshire Express of October 14th 1916 expands on the event, using a letter he wrote to his parents on September 24th, '*I have had the pleasure of a trip across to the German trenches, a party of us pulling off a raid one*

The wounded Arthur Walker.

night, the bombing officer and myself being in charge; everything went off O.K., and the raid was quite a success. We got all kinds of praise for our work. It was quite an experience, and now it is over I am glad I had it, although at the time it was a bit hard on the nerves, for we had to go in under cover of a bombardment by our artillery and shells were falling all round us, but things worked very smoothly and we came through fine, bringing a prisoner back with us. I was recommended for my part in it, but I don't expect to get anything out of it.'

Five days later, he wrote again '*I heard about Tom Abbiss* (another Pirton man) *being wounded. I saw him and was speaking to him the day before he went out on a raiding party (the same night that I was), and he was unfortunate enough to get wounded. I think I told you that I had been recommended for my part in the raid, and I was much surprised yesterday to learn that I have been awarded the Military Medal. I have received all kinds of congratulations, from the General down.'* He had been awarded the Military Medal for '*the gallant part he played in a bombing raid on the Somme.'*

On April 9th 1917, for his actions on the battlefield, he was appointed to the Commission Rank of Lieutenant and, at around the same time, he was fighting at Vimy Ridge in France - one of 30,000 Canadians who had arrived on the April 8th. In a letter to his parents dated April 15th 1917, he wrote '*I don't suppose the censor will object to me mentioning where we are now, for it was in all the papers that Vimy Ridge was captured by the Canadians, and I can tell you that it was a great satisfaction for us to get 'him' off and look down the other side, for we had to take to take a lot of dirt from the Hun up there and we had a lot to pay back.'* He went on to write, '*We licked some of the best troops that the Germans have, and, naturally, we are proud of our success. I don't think that I will be saying too much when I say that the whole Empire will be proud of the Canadian troops.'*

In August 1917, he had been home on leave to Pirton but, by the 17th, was back in France and by the 19th he was back in the line and occupying the German trenches near Lens. It was there, two days later, in the battle for Vimy Ridge, that he was wounded in his right hand. He was hospitalized in Camiers, France, then moved to Western General Hospital in Fazakerley, Liverpool, '*Here I am quite safe in Blighty and doing fine. You have no cause to worry. I have my right hand rather badly smashed up, the index finger having to be left in France.'* When discharged from hospital, he went back to Bramshott as a bombing instructor.

On December 2nd 1918 he was ordered to London for embarkation orders and, on the 5th, sailed for Canada on the S.S. Minnedosa, where he was discharged from the army on January 6th 1919.

After the war he returned to farming for a year and then, on February 1st 1920, joined the Manitoba Provincial Police. He served with them until they amalgamated with the Royal Canadian Mounted Police on April 1st 1932 and he continued to serve until retiring on May 31st 1945, when he moved to British Columbia.

At some point, soon after the war, he married Belle (Isabelle) MacLennan and they had one child, Robert Barryford (Barry), before Belle sadly died from tuberculosis. Arthur remarried in 1933 to Gladys Lucille Workman and they had three children: Patricia Carine, James Arthur (Art) and Elizabeth Margaret Rose (Margaret). He died in Victoria B.C. on October 8th 1969.

Arthur's medals: war and the Royal Canadian Mounted Police.

Note: *Four men with a Pirton connection were to be awarded a medal. Military Medals were awarded to Lieutenant Arthur Robert Walker, born in Pirton but who had been living in Canada, Sidney Cox, baptised in Pirton, and Charles Furr, born in Pirton, and a Distinguished Conduct Medal to Henry George Chamberlain, born in Pirton and who was killed in the war.*

WALKER, BERTRAM J.

Bertram appears on the School War Memorial, confirming that he attended the school.

Parish and census records suggest two possible men:

The first was born on January 30th 1884 to James and Martha Walker, but it was thought that he was unlikely to have served because he was in Canada. No attestation papers have been found and the family in Canada is not aware that he went to war (although information recently came to light which suggested he may be the man who served). The North Herts Mail dated March 15th 1917 suggests that the sons of Mr and Mrs James Walker - Edward, Charles and Bert - were all serving, but the paper also records '*A Wilshere*' as a brother. The first names do not all seem to be relevant to one family, Walker or Wilshere. Therefore, this information should be treated with great caution, as it may be wrongly attributed.

The second possibility is Bertram John and, with the confirmation of the middle name and the fact that school records also confirm that this man attended, he is almost certainly the correct man. He was born on March 9th 1891 to Thomas and Clara (née Lawman), and so he would have been twenty-three at the outbreak of war. Baptism records list two children: Bertram John (b 1891) and Beatrice May (b 1893).

Bert photographed on a pub outing from The Red Lion in the early 1930s.

Bertram is recorded in the Parish Magazine of September 1917 as enlisting during 1914, but after July, and serving in the 1st Bedfordshire Regiment. It would have been late in 1914, as the Hertfordshire Express of October 17th 1914 records him as being involved in an '*infamous fracas*' in Pirton on October 3rd. The paper headlines this event as '*War Against Special Constables*' *1. Bertram was one of the special constables assaulted.

The North Herts Mail of February 3rd 1916 reported that he had written that '*as he was leaving the trenches he had met several Pirton boys as they were going in to the trenches. They were cheery and fit as usual. He also met Sgt Major Arthur Langford 'who wished to be remembered to Mr Franklin and other Pirton friends.*'

It would appear from a memorial in St. Mary's churchyard that Bertram had a wife named Grace. He died on April 12th 1946, aged sixty-two and Grace on December 8th 1954 aged seventy-nine.

*1 *The full report is included in the reference section of this book.*

WALKER, CHARLES

There were several families named Walker in Pirton at the time of the Great War, and some names are common across these families making identification difficult. However, an undated newspaper cutting in the village scrapbook names Corporal Charles Walker and reports that he had two brothers, William and George, who were also serving. Assuming this information is correct, by cross-referencing this with parish records only one possible family is identified. However, for the reason explained below, caution is necessary in case the parish records are incomplete.

From the information available, Charles would seem to be the son of James and Selina (née Goldsmith), and he was baptised on August 5th 1866. This would mean that he would have been about forty-eight at the outbreak of war. This is rather old to have enlisted; the upper age was normally thirty-eight, but could be forty-five if the man had previous army service. For this reason he may not be the man who served and survived. However, it is possible that he lied about his age – unusual, but not unheard of, so his details are provided here.

Baptism and census records list nine children but, by 1911, two had died. At this time only eight can be identified with certainty. They are Emma (bapt 1862), John (bapt 1864), Charles (b 1866), Anise (bapt 1868), Martha (bapt 1876), William (b 1878), John (b 1880) and George (b 1882). It is believed that both William and George also served and both survived.

The North Herts Mail dated March 15th 1917 suggests that the sons of Mr and Mrs James Walker, Edward, Charles and Bert, were all serving, but the paper also records '*A Wilshere*' as a brother. The first names do not all seem to be relevant to one family, Walker or Wilshere. Therefore, this information should be treated with caution, as it may be wrongly attributed.

By 1911, the only child still living in the family home was William. Charles is not listed in the Pirton census, so he must have been living or working away.

The cutting mentioned above reports that Charles was acting Serjeant in the Royal Engineers and '*got his discharge from the Army owing to rheumatic fever.*' He had been in France for six months.

WALKER, EDWARD

Edward appears on the School War Memorial, confirming that he attended the school. Parish records suggest only one man of this name who could have served; he was baptised on May 24th 1885 and was the son of Albert and Mary Ann Walker. He would have been about nineteen at the outbreak of war. Baptism records list nine children: William (bapt 1876), Lily (bapt 1878), Robert (b 1880), Harry (b 1882), Edward (bapt 1885), Joseph (b 1887), Philip (b 1889), Marguerit (b 1893) and Leonard Charles (b 1896). His brother Philip also served and survived.

The North Herts Mail dated March 15th 1917 suggests that Edward was in the 'South African campaign', had to have his leg amputated and was therefore in hospital. However, this information must be treated with caution as the paper confusingly mentions the surname as Wilshere *and* Walker and lists Mr and Mrs James as his parents and 'A Wilshere', Edward, Charles and Bert (Walkers) all as brothers. Therefore, this information should be treated with caution, as it may be wrongly attributed.

WALKER, FREDERICK

There were two Frederick Walkers who served. Two undated newspaper cuttings from the village scrapbook record this Frederick as one of four brothers serving. Parish and census records confirm they were the sons of George and Sarah Walker (née Odell), who both died before the war. The family lived in Bury End, near Great Green and baptism records list eight children: Charles (bapt 1864), John (bapt 1868), Alice (bapt 1871), Frederick (bapt 1882), Gertrude (bapt 1885), Sidney (b 1888), Herbert (b 1890) and Arthur (b 1892). Frederick was baptised on March 5th 1882. His brothers, Sidney, Herbert and Arthur all served. Arthur, the youngest, was killed and is recorded on the Village War Memorial.

In 1911, his brothers Herbert, Sidney and Arthur and his sister Gertrude were all still living in the village but Frederick was absent, working or living away.

The Hertfordshire Express dated December 4th 1915 confirmed that he was at the Front and had previously been wounded from a 'serious accident with his horse'.

He is recorded in the September Parish Magazine of 1917 as enlisting during 1914, but after July, and serving as a Serjeant in the 11th Hussars. He would have been about thirty-two years old when he enlisted.

WALKER, FREDERICK, (FRED)

There were two Frederick Walkers who served; one is positively identified above. The Parish Magazine of September 1914 records this Fred as one of the men 'Belonging to the King's Forces to defend the honour of their country'. This is confirmed by the Hertfordshire Express of November 20th 1914, which records him as serving in the 12th Reserve Regiment.

Parish and census records suggest the following possible men:

The first was baptised on March 19th 1877 and was the son of William and Ann (née Titmuss). However, it would appear that he died aged five months.

The second, Frederick Goldsmith Walker was born to Emma on July 1st 1879. He would have been thirty-five at the outbreak of war. By 1911, he had been married to Mary Ann G Walker for nine years. They had three children, but one had died; the two surviving were Jessica Mabelle Mary G (b c1907) and Frederick Benjamin G (b c1908). Fred (senior) was a farm labourer on one of the local farms, and they were living around Little Green. A headstone in St. Mary's churchyard records that he died on October 31st 1966 aged eighty-seven.

The third was baptised on September 7th 1884 and was the son of Stephen and Emma Walker (née Weeden). He would have been twenty-nine at the outbreak of war. Baptism records list five children: Charles (b 1880), Albert (b 1882), Frederick (bapt 1884), Ellen (b 1887) and Joseph (b 1890).

Unfortunately it is not absolutely certain which man is referred to since, although the latter did serve and was born in Pirton, he was probably living in Offley when the war began. However, as his brother Albert also seems to be listed, it seems almost certain that it is the latter if the two who served.

Sometime after 1901, but before the war, at least some of the family including both parents and Joseph moved to Offley and lived in one of the Claypit Cottages. Albert, Fred and Joseph all served. Albert and Fred survived but Joseph suffered a terrible death and appears in the chapter 'Should These Names Be On Our War Memorial?'

In December 1915 this man was stationed at Dovercourt in Essex.

WALKER, GEORGE

By cross-referencing the undated newspaper cuttings in the village scrapbook with parish and census records, only one possible candidate has been identified. He was born on June 23rd 1882 to James and Selina Walker (née Goldsmith). In all it would appear that three brothers served and survived - refer to Charles Walker for more family details.

The 1911 census reveals that he was living around Great Green and had been married to Ellen for four years. Four children had been born, but two had died. At this time only two can be identified with certainty; they are Alice (b c1908) and Bernard (b 1910). So, by the time he went to war he was married and a father.

George is recorded in the Parish Magazine of September 1915 as enlisting during 1914, but after July, and serving as a Gunner in the Royal Garrison Artillery (RGA). Two undated newspaper cuttings confirm this, and so he would have been thirty-three when he enlisted. The discovery of his service record reveals his military background but little about his war service.

In fact he had served with the RGA before the war, enlisting at eighteen and signing his attestation papers on March 14th 1900 whekijDecember 1914, names this as Bantry Bay, West Ireland. He wrote that he was grateful for the gift of a jersey and added that '*It's rained and rained and land's like a pond. I'm position finder for the guns*'. In another letter to the vicar of Pirton, he wrote '*a soldier must do his duty and do it well.*' On a short visit home his friends described him as looking well and fit. The North Herts Mail reported that he was home between January and February 1915, presumably the same leave, and adds that '*he is sight ranging on coastal defences. Looked well. His section had come out A1 on firing contest with regulars.*'

Another, the undated newspaper cutting, recorded that he had rejoined his Regiment after being in hospital for a leg wound – this would have been in 1917 unless he was wounded twice.

The North Herts Mail of April 12th 1917 reports that '*home*' was opposite the post office, and that his parent lived in Pollards Cottages. He had been in France since August 1915, but he had also been to South Africa with his Regiment and had been promoted from Corporal to Serjeant. A later edition, dated June 7th 1917, reports that Serjeant George Walker had been shot below the knee.

The 1918 Absent Voters' List records him as Private (contradicting the North Herts Mail) 2158 Royal Garrison Artillery, with his home address as Great Green.

WALKER, HERBERT

Herbert appears on the School War Memorial, confirming that he attended the school. An undated newspaper cutting from the village scrapbook reports him as one of four brothers serving, whose parents had died.

Parish and census records confirm that they were the sons of George and Sarah Walker (née Odell) who both died before the war. The family lived in Bury End, near Great Green. In all it would appear that four brothers served, of whom three survived - refer to Frederick Walker for more family details.

In 1911 he was sharing a house around Great Green with his brother Arthur and sister Gertrude; all were single. Herbert worked as a road-man for Hertfordshire County Council.

He is recorded in the Parish Magazine of September 1915 as enlisting sometime during 1914, but after July, and serving in the transport section.

The North Herts Mail of May 27th 1915 reported that he had written to his sister at 'Big Green' Pirton, '*a shell burst near the transport and killed all the horses in that section (five, we believe), and six of his chums were also killed.*' It also describes that, sometime before this incident, he had been injured by shell and had spent eight weeks suffering from blood poisoning.

His Company, Battalion and Regiment are confirmed as the 1st Battalion, Hertfordshire Regiment, "G" Company by the North Herts Mail of March 2nd 1916. The cutting reports that he had returned to Pirton, having completed his service of twelve-and-a-half years; he had served with the Militia before the war.

Although in the transport section, he was known to have spent a considerable time at the Front and had been shelled '*on more than one occasion has been in supreme danger though bursting shells*'. He had often been very lucky, escaping serious injury, '*horses he has had charge of have been killed.*' On another occasion, '*he fell into a hidden ditch, with the horses on top of him, but again escaped injury.*' However, he was not completely unscathed; he did suffer '*bad feet*' - probably trench foot, which was so bad that he was hospitalised in France for several months. The North Herts Mail of March 2nd 1916 reported that, by that date, he had been in hospital for a month.

By 1918, he was recorded as Private 109, Labour Company (probably Corps), with his home address as in Bury Lane.

Some time after the war Herbert married his brother Arthur's widow Rose (née Males) and continued to live in Pirton with Arthur and Rose's son (his nephew Stanley) and their own two sons. Stanley lived in Pirton until the last few years of his life.

WALKER, HUBERT JAMES

The name H J Walker appears in the Hertfordshire Express of July 11th 1914, which reports him as being a steward at the Pirton Transept Fête.

Given the middle name, the parish and census records suggest only one possible candidate. They confirm that Hubert was born on August 1st 1883 to James and Ann Walker (née Kingsley), and so he would have been thirty-three at the outbreak of war. In all it would appear that two brothers served and survived - refer to Arthur Walker for more family details.

In 1911 he was living and working on his father's farm, Little Green Farm. Like his brothers Jesse and Arthur, '*A Farmer's son working on farm*'.

An undated newspaper cutting from the village scrapbook incorrectly refers to *Herbert* James Walker, but confirms his parents as Mr and Mrs James Walker. It goes on to add that he was serving in the Beds Yeomanry in Egypt. Another brother, who must have been either Harry or Jesse, was at home working on the farm as their father was an invalid.

By 1918, he was recorded as acting Corporal 11092, County of London Yeomanry, with his home address the same as his brother Arthur's, Little Green Farm.

He married Ellen and they probably continued living in Pirton for the rest of their lives as they are buried in St. Mary's churchyard. Hubert died on June 19th 1974 aged ninety and Ellen on December 29th 1977 aged eighty-eight.

WALKER, JAMES

James appears on the School War Memorial, confirming that he attended the school.

Parish and census records suggest the following possible men:

The first was baptised on April 2nd 1873 and was the son of George and Mary Ann Walker (née Taylor). He would have been about forty-one at the outbreak of war. Baptism records list nine children: James (bapt 1873), Joseph (bapt 1875), George Edward (bapt 1875), Florence (bapt 1878), Emma (b 1880), Isabella (bapt 1883), Kate (bapt 1885), Rose (b 1886) and John (b 1889).

The second was baptised on March 28th 1875 and was the son of William and Ann Walker (née Titmuss). He would have been about thirty-nine at the outbreak of war. Baptism records list nine children: William (bapt 1867), John (b 1868), Samuel (bapt 1870), Joseph (bapt 1871), Alice (bapt 1873), James (bapt 1875), Frederick (bapt 1877, died, aged five months), Charles (bapt 1878) and Anise Emma (b 1880).

The third was baptised on April 5th 1885 and was the son of John and Lucy Walker (née Presland). He would have been about twenty-nine at the outbreak of war. Baptism records list six children: Florence Ann (b 1879), Albert John (b 1882), James (bapt 1885), Eleanor Rose (b 1888, 1901 census records Helena), Daisy (b 1893) and Nellie (b 1897).

The fourth was born on October 20th 1886 to Emily Walker, and so he would have been about twenty-eight at the outbreak of war.

Unfortunately it is not certain which of these men served.

WALKER, LEONARD JAMES

Leonard appears on the School War Memorial, confirming that he attended the school. Given the middle name, the parish and census records suggest only one possible candidate. He was born on April 8th 1900 and was the son of James and Alice Walker (née Titmuss). The 1911 census identifies five children: Annie Ethel Titmuss (b 1898, before the marriage), Leonard James (b 1900), Frederick Charles Walker (b c1903), Doris Eleanor (b c1906) and Mildred Emily (b c1908).

Leonard would have only been fourteen at the outbreak of war so, if he is the right man, he is unlikely to have served until late in the war. This is confirmed in the Parish Magazine of September 1918, which records Leonard as being '*called to service*' and by then he would have been eighteen. The later Parish Magazine of November 1918 recorded him as serving in the 51st Queen's.

WALKER, PHILIP

Philip appears on the School War Memorial, confirming that he attended the school, but he must have emigrated at some point as he served with the Canadians. Parish records suggest only one man of this name who could have served, and he was born on November 16th 1889 (although his attestation papers record 1890) to Albert and Mary Ann Walker. In all it would appear that two brothers served and survived - refer to Edward Walker for more family details.

The North Herts Mail of December 14th 1916 reports that Philip had worked as a cleaner at the Hitchin Great Northern Station. After emigrating to Canada in 1909 or 1910, he initially worked on a boat on which Philip Trussell, the son of the well known Pirton post office man, who had also emigrated, was the engineer. Like a number of other Pirton men, he had settled in New Westminster.

An undated newspaper cutting confirms him as the son of Mr A Walker. The oath was taken in Vancouver on March 15th 1916 and so he was twenty-five when he enlisted. His attestation papers record him as living in New Westminster, a fireman and not married.

The Parish Magazine of June 1917 records him as serving in the Duke of Connaught's Own and wounded. The Parish Magazine of October 1918 records him as a casualty, after being gassed, and the North Herts Mail of September 5th 1918 confirms that he was 'Badly gassed and was now in Napsbury Hospital, St. Albans.' Apparently, the gassing took place several months before, but 'he pluckily made light of it. A nurse saw it as serious and he was sent to England.' He first went to France around Christmas 1916 and was wounded at Vimy Ridge - the battle commonly recognised as giving the Canadians their distinct national identity.

A headstone in St. Mary's churchyard lists a Philip Walker of the right birth date, so it is possible that Philip returned from Canada, married and remained in Pirton. If so, then he had a wife named Florence and died on January 5th 1946 aged fifty-six.

WALKER, SIDNEY

Sidney appears on the School War Memorial, confirming that he attended the school. An undated newspaper cutting from the village scrapbook reports him as one of four brothers serving, whose parents had died.

Parish and census records confirm that they were the sons of George and Sarah Walker (née Odell), who both died before the war. The family lived in Bury End, near Great Green. In all it would appear that four brothers served, of whom three survived - refer to Frederick Walker for more family details.

By 1911 he had a wife, Susan. They had been married for three years and had two children: Edith Sarah (b c1909) and Ivy May (b 1910). They were living around Great Green and he was a cowman on a local farm. By the time he went to war he was married and a father.

An undated but war time newspaper cutting confirms a third child. It also reports that before the war they had moved to Knebworth, with Sidney working as a cowman on Lord Lytton's Estate. However the family, with Sidney away at war, moved back to Pirton.

Sidney is recorded in the Parish Magazine of July 1916 as enlisting between October 21st 1915 and March 2nd 1916, and serving in the Royal Garrison Artillery. He would have been about twenty-seven years old.

WALKER, WILLIAM

Note: See Charles Walker for notes on the identity of this branch of the Walker family.

Cross-referencing an undated newspaper cutting in the village scrapbook with parish and census records, suggests only one possible man of this name who could have served, and he was baptised on March 10th 1878, the son of James and Selina (née Goldsmith). In all it would appear that three brothers served and survived - refer to Charles Walker for more family details.

By 1911 William was thirty-three, still living in the family home in Holwell Road and earning a living as a labourer.

He married before the war and the Parish Magazine of October 1915 congratulates William for enlisting with the comment 'To the list of names published in the last Magazine is now added that of another married man, William Walker. Why don't more unmarried men come forward?' He would have been about thirty-seven when he enlisted. The Parish Magazine of July 1916 records him as serving in the 9th Labour Battalion of the Royal Engineers.

WEEDEN, ALBERT, (BERT)

Albert appears on the School War Memorial, confirming that he attended the school. Parish records suggest only one man of this name who could have served, and he was born on June 16th 1889 (18th on Church headstone) to William and Hannah Weeden (née Walker). Baptism and census records list ten children but by 1911 two had died. The children were Mary Ann (bapt 1870, d 1870 aged fourteen days), George (bapt 1872), John (bapt 1874, d 1895), Alice (bapt 1878), Mary (b 1880), Ellen (b 1882), William (bapt 1885), Fred (b 1887), Albert (b 1889) and Lily Jane (b 1893). His brother Fred may also have served and his nephew, Leonard, served and survived.

In 1911 Albert was twenty-one, still living in the family home and earning a living as a horseman on a local farm. In 1915 he was recorded as a farmer, but having heard the call to arms aged twenty-five he signed his attestation papers on January 5th 1915, joining the Royal Horse Artillery as Driver 77744 and being sent for training at Woolwich. In early May 1915 he was posted to the Mediterranean Expeditionary Force and joined the 29th Division. As part of "P" Battery, they embarked on the S.S. Orsova from Devonport on May 10th, arriving in the Dardanelles later that month. He had a fearsome welcome, arriving during shelling by the Turks. A report in the North Herts Mail of July 15th 1915 records a letter that he managed to write home shortly afterwards. It provided news and some reassurance for his parents; 'Just a line to let you know that I am still in the 'pink'. We landed here Wednesday night receiving a hearty welcome from the Terrible Turks, who were showing us A1, all the lot of them falling in the water. We had a fine journey, travelling second class. We called at Alexandria and stayed there two days but would not let us get off, and the niggers*1 would not let us do any fatigues. I am writing this with the shells pinging over me about every five minutes so you can guess I am not far from the firing-line. We have plenty to eat and drink, and me and my pal have a nice little house which we dug ourselves, about six feet in the ground, so we lay and count stars at night. We lost scarcely any men, only a few horses have dropped since I have been here so I don't think we shall be here long. The Old Turk will never stand the pepper he is getting. We are getting served out with tobacco tomorrow so will you send some packets

Albert Weeden

of fag papers? It is no use thinking of buying anything here as there are no houses, much less any shops, and writing paper is hard to get. We have no time for writing, what with digging holes for horses and gun-pits. We have just had an argument about when was Whit-Sunday. Some say it was last Sunday. If so this is Friday.

On the 26th, he was posted '*in the field*' to "Y" Battery. He did not have a good time and on June 30th was admitted to Hospital with Enteric Fever, a tropical infection. Enteric fevers include typhoid and paratyphoid fevers and gastroenteritis. A week later the hospital in Mudros recorded him as '*Dangerously ill*' and wired the news. The above newspaper report mentions that he was in hospital through illness and reported that his parents had been '*wired*' from the Royal Dock Yard Woolwich, informing them that their son Driver Albert Weeden, "Y" Battery Royal Horse Artillery, had become dangerously ill on July 8th but gave no further particulars. Obviously, his parents would have been dreadfully worried, but his health improved and, on the 21st, the hospital wired to say that he had been removed from the danger list. He was invalided from Mudros to England and was admitted to the Military Hospital in Lewisham on September 15th 1915.

Albert's service record is faded and therefore parts are hard to read but, after recuperation, he certainly remained on home service, stationed at Woolwich, joining "G" Battery until June 29th 1916 when he embarked for France and, a short time later, joined the 19th Anti Aircraft Battery (AAB). While he remained in France, on October 12th 1916 Albert's mother died. In December his AAB was reorganised and became "T" Battery AAB. On January 5th 1917 he was granted class II proficiency and was also awarded a Good Conduct Badge. Albert continued his service with a posting to "R" Battery AAB and then, on January 4th 1918, to "U" Battery AAB. He became ill again and on April 20th 1918 was admitted to hospital with mild '*Inf Accessory Sinuses*'. It was presumably not that mild, as he was not discharged until May 4th and then, not back to service, but to the St. Martin Rest Camp. He returned to active service on the 18th and posted to "G" AA B on June 22nd.

The Hertfordshire Express of October 26th 1918 confirmed some of the detail above and added that Albert had been a smallholder in Pirton, that he had been in the army for three years, was serving in France and that, on October 5th, he was wounded. His service records are badly faded at the entry for this date, but they confirm that he was wounded in action, on or just before this date, and that he was admitted to hospital. He was then discharged on the 8th or possibly the 9th.

Rodney Marshall, Albert's grandson, confirms that Gunner Albert 77744 was in the artillery and was at Gallipoli and also in France. Like most of the men who served, Albert rarely spoke about it. The only things that Rodney remembers him saying were, in reference to Gallipoli, that he was staggered by the '*sheer number of bodies of men and horses he saw floating in the sea,*' and that when he was billeted in France, '*the serjeant used to come round early every morning and yell 'gas', at which everyone would jump out of bed and don their masks, there was never any gas.*' '*So one morning my Grandfather and his mate decided to stay in bed;*' '*that's how I lost all my teeth*'. Rodney adds, "*Whether this is true or not who can tell, but he never had any teeth that I remember.*"

The 1918 Absent Voters' List confirms Albert as Gunner 77744, 221st AA (Anti Aircraft) Section, Royal Artillery, with his home address as Dead Horse Lane (now Royal Oak Lane).

In 1921 he married Ruby Goodwin Gaff, who came from Ipswich, in St. Marylebone, London. They had three children Denise (b 1921, Rodney's mother), who married John Marshall, Ronald (b 1924), who married Patricia Wooley (buried Pirton churchyard) and Ruby (b 1927), who married Rex Allingham from Barton. Both Ron and Ruby, together with their families, emigrated to Australia in the early 1960s.

After the war, in various censuses, he is recorded as a farmer at Hammonds

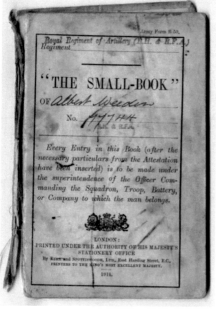

Albert's service book 'The Small Book'.

Farm (Burge End Lane). He was also Vice-President of the Pirton branch of the British Legion. Albert and his wife spent the rest of their lives in Pirton and are buried in St. Mary's churchyard. Albert died in 1958 aged sixty-eight and Ruby in 1971 aged seventy-eight.

*1 *We have no wish to offend, this is a direct quote. Remember acceptable word usage was different 95 years ago.*

WEEDEN, ALBERT WALTER

The Parish Magazine of October 1915 records Albert, who was serving in the Coldstream Guards, as '*indirectly connected to Pirton*'.

This man is a curiosity; the 1918 Absent Voters' List records him as Lance Corporal RTS/5567 Machine Gun Corps (Guards), with his home address given as Dead Horse Lane (now Royal Oak Lane). This suggests that Albert Walter was living at the same address or at least reasonably close to the other Albert Weeden, who also survived, perhaps a cousin or other relation. However, current family members have no knowledge of him.

It was not until the release of the 1911 census, and the discovery of his service record, that more information could be established. Albert Walker was the son of Frederick Weeden, who had married a girl named Elizabeth. Both were from Pirton, and by 1911 they had been married for fourteen years and were living at 20 Moreland Street, Finsbury Park. The census lists two children: Albert (b 1892) and Alice (b c1906). Albert was born in Pirton and Alice in Finsbury Park. With Albert being eighteen and the marriage only being fourteen years old, it could mean that Elizabeth was Frederick's second wife. Albert was single and working as a dairy clerk.

He enlisted on July 29th 1915 in London, aged twenty-six. His father's address was still Moreland Street. Albert was recorded as a clerk (elsewhere as dairyman) for H J(NB: this is hard to read from the records) Pring, 216 High Road, Leyton. He joined the Coldstream Guards as Private 16559. After training and home service he embarked for France on August 29th 1916 and the 4th Battalion. After a month at the Base depot he joined his Battalion in the field. On October 21st he transferred to the 2nd Guards Brigade, Machine Gun Corps (MGC), as Private 736, and qualified as a machine gunner.

Albert became sick in early May 1917 and rejoined his Company on the 18th but, within four days, was sick again and was admitted to hospital in Gailly on the 23rd, where he was treated for an '*Abs L buttock*' (presumably - abscess left buttock), but was discharged on the same day, rejoining his Company on June 26th. On October 12th he was shot in the thigh, admitted to the 47th General Hospital and by the 29th was well enough to be discharged to the base depot.

Between March 13th and 27th 1918 he was given well earned UK leave and did not return to action with his Battalion until April 21st. In June he was appointed to the rank of Lance Corporal. Then, on September 9th 1918, he was mildly gassed and was again admitted to hospital. He was discharged on the 12th but, a month later, on October 11th was gassed again, with phosgene gas. This time it was more serious and on the 20th he was invalided to England and admitted to Military Hospital, Sycamore Road, Nottingham, where he spent the remainder of the war. It was not until December 4th 1918 that he was well enough to be discharged.

In his final medical, although he complained of chest pains, he received no disability award and was demobilised on February 11th 1919, having served for three years and 198 days, of which two years and two months were in France.

Perhaps his parents had moved back to Pirton by then but, in any case, his home address was given as Royal Oak Lane, Pirton.

WEEDEN, FREDERICK, (FRED)

It is not certain that Fred served, as the North Herts Mail of October 26th 1916 reports that Frederick Weeden, aged twenty-seven, a Pirton small holder, was given three months exemption from service. This would have been following his appeal against being called up, which would have been heard by the Hertfordshire Appeal Tribunal. The report also mentions that his brother (Albert Weeden) was serving. It is possible that the exemption could have been extended. However, as it was for such a short period it is assumed that it is likely that he would have gone on to serve.

Parish and baptism records reveal only one possible man who could be correct, although he would have been twenty-nine not twenty-seven at the time of the report. With everything else fitting this is assumed to be an error in the report, in which case he was born on April 9th 1887 to William and Hannah Weeden (née Walker). In all it would appear that two brothers served and survived - refer to Albert (Bert) Weeden for more family details.

By 1911 Fred was twenty-three, still living in the family home and earning a living as a domestic gardener.

WEEDEN, LEONARD STANLEY, (LEN)

Leonard appears on the School War Memorial, confirming that he attended the school. Parish records suggest only one man of this name who could have served, and he was born on March 29th 1899 to George and Ellen Weeden (née Handscombe). He would have been fifteen at the outbreak of war and therefore he is very unlikely to have served until the latter stages. Baptism and census record three children but, by 1911, one had died. At this time only two can be identified with certainty; they are Alice Miriam (b 1896) and Leonard Stanley (b 1899). Norah Lake kindly adds that Leonard (Len) was Albert Weeden's nephew. Albert also served in the war and survived. Len's sister Alice married Thomas Lake, also listed as a survivor of the war.

The Parish Magazine of October 1918 records Leonard as serving in transport and having been wounded. The Parish Magazine of November 1918 confirms that this was with the Royal Warwickshire Regiment.

Len died on November 26th 1967 aged sixty-seven and his ashes are interred in the St. Mary's Church, Garden of Rest.

WELLS, ARTHUR

The Parish Magazine of October 1915 records Arthur, who was serving in the Royal Engineers, as '*indirectly connected to Pirton*'. Parish and census records currently provide no further information.

WESTON, FRED

Parish records suggest only one man of this name who could have served, and he was born on April 10th 1883 to Charles and Jane Weston, who lived in one of the Wellbury Cottages on Hexton Road. Baptism and census records list seven children: Walter (b c1868), George (b c1871), Mary (b c1875), Kate (bapt 1876), Louisa (bapt 1878), John (b 1881) and Fred (b 1883).

The 1911 census shows that he was living next door to his parents in Wellbury Cottages. His father was recorded as a retired gamekeeper and Fred as gamekeeper. A later newspaper cutting confirms that he had followed his father into the job of gamekeeper for Highdown. Fred had been married to Rose Jane for two years and they had two young children: Hilda Mary (b c1909) and Lucy (b 1910). He was married and a father when he went to war.

He is recorded in the Parish Magazine of September 1915 as enlisting during 1915 and serving in the 2nd Bedfordshire Regiment, so he would have been about thirty-two years old when he enlisted. The North Herts Mail of July 1st 1915 reported that he was about to go to the Front and then later, the Hertfordshire Express of May 5th 1917 reports him as wounded, but he was '*lucky*' as '*a piece of shell entering at his chest emerged from his back without breaking a bone or doing any vital injury.*'

WILSHERE OR WILSHER?

It is difficult to be sure which is the spelling to use, as usage, even between parents and children, seems to change. There are also a number of contradictory spellings of this surname, e.g. Charles Wilshere is listed on the Village War Memorial, but the same man appears as Charles Wilsher on the Arras Memorial, which records his death as a missing soldier. The spelling of Bert is confirmed as Wilsher by a family member, by his signature on his attestation papers and on his monumental inscription in St. Mary's Garden of Rest, but his parents are recorded as Wilshere and signed with that spelling in the 1911 census. Wilshere has therefore been used for all the men except Bert.

WILSHERE, ARTHUR

Arthur appears on the School War Memorial, confirming that he attended the school. The Hertfordshire Express of April 28th 1917 reports him as one of four brothers serving whose parents were Mr and Mrs J Wilshere of Andrew's Cottages - the three cottages at the bottom of the High Street.

Parish and census records confirm they were James Wilshere and Sarah (née Larman). Baptism records list seven children but by 1911 one had died. At this time only six can be identified with certainty. They are Martha (b c1876), Charles (bapt 1878), Frederick (b 1882), Robert (bapt 1885), Arthur (b 1887) and Bertram (b 1890). Arthur was born on April 29th 1887. His brothers, Charles, Frederick and Bertram all served. Frederick was wounded and sadly lost a leg. Charles was killed and is recorded on the Village War Memorial.

Arthur was married before the war to Lily, whose surname has not been found, and they had at least one child, Irene Bertha (b 1910). In 1911 he was living with his wife and child in their own home. A later report records that, like his brother Bert, he was earning a living as a cowman on one of the local farms.

He is recorded in the Parish Magazine of July 1916 as enlisting between October 21st 1915 and March 2nd 1916 and serving in the Bedfordshire Regiment. He would have been twenty-eight years old. The Hertfordshire Express of March 10th 1917 reports him as being wounded. This is confirmed in the North Herts Mail dated March 15th 1917*1, with the date

Arthur and Lily Wilshere

of his injury given as February 26th. He was taken to Rouen Hospital with gunshot wounds to the head. It noted that he was married with four young children, and that, before joining up (a year ago), was a stockman for Mr Perkins of Little Offley. He was thirty and had been in France for eight months.

It is likely that Arthur and his wife spent the rest of their lives in Pirton, as they are buried in St. Mary's churchyard. Arthur died in 1942 aged fifty-five and Lily in 1961 aged seventy.

*1 *Unfortunately it is possible that this information has been confused with one of the A Walkers who served, as the paper mentions both surnames; the information from this paper should be treated with great caution.*

WILSHER, BERTRAM, (BERT)

The name Bertram Wilsher appears in the Hertfordshire Express of July 11th 1914, which reports him as a member of the organising committee for the Pirton Transept Fête.

Bertram appears on the School War Memorial, confirming that he attended the school. The Hertfordshire Express of April 28th 1917 reports him as one of four brothers serving, whose parents were Mr and Mrs J Wilshere of Andrew's Cottages - the three cottages at the bottom of the High Street.

Parish and census records confirm they were James Wilshere and Sarah (née Larman). In all it would appear that four brothers served, of whom three survived - refer to Arthur Wilshere for more family details.

By 1911 Bert was the only one of the children recorded as living in the family home. He was twenty-one and, like his brother Arthur, was earning a living as a cowman on one of the local farms.

Bert is recorded in the Parish Magazine of July 1916 as enlisting between October 21st 1915 and March 2nd 1916 and serving in the Bedfordshire Regiment. In fact, he signed his attestation papers on November 12th 1915 in Hitchin, aged twenty-five. Previously a labourer, he became Private 23186, Bedfordshire Regiment, joining his Regiment on

the 17th at the Ampthill Depot for training. He was unmarried and his next of kin given as his mother, Sarah. Later, after he married on February 19th 1916, this was changed to his wife Mary (née Males) of Holwell Road Cottages, also known as the 'Twelve Apostles'.

Bert transferred to the Machine Gun Corps (MGC) as Private 31538 on April 12th 1916 and embarked for France on June 18th and, after a period in the Base Depot, was posted to the 107th Company on July 4th.

The Hertfordshire Express of April 28th 1917 reported Bert as serving in France and the North Herts Mail, dated two days earlier, states that Bert had been wounded. This may be an error, perhaps confusion with one of his brothers, because this wound does not appear in his service record. However, he was wounded on August 10th 1917. It is not clear if he returned to France, but he was posted three more times in 1918 and was demobilised on March 3rd 1919.

Maureen Worsley (née Wilsher) adds '*My paternal Grandfather, Bertram served in World War 1 as a private in the army. Whenever anyone asked, 'What did you do in the war?' he would say 'You don't want to know about such things as that' and then shut up like a clam and refuse to say anything further!*'

Bert Wilsher

'*He married Mary Males in St. Mary's Church, Hitchin, I think it was on February 19th 1914* (in fact it was 1916). *After the war he worked on the railway up until he retired in 1925, living with Mary in Pudding Bag Alley*1 *until retirement when he moved to 11 Davis Crescent with their children: Alan, Dulcie and Patty, three of their seven children.*'

Another grandchild, Martin Wilsher added '*I know my Grandfather, Bertram Wilsher, was a participant in the Great War, and I have a memory of him playing tunes on the harmonica he had given to me for my seventh birthday that he had learnt while he was in the trenches.*'

His Pirton monumental inscription reads "*Bertram Wilsher born 1890 died 1976*". Also "*Mary Wilsher born 1895 died 1980*".

*1 *Pudding Bag Alley was the name given to the alley way running behind the row of terraced cottages in West Lane at the junction with the High Street.*

WILSHERE, FREDERICK

Frederick appears on the School War Memorial, confirming that he attended the school. The Hertfordshire Express of April 28th 1917 reports him as one of four brothers serving whose parents were Mr and Mrs J Wilshere of Andrew's Cottages (the three cottages at the bottom of the High Street). In all it would appear that four brothers served, of whom three survived - refer to Arthur Wilshere for more family details.

By 1911 only Bertram was living with his parents; all the others were making their own way in the world. Frederick is not recorded in the Pirton census, so he was working or living away from the village.

Frederick is recorded in the Parish Magazine of September 1915 as enlisting sometime during 1914, but after July, and serving as a Corporal in the 13th Royal Fusiliers. The Hertfordshire Express of April 28th 1917 informs readers that Frederick had a leg amputated and was home on leave waiting for his discharge.

WRIGHT, JAMES WILLIAM

All that is known of this man comes from the 1918 Absent Voters' List. He was Lance Corporal RTS/5567 XI Squad No. 1 Base, Remount Depot, British Expeditionary Force, with his home address as The White Horse Inn, which was where The Motte and Bailey now stands on Great Green. This is the same address as given for Percival Harry Wright, who also served and survived - perhaps his brother, and for Alfred Nightingale, another soldier who served and survived.

WRIGHT, PERCIVAL HARRY

Most of what is known of Percival comes from the 1918 Absent Voters' List. He was Private 126341 Royal Horse Artillery, with his home address given as The White Horse Inn, which was where The Motte and Bailey now stands on Great Green. This is the same address as given for James William Wright, who also served and survived - perhaps his brother, and for Alfred Nightingale, another soldier who served and survived. The Kelly's Trade Directories provide further information. It appears that after the war he had several occupations, as the various directories of 1929, 1935 and 1937 list him as motor engineer, motor coach proprietor and taverner, all located at The White Horse PH. He ran the 'Pirton Belle', a bus service that ran from Pirton to Hitchin, Pirton to Luton and Pirton to Letchworth. That business was sold to Birch Brothers, together with the routes, in January 1938.

His headstone in St. Mary's churchyard records that he died on January 31st 1949 aged fifty-nine, so he would have been born around 1890 and would therefore have been about twenty-four at the outbreak of war.

TOM (SURNAME UNKNOWN)

An undated newspaper article provided by Jim and Mary Moffatt of Pirton Grange gives us a tantalising fragment of information about an unknown Pirton man, Tom:

The article, which reports the post war visit of King George V to Pirton, ends with *'Suffice to wind up with a story of a grandson of a Pirton man also named Tom, who sums up the bizarre but yeomen traits of the character of Pirton. This grandson was presented to King George V for bravery and skill as a bomb aimer in the First World War. 'I suppose,' said the King 'that you would find it an easy matter to drop a bomb in an egg cup?' 'No, your majesty,' came the reply, 'on an eggcup'.'*

Further positive identification of this man has not proved possible. His information does not fit with any of the 'Toms' which are already listed, i.e. Tom Lake or Thomas Abbiss. All Toms and Thomas' of an appropriate age who are listed in the parish and census records were investigated and then traced back to find those with a grandfather of the same name. The only likely man appears to be Thomas Charles Trussell, who is listed above as Charles Trussell (baptised as Thomas Charles). George's parents were Thomas and Esther Trussell. Perhaps this man is the right Tom, but as he was a soldier not an airman, he seems unlikely to be the right man.

For Reference, Interest & Curiosity

Contents

Notes on Research

The research for *The Pride of Pirton* began in 2003 and was undertaken by Tony French, Jonty Wild and others who volunteered their services. The vast majority of the information gathered has come from the following sources:

The Pirton War Memorials
There are five; four list the Pirton men who died and the other, the Pirton School Memorial, lists the pupils who served - both those who died and those who survived. The details of the men who died enabled the following databases to be investigated:

The Soldiers Who Died
The Commonwealth War Graves Commission provides free access to its database on the internet (www.cwgc.org). The other major database is the 'Soldiers Died in the Great War 1914-19' available on DVD or pay per view.

Pirton Parish Magazines
A collection of these magazines is held by Clare Baines and includes an almost complete set for the war years. They include lists of the Pirton men who joined the forces, which regiment they joined and when. They also provide some information on those wounded, missing or killed. Unfortunately in the case of those described as *'indirectly connected to Pirton'* it does not explain their connection to Pirton. Without more information we can only assume that they are relatives of Pirton families, were people living or working in Pirton or that they once lived in Pirton.

The Hertfordshire Express and the North Hertfordshire Mail
Local newspapers are a good source of information and photographs, particularly for those killed or wounded. Some of the war year editions of the *Hertfordshire Express* were saved from a skip by Hitchin Museum. They were painstakingly investigated and scanned by Tony French and Jonty Wild in 2005. Although bound, they were in a very delicate condition and it was worrying to handle them for fear of the damage that might occur. Because of this we are particularly grateful that Hitchin Museum granted us access. The missing issues were researched at the British Library. The *North Herts Mail* was available in the British Library and was researched by Tony French, Jonty Wild and Irene Fussell. These papers are also in a delicate condition and it is understood that since our research they have been withdrawn from public viewing pending their digitisation. It seems that we were quite probably the last members of the public permitted to view and handle them.

Baptism, Census, Marriage and Other Official Records
These are an obviously excellent sources of information. Their research is a daunting proposition, very time consuming and interpreting the information can be surprisingly complicated and confusing. However, the task was made substantially easier by the use of the Pirton Local History Group's superb website at www.pirtonhistory.org.uk. In addition, copies of the 1891, 1901 and 1911 local censuses were purchased and used along with other internet research. The 1911 Census was released in 2009, earlier that normal, and this added considerably to our knowledge of the Pirton men. However, it should be noted that because of time constraints for research at Kew and the cost of researching these records on the internet, use of this was restricted to the Pirton section, except for the men who died. The Pirton Heritage Support Group provided the Pirton census to the Pirton Local History Group and they are now available via their website, for the benefit of all.

The Village Scrapbook
A contemporary scrapbook exists and was given to Rodney Marshall's father, Jack, and then passed to Rodney. The newspaper cuttings seem to fall into two types; those that relate to Pirton men, and general articles about the local regiments in which they served. This was a key source of information, but, unfortunately, often lacked dates and details on their source.

The Pirton School Admission Records
A copy is held by Hertfordshire Archives and Local Studies (HALS).

The 1918 Absent Voters List
A copy is held by Hertfordshire Archives and Local Studies (HALS). It lists the names of the men over the age of twenty-one who were on active service and who were eligible to vote in their home constituency. It was compiled from details supplied by the men themselves before the closing date of August 18th 1918.

The British Army World War One Service Records
These were obtained for all the Pirton men, where available; however, the number of men for whom such records exist is limited, as approximately sixty percent of all these records was destroyed by bombing in World War Two.

Battalion/Regimental War Diaries and Naming
They are factual records of a battalion, battery or larger military group's movements and actions. It should be remembered that they generally '*play down*' the experience of war and rarely describe the horrors of that experience. They can occasionally be found for free on the internet, but it is often necessary to visit a regimental museum, use the National Archive website or the fantastic facilities that are offered by the National Archives in Kew.

These diaries are essential research for anyone wishing to trace the movements of a soldier's battalion and therefore a soldier's experience of the war, but as they rarely mention men's names, it has to be assumed that a man was present, when, of course, it is possible he could have been absent due to illness, injury or leave.

Battalion naming and numbering can be confusing. For instance, 8th London Regiment means the 8th Battalion of the London Regiment. The 2/8th means that there were two 8th Battalions the 1st 8th (1/8th) and the 2nd 8th (2/8th). It is common to abbreviate the name, for instance the 1st Battalion Hertfordshire Regiment is often abbreviated to 1st Hertfords, 1st Herts or even just Hertfords.

Where possible, we have given information about the regiments that the men were in. It is probable that this information is correct, but there may still be confusion, e.g. a man may be listed as in one regiment and then later in another. This movement was not unusual; a man may have been transferred to another regiment following an absence due a wounding or illness. Also, such was the carnage of the war that individual men or groups of men were often re-assigned to other regiments to bring them back up to strength.

Casualty Figures
The accuracy of casualty figures can vary considerably between different sources. When the numbers given in the book are from a war diary they should be accurate. When larger numbers are given, as in the case of total casualties for various battles, the reader should not to be too concerned with the accuracy; often it is the sheer scale of the numbers that is important. It is also worth noting that numbers given for the British Army generally include all Commonwealth soldiers.

Visits to Memorials and Cemeteries
Personal visits were considered to be absolutely essential by the book team. We felt, and still feel, that this is the only way to properly understand our men and to demonstrate our respect for them. The book team members have all made numerous visits, including locations in Pirton, France, Belgium and the Netherlands. The last remaining man from the Village Memorial, Frank Abbiss, whose grave is in Egypt, was visited in October 2010. Both Tony French and Jonty Wild have, together, visited and paid respects to all those men and will perhaps, given the time and effort involved, be the only people ever to complete that pilgrimage. Many photographs were taken and these can be made available in digital or photographic form. For relatives this would be either free or for a small charge to cover costs. Contact history@pirton.org.uk; however copyright will remain with the originator.

Other Sources
Of course there have been many other sources of information, including the written sources, relatives and the Internet. Although difficult to do thoroughly, we hope that we have acknowledged all of these in the reference section of this book. If any provider believes that we have failed to do so, we apologise and ask that you notify us so that we can rectify the omission as soon as possible. This can be done via history@pirton.org.uk.

Mistakes
We have tried very hard not to make errors; however it is all too easy to make mistakes even when, or perhaps, *especially when*, we cross reference multiple sources. Often the spelling of a surname varies, even between parents and children; if born out of wedlock sons carry their mother's maiden name and, occasionally, men preferred to use their middle name rather than their first name. Sometimes men are even recorded by their 'nickname', for example Francis John Pearce died but Jack Pearce was listed amongst the survivors until we discovered that they were one and the same man. There are also many examples of men with the same name; we believe that we have identified three Fred Baines, all of whom fought in the war. One died. It is therefore not difficult to understand how easy it might be to transpose background information.

Mistakes are all too easy to make and the authors of this publication apologise for any and all that may have been included – please help us correct them if you can - see the contact details below.

Sharing Our Research and New Information

The aims of the Pirton World War One Project are to document the Pirton men's live and their experience of the war; make all the research available to all and for new and additional information to be captured and recorded for posterity. This book goes some way to achieving this, but ultimately it is intended to provide all the information via the Pirton Historical Photograph and Document Archive. To that end in due course and copyright permitting, it will appear on www.pirton.org.uk. This and other research may also be available digitally or in paper form. All enquiries should be addressed to history@pirton.org.uk.

If you find any new information or photographs relating to the Pirton men included, or indeed of any man who may have been missed, please contact any of the authors or jontywild@pirton.org.uk.

Additional Notes:

Serjeant, rather than sergeant, is the spelling used in the book because that reflects the use by the Commonwealth War Graves Commission on the headstones and memorials.

Abbreviations used in the following text: b = born, bapt = baptised, c = circa and d = died, DCM = Distinguished Conduct Medal, MM = Military Medal, OR = Other Ranks (i.e. not officers)

Additional information can be found at www.pirton.org.uk/ww1book.

SELECTED FACTS, FIGURES AND ITEMS OF CURIOSITY FROM WW1

Some things that began during World War One still impact on us today. Borders established or re-established in Europe at that time still stand. The regions of Alsace and Lorraine, for example, lost in earlier wars, were returned to France and remain French to this day. British summer time that we experience every year was brought in as part of the Defence of the Realm Act (DORA) and even though pub opening times have changed in recent years their basic restrictions were also brought in as part of DORA.

Many daily conversations still reflect expressions brought in to usage at that time. The following are just a few:

A1	If you're feeling A1, then you are referring to the highest army grade for health and fitness.
Chat or chatting	The lice that were endemic to the fighting soldiers were known as chats. The soldiers would sit in groups during rest periods having a conversation and trying to kill off the lice one at a time – they were just chatting.
Lousy	If you feel lousy then you may not be feeling A1, but it was how you felt when infested with lice.
No man's land	The name given to the area of land between the two front lines, not controlled by either side.
Plonk	A bottle of plonk was the name given to cheap French white wine.
Over the top or OTT	How the soldiers left their trenches to attack the enemy.
Shell-shocked	This expression was first used then, 'unofficially', to describe those deeply affected by the bombardments or close calls with explosions.
Shot down in flames	We may do it to people, ideas or arguments, but it had more serious connotations for pilots over the Western Front.
Zero hour	Might now refer to any deadline, but it was the countdown to the time for the men to attack.

WHAT OFTEN STANDS OUT FROM WORLD WAR ONE ARE THE INCREDIBLE STATISTICS

THE STATISTICS OF THE WESTERN FRONT

The Western Front varied in length during the war, following gains or losses. In general terms it was up to 400 miles long and stretched from the Belgium coast to the Swiss border. The British Army held about 20 miles in 1914, rising to 120 miles in 1918.

BATTLE FACTS

There were many huge and terrible battles along the Western Front and of course elsewhere; here are some statistics from just a few:

THE BATTLE OF THE SOMME

Preparation for the battle: In the seven days before the Battle the British artillery fired 1,750,000 shells (250,000 a day for 7 days).

The first day: July 1st 1916, 120,000 men of the British Army advanced at walking pace – due to the distance and the weight they were carrying. British casualties were 57,470, including 19,240 dead.

From July 1st To November 1916: British casualties were 654,751 including 127,419 dead. French casualties were 204,253 and German casualties estimated as 465,000 to 680,000. In some places the British gained as much as 7 miles!

For the British these figure equated to 893 British Army deaths per day or 18,250 British lives per mile.*1

*1 *As with everything about World War One things are rarely as simple as they first appear; one of the main aims of the Somme was to deflect the Germans from Verdun, where a German victory over the French would probably have lost the war.*

The Canadian Newfoundland Regiment: They went into action with 801 men, when the roll call of the unwounded was taken the next day it counted 68 men.

OTHER BATTLES

The 'Minor' Battle of Derville Wood: Derville Wood was defended by 3,250 South Africans. They held out against overwhelming German forces for six days; 140 soldiers and three officers survived

Third Battle of Ypres (or Passchendaele): 310,000 British casualties, 260,000 German casualties.

Total for the Three Battles of Ypres: 1,700,000 soldiers on both sides were killed or wounded.

Verdun: Lasted 300 days and nights, with 26 million bombs and shells fired (six for every square metre of the battlefield). The French lost 550,000 men of which 300,000 were simply 'missing'. German casualties were 434,000.

COMMONWEALTH WAR GRAVES COMMISSION (CWGC)

Some 908,371 Commonwealth soldiers, sailors and airman died; 200,000 in Belgium and 500,000 in France, the rest elsewhere. They are marked in over 1000 war cemeteries, 2000 civil cemeteries or on memorials - six in Belgium and 20 in France which name more than 530,000 men with no known grave.

The CWGC is responsible for maintaining all the official war graves and monuments from the local single grave in Holwell Churchyard to the massive cemetery at Tyne Cot (11,853 graves). By the end of the Great War the CWGC was responsible for 580,000 identified graves (52% of the total), 180,000 unidentified graves (16% of the total) and 530,000 commemorations on memorials (48% of total). These numbers change when men's bodies are discovered and/or are identified, which still happens.

MEMORIALS AND CEMETERIES

The memorials commemorate the men with no known grave. They may, in fact be buried in a cemetery and marked as 'A Soldier of The Great War', 'Known unto God'. Statistically it is more likely that their bodies were completely obliterated or still lie under the battlefields. Here are details of just a selection:

Tyne Cot Memorial (British Army)	Names 34,874 men with no known grave. The grounds also contain 11,853 graves of which 8,366 of the burials are unidentified.
Verdun Ossuary (French Army)	Contains the bones of 130,000 French soldiers and is still being added to. The grounds contain 15,000 graves.
Thiepval Memorial (British Army)	Names 72,116 men with no known grave.
Menin Gate (British Army)	Names 54,344 men with no known grave.
Arras Memorial (British Army)	Names 34738 men with no known grave.
Langemark (German Army)	Contains 44,234 graves. Most are mass graves or Kameraden Grab (Comrades Grave), 7,575 are identified. The 'Kameraden Grab' graves usually contain eight bodies below a single flat stone, but one mass grave contains the bodies of 24,917 men. Two British soldiers also lie within this cemetery.

THE HUMAN COST OF THE WAR - MILITARY CASUALTIES

Country Allied Forces	Mobilised	Killed	Wounded	POW/ Missing	Total	% of Those Mobilised
Russia	12,000,000	1,700,000	4,950,000	2,500,000	9,150,000	76.3%
France	8,410,000	1,357,800	4,266,000	537,000	6,160,800	73.3%
British Empire	8,904,467	908,371	2,090,212	191,652	3,190,235	35.8%
Italy	5,615,000	650,000	947,000	600,000	2,197,000	39.1%
USA	4,355,000	126,000	234,300	4,500	364,800	8.4%
Japan	800,000	300	907	3	1,210	0.2%
Romania	750,000	335,706	120,000	80,000	535,706	71.4%
Serbia	707,343	45,000	133,148	152,958	331,106	46.8%
Belgium	267,000	13,716	44,686	34,659	93,061	34.9%
Greece	230,000	5,000	21,000	1,000	27,000	11.7%
Portugal	100,000	7,222	13,751	12,318	33,291	33.3%
Montenegro	50,000	3,000	10,000	7,000	20,000	40.0%
Allied Total	**42,188,810**	**5,152,115**	**12,831,004**	**4,121,090**	**22,104,209**	**52.4%**

Country Central Powers	Mobilised	Killed	Wounded	POW/ Missing	Total	% of Those Mobilised
Germany	11,000,000	1,773,700	4,216,058	1,152,800	7,142,558	64.9%
Austria-Hungary	7,800,000	1,200,000	3,620,000	2,200,000	7,020,000	90.0%
Turkey	2,850,000	325,000	400,000	250,000	975,000	34.2%
Bulgaria	1,200,000	87,500	152,390	27,029	266,919	22.2%
Total	**22,850,000**	**3,386,200**	**8,388,448**	**3,629,829**	**15,404,477**	**67.4%**
All Total	**65,038,810**	**8,538,315**	**21,219,452**	**7,750,919**	**37,508,686**	**57.7%**

Source - Microsoft Encarta 2002 and other website

CIVILIAN CASUALTIES

In addition to the military losses, there were hundreds of thousands of civilian deaths; in France after the war there were an estimated 600,000 widows and 700,000 orphans.

Source - www.spartacus.co.uk/FWWgasdeaths.htm

THE MISSING MEN

The CWGC estimates the number of commemorations on memorials at 530,000 and the number of graves where the occupant cannot be named at 180,000. That means there are still some 350,000 bodies of British and Commonwealth soldiers lying beneath fields and land in unmarked graves in France and Belgium - the total number of men with no known grave from the First World War is more that the total number of British servicemen killed in the Second World War (about 450,000).

THE DAMAGE

Clearance Required	Destroyed	Need of Repair
10,000 square miles of farmland	11,000 public buildings	1,154 miles of canals
233,000 miles of barbed wire	350,000 houses	Over 3,000 miles of railway track
2,300 square miles of building land	38,500 miles of roads	

Source - Commonwealth War Graves Commission

THE FINANCIAL COST

Allied Powers	Cost in Dollars in US 1914-18 Value	Central Powers	Cost in Dollars in US 1914-18 Value
United States	22,625,253,000	Germany	37,775,000,000
Great Britain	35,334,012,000	Austria-Hungary	20,622,960,000
France	24,265,583,000	Turkey	1,430,000,000
Russia	22,293,950,000	Bulgaria	815,200,000
Italy	12,413,998,000		
Belgium	1,154,468,000		
Romania	1,600,000,000		
Japan	40,000,000		
Serbia	399,400,000		
Greece	270,000,000		
British Colonies	125,000,000		

Source - www.spartacus.schoolnet.co.uk/FWWcosts.htm

WEAPONS AND KIT

HELMETS

The British army was not issued with helmets until late 1915 or early 1916. They were provided not as protection from bullets, as they would not stop a direct hit, but for protection against the air bursting shrapnel shells. They were made from forged steel with steeply sloping surfaces, which was most effective for deflecting debris, shrapnel and small shell splinters.

MACHINE GUNS

Next to bombardment shelling these caused most deaths. The British Vickers machine gun fired about 500 rounds a minute and the German Maxim about 600 rounds a minute.

RIFLES

The British Lee Enfield 0.303 rifle had a ten bullet capacity and with practice could be fired rapidly and accurately. At the Battle of Mons, the advancing Germans believed that they were under fire from British machine guns, but it was the British Expeditionary Force using the Lee Enfield.

The French had either the Lebel or the Berthier rifle. The magazine of the Lebel held eight bullets and the Berthier six.

The German Mauser rifle was very reliable, but only held five bullets.

War Against Special Constables

EXCITING NIGHT SCENES AT PIRTON.

BATCH OF DEFENDANTS AT HITCHIN SESSIONS.

STRONG MEASURES BY THE BENCH.

A remarkable story of the night adventures of two Pirton special constables was told at the Hitchin Sessions on Tuesday, when, before F. A. Delmé-Radcliffe, Esq. (chairman), and other magistrates, Frederick Buckett, labourer, Pirton, was summoned for assaulting Bertram Walker, a special constable, while in the execution of his duty at Pirton on October 3.

Mr. E. J. Jackson, of Messrs. Jackson and Wade, solicitors, Hitchin, defended.

Bertram Walker, the Bury, Pirton, said he was a special constable for the district of Pirton. He came on duty on October 3 at 8 p.m., and was going off duty at 10.30 p.m. He was accompanied by special constable George Charlick. At 9.45 they entered the White Horse publichouse, and were at the time wearing armlets, showing that they were acting as special constables. When complainant got into the publichouse someone in the bar shouted, "You have no business here." Buckett then came up and struck witness on the face without any provocation, and said, "If I catch you and Newbury round my places to-night I will blow your brains out." Witness and Charlick then walked outside, and Buckett and some other men followed, using threats and bad language.

Cross-examined: He had been a special constable for about one month. He stopped in the publichouse for about five minutes, and not until two or three minutes to ten. His wife was present, and they stood in the passage just outside the bar. He did not call out "Stop that row." He did not strike or push Buckett. Buckett asked who gave him permission to look after his fowl-house, and he replied that they had to do their duty. He did not hear Charlick say to Hoye, "I shall have you before Christmas, and Buckett will follow."

By Superintendent Reed: There had been several fowl robberies in the district, and the police were paying special attention to the fowl-runs.

George Charlick, a special constable, said he entered the White Horse publichouse with Walker. A man named Charles Tomlin said, "You have no business in here." They did not enter the bar, but stood in the passage. Buckett came up to Walker, and with abusive language said, "If I catch you and Bill Newbury behind my place to-night I will smash your brains in." He then struck Walker on the face. When they left the house they were followed by Buckett and some other men. Witness asked them "to be men."

Cross-examined: Walker did not shout into the bar, "Stop that row," but said, when Buckett struck him, "Stop it, Dick." Walker did not push Buckett. Hoye said to him, "You are not sharp enough to catch us," and he replied, "I don't know about being sharp enough, but mind I don't have you before Christmas." Buckett did not interfere with him.

Buckett, on oath, said that he was in the White Horse publichouse with William Hoye, Charles Tomlin, Reginald Lake and his brother Harry. He went in at 7.30 and remained until five minutes to ten. He saw the constable come in, and Walker looked in at the door and said, "Don't make so much noise," and he replied, "What is that to do with you?" He then went up to Walker "like a man" and asked him who gave him permission to watch his fowl-house, and Walker said, "Grotrian." Defendant told Walker that if he found him round the fowl-house again he would put the matter in other hands. Walker then pushed him into the bar, and said "I want none of your nonsense." He was certain he did not strike Walker.

Superintendent Reed said the Chief Constable desired him to state that the special constables of the county were doing excellent work. There were about ninety in Hitchin alone doing duty three times a week. If the Bench decided to convict, he hoped they would view the case as a serious one, as special constables must be protected in the work they were doing.

Mr. David Simson, Ickleford Manor, said that he was section leader of the special constables in the Hitchin northern district, which included Pirton. The men were trying to serve their country in this time of emergency, and he submitted that they ought to be properly protected, and he hoped the Bench would take a serious view of the matter.

The Chairman said the Bench considered it a most serious charge. Fortunately for defendant it was the first case of its kind before them, and therefore they would deal with him comparatively leniently. But he wished it to be understood that any further cases of this description would be rigorously dealt with, and with the greatest severity the law would permit. Defendant would have to pay £2, or go to prison for one month. Special constables must be protected in the execution of their duty.

Henry Chamberlain was summoned for assaulting Bertram Walker and George Charlick at the same time and place. He pleaded "Guilty."

Charlick said that Chamberlain followed them out of the publichouse, struck Walker on the face and then struck witness on the shoulder.

Walker said that Chamberlain struck him on the nose, turned and struck Charlick and then struck witness again.

The Chairman said that it was a more serious case than the previous one. Chamberlain must pay £2 and 7s. 6d. costs, or go to prison for one month.

Frederick Buckett, Henry Chamberlain, William Hoye and Charles Tomlin were summoned for using obscene language at the same time and place.

Bertram Walker and George Charlick said that the four defendants followed them out of the White Horse publichouse. They all used obscene language to them. Buckett was using obscene language inside the house.

The case against Buckett was dismissed. The others denied using the language (produced), but each was fined 5s.

Henry Chamberlain was further charged with assaulting Ellen Maud Hubbard on the same night.

Mrs. Hubbard, wife of Alfred Hubbard, Great Green, Pirton, said that at 11.30 p.m. she heard police whistles being blown and cries of "police," "murder" and "help." Her husband went out to see what was the matter, and she went with Mrs. Newbury to the back entrance of Mrs. Newbury's property. Three men came along the lane, and Chamberlain was threatening her husband. She said, "You dare to hit my husband." Chamberlain then sprang at her and grasped her shoulder. Then he struck at her, but her husband stepped in front and received the blow on his eye.

Alfred Hubbard said he heard the cries and the police whistles, and went out to see what was the matter. He met Chamberlain, Buckett and Hoye. They used threats to him, and Chamberlain jumped at his wife and later struck at her, but he got in the way. The men were using threats against special constables in general.

Mrs. Newbury corroborated.

Chamberlain was fined £1; in default, 14 days, the sentence to run consecutively with the previous one of one month, making six weeks' imprisonment in all.

From the Hertfordshire Express of October 17th 1914.

Acknowledgements

It would have been incredibly difficult to have written this book without the excellent professional reference sources provided by the **Hitchin Museum**, the **National Archives** at Kew, the **British Library** (Newspapers at Colindale) and those provided on the internet by the **Pirton Local History Group**. Many individuals have also taken the time to help the Pirton WW1 Project by providing information, photographs, documents and artefacts; some arriving from as far away as Canada and the USA. A huge amount of help was also received via the wealth of internet websites that do so much to supply the information and facts that keep this part of our history alive and accessible.

This section is divided into the following sections:

'Sponsors', 'People', 'Organisations', 'Documents, Books and Databases', 'Websites' and 'Photographs and Artefacts

Here we try to thank them all. This is difficult as there are so many, but we have done our best. Please forgive us if we have inadvertently missed any individual or source and please let us know so that we can correct that omission at the earliest opportunity.

We are pleased to acknowledge the supporters and sponsors of this project who provided the essential financial backing to enable us to complete the book. We hope that we have enabled you to be proud of the result.

Except for the photographs, the listings are in alphabetical order against the relevant section/chapter in the book:

Sponsors

Jeremy Abbiss - Mr E Angell - Mrs S Attewell - Diane Bailey - Bob Barton - Sandy & Alison Bierrum - C Bowyer - James & Ian Brakenbury - John Brewster - Lynn & Angela Bristow - Carol Brown - Alan Brundell - Ken Burton - Zoe Burton - Ron Burton - Chase Park Developments - Mick Child - Rob Clayburn - Mel Cole - Kev Cumberland - John & Pauline Davis - Peter Donovan - Caroline Elen - Richard Farrimond - Aubrey Fisher - Tony French - Irene Fussell - Michael Goddard - Ian Halls - Rosie Hamilton-McLeod - Alan & Rhoda Hartley - Trevor & Jayne Healey - The Holwell Shoot - Derek Jarrett - Peter Johnson - Malcolm Kelsey - Paul Kerswill - Steve Kitchener - Chris Knights - Doug Lake - John & Leila Lauder - Rt Hon Peter Lilley MP - Graeme Low - Colin Maclaughlan - G Maidmont - Mr & Mrs S Maple - Mr S Marks - Liz Martyr - Morris Builders Ltd - The Motte & Bailey - Mrs M M Parkin - Mark Payne - Mark Pearson - Simon Penny - Pirton Pumpkin Club - Adrian Pitts - Village Fair Committee - Zoe Railton - Dave Randall - J Randall - Charlotte Rhodes-James - RPB Building & Roofing Contractors - Chris Ryan - Alan Scrimageour - Duncan Scrimshire - Brian & Rosi Somerville - Shirley Taylor - Bren & Dave Timson - David Tree - Paul Trelford - Colin Trevillion - Mr & Mrs Tullett - Jim Walker - Richard Walker - Peter Warner - Anne Watson - Jonty Wild - Peter Wilshere - Ann Wilshere - Stephen Wood

People

Richard Abbiss - Stanley Abbiss - Ron Albon - Stanley Ashton - Diane Bailey - Clare Baines - David C Baines - Roger Baines - Len Blackburn - Brian Bristow - Geoffrey Colin (Colin) Budd - Gil Burleigh - Charles Burton - Ken Burton - Tracey Chamberlain - Rita Chambers - Ron Crawley - Brenda Dawson - David Doorne - Audrey Ford - Dick Franklin - Caroline Frith - Steve Fuller - Dan Furr - Rod Furr - Irene Fussell - Christine Gammell - Taff Gillingham - Allan & Liz Grant - Mac (Meckenzie) Gregory - Graham Halsey - Andy Lomas - Rosie Hamilton-McLeod - Peter & Beth Harding - David Hodges - Helen Hofton - Ian Hook - Margaret Ingram - Roy Jarvis - Elspeth Johnstone - Jean Keane - Rev. W Kemm - Edna Lake - Norah Lake - Peter Lake - Bob Lawrence - Ivor Lee - Grace Maidment - Alan Males - Andy Males - Colin Males - Denise Marshall - Rodney Marshall - Mary Millen - Jim & Mary Moffatt - Martin Morris - Alan Morrisson - Gary Moyles - Michael Newbery - Phyllis Pearce - Pat Pickering - Adrian Pitts - Gill Riding - John Ridler - Sharon Ryan - Patti Salter - Lorna Sexton - Linda Smith - Lynda Smith - Tony Sprason - Gwyn Thomas - Muriel Timbury - Alan Titmuss - Joe Titmuss - Grace Tomlin - Gladys Tullett (nee Abbiss) - James Vaughan - Art Walker - David Walker - Liz Wallace - Kim Whitaker - Patsy Willis - Barbara Wilshere - Peter & Ann Wilshere - Maureen Worsley (Nee Wilsher)

Organisations

British Library - Essex Regiment Museum - Fusiliers Museum - Gloucester Regiment Museum - Hitchin Museum - Imperial War Museum - National Archives - Pirton Heritage Support Group - Pirton Local History Group - Suffolk Regiment Museum - Royal Star and Garter Home - Western Front Association

Documents, Books And Databases

1911 Census (National Archives) - A Foot on Three Daisies, 1987 (Pirton Local History Group) - Hitchin Express, 1914, 1917, 1918 (Hitchin Museum) - Hitchin Express, 1915, 1916, 1919 (British Library) - History of the Post Office Rifles, 8th Battalion City of London Regiment 1914 to 1918 (One of the battalion commanders) - Memories of Old Joys (Joy Franklin) - Monumental Inscriptions of St. Mary's Pirton, 1990 (Laidlaw, Jean, Series no. 40, Hertfordshire Family & Population History Society) - No Labour, No Battle (J Starling and Ivor Lee) - North Hertfordshire Mail 1914-1919 (British Library) - Pirton School Admission Register (Hertfordshire Archives & Local Studies, Hertford) - Portrait of Pirton, a Century of Change, 2005 (Pirton Local History Group) - Scrapbook of WW1 Newspaper Cuttings (Rodney Marshall) - Soldiers Died in the Great War 1914-19 - St. Mary's Pirton Parish Magazine, 1911-1918 (Clare Baines) – The Suffolk Regiment, 1914-1912 (Col C C R Murphy) - War Diaries (National Archives)

Websites

138th Heavy Battery (www.hampstead-heavies.com) - 1911 Census (www.1911.com) - Ahoy (ahoy.tk-jk.net) - Bedfordshire Regiment (www.bedfordregiment.org.uk) - Berks & Wilts Museum (www.thewardrobe.org.uk) - Canadian Virtual War Memorial (www.vac-acc.gc.ca) - Census, war service & official records (www.ancestry.co.uk) - Clydesdale Built Warships (www.clydesite.co.uk) - Commonwealth War Graves Commission (www.cwgc.org) - Country Bus (www.countrybus.co.uk) - East Surrey Regiment (www.queensroyalsurreys.org.uk) - East Surrey Regiment (qrrarchive.websds.net/menu1.aspx?li=1) - Gloucester Regiment (www.glosters.org) - The Great War 1914-1918 (www.greatwar.co.uk) - Highclere Castle (www.highclerecastle.co.uk) - History Learning Site (www.historylearningsite.co.uk) - Imperial War Museum (collections.iwm.org.uk) -Library & Archives Canada (www.collectionscanada.gc.ca) - The London Gazette (www.gazettes-online.co.uk) - The Long, Long Trail (www.1914-1918.net) - Middlesex Regiment (freespace.virgin.net/howard.anderson) - Military History Encyclopaedia (www.historyofwar.org) - National

Archives (www.nationalarchives.gov.uk) - Northumberland Fusiliers (www.4thbnnf.com) - Old Front Line Battlefields of WW1 (battlefields1418.50megs.com) - Pirton Historic Photograph & Document Archive (www.pirton.org.uk) - Pirton Historical Records (www.pirtonhistory.org.uk) - Queen's Royal Surrey Regiment (www.queensroyalsurreys.org.uk) - Queen's Royal West Surrey Regiment (qrrarchive.websds.net/menu1.aspx?li=1) - Roll of Honour (www.roll-of-honour.com) - Royal Norfolk Regiment (www.rnrm.org.uk) - Royal Star and Garter Home (web.ukonline.co.uk/sheila.jones/stargart.htm & www.starandgarter.org) - Royal Surrey Regiment (www.queensroyalsurreys.org.uk) - Soldiers of Gloucestershire Museum (www.glosters.org.uk) - Spartacus Educational (www.spartacus.schoolnet.co.uk) - Suffolk Regiment (www.suffolkregiment.org) - Union Castle Line Ships (www.simplonpc.co.uk/UnionCastle3.html) - Western Front Association Forum (www.westernfrontassociation.com) - Wiltshire & Berkshire Museum (www.thewardrobe.org.uk) - World War 1 Naval Combat (www.worldwar1.co.uk) WW1 Battlefields (www.ww1battlefields.co.uk)

PHOTOGRAPHS, IMAGES & ARTEFACTS

The Pride of Pirton Book Details Book Team - Irene Fussell. **The First World War – 'THE GREAT WAR?'** Hertfords and Bedfords (x2) - Alan Morrison. **1914 The Rush to War** Newspaper extracts - HM-HE 8/8/1914 (x2), HM-HE 26/9/1914, HM-HE 29/8/1914, HM-HE 20/11/1914. **The Men That Died** *Frank Cannon* Frank Cannon – BL (x2). Last view of cemetery – RM. *Albert Abbiss* View of cemetery – RM. Albert Abbiss – BL. Newspaper extract – RM-SPB. *Frank Handscombe* Frank Handscombe – Margaret Ingram. View of Burge End – Sarah Burton (also available for HM ref: 366-08). Newspaper extract – RM-SPB. Frank Handscombe – BL. *Joseph French* Joseph French – BL. Joseph French – Brenda Dawson. *Alfred Jenkins* Newspaper extract – RM-SPB. Alfred Jenkins – BL. *John Parsell* John Parsell - RM-SPB. PM-CB. Grave registration form – Ron Albon. *Arthur Walker* Death Penny and Medals – Andy Males. PM-CB. *Sidney Baines* Sidney Baines – CB. *Edward Burton* Edward Burton – Maureen Bygraves. *Harry Crawley* Death Penny and medals – Dave Britnell. PM-CB. *Joseph Handscombe* Newspaper extract - HM-HE 19/5/1917. *Harry Smith* Harry Smith - HM-HE 15/9/1917. Last view of cemetery – RM. *William Hill* PM-CB. Penultimate – view of cemetery – RM. *Albert Titmuss* Albert Titmuss – HM-HE 1/12/1917, HM-HE 17/11/1917. *Fred Burton* Fred Burton and memorial card - Audrey Ford. HM-HE 29/12/1917. *Walter Reynolds* Walter Reynolds and memorial card – Grace Tullett. Newspaper extract – RM-SPB. Death Penny – JW. *Arthur Odell* Arthur Odell – BL. HM-HE 23/3/1918. *Bertram Wilson* Cap badge – Stanley Abbiss. *Henry Chamberlain* Henry Chamberlain - RM-SPB. View of The White Horse – Pat Courtney, HM-HE 16/2/1918. *George Charlick* Last 2 views - RM. *Fred Anderson* PM-CB. *Albert Reynolds* Albert Reynolds and newspaper extract – HM-HE 14/9/1918. *Francis Pearce* Francis Pearce and group photograph - Phyllis Pearce. PM-CB. *Frederick Baines* Bowman's Mill – Ken Burton. *Sidney Lake* Hampstead Heavies photograph - Brian Bristow. *Frank Abbiss* Sepia cemetery photograph - Alan Morrison. Headstone and cemetery – CWGC. *Frederick Odell* View of St. Mary's - Howard Etherington. **Should These Names Be On Our War Memorial?** *Herbert Clarke* Herbert Clarke – Ron Albon. *E Southgate* HM-HE 19/1/1918, VAD photograph – Ken Burton. *Francis Tarrier* Francis Tarrier – HM-HE 19/6/1917. *Joseph Walker* Funeral drawing - RM-SPB. **The Pirton War Memorials - We Will Remember Them** *The Village War Memorial* PM-CB. 1920 ceremony – HM (Ref: 376-02). Cenotaph walkers – Sarah Butikofer. 1950 and 1984 ceremonies – Roy Brittain. *School Memorial* Classroom photograph – Sheila Sanders. **Remembrance in Perpetuity** Jewish headstone – RM. **Was It Worth It?** Certificate – Ken Burton. Trenches today – RM. **Pirton's Survivors of the Great War** *Frank Abbiss* Frank Abbiss(x2) – Stanley Abbiss. *Harry Abbiss* Harry Abbiss, Abbiss group and unknown Abbiss – Richard Abbiss. *Frank Ashton* Baker's cart – HM (Ref: hm439-10). *Bertram Baines* Bertram Baines - Muriel Timbury. *Ernest Baines* Ernest Baines and group photograph – Roger Baines/Jean Keane. *John Bedale* H.M.S. Bacchante – Cassandra Murdoch (gone_off_the_rails). *Oscar Cherry* Oscar Cherry group – Grace Tomlin. *Harry Davis* Harry Davis – Vera Farey. *Bertie Dawson* Bertie Dawson – Gillian Bethell. *Laurence Franklin* Laurence Franklin – Dick Franklin. *Charles Furr* Charles Furr - RM-SPB, extracted from pub outing HM (Ref: 378-08), medals – Rod Furr. *Hedley Handscombe* Hedley Handscombe – Ronnie Mead. *Horace Handscombe* Horace Handscombe – Margaret Handscombe. *Eldred Hubbard* The Gloucester Castle - Mackenzie Gregory/ahoy.tk-jk.net. *Edward Lake* Edward Lake – Norah Lake. *Reginald Lake* Reginald Lake - David Gooch. *Tom Lake* Tom Lake(x2) – Norah Lake. *Jack Laurence* Jack Laurence – HM (Ref: 491-04). *John Males* John Males – Ronnie Mead. *Michael Males* Michael Males – Alan Males. *John Pearce* Shell fuse – Ron Burton. *William Reynolds* William Reynolds – Gladys Tullett. *Sidney Smith* Sidney Smith - David and Linda Smith. *Fred Titmuss* Fred Titmuss – Pirton Sports & Social Club. *Albert John Walker* Albert Walker – David Walker. *Arthur Robert Walker* Arthur Walker – BL, Arthur Walker (wounded) and medals – Art Walker. *Bertram Walker* Bertram Walker - extracted from pub outing HM (Ref: 378-08). *Albert Weeden* Albert Weeden and service book – RM. *Arthur Wilshere* Arthur Wilshere – Peter/Ann Wilshere. *Bertram Wilsher* Bertram Wilsher – Maureen Worsley. **For Reference, Interest & Curiosity** War Against Special Constables HM-HE 17/10/1917.

BL = British Library newspaper*[1]
CB = Clare Baines
CWGC = Commonwealth War Graves Commission
HM = Hitchin Museum*[2] *[3]
HM-HE = Hitchin Museum's Hertfordshire Express*[2]
PM-CB = Parish Magazine extract from Clare Baines
RM = Rodney Marshall
RM-SPB = Rodney Marshall Scrapbook

All other photographs are by Chris Ryan, Tony French or Jonty Wild

[1] Reproduced with the permission of the British Library, licence and copyright paid for.

[2] Reproduced by kind permission of Hitchin Museum, Paynes Park, Hitchin, Herts. SG5 1EH. Telephone number 01462-434476. Copies can be obtained from Hitchin Museum.

[3] Some of the photographs obtained from Hitchin Museum are also held in the Helen Hofton Collection.

Professional proof reading advice and guidance provided by Martin Morris, Literacy Ltd., 07768 627344. www.copy4.eu